WHITE TRASH

John King is the author of four previous novels: *The Football Factory*, *Headhunters*, *England Away* and *Human Punk*. He lives in London.

John King

WHITE TRASH

V

VINTAGE

Published by Vintage 2002

4 6 8 10 9 7 5 3

First published in Great Britain in 2001 by
Jonathan Cape

Vintage
Random House, 20 Vauxhall Bridge Road,
London SW1V 2SA

Random House Australia (Pty) Limited
20 Alfred Street, Milsons Point, Sydney,
New South Wales 2061, Australia

Random House New Zealand Limited
18 Poland Road, Glenfield, Auckland 10,
New Zealand

Random House (Pty) Limited
Endulini, 5A Jubilee Road, Parktown 2193,
South Africa

The Random House Group Limited Reg. No. 954009
www.randomhouse.co.uk

A CIP catalogue record for this book
is available from the British Library

ISBN 0 09 928306 9

Papers used by Random House are natural, recyclable
products made from wood grown in sustainable forests. The
manufacturing processes conform to the environmental
regulations of the country of origin

Printed and bound in Great Britain by
Bookmarque Ltd, Croydon, Surrey

FOR MY FAMILY

'Old clothes are beastly,' continued the untiring whisper. 'We always throw away old clothes. Ending is better than mending, ending is better than mending, ending is better . . .'

Brave New World, Aldous Huxley

THE MAN IN the white coat comes when good girls are tucked up in bed dreaming of talking dolls, the bell tinkling once, ever so quick, so the sound slides away and it seems like the fairies who live by the garages are giggling, in the dark, the ring of a bottle breaking outside a pub, far far away, and it's safe in bed, warm and snug, this man in the white coat clicking the door shut, tiptoeing into the living room where Ben is stretched out on the couch with his great big head resting on Mum's lap, dozing and dreaming and chasing rabbits through sunny green fields, fluffy bunnies he's never seen and couldn't catch even if he wanted to, because, you see, Ben's not a puppy any more, he's all grown up and lived out, tired after his last walk, the joints in his knees swollen, cancer eating into his belly, dumplings under grey-specked fur that used to shine it was so black, he's always been a beautiful boy, and very friendly, even now he moves his tail in half a wag, for the stranger, Ben doesn't have a bad bone in his body, and he loves his walks, the fresh air and chance to have a sniff, a wee and a poo, he loves the summer, laying in the sun, and today he just about made it out, his body swaying, crying gently, to himself, limping, he wanted his walk same as when he was a puppy, it's his body that's the problem, his age, but now he's tired out and stays on the couch, smiling, just smiling.

BEN ONLY REALLY sees shapes, eyes misty and cataracts taking him back to when he was newborn and trying to work out what the outlines held, that's what Mum says anyway, Ben's puppy face stuck in photo frames around the room, rubber nose twitching as he sniffs the man, a mixture of aftershave and antiseptic, Ruby bets it's strawberry flavour, sitting at the top of the stairs out of sight, Mum's read her a story and told her to sleep tight, don't let the bed bugs bite, stroked her eyes and hair, and usually she's a good little girl but tonight she can't sleep, Mum's eyes red, like she's been crying, so Ruby's peeking through the banisters, Mum's long fingers stroking Ben's head, moving over his lids, ever so gentle, the sound of her voice whispering, a good boy, a beautiful boy, Ben's eyes shut again, sighing deep down in his chest, in his heart, happy, so happy he doesn't have to move, it doesn't hurt when he keeps still, the warm of the electric fire and the touch of Mum's hand all he needs, Ruby looking towards the man in the funny white coat who's talking in a quiet voice so she can't hear what he's saying, his hair combed to one side, a tie around his neck, he's leaning forward and touching Ben, Ruby can't see any of Ben's toys handy, no bouncy ball or plastic bone, doesn't know what she's seeing really, she's only a kid.

POLICE CARS STEAM down the hard shoulder blue lights flashing epileptic fits tyres screaming as they brake and unload, Ruby counting three cars with two vans right behind, numbers on the roofs for their chopper copper mates, riot mesh pulled down over the windows, asylum sirens screaming drowned puppies, floppy dog corpses, giant body-armour men swinging truncheons as they run along the side of the motorway, handcuffs snapping, their fuck-fuck-fuck language mixing with the drone of engines, three boys climbing the embankment, mechanised Old Bill too heavy and slow to catch these scruffy skin-and-bone herberts churning up rocks and gravel as they scramble to safety, parched earth crumbling, the first two boys reaching the ridge and running into the brambles, the last one stopping and turning towards the flashing lights and robocops struggling in the dirt at the bottom of the embankment, electric rozzers weighed down with toys, the boy raising two fingers in a fuck-off V-sign, grinning inside a death-head skull, red skin peeling burnt under a heatwave sun, hair sliced to the bone, counting stitches and feeling scar tissue, a nurse's fingers tracing the line, easing the pain, and he picks up a bottle, glass catching thousands of glittering cars, lorries, vans, coaches, lobbing it at the police before he follows his friends through the brambles, out of sight of the police now, laughing as he picks a track through ripe fruit nobody comes to pick, oozing black juice against his legs, rotting, fermenting, leftover rubble and masonry nails rusted down turning to dust, flowers on the rougher land behind, pricks of yellow, red, blue.

THE FLASHING SILVER blades of a police helicopter cut across the sky, chopper coppers linked to millions of television sets, the light turning blue to grey, smeared orange and purple razor nicks, thermal technology targeting three fleeing suspects, and the pilot has a brilliant view of the town, motorway ticking red-white-red-white, the spread of houses and factories same as a plastic model, the place ready to explode along the power grids, industrial ley lines melting down as the sun scorches the earth and the reservoirs boil and sink, slow columns of steel and rubber oozing past concrete blocks, slate terraces fanning out from the train track, car parks and gas tanks, patches of asphalt and prefab factories, a wood to the east, patches of yellow where the fields have died, a square of caravans, local roads and the hum of computers, chemical visions and exhaust hallucinations, non-stop tunes, sweating truck drivers loaded down with electrical goods and live exports, ticking indicators and smoking pipes, choking pigs, the motorway a road to somewhere else, the pressure and heat helping to raise top-quality skunk for hooligan farmers who've created a tropical paradise off the hard shoulder, a little bit of heaven where hemp-hungry peasants sow their seed and tend the soil, working the land and loving the earth, the perfect factory farming, concrete cows in a concrete paradise, the black-tarmac snake of the motorway passing through dreamland.

BECAUSE THIS IS the worker's dream, make no mistake.

THE MAN IN the white coat has perfect manners and a sympathetic tone, a black bag by his side, crouching down next to the couch, Ben opening his eyes, nose sniffing, mind floating, catching ghosts, lip pulling back and showing fangs, the man's hand on a sore paw, and Ruby wonders what he wants, who he is, running her palm over the legs of her pyjamas, pretends they're made of silk like that princess in the film, and the man is friendly to Mum, maybe he's a doctor, and he opens his bag and takes out a small pair of scissors, that's it, he's come to give Ben a haircut, that's going to be funny, she's never seen a dog have a haircut before, he's a hairdresser, they wear white coats and use scissors, she wonders if he's got a comb as well, or if he'll use Ben's brush, the one with two sides, he loves being brushed, and the man strokes Ben's leg again, keeping away from the paws, nails long, too long, he won't let anyone near them, Mum tells the hairdresser to be careful, and he nods, smiles, smooths the fur on Ben's leg, and Ruby imagines the feeling, his fur soft and smooth, and people and animals have skeletons inside them, lots of bones that join together and hold the skin up otherwise it would fall down, and for some reason she thinks of a skull grinning, glad the hairdresser is gentle with Ben.

THE POLICE GIVE up trying to climb the bank and hurry back to their machines, stand at the doors brushing earth from their armour, the ridge empty, one man talking into a radio, looking around, shaking his head as he says something to the controller, sun dipping further down, it'll be dark soon, and he shakes his head some more, listening, another police van roaring in from the opposite direction, cutting through a gap in the central reservation, traffic slowing, picking up speed, blue lights flickering, it's a great sight, small balls of electricity casting shadows, and Ruby can see it all from where she's sitting near the top of the opposite bank, the boys have reached their car, a rusty Ford parked by a stack of breeze blocks, the last boy catching up with the others, suddenly injected with adrenalin, turning and looking towards her, and Ruby feels air smack into her face as the chopper sinks down, waves off the blades flattening the straw in front, the thumping rhythm of its massive scythes building a long track over the hum of the motorway, radio messages confused, and for a second or two she loves the feel of the air on her skin, finally realises what's happening.

THESE CHOPPER COPPERS are zeroing in on Ruby, everything else forgotten now as thermal-imaging equipment picks up the nearest shape, sitting by the embankment leaning against a tree, and the turbulence rattles the branches so hundreds of crisp leaves snow down on her, she looks up at the chopper and sees the lights, the sleek body, the blur of the blades coming to chop off her head, and she's all grown up and full of life, but minding her own business, sitting at the top of the stairs, sitting on the embankment watching the cars pass through, wondering who's driving them and where they're going, loving the smell of burnt petrol, and sometimes she comes early Sunday morning, when the road's empty, imagines the world has no people in it, the tarmac so powerful when it's empty, these things stand out when you're high up, in the clouds, and she's just sitting in the background, doesn't have a bad bone in her body, wrinkles her nose and sniffs the leaves, picks one up and holds it to the fading light, sees parched human skin and thin veins, a crinkly feeling of age, the chopper edging down, Ruby stuck on the lines of the leaf, imagines the pilot talking to his controller who passes the information on, something lost in the system, and Ruby doesn't have a face now, no name, no number, just the heat of her body, she's sexless, hardly human, more threatening than a photofit, the police on the road looking towards her, the man with the radio pointing a finger.

THE POLICE RAISE their truncheons, excited, one of them stepping forward to hold up the traffic, the rest beginning to cross the motorway, and Ruby knows there's a path cut into the embankment on her side, that the footbridge means they think she's one of the skunk farmers who's snuck back over the motorway, and they're obeying orders, they'll be here soon, huge men stuck in the central reservation now, a van moving to block the road, and she's laughing, they don't know what they're doing, wonders why they're wasting time on these boys anyway, and she's on her own, just sitting against a tree having a smoke, relaxing, something a bit stronger in her pocket, and the police are over the last lane now, angry and hot inside their uniforms, bitter pills to swallow, the town simmering, tension in the air specially after last week's riot, and she was one of the people who had to clean up the mess, the Old Bill were caned, everybody knows that, knows it was their own fault as well, there's too many kids out and about for them to take liberties like that, and anyone will do right now, she's no fool, has to sort things out, stands up and takes a

deep breath, the chopper sinking lower, a spotlight
bursting out, the voice of authority through a speaker.

AND SHE'S OFF.

RUNNING IN THE opposite direction to the boys in the
Ford, and she hopes they'll get away but doesn't want
to be the diversion, she's only up here for the cars and
the sunset, relaxing, chilling out, and the Ford's
cranking up and puffing dust as she heads across the
empty ground that separates the nearest houses from
the motorway, hoping she doesn't cut her ankles on
broken glass, rubbish and plants heaped together, a
long wooden fence ahead of her marking the boundary, where the houses begin and the empty land ends,
she always wonders why the council doesn't do
something with it, turn it into a garden or something,
allotments, maybe it's because it lines the motorway,
and she can feel the chopper locking in on her, the
sound of its engine pushed back by her breathing, the
beat of her heart, and she's trying to think where to go,
watching her step best she can, a minefield of nails and
broken glass, the long splinters of cracked planks,
swerving right and speeding towards a hole in the
fence.

RUBY SEES HERSELF on the police monitor, she's been in
these helicopters before, on the telly, the LAPD
chasing gang bangers along burning freeways and into
a McDonald's parking lot, the producers mixing hip-
hop effects in with the voice of a controller, Los
Angeles police chasing kids through the streets of

England, the long old urban sprawl of the provinces, vans unloading outside McDonald's, the same tunes, new computer sound effects, and she knows she's a blur on the silver screen, a white spirit crashing through the fence and disappearing behind the point of a terrace, walls and roofs protecting her, coming back into view, a thermal image on a game show, presenter serious about the threat posed to society by these running shapes, speed freaks racing cars through new model estates, banging into walls and bailing out, off across football pitches as the monitor shows police arriving, more shapes joining in, and Ruby knows she has to merge with other spirits, knows where she's going now, the mass of houses will give her time to work out the best way, they've spent money getting the chopper up and will be looking for a result, it's not fair but she has to treat it like a game, harmless fun, she's been on her feet all day, had a smoke, she's tired and doesn't fancy running for fifteen minutes.

BUT THE MACHINE has seen her acting suspicious, sitting on wasteland, there's no pubs or takeaways, no flower beds or climbing frames, only tramps and kids up to no good hang around there, people walking dogs, and boys wee through the railings when they see a Porsche or Mercedes, politicians call it the hooliganism of envy, but Ruby knows it's just kids being kids, it could be stones and bricks, that's dangerous and happens sometimes, and even though she's done nothing wrong they'll arrest her, no doubt about it, but the chopper has to pull back up and hover, trying to see where she's heading, the police will be back in their vans now, following directions, aiming to cut her off, and she stops to look at the chopper, the controller is busy, she's a target all right, the system on full alert, there's nobody to talk to, no chance to explain, there's alleyways and short cuts, she doesn't need the bother, has people to meet, everything out of control suddenly, she has to be with people, on her own she's dead.

RUBY JOGS NOW, running full pelt is only going to make people stop and stare, she passes along the street, turns right, keeps going, television stars floating out of open windows, around the corner and past an overgrown verge, she hears the wolf whistle of a boy sitting on a burnt-out car with his friends, brothers by the look of two of them, a hundred shades of black, torched Ford textures, and she knows the helicopter won't dip low here, the pilot has to remember the guidelines and stay sensitive to the needs of the community, can't risk hitting a house, stirring people up, trouble spreads, copycat riots they call them, kids with red peeling skin and nothing better to do than sit on dead cars sipping fizzy drinks, small boys playing football, bare-chested so she can see ribs sticking out, a couple of girls stroking a cat, the purr of the chopper, heads snapping back, she knows he wants to dip right down and buzz her, make her scared, the pilot wants to have some fun but has to stay in the background, directing the troops.

RUBY IS QUIET as a mouse looking at Ben's left leg sticking out over the edge of the couch, the hairdresser snipping at the fur, a small patch of grey skin showing through, and Ben's lips slide back again, he doesn't want his fur cut, it should be his head, but then he'd look silly having more hair on his body, somehow things don't seem right to Ruby, he's a good boy, loves everyone and everything, in love with life, even tries to play with the cat next door sniffing at her till she pats him on the nose and he runs off, and he smells Ruby when she's been stroking the cat, interested, and when Ben sees another dog he bounces forward to say hello, he's only ever had a fight twice, both times with boy dogs his own age, they started it as well, and Ruby is standing in the road somewhere, laughing, pointing, asking Mum if cats and dogs speak the same language, his ears are big and flop around, Mum calls him a cartoon dog, too friendly by half, he wouldn't be much good if burglars came knocking with a chewy, but when those other dogs attacked him he had a go back, then wagged his tail after, no hard feelings, he's just defending himself, sees the good in everyone, the same as Ruby, that's what people say about her, they've always said that about Ruby, that she's kind-hearted.

THE MAN IN the white coat isn't a hairdresser though, reaching in his bag and taking out a ball of cotton wool and a tub of ointment, a syringe with a long needle, a small bottle of liquid, and she's wide-eyed, shuts her eyes now, remembering, running, opens them again, thinking instead of Ben when Mum and Dad first brought him home, before she was even born, she loves hearing about that, how he was a three-month-old pup who gobbled his food down so they thought he was going to be sick, he still loves the jelly, the meaty chunks, just a baby living in the corner of someone's garden, scared at first, Mum says he thought he'd died and gone to heaven, to end up in a house where he was so loved, people can be cruel, imagine that, he'd never been inside a house before, another three months in the dog's home, and he's such a beautiful boy with this tuft of white at the back of a black neck, white on his tummy, loves having his belly rubbed, he was scared to go outside in case he wasn't allowed back in, and when he ran to jump on the couch he missed because he'd never done it before, tried again and again until he got it right, it took him ages to work out how the stairs worked, Mum had to lift him up and move his front legs, and he understood after a few goes, running up fast as he could, the chopper firing a light down, it's dark now, cutting into memories.

RUBY GETS OFF the wider streets and runs down an alley cutting through the one-parent flats, small starter homes where flaking cement hangs like icicles, frozen Arctic sculptures, the woodwork a two-tone mix of wood and paint, gravel earth and dried-out housing association trees, a square of grass that hasn't caught on, squashed fag ends and the smell of fish fingers from a ground-floor window, electronic heartbeats, a new orange bike and a fluorescent skateboard, leftover building materials, bricks and mortar, worm-shit blobs of concrete left behind the same as when the tide goes out at the seaside, and Ruby stops for a breather, maybe she's lost the police, checks this way and that, sweat covering her skin, should she turn left or right, one way is quicker but the other is safer, the roads tighter, lots of bollards and alleys, the street lights on, but dim, two fat women in trainers and joggers standing outside their front door chatting, drinking cans of Diet Pepsi, and suddenly there's a roar and the air whooshes again, the helicopter breaking all the rules, scaring children, and it takes the women about one second to realise who it's chasing, telling Ruby to duck down that road over there, she'll be all right if she goes between the houses, and she thinks for a moment, frozen in the light, brain counting down.

BEN'S OLD HEART ticking in his chest, all grown up and worn out by time, lying on the couch with a patch of fur cut away, the vet pushing the needle of the syringe into the potion, pulling the lever back, removing the needle, moving forward, Mum's hand over Ben's eyes so he doesn't see what's happening, the vet leaning forward and slipping the needle into Ben's leg, a second when he tries to move, the soft feel of Mum's hand moving over his eyes, stroking his forehead, whispering gently like she's singing, a good boy, his fur soft, such a beautiful dog, a good good doggy, and the man moves his hand and Mum is crying, he pulls the syringe away and stands up, moves off, and Mum is stroking Ben's head, sobbing now, choking, and somehow Ruby thinks that Ben is dead, that he's in heaven, in his dream chasing rabbits and running through great big fields, she doesn't know how it happened so fast, she isn't sure, hears the vet talking, maybe she's wrong, sitting there until he lifts Ben's floppy body off the couch and wraps it in the blanket he always sleeps in, a fluffy old red blanket with hairs mixed in with the blobs of wool, and the vet takes him out of the house, Ruby going back to her room and, looking out of the window, she sees Ben being put in the boot of the vet's car and driven away.

SHE RUNS BETWEEN the houses same as she did that night when she was a little girl, an hour later after she went downstairs and Mum told what had happened, she slept in a garden till morning before going home, it must be fifteen years since Ben died, it's in her dates book, a long time ago and just like yesterday, there's no cradles and no graves for animals, just syringes full of special medicine, that's what her mum called it, when she sat down with Ruby the next day and explained that it was kinder to him because he was dying and in pain and didn't have very long to live, and he was happy now, he was in heaven, and she held her little girl in her arms, Ruby asking about heaven and what happened to people when they were like Ben, and when you were in heaven did it mean you could see all the people who were dead and could you come back or was it for ever, and where did this special medicine come from, was that the vet in the white coat, and Ruby never told her mum she'd been sitting on the stairs watching.

RUBY KNOWS WHERE she's going now, five minutes later climbing the sagged corner of a wire fence, off along another terrace and cutting across a petrol-station

14

forecourt, past more houses and a curry house, out on to the high street next to the pet shop, the helicopter higher in the sky but still in touch, this is the crunch, the chopper's tracked her the whole way but is going to lose contact any second, she's out in the open on a main road and this is their last chance, if they can get a van down here now they'll have her, but she's moving through other shapes, she has no face, sex, age, the man on the monitor doing his best not to mix her up, and there's three pubs up ahead with at least a hundred people standing outside drinking, and she goes into the first one, safe, laughing, and she stays for a minute, the music and conversation battering each other, a smell of drink and cigarettes and perfume and sweat, and she's thinking of Ben and how he died, how she ran away from home but only for one night, the press of a cold glass on her arm, she could murder a drink, and it's the pub across the road where she's meeting the others, in half an hour, so she goes back out and strolls over, looking into the night sky as a police van passes at street level, packed with armour and frustrated police who aren't about to steam into a busy pub chasing shadows, they probably think they're after a young man with a shaved head, or a ponytail, one of the stereotypes, already people are waving at the van, things are tense and they withdraw, the chopper peeling away, giving up, they've lost a dangerous criminal and Ruby's safe with the masses, orders a drink that smells of raspberries and is laced with vodka, the bottle icy cold, the taste sweet on her tongue.

R uby reached over and slid the switch sideways, the jolt of the radio's alarm replaced by the easy hum of *On The Parish*, her favourite DJ, Charlie Boy, easing her into the new day. Police sirens weren't the sweetest sound first thing, but they turned her head and opened her eyes. She couldn't afford to oversleep. People depended on her. She stretched out over the mattress lifting her arms above her head, heard the veins buzz and valves pop, big surges of energy racing into her brain. She saw muscles under the skin, dazzled by the colours, glowing red and orange, held her right hand up to the sunlight for a proper X-ray effect, a skeleton outline of fingers, thumb, knuckles. She wasn't religious, but there was no way this was accidental, her body too complicated, a jigsaw that was taking the best scientists hundreds of years to work out. The sun fed her, long bamboo shafts reaching deep into the room, turning to elastic fingers as she watched, relaxing her same as a massage, cracking joints, releasing tension, pressure on her skull tapping a pulse, meridians on fire. She felt brilliant. It wasn't even half six yet and she was already warm, the sunlight catching billions of dust particles spinning same as a slowed-down fractal, waves of motion taking her breath away. She rolled on to her tummy and really listened to the music, a long track that eased back and forward over a central rhythm, boring to some people but trance-like to her.

On The Parish came out of the best pirate station around, Satellite FM, the sound cutting into the M25, broadcasting for six months then disappearing off the air. The DTI had shut them down before, the RA running riot with the bolt cutters and angle grinder, confiscating the station's aerial and transmitter, at other times those concerned having a break, then coming back twice as strong. It was a lot of work for no real financial return, just a love of music, and Ruby sometimes wondered where their studio was, what the DJs looked like, she could picture the turntables all right, the mixing desk and mic, the speakers, but not the faces involved. As well as Charlie Boy there was DJ Chromo and DJ Punch, Ruby remembering the time Chromo told his listeners about FM and medium wave, the regular Chromo Zone lecture, how with medium wave the stratosphere was like a cushion and bounced the waves back down to earth, since then she'd felt safer than ever, could almost see the dome protecting her, keeping the goodness in and the evil out, a shimmer of skin, every single fish scale glittering in the wind. Charlie played a couple of times each week and had been going since midnight, coming through with the insomniacs and speed freaks, the hypermanics, night prowlers and other barmies, kick-starting anyone lumbered with the early shift.

For a moment Ruby could feel Ben at the bottom of her bed, tried to forget but couldn't stop herself going back, and that dog really loved the sun, stretching his panting body across the floor in summer as his fur cooked, lids jammed shut and his tongue lolling, and when she woke up in the morning he was always there waiting to lick her face, the bang of his tail on the mattress, Ben her drummer boy, turning to scratch his ear and lick his balls, innocent and carefree, a bell ringing somewhere, fast, lost in the drizzle, the clink of bottles and the yawn of a milk float, a man in a white coat with six eggs in his hand, passing another figure with a black bag, and she thought of Jack the Ripper, a professional passing a tradesman in the street, a surgeon or a butcher, no, a milkman, the milkman of human kindness, milk and eggs and sliced bread on your doorstep, birds pecking through foil tops sipping cream, and Ben was trying to lick her face again, little Ruby screaming and laughing and pushing him back, not after licking his willy, and she's going downstairs to meet this man with the special medicine, a magic potion that puts you to sleep when you're very sick, Mum says it takes you to a beautiful place where you live for ever and everything is nice, a place where you never get sick and everyone's happy and smiling all the time, there's no worrying about money, no working yourself into an early grave, and Dad's there, throwing Ben's favourite rubber ball into a stream so he can bellyflop in and grab it with his mouth, bring it back out, shaking his fur dry, fluffy same as after a bath or when he's been in the rain, Ruby shouldn't be too sad because we'll all be sitting next to God one day, up in heaven, life will be perfect and it'll never end, that's our reward for being good people while we're alive, and the bad people, they go somewhere else. To hell.

Ruby blinking and shivering and goose pimples covering her skin, a hard coldness in her bones as Charlie's voice pulled her up above the surface.

– This next track is for the chaps who helped us out the other night. I know one of you is listening, so thanks again, it was much appreciated. And a question for the boys who kicked it off, just asking you, what was the point? You must know you got a slap when you deserved a spanking. Why shit on your own doorstep when there's plenty of people dumping on us who don't even live here. And just because you never see them it doesn't mean they're not out there. Just because they don't turn up mob-handed doesn't mean they're not ten times as deadly. So let's calm down and live in harmony, man. And for anyone who thinks I'm turning into a smelly hippy, and for all the people who keep tuning in, this one is for you, and if anyone's interested . . .

Ruby got out of bed and had a shower, dried herself off and dressed. One of her work shoes had a small hole in the sole so she could feel the road when it was hot, reckoned she could get by for a while yet, as long as it didn't rain, but the tarmac felt good coming in like that, small jets of heat where her foot touched down, shoes expensive. It was early but she wasn't going to hang around sitting indoors. She hadn't eaten anything last night and was starving, the fridge empty except for some jam and half a bottle of flat Coke. She could smell bread baking downstairs, her mouth watering as she imagined the food.

Ruby lived on top of an electrical shop, but next door was Dilly's Dozen, a baker's dealing in bloomers, filled rolls, turnovers, iced buns and doughnuts, plus sausage rolls and meat pies, a fridge with cold drinks and a pot of coffee on the go, a kettle for tea and hot chocolate. Dilly ran the counter while her husband Mick did the baking. They opened at six for the first wave of workers on their way to the trading estate, Mick coming out front to help when things got busy, when the baking was done.

– It's funny how you can jump back and jump up to different styles, and today's Deep South selection is five-strong, kicking off with the original version of 'Brand New Cadillac' by Mr Vince Taylor, and thanks to Jim in the market for this one. If you fancy trying some rockabilly, go and visit him, he's right between the saris and the livers, he's got a load of psychobilly vinyl as well, mutant stuff by the Meteors and Tall Boys, but going back to Vince Taylor, if you were going to buy yourself a Cadillac, what colour would you choose? Me, I'd . . .

Ruby clicked the radio off and left the flat, made sure the door was locked and went down and out on to the street, turned towards the baker's and just missed a pool of sick, looking at the colours and doing her best to see good in bad, struggling, but just about doing it, Mick coming out with a bucket of water and washing most of the mess into the gutter, raising an eyebrow and shaking his head.

– She almost had me out rowing with them last night, he said. Fifty-five years old and she wants me to have a go at a couple of drunks in their thirties.

He shook his head and went back into the shop for more water, Ruby following him in through the door.

– Morning, dear, Dilly said, arms folded. Did you hear the noise last night? Bloody hooligans effing and blinding when we're trying to sleep, kicking bottles around. I got up and gave them an earful, then one of them threw up. They got a move on when I said I was letting the dogs out.

Mick went back outside and Ruby smiled.

– What can I get you, dear?

– A black coffee and a cheese roll please. One of those buns as well, that one at the front with the icing down the side.

Dilly was nice enough, but a nosy parker.

– Been out, have you, love?

Ruby nodded, watched as Dilly's face shivered in front of her, the edges of her eyes lined with red, then purple, finally smashing back into yellow, and she could see the drunks looking up and seeing this woman hanging out of a window, eyes burning into them, and Dilly was well built, could look after herself, Ruby wouldn't want to get on the wrong side of her, and the head was growing, eyes huge, deep and interested in anything Ruby had to say, she was thinking about the boys Dilly caught breaking in two months back, how she knocked one out with Mick's rolling pin, punched the other and broke his nose. She didn't call the police either, believed in instant justice, told Ruby she wasn't a grass but made them squirm, waited until the weedy one came to and gave them a lecture, she could see they were embarrassed, being sorted out by a middle-aged woman. Ruby kept smiling politely.

– Busy at work? Suppose that's a silly question

really, isn't it, you're always busy. At least here you can stop, there's a beginning and an end, you get up early but finish early as well. It's not a bad way to make a living. Not bad at all. You look at some of the people who come in, working with metal all day, stuck on production lines, things like that, and we're lucky, working with flour and yeast. Jam and tea.

Dilly's face shrunk back to normal size.

– It never stops, Ruby said. The more people get well and go home, the more seem to turn up needing a bed. You get used to it, have to remember that every case is separate. I wouldn't change it for anything.

– You're a good girl. Kind-hearted.

The BBC was playing a song with a chorus about rocking in the free world and Ruby couldn't help tapping her foot as Dilly put her breakfast together in a paper bag. She was free and in love with life, and looking at the woman on the other side of the counter she thought again how Dilly was big for her height, it must be tempting in a baker's, you'd want to eat all day long, but Ruby didn't reckon fat meant ugly, never thought like that about people, Dilly big and strong and generous.

– Here you are.

Ruby handed over the right money.

– Thanks.

– See you.

– Bye, love.

Ruby left the shop and turned right, walking along the length of the parade, three skinhead dustmen on a wall opposite with their lorry parked a few feet away, the youngest one whistling, and she flashed him a smile for the compliment, these men sipping three hot drinks and chewing three rolls, the smell of rubbish hanging in the air. Ruby made sure she only picked up the tea, coffee, sugar, wasn't interested in rotting food and dirty nappies. She saw these three every week, loved the fine hair on their heads, white skin showing through all that individual stubble, the black and brown and grey razored right down. The one whistling was the nicest, a red cross cut into his right forearm, and when he moved the polystyrene cup to his mouth a ripple of energy raced towards the older man next door, a box-like head more interested in newspaper models than a passing nurse.

– You're happy this morning, the youngest skinhead shouted.

Ruby smiled again and crossed the empty road, heading towards the hospital, a car turning and the smell of exhaust fumes in her nose, the rubbish gone, petrol floating up and through radio waves that were all around her but which she couldn't hear, trying but getting nowhere. She could feel the tarmac on the bottom of her right foot, surface gently rubbing. She'd go and buy a new pair at dinner time, it was just the money made her put it off, but if she didn't go to Dilly's for a while, made her own breakfast instead, then she could save a bit, but it was never enough, and she wasn't good with domestic stuff, couldn't be bothered cooking. She spent a fair bit going out, but it was to do with priorities, she wasn't the sort to sit at home, she liked having a laugh, listening to music and dancing, talking to people, feeling alive and free and part of the world, really loving it when the ground was hot and the heat surged into her like this, thinking again about the meridians and all the different medical systems people had worked out, wished she could see the power flashes, looking back at the shops, the flats above, her home in the bricks, the outside giving nothing away. There were no ornate decorations or plaster casts, creeping vines or stained-glass windows, just bricks and glass in metal frames that were peeling and spotted with rust, and it was perfect, so many lives being lived there, by people she knew. It was a proper home.

It didn't take long for Ruby to get to work, and she was early, sat on the grass to the right of the main entrance and had her breakfast, sipped her coffee and enjoyed the caffeine straightening things out. The bus stop was next to her, but empty, daisies and ants moving through the grass, stubble on a man's head, and she dug into the roll, Dilly always loaded them up, thick slices of Cheddar that said so much about the woman, the same quality that let those boys go free. It didn't matter that she was a nosy parker, a tough woman with her arms crossed, bossing Mick around, because the cheese showed she had a generous spirit, and that was the best quality going. The coffee was a good blend as well, she didn't have to do that, could've got away with a cheaper make. People took what they could get. The roll filled her up, the bun big and chewy, and it made sense that Mick was the same. They were all right those two. The world was full of decent people, every single one of them with a story to tell, things that made you smile, thinking of Dilly's hard stare and Mick's scrunched-up face, his dry humour and the way she crumbled when he had a go at her, she'd only ever seen it happen once. He'd been a baker all his life, after doing his national service, the army teaching him a trade. He collected beer mats for a hobby. A funny thing to collect really.

Ruby sat on the grass till it was time to start work, running her hands over the ground, a spider in her palm. When it was time she jumped up, went in through the main entrance and off along the corridors of her life, passageways that had been planned to link certain departments, the quickest route from A to B, connecting expertise, and the place smelt good, clean and efficient, a centre of excellence without a snobby tag, corridors of dedication and selflessness, a job worth doing, a place worth being.

She saw Boxer up ahead, pushing a bed, a nurse next to him carrying a bag. Ruby caught up with them and Boxer smiled when he saw her, falling into step. He was twice her size, a huge man who was kind, generous, maybe naïve, what some people would call slow. He didn't read too well, and had trouble telling the time, but he'd do anything for you, was well liked by the other porters and the nurses, the people he worked with, the doctors more removed, in their own world. He was strong as well, eased beds and trolleys along that other porters struggled to move, brought the nickname with him, said that's what he'd been called at school. Ruby felt good about Boxer, and Dawn was helping him with his reading, children's books he thought were silly at first, till she made him understand it was just a start. Ruby loved Boxer, wanted to hug him right now, squeeze him like a baby. She was showing him how to use a watch, and he nearly had it now, but it was more work for Dawn with the reading, she wasn't a teacher or anything, just had this heart of gold, even if she was a tart, Ruby smiling to herself, they were always teasing each other.

– You look tired, Ruby, Boxer said. Didn't you sleep very good last night?

– I slept all right, had a late night, that's all. I'm fine.

– You've been drinking. You shouldn't drink too much. It's not good for you.

The nurse on the other side grinned and leant forward to catch the patient's pillow, the man's face wet and red and his breathing stuck in congested lungs. Ruby squeezed his shoulder, knew that he was scared, asking God why his life was blocking up inside his chest, he didn't want to drown in his own spit, and he wasn't seeing the beauty right now, but they'd get him well, he was in the right place, in safe hands, his pyjama arm damp on her hand, trying to reassure him.

When he walked back down these corridors, discharged and fit and using his own legs, bursting with a new lease of life, he'd see the drawings he was missing now, all sorts of crayon houses and insect people from the children's ward, mums and dads and boys and girls holding hands, a red boy kicking a blue football, a church full of heads, a ship on the sea and a man on a motorbike, a car with the driver's neck and head sticking out of the window twice the size of the bonnet, a forest with tiny people sitting on tree stumps, a spider in a web, and then there were the notice-boards with brochures pushing a diet of fresh fruit and vegetables, good hygiene, a sheet on bowel cancer, prevention the key, purple drawing pins nailed into cork, colour photos of broccoli and lettuce and a bowl of cereal, a section on bran.

They passed the doors of the gastroenteritis ward where a man stood still, waiting, just waiting, no slippers on his feet, head bald and pocked with craters, burnt-out meteor showers, staring into Ruby for a second, steam coming off the mug in his hand, a long row of plastic pots filling the ledge leading into the ward, and she could see Davinda behind the man, waved but didn't catch her eye, the man nodding at Ruby, keeping his dignity best he could in his bare feet, waiting for something to happen inside him. Ruby would see Davinda later on, when they had their break.

When she reached her ward, the next one along, she left Boxer and the others and went in, noticed her legs were stiff. She'd been dancing till two, before that running from the helicopter, and she couldn't believe that had happened. Maybe she was paranoid taking off, but no, they'd have had her, she did the right thing. She wondered if they'd keep the video, she was sure now she'd been taped, part of an archive on Britain's most wanted. Maybe they were sending the film to the TV people, turning it into a drama, adding a righteous commentary and creating startling news. It was a joke, the whole thing, but the mornings were busy and last night was in the past, the hospital waking early, same as the army according to some of the men on her ward, the ones old enough to have done national service or fought in the war. They were probably right as well. Morale was important, and you had to have discipline, a routine. Sister was at the other end of the ward, and when Dawn followed Ruby in five minutes late she was glad to see her still down there. Sister was Maureen when she was off duty and game for a laugh, but strict when she was working. It was rosary beads and a crucifix in uniform, the Irish Club when she was out socialising with her husband.

– I had trouble walking in, Dawn said, once she'd settled in, winding Ruby up first thing. I met King Dong last night.

Ruby smiled and got on with the day, fell into the routine, losing herself in jobs she did like clockwork, the thing that kept her going the people, patients as well as staff, stripping a wet bed, the man concerned sitting in the television room and probably feeling ashamed of himself, it was a normal reaction, but she didn't mind, she'd seen everything in this job, gallons of piss, blood, shit, mucus, pus, it was part of life, didn't mean much any more, the mechanics of living, it was the people that mattered, the personalities she met, the things they'd done in the past and their plans for the future. She didn't know much about the bed-wetter, a new arrival, middle-aged and thin, and she worked on the mattress, stains you had when you were a kid, thinking of her bed this morning, the yellow ground in, years old, a bed Dez's mum gave her when she moved in.

With the bed stripped the wet sheets were forgotten, and she was running her hands over the new ones, crisp and clean, holding a pillow case up to her nose and imagining a line of coke but with a fresher smell, and she had to turn the mattress first, hauling it over, easy-peasy, making it up, the angles straight and creases brushed out, it was a thing you did over and over, cleaning and maintaining standards, caring for people. It was to do with hygiene, but also for morale.

The tea trolley rattled in the hall and Ruby went to the television room, a news programme on a war somewhere, lines of bodies on the ground, stupid wars about nothing, she had no time for any of that, there was enough disease and sadness around without these idiots making more problems, and she told the man in the television room, Colin, that he could go back to bed if he wanted, smiling and moving on quickly so he'd feel it was okay and wouldn't have to look her in the face, she knew how he'd be feeling, went into the first section as the trolley arrived, voices dipping as she entered.

– Morning, nurse, Percy called.

Ron waved at her, sitting up in bed. He had been in for a while now, but would be going home soon, a proper character with stories to spare and a twinkle in his eye. She talked with all the patients, but Ron was special. When she had time she sat with him in the TV room and made him tell her stories about Calcutta and Lima and all the places he'd seen when he was in the merchant navy. She really liked Ron, he had a quality about him, like he knew so much but was humble with it. If she had a granddad she'd want him to be like that.

Percy was all right as well, he liked the nurses but wasn't sleazy, not like that Mr Robinson, or Tinky Winky as Dawn called him, the other two in this section quiet. Warren stuck behind his oxygen mask and only in one day, Mr Hay keeping to himself, more interested in his crossword book than what was going on around him, not rude or anything, a bit superior but no trouble.

– How are you feeling? she asked Percy, holding the thermometer up.

– Not bad. I dreamt about you last night, nurse.

– I hope it wasn't rude.

– No, it was nothing like that.

She knew he was lying, he'd gone ever so slightly red, but even then it was probably innocent, holding hands, something like that. She'd seen hundreds of Percys over the years, men adjusting to old age and finding their bodies were slowing right down, the responsibilities they had no longer there, that the world had moved on and they had to find a place in it. They'd been raised to block things out, to be strong and ready to fight, it was up to them to take on the world and worry where the money was coming from, raising families, but in their later years they could let this go, if they wanted, if they were able. Women had more to look forward to, got stronger with age. Ruby felt sorry for men. Who'd want to be born a man? They said it was a man's world but she wasn't so sure. She was glad she was a woman. She shook the thermometer.

– We were going to the pictures. My girl was there as well, you've seen her when she's come to visit. She brought those flowers over there. Must've paid a few bob for them as well. I told her not to bother. Better saving your money. They're only going to wilt in a few days. But they're nice flowers. Add some colour.

A bunch of daffodils sat on his bedside table. Ruby remembered his daughter, a worn-out woman with four kids jumping on granddad's bed, worried when they first came in because of his enlarged heart, something that was common enough but still a fright when you didn't know what was going on, when his face was puffed up and he was losing his temper, losing his marbles the daughter said, laughing and worried. The heart slowed down, didn't pump the blood fast enough so water seeped out and built up on the lungs, cut down the oxygen reaching the brain.

People just didn't know what was going on most of the time. Most illnesses were a mystery. Once things were explained they cheered up, specially when Percy started improving, sitting up and eating, cracking jokes that weren't funny. She could see the relief in the faces of his grandkids, and they brought pictures in, the same drawings that came out of the children's ward, houses and people, all the colours of the rainbow.

Sometimes she wondered about the doctors, they were well meaning, overworked and stressed, but their social skills weren't very good. Percy's girl was told he had heart failure in emergency and it was two days before Ruby explained that it was a term that sounded worse than it was, in the meantime his family stuck with this notion that his heart was no good. A lot of the doctors couldn't connect with the people they were dealing with, assumed everyone knew what they knew. It was a pressurised job, she wasn't criticising, but had to smile when Percy lost his temper about it, told one of the doctors off. Some of the nurses got wound up by the doctors, but she didn't pay much attention. With some of them it was their background, with others tiredness. She didn't care, life was too short.

– What film did we see?

– We never got to see it. It was one of those adventure films, don't even know the name, they're all the same these days, just special effects. We had our popcorn but got lost on the way. The place had ten screens and we didn't know where it was showing. We were walking for ages and ended up going in a circle.

– Come on then, open wide.

She put the thermometer under his tongue and went over to Warren. He was in his mid-twenties and had trouble breathing, his test results due back this morning when the doctors came round, and she hadn't spoken to him properly yet, it took a few days, it was the same with all of them, then Warren would have his mask off and be mixing with the others. She saw it every time, how people got together. Some were straight in, laughing and joking, while others took longer. Something formed out of nothing. They were in the same boat. It was nice to see this happen, it didn't matter what their background or age was, and for the lonely ones it was hard when they had to go home. That was sad. There were some people who never mixed, but not many. Once a patient was out of danger and knew they were going to be okay, it was a chance to have a holiday and recharge their batteries. Waiting outside were responsibilities, the roles they had to play. But beds were in short supply and they were sent on their way.

She loved seeing people get well again, building up

their strength, innocence and dependence replaced by the usual masks. She could handle things when the old-timers started playing up as well, they liked it with the tables turned. They were like little boys. The threat of an enema or laxative did wonders for discipline. Talking of which, Dawn had lined Tinky Winky up for an enema this morning. The dirty bastard had slipped his hand up her dress yesterday, almost got inside her pants as well.

– What's funny? Boxer asked, strolling past.

– Nothing, she said, moving away from Warren and heading towards the room where Mr Wilkins was calling for help.

– Nothing at all.

Mr Wilkins wasn't heavy and she eased him into his wheelchair, pushed the man over to the toilet. She eased him into the room, locked the door, pulled his trousers down and positioned him on the seat. Mr Wilkins drifted off waiting for his bowels to empty and forgot Ruby was there. She looked away and followed the hand rail, the sweet smell of disinfectant and soap. He was eighty-six and virtually alone in the world, going senile and suffering from lung cancer. He would soon be a baby again, if he didn't pass away first, going the full circle, totally dependent, his strength withered and a shell left. She never thought like this for more than a second or two. He'd have done things in his life, she just didn't know what, eighty-six was a good age, and she saw him as a young man, one for the girls, drinking and loving and enjoying a good knees-up, dancing to jazz and all sorts, she'd have to ask Ron what they listened to, what they drank, imagined it was mostly bitter, smoking Woodbines, and drugs were legal back then, cocaine and opium, things like that.

Ron would know, he was eighty-four, two years behind Mr Wilkins but a million times fitter, sharp as they came. Mr Wilkins had a nephew who visited once, but apart from that nothing. Ron had lots of family, there was always different generations coming to see him, he was more like a healthy sixty-five than eighty-four. Maybe it was in the genes, but he had a lot to live for, a rich life, some good years ahead of him. Mr Wilkins's first name was John, and she imagined Johnny Wilkins charming the girls, making up stories, a young face on old shoulders, hair slicked back, a comb in his pocket, eyes bright, loving and leaving them, till the night he met the girl of his dreams, going in the toffee-maker's and charming her to the altar.

When Mr Wilkins was finished, Ruby cleaned him up and flushed the toilet, washed her hands and lifted his back into his wheelchair, took him back to bed, made sure he was comfortable. She looked into the misty eyes and saw morphine merging with the Alzheimer's, wrinkles covering his face, lines sliced into yellowing skin, and he would've been a proud man, it was just as well he couldn't see himself, that the faculties that gave him his pride were gone. Morphine was a good drug, anything that eased the pain had to be good, dealing with the cancer he didn't even know he had. Maybe senility was a blessing in disguise for some people, they said Alzheimer's was hardest for the sufferer's family, but she pushed this away. It was unlike her to have sad thoughts. It was thinking of Ben that had done it, and she jumped back into her work, soon rushed off her feet, the morning passing quickly in a whizz of showers and bed-baths, breakfast served, the doctors doing their rounds, giving medicine out, the run of duties that meant everything happened right away, the banter she loved, tired by twelve and ready for her dinner.

Ruby passed back through the same corridors, and they were busy now, looking into the chapel as she passed and seeing the back of a teenage boy sitting on his own staring at the carpet, the sound of a child laughing ahead of her, two men swinging her by the arms, and Ruby was knackered, her legs so heavy she wished she could afford a massage, and she was thirsty as well as hungry, nothing better on a hot day than sitting in the sun with a cold pint of lager in her hand. In the canteen she got herself a pie and chips, the coldest can of Coke on offer, a yogurt for dessert. Dawn had nipped off a few minutes earlier and was sitting with Sally, Ruby going over and joining them, the other two having a friendly argument about funding, Davinda arriving right behind Ruby, the four of them taking up the table.

– If people weren't so selfish and didn't mind paying a few pennies extra in taxes they wouldn't have to worry about waiting lists and a shortage of beds. Most people are just thick and can't see past the end of their nose.

– I know, but for a lot of them every little bit counts. They're forced to be selfish. Anyway, I don't want to talk about work in my lunch break, do I? It doesn't make any difference.

Dawn was to the point, a good laugh and with a dirty mouth on her, while Sally was much more serious, outspoken when it came to politics, played an active part in the union, Davinda quieter, very straight. Ruby liked them all, but she was closest to Dawn, saw her socially as well as at work.

– All right, but you started it.

– Did you see that bloke they brought in today? Dawn asked. Jesus, I had to hold his dick when he wanted a pee and it was the size of a cannon. He was out of it, didn't know it was me helping him. If that's what it's like limp I wouldn't want to be on the end of it when he's got a hard-on.

– You would, Sally smiled. You'd love it.

Dawn raised her eyes and acted bashful.

– Haven't seen a piece of meat like that since Studley stayed with us. You remember him?

– I'm not going to forget Studley in a hurry, Sally sighed. He should've been locked up. He's as bad as Mr Robinson.

– I walked in on Studley that time and there he was screwing this woman from along the corridor, right there on his bed with only the curtain around them. She had a glazed look on her face and I'm not surprised, she must've been on some heavy drugs to get off with him. And there was me trying to keep a straight face and at the same time give them a bollocking.

– He was going on about his lover's balls for all the

next week. Always talked to your tits instead of your face. I got him though. Laxative in his tea.

Ruby drifted away from the conversation and looked at the hospital staff scattered around the tables, enjoying some peace and quiet before going back to work, reading papers and talking, staring into the distance thinking about another place and another time, everyone with healthy appetites making the most of food that was filling and cheap. A good meal here was worth a few pounds each week saved on food at home. She looked out of the window at one of the squares of grass set in the middle of the building, a good design idea, daisies running in a line tied together in a chain under the earth, windows open, the temperature high, the morning cooler on the ward due to the angle of the sun, and Ruby knew the last few hours were going to be a hard slog.

No way would she get away this year. She'd love to go on holiday, but she was in debt as it was. She thought of Dawn talking about renting herself out. It was pretty sad when you couldn't live on your wages. It wasn't right. She called Dawn a tart for a laugh, but really it was a shame Dawn was so disillusioned. Your body was special, you couldn't separate it from what you were as a person. She didn't know, she wasn't being moralistic, and Davinda was hiccuping opposite, Ruby looking up and seeing that she was in tears, realising she was laughing so hard she was going to wet herself.

– No, I sorted Tinky Winky out this morning. He had an enema to wash out his dirty mouth and he wasn't smiling. The last thing on his mind now is touching up a nurse. It serves him right. He'll be good as gold. I told him that if he ever touches one of us again I'll get my boyfriend to sort him out, once he's home from hospital. I showed him Boxer and he nearly shat a brick. Well, not a brick really, more like a lager shandy.

Everyone laughed. Dawn grabbed the ketchup and squirted sauce all over her chips, the plastic sucking in air and farting. They laughed harder.

– He probably enjoyed it, Sally said, after a while. Robinson's the sort of bloke for who an enema is one of life's pleasures. He'll be back for another one.

– Not him, Dawn said, thinking. I fucking hope not anyway. Don't worry, girls, he's only a fucking Teletubby. If he wants another dose he can go private. This is the National Health Service we're talking about here, not Moody's Massage Parlour.

Jonathan Jeffreys dabbed at his mouth then carefully refolded his serviette, checking that the creases were exact before wedging it between the rim of his empty dessert bowl and the plate below. He signalled to the waitress and watched intently as she brought him his cognac, guessing that she suffered from varicose veins and an underactive thyroid. His heart went out to the poor woman. He waited until she had cleared the table before lifting the glass to his mouth. Already in high spirits, the cognac gave Mr Jeffreys an increased sense of well-being. He felt such contentment it was a pity he had to leave. He watched the waitress walk into the kitchen. A middle-aged woman with fat calves and a slight hunch. Her life was no doubt hard and he sympathised, instantly shifting his attention to the Piano Bar next door, separated from the hotel restaurant by a wall of tinted glass.

The pianist wore a white tuxedo and played a baby grand. The piano matched the jacket. Notes reached Mr Jeffreys. If he listened closely enough and ignored the conversation around him he could make out a tune. A relaxing strand of five-star jazz. He nibbled a mint and wondered at the sheer enjoyment to be found in such simple pleasures. The ambience was perfect, the food excellent. French cuisine at its finest. An elderly couple passed along the glass, well dressed and well mannered. Hidden now by a huge cactus neatly bathed in soothing blue light. The pianist smiled. He obviously enjoyed his work. Mr Jeffreys was tempted to order a second cognac but resisted. He did not want his thought processes clouded.

Entrusted with a brief far wider than that of a mere doctor, it was vital that his head remain clear. Nothing less that the welfare of the state and the stability of the masses was at stake. His role was, quite frankly, essential, although he would never have said so, or even thought as much. He was a modest man. But as a highly trained professional with a knowledge of economics as well as medicine, he was observing the nation's health from a higher plain than a physician. Removed from the daily grind he was able to grasp the broader issues involved. It was his job to monitor the distribution of funds and help guide resources to where they were most needed. He considered every factor. The cares of the hospital weighed on his shoulders. A microcosm of the nation. The more professional element at the hospital, the consultants and doctors, treated him fairly, once they understood that he was not there to cut funding. The lower levels, the nurses and auxiliary workers, had taken longer to convince. This he explained in terms of education, specialists generally from better stock and more able to control their emotions. They understood the logical argument while the labour force was more irrational and short term in its thinking, governed by sentiment. But he had won the workers over through sheer force of manners. He was a modest man and people soon warmed to him. It was a hard job, but somebody had to do it. He chuckled at the cliché.

When the waitress reappeared he signalled for his bill. Concentrated on the poor woman once more as she approached. The face was tired, skin creased with worry. The eyes misty before their time, from tiredness rather than age. He tried to imagine her life and saw nothing but long hours and poor pay. The lack of a decent vacation. The optimism of youth destroyed by her grim reality. He felt so sorry for the woman. Knew that her name was Sandra from having used the restaurant regularly since he came to stay at the hotel. He would never call her by her first name of course. This would show a familiarity that could easily be misinterpreted. There was a working arrangement that had to be respected. He had seen businessmen and tourists treating her rudely and found their behaviour repugnant. He carefully placed his card on the plate and signed his name with a flourish. He thanked her for the meal. Smiled. The waitress returned this smile and thanked him.

Mr Jeffreys understood that she was on a treadmill. She paced across the carpet in shoes that bit into her heels, most likely struggling with the hot flushes of menopause. Her children had no doubt turned from her, towards drugs, yet despite her hard life she was forever smiling. Making the effort her work demanded. He appreciated this. Had done it himself as he tended the sick and dying, frail bodies broken by heart failure and the numerous forms of cancer. She had always been friendly towards him and once, when he had overheard her talking to a colleague, she had referred to him as a gentleman. This made him proud. Knowing that he did not possess the same arrogance as far too many of his contemporaries.

Times had changed and the nation was now managed according to consensus. Britain had evolved into a more fair and classless society. It was true that today you truly reaped what you sowed. He placed a healthy tip on the table and left the restaurant, smiling again at the waitress as he left. He wished there was something he could do to ease the pain of her existence, but knew that his life's work was within the hospital, that unless she was admitted she was beyond his assistance. He stopped by the door and looked over at the pianist. Waved when he caught the man's eye. The man beamed back. He appreciated the sophisticated yet easy atmosphere of the Piano Bar and the sheer love of good music displayed by its clientele.

Mr Jeffreys passed through reception and smiled at the girl on the desk, went outside and straight into the waiting taxi. He was pleased to see that the cab driver was punctual to the minute. He was staying in one of the airport hotels, a short drive from the satellite town in which he worked. He loved the feel of the hotel. The steady turnover of guests and the empty hush of the corridors. The rich carpets beneath his feet. Quality prints lined the walls leading to his room. His bed was made and room cleaned on a daily basis. He fully appreciated the plush restaurant and bar. Heated swimming pool and first-class gymnasium. Room service whenever he was peckish, no matter what hour of the day or night. He loved the sheer efficiency of the place. The impeccable behaviour of the staff. If only the hospital could match its standards. One day perhaps. Of course, he could make the trip out from his central London apartment each day, yet the journey was stressful and merely emphasised the shabby nature of these outer zones. He was more than willing to pay for a hotel room. His work was sensitive and the core of his existence. He was certain of at least another six months at the hospital, perhaps longer. He had worked in further flung regions than this one, and each had its own problems. As such he was used to hotel living. Quite enjoyed the anonymity in fact.

As the cab pulled away he noted the cropped hair of the man driving. A skinhead. As a sensitive man he naturally abhorred the thuggish element within society, but was willing to give each individual a chance. The smell of mint wafted back. From a packet no doubt. So different from the sealed mints served in the hotel. The man was playing a tape with an irritating beat, a voice talking in a strange tongue he did not understand. It was a primitive rhythm and he thought of the Tower of Babel, likening popular music to a technically enhanced version. He wondered if his driver had ever heard of the great European composers he himself adored. When the car stopped at a set of traffic lights he very politely asked the skinhead if he would mind turning the music down as he had a splitting headache. The skinhead silenced the racket but Jeffreys suspected irritation. He had only wanted the volume reduced a little so that he could focus his thoughts. The white lie of a headache was merely a polite means of achieving this end and avoiding unnecessary conflict. The skinhead had to react and turn the radio right off. It was not his fault if the music was annoying. He wondered whether he should try to explain himself, but decided to let the matter rest. He was a customer and the skinhead was there to provide a service.

The taxi eased forward across the crossroads, circled a roundabout and joined the motorway. Mr Jeffreys enjoyed this section of road, which was only the distance of two junctions. The houses and factories were blacked out for a while and he was able to peer at the faceless shapes driving nearby cars, staring straight ahead, intent on reaching their destinations. He considered the movement of the soul, the shifting of the intellect to a higher level of consciousness. At least for those citizens who spent their lives doing good. He shuddered at the horrors awaiting those who committed evil acts. Felt sorrow for them despite their crimes.

The dark stretch lit up and they were soon rising on to an elevated section of road, the lights of the town twinkling to his right. It was a view that masked the grinding monotony of life in this place. The mindless violence and spirit-sapping drug addiction. People lived and died under those artificial stars. Stuck in the same streets for entire lifetimes. Doing nothing. Going nowhere. He wished he could instruct the skinhead to keep driving. Deep into the countryside. He imagined small hamlets and green fields, ancient country pubs and a village cricket match. This was a no-man's-land in many ways, neither here nor there, a brief feeling of despair just that. It would soon pass. He would do his duty. Dealing with sickness and death left its mark on everyone involved in the eternal fight of Good against Evil. It was an inevitability.

Once off the flyover they left the motorway. The driver contined to another set of traffic lights. There were houses on either side, terraces coming right up to the edge of the dual carriageway. To the left were flats. Beneath them a parade of shops. These shops sold newspapers and tools. Beyond the lights and near to the railway tracks there rose a factory, consisting of dull brickwork and flaking windowpanes. Mr Jeffreys sighed. A pub flew the Union flag. From now on the journey would be slow. The scenery mundane. The cheap housing and tacky shops lacked character. Oozed mediocrity. He was forever aware of the poor clothing of the masses, the hunched shoulders and hacking lungs of the elderly. The belligerence of middle-aged men and women. Overweight and undernourished. The indiscipline of the young. He felt so sorry for these people.

Traffic backed up from the red lights and he looked into the car next to the taxi, which was full of teenagers. Boys and girls slapped at each other in a mock fight and one of the girls raised a bottle to her mouth. The glass was brown and her lips bright red under the street lights. It was nothing more than high spirits and he smiled. He himself had larked around as a young man. It was a part of growing up. He remembered his own youth, how even as a child he had wanted to help others, although never to be a surgeon like his father. But death had always terrified him.

The lights changed and the teenagers accelerated

away. A smell of burnt rubber entered through the taxi's vents. Mr Jeffreys looked ahead hoping that no poor soul was in the way of this act of bravado. He understood the need for excitement in the young, but as a medical man had seen the consequences of such behaviour. It was a problem within society.

People were forever rushing, lost in turmoil. Not thinking before they acted. Or spoke. They were unable to quietly reflect on life and its deeper meaning. The young were the worst offenders, unaware of their own mortality, not to mention the mortality of those around them. But it was a general truth. People's minds were confused, actions haphazard. Education channelled the energy of youth and helped to create useful patterns of behaviour. This in turn shaped civilisation. Without control, human beings was no better than apes. His own education had been impeccable, yet he had worked hard at his studies, pushed himself and avoided temptation. Too many teenagers wasted their opportunities. He lived in a meritocracy and was where he was today through sheer hard work and self-sacrifice. The youngsters vanished beyond the curve in the road and he wished them well.

His taxi followed, but at a more dignified pace. They passed a pub–cum–steakhouse. One day he would eat a meal there. When he was about to move on perhaps. It was the type of place where families gathered to celebrate birthdays and anniversaries. He pictured small plates of steak, served with processed chips and peas. This would follow a prawn cocktail of course. The accompanying sauce would be made with supermarket mayonnaise and tomato ketchup. The prawns frozen. For dessert there would be a slice of apple pie and custard. He had seen this on television. People also gathered in these steakhouses after funerals. They sipped at glasses of lager and ate sandwiches made from nutritionless white bread. They ate pickled onions. Gherkins. Sausage rolls. Buns with layers of sugar on top. Small pieces of Cheddar on wooden sticks, next to tinned pineapple chunks. All this was in stark contrast to the meal he had just enjoyed. The asparagus. Veal. Gateau. A salad sprinkled with extra-virgin olive oil. An expensive cognac.

He thought of the waitress who had served him. Sandra. Her family would toast her in just such a place. Mourners would look through the dirty glass and see passing lorries instead of cacti and framed prints. A pop song would replace the subtle jazz of a trained pianist. A cheap stereo system rather than a baby grand. A few words would be said and that would be that. He noticed Christmas tinsel lining a window. In the middle of summer as well. It was so sad. But again, everyone could prosper if they so chose. All it took was determination. This was in-built of course. A part of what you were. Yet these were the two strands of existence with which he toyed. The inevitability of death suggested fatalism while his own success insisted on free will. He had long fought the notion of fate. Believed that even in death it was possible to influence the future.

The sports centre ahead was also without any discernible character. A block of stone. Concrete dominated the town. Sheets of glass filled the gaps. There was no fine architecture to raise the spirit. Inside the sports centre, the gym would be occupied by men dedicated to violence. Thugs and bouncers. The swimming pool full to the brim. He remembered his last visit to a public baths and how he had spent the entire time trying to avoid what were termed dive-bombers. Horrible little boys with shaven heads and skin so white it resembled marble. These guttersnipes never tired. They churned the water and harassed him to such an extent that his normal composure had almost cracked. The taxi driver's son would be a dive-bomber. This was a certainty. Like father, like son. Mr Jeffreys was used to health-club pools. The hotel offered everything he needed. The gymnasium was sparsely used, while the pool was often empty. He could exercise in peace. There were no bouncers or urchins to disturb him.

He craved peace above all else. It was a different way of life, he admitted that, and did not wish to appear arrogant or snobbish. Of course, the dive-bombers were lovable little rogues. Innocent enough, but badly disciplined. Some people expressed themselves in a physical manner while he was more of an intellectual. He imagined the bouncers and dive-bombers as patients in his hospital, saw these men and boys attached to monitors. Rows of shaved heads and pale faces. He felt the beat of a child's heart, blood-sugar levels running wild, the gentle prick of a sedating needle giving him the rest he needed. His mood cheered. He saw these men and boys being reunited with loved ones. Wives and sisters. Weeping mothers. They would have welcome-home dinners. Eat peas and chips and hamburgers. They would add ketchup and brown sauce. Vinegar would soak the chips. That was the best thing about his work. He was able to help everyone, his life dedicated to their well-being. It sounded a grand statement but was not intended as such. It was thanks to people such as Mr Jeffreys that the dive-bombers were able to dive-bomb, the waves they created a minor irritant.

Light filled the windscreen and they were passing more stone blocks. Then a busy supermarket. Trolleys lay on their side. In a place where nothing ever happened the supermarket was a focal point. He saw children waiting by the side of the dual carriageway, preparing to cross. They breathed exhaust fumes. Lead accumulated within their brains. They had little hope for the future. Lacked self-belief. He lowered his head and closed his eyes, shut down completely.

He imagined that he was on holiday. Sitting on a beach in the Maldives. He would go fishing and return home with dinner, then sit in a jacuzzi with a refreshing cocktail. Follow the walkways and feel the sun on his back. At night enjoy the deepest of sleeps, his room cool and comfortable. During the day he would read classic literature and chat with his fellow guests. He would forget the sorrows of mankind for a short while. Make love to a beautiful woman. Sip champagne. Recharge his batteries. Escape his responsibilities for a short while and revel in silence.

The skinhead's voice ripped into this idyllic vision. They had arrived at the hospital. Mr Jeffreys tipped the man generously, and this brought an embarrassed smile to the driver's face. Good relations were restored. Bad feelings could not be allowed to fester. Misunderstandings only existed to be smoothed out. It was a basic rule of his.

Mr Jeffreys passed through the first set of glass doors to enter the hospital and was struck by the ferocious, trapped smell of old books. There were two shops to his right. The first sold newspapers, pads of paper and envelopes, carbonated drinks and heavily sugared candies. This was closed. The second was empty bar two rows of collapsible tables. These were heavy under stacks of used CDs, videos and books. This shop was open, its stock donated in order to raise funds for the hospital. Acting on a whim, he went inside. The CDs were easy listening, country and western, Irish ballads and movie soundtracks, plus a small number of pop singers whose names he did not recognise. The books were a mixture of crumbling war stories and cheap romances. He scanned a pile of videos. Suntanned musclemen fired automatic weapons at him. He smiled at the volunteer who was preparing to close for the night. Mr Jeffreys was surprised by the quantity of goods donated but not by the quality.

He left the shop and went into the main reception area, through a second set of doors. He said hello to the woman on the desk and weaved through the last visitors of the day, noticed a skinny girl sitting on one of the benches arguing with an older man who could have been her father. She looked like a drug addict. He did not mean that in a moralistic way of course. Heroin addiction was an illness and its sufferers deserved sympathy rather than condemnation. Nevertheless, this disease was a clear example of personal weakness affecting the majority of hard-working, decent folk. He smiled at her as he passed and she smiled back.

The cafeteria was closed. It was a place where he often sat and observed those who came to visit family and friends. This was an important element of his work. Knowing the rhythm of day-to-day life. The hospital's human side was so much more than just the staff. The cafeteria revealed a good cross-section of locals. Here he saw healthy versions of his patients. In all their glory.

Different hospitals had different needs. Prior to this assignment he had worked on the south coast where the hospital served a very different clientele. The population was far more elderly and this was reflected in the nature of the illnesses with which the hospital dealt. His first winter had seen an influenza epidemic sweep the country and this had hit the elderly hard. A great strain on resources was the inevitable result. Staff had come under unbearable pressure. In the short term it had been necessary to control the situation as best they could. In the longer term, contingency plans were required. There were other illnesses associated with old age and he had studied the effect that the outbreak had had on efficiency. His expertise had proved invaluable. Resources had been maximised. Money saved and redirected.

As he walked to his office, Mr Jeffreys felt a surge of pride. He made a difference. The corridors around him were dull and devoid of life, but his office offered sanctuary, somewhere he could work undisturbed. An intellectual haven in a material world. He unlocked the door and went inside. The room was small but adequate. The knockers could say what they liked about the NHS, but it worked. Against the odds. It was a balancing act of course, and a rethink was long overdue, yet for the moment the state coped.

He switched on his lamp and stopped for a moment to admire the image of the Acropolis decorating his calendar. He had touched those columns with his own hands. He thought of the Hippocratic oath and recalled the fumes of Athens. The air-conditioned cool of the Hilton. He fired up his computer and settled down to work.

It had been a hard day and Ruby was exhausted when she got home. With just a few hours of sleep the night before she should've been staying in with the remote in one hand and a mug of cocoa in the other, patrolling the mean streets of Britain with a TV crew, spying on herself from a helicopter gunship, firing into a shopping-centre pub, flushing out the hooligan element, but she wasn't bothered about the ratings war, had tomorrow off and was going out. She had a shower and washed her hair, painted her fingers and toes, dressed in front of the mirror. When her lift pulled up outside she ran down, the tiredness gone, tingling by the time she jumped in the back seat next to Paula.

Des was driving, his twin brother Don in the passenger seat, radio turned right up as they pulled away. Don was the perky one, always making plans, fiddling with a pack of cards, shuffling kings and queens, hearts and diamonds, training for this new life as an international card shark. He'd soon be on his way to Monte Carlo to relieve those chinless jet-setters of their excess millions, once his moves were perfect. Last week it was gun running, next it would be gold prospecting. He always had a dream, an adventure waiting to happen. And because Don was always perky, it meant Des was Pinky. For Ruby and Paula the twins were a couple of easy-going guys who liked a laugh.

Ruby couldn't hear Paula talk the music was so loud, but they nodded and shook their heads, knowing exactly what was being said. It happened like that, in a pub or club, talking for hours and not hearing a word, reading minds instead. Pinky and Perky should've been good at ESP, but they came from different eggs, so even though they looked similar there was no way you'd get them mixed up. It wasn't like they were identical and you could go out with Des, say, then end up having it off with Don by mistake. Not that Ruby fancied either of them, they were her friends, but she'd heard about that happening, when she was at school and her best friend at the time, Viv, was going out with a boy for three months before she found out he was sharing her with his twin brother. That was nasty, not far off rape, but Viv got them back with bells on, first by taking it in her stride so it looked like the joke was on the twins, laughing in her boyfriend's face after she'd done it with his brother, pretending she knew all the time and preferred it with the other boy, and the funny thing was, he got jealous and started slagging her off, couldn't handle the tables being turned, and then she went and told *her* brother about what had happened, made up some extra stuff about them going around calling her a slag and trying to sell her smack.

Viv's brother Bobby was the sort of nutter who had lots of nutty mates so she must've had some idea of what was going to happen. Bobby found the twins and sliced them up badly with a Stanley knife. Ruby never saw it happen but had been around enough cut faces since to know it was a horrible thing to do to another human being, never mind the shock and trauma involved. She hated violence. It was wrong what the twins did to Viv, but there was no excuse for slashing someone and scarring them for life.

Bobby was handsome and she'd had a crush on him, at least till he hurt the twins. She saw one of them a month later in the street and the marks on his face made her feel sick. Nowadays she wouldn't think it was ugly, but was fifteen at the time and had a different view. Nursing changed the way you saw things. Now a scar was the leftovers of a successful mending process, something magical, like a miracle. Thing was, Viv wasn't that upset about what had happened to her. She almost saw the twins as one person anyway. It was more her pride. But the vicious stuff, the knives and glasses, were rare when you compared it to the good that went on, the way people socialised and helped each other out.

Violence wasn't just physical either, it was mental as well, and she might've believed in love and peace but that didn't mean she was thick. You learnt early that sticks and stones could break your bones, but they would mend, that it was the words that really hurt you. Words stuck in your mind same as a cancer, lumps of rotten thought that seeped into your blood and spread, ruining everything. There was the scorn of someone you knew, words that were bitter and twisted but somehow wrapped up with love, like her mum when she got sick, the rage unplanned and confused. Then there was calculated cruelty, the poison of strangers, snobs who looked down their noses at you. That was to do with power. Some people used their fists, others their tongues. She wondered where the twins were, if people felt sick seeing their scars. At least you could improve your manners, make yourself a better person. That's what she tried to do, did her best not to dislike anyone, to see the good in them and the reasons for their actions.

Des and Don were nothing like those other twins, she couldn't even remember their names now, and she reckoned she was a good judge of character, most of the time. Desmond and Donald were old-fashioned names and maybe they'd been in the family for generations, and she was imagining what she'd call her kids, if she had them one day, if she met the love of her life, and Paula was leaning over and asking if she was all right, Ruby nodding, she felt brilliant, honest, and the two of them grinned great big massive smiles at each other and it was a shame she hadn't brought a CD with her, she wasn't mad about the stuff on the radio, it was harder music than she listened to, but she wasn't moaning, no chance of that, she wasn't one of these women who put on airs and graces and gave the boys a hard time when they were doing her a favour giving her a lift. She believed in equal opportunities, the colour around Paula's eyes wobbling same as a bubble you blew through a hoop, washing-up liquid in a fancy container, rings coming off her eyes and filling with air, tumbling out of the window, and Paula was salt of the earth, it was a struggle for her to get by in life, but she never complained, made the most of things.

Des was busy nodding his head to the music, acting

more confident than usual and Ruby guessed he was covering up his shyness for Paula's benefit. There was a smell and cherry air-freshener in the car, and she just knew Des had gone out and bought it specially for tonight, for Paula.

They were going for a drink first, an hour in the pub then on to Detroit's. She hadn't been there for months and was looking forward to it.

– Fucking hell, Don said, Des slowing down as the traffic in front backed up. Look at that.

Over the other side of the central reservation was a king-size Tesco's, and in the car park something was burning, big puffs of smoke rolling into the sky, a smell of ash and petrol heavy in the air, a fire engine coming up fast. Des pulled into a bus stop and they got out, the police blocking the road at the roundabout. Flames were starting to rise up, pushing the smoke higher into the atmosphere, the fire getting a proper hold, a bang thudding out as the fuel tank exploded.

Ruby could see it was a car, and knew she had to go and find out if anyone was hurt. There was no ambulance on the scene yet, so she didn't waste time, back to being a nurse and crossing over, cutting through the shrubs next to the service station, worried about what she was going to find. The fire wasn't that far from the petrol pumps either. She hoped no one was burnt, those were horrible injuries to treat let alone have, and there was another car right next to the one that was burning, and it was starting to smoulder where the flames had reached over and dug into the upholstery. Ruby went over to one of the policemen, but he was too busy talking into his radio about car thieves and arson, so she checked for herself and couldn't see anyone who was injured, and the car was empty so she walked over to the front of the supermarket in case they'd been dragged out, but there were no casualties there and the weight really did lift off her, she could feel it going.

She could also feel the heat of the fire on her body and smoke in her nose, so glad nobody was screaming out for their mothers, the fire was beautiful but it was a stupid place to torch a car, there were people shopping and it was near the pumps, but she couldn't help looking on the bright side, there was no real danger, the fire was going nowhere, just up into the sky, and the smell was fantastic, the colours exotic, like Bonfire Night had come early, Guy Fawkes out joyriding, loading up the boot with gunpowder thieved from B&Q, putting on a show, celebrating life, long licks of orange dancing in front of her, and there should've been fireworks as well, and a hot-dog van.

A crowd had quickly gathered, people coming from the pub over the road to have a look, post office workers from the sorting office, shoppers with bags and trolleys, passers-by, gangs of kids who hung around the car park doing wheelies, and it was turning into a spectacle all right, Ruby feeling the same excitement as when she was a kid, remember remember the fifth of November, the only thing missing was the cold air, the drizzle and dampness of a dark night, bundled up in her coat and scarf holding Mum's hand, toes frozen and a sparkler in her hand, the white fizz of powder, and it was like she was looking into the head of the sparkler right now, something on the car sizzling white for a few seconds, shooting stars and sparkling dreams, and she was so happy she almost wanted to cry, all these years later she was warm and the sky wasn't pitch black, another fire engine arriving as the first hose blew water into the flames, the smouldering car bursting alight at the same time, the police telling everyone to move back in case it blew up same as the other one, and everyone was just watching the fire, really enjoying themselves, and she bet they were thinking the same thing as her, Guy Fawkes with his straw heart inside a jumblesale body stitched together by Frankenstein, a smiling face topped with an old hat, a happy dummy glad to burn and make people smile, she heard someone shout out PENNY FOR THE GUY, everyone laughed and she was right, they were all thinking the same thing, similar memories, Ruby half expected someone to come out of the store with a trolley full of potatoes to wrap up in foil and stick in the fire, but the hoses were strong and she couldn't help feeling disappointed when the first fire was put out, standing next to three boys who'd taken advantage of the distraction and nicked some beer from inside, frothing it up and spraying each other with foam, they cheered when the second car exploded and everyone shifted back oohing and aahing, but a policeman came and pushed one of the boys with his truncheon so Ruby moved away as the argument started, more police arriving in a van and going over, the first car soon soaked and just a heap of bones, its black frame steaming, the second fire quickly going down, and the focus of everyone was moving from the fire to the police and youths, a mob forming out of nothing, more youths and men from the pub getting involved, it wasn't necessary, she hoped there wasn't going to be any trouble, things always had to spill over, and then as quick as it all flared up people drifted off and the police seemed to lose interest, the excitement over as the second fire was doused.

Ruby waited for five minutes, watching the police and fire brigade left behind to clear up the mess, an ambulance by the pumps that she hadn't even seen arrive, a few people lingering in ones and twos. She felt sad suddenly, walked back over to the car, the road clear again, traffic moving.

– You took your time, Don said. What did you go running over for?

– I thought someone might've been hurt. I couldn't stand here watching.

He nodded.

– Where's Paula? she asked.

– She went to find you. Didn't you see her?

– No.

– Maybe I should go look for her, Des said.

– She'll be back in a minute. Come on, we'll wait here. Then we can get going.

Des sat on the bonnet while Don juggled his cards. Ruby watched and had to admit he wasn't bad. Ten minutes passed, and then Paula appeared carrying a plastic bag packed with tins of spaghetti shapes.

– They had a special offer on. The kids love them. Some of the girls on the till went out to watch the fire, so it took me longer than I thought. Sorry.

They didn't bother with the pub now, went straight to Detroit's. Des parked and they walked over, the twins well impressed when Ruby waved to one of the bouncers and was called over, a long queue watching them, keeping quiet. There were four men on the door, and Ruby's bouncer was a vintage forty-odd-year-old with a gold-coin ring on his middle finger and shoulder-length hair, a big collar and a crucifix dripping off his left ear, a face that had seen and done it all, a throwback to a tougher time, an old-school hard man who took no lip off anyone but went soft when he saw Ruby coming, seeing as she'd been on his ward for the two days the doctors kept him in after he was admitted at one in the morning, glassed during a lock-in, when he was socialising, off duty, a sliver of glass wedged near his eyeball, luckily working its way free.

Ruby ran a finger over the length of his scar, very slowly, turning him to mush so he blushed and turned his head away from his mates who were rocking back on their heels, the same age but moving with the times, shaved heads and Stone Island, arms folded, Ruby'd heard about them when he was in hospital, this lot drank, trained and worked together, been a team for years and made good money. She tried to remember their names, only knew Terry. He'd told her he was going to do the men who glassed him, they were as good as dead, and she'd done her best to calm him down, what good did it do hurting people like that, she was the one who had to clean up the mess, and he nodded but she guessed he'd do it all the same, understood that it was as much about his self-respect as revenge, then convinced herself he'd take some notice of what she said.

When you saw someone in a hospital bed, worried

about what was going to happen to them, if they'd end up maimed or dead, they went back to being a child. The hardest hard man crumbled once you gave him a bed-bath. They relied on you same as they used to rely on their mums, and you developed a special bond. Their mums were never impressed with them acting up once they'd cleaned their bums as babies. That's how it was with Terry. She had his number, loved the collar and yellow hair dye, a seventies face raised on glam rock, the cheesy sounds of Mud and Hot Chocolate.

– Is she with you? he asked, looking at Paula in the background, the other bouncers staring at her bum and licking their lips.

– These two as well. We're all together.

He gave the boys a different sort of look.

– Go on then.

– What about us, someone asked at the head of the queue, too pissed to keep quiet.

– Fuck off, mush, he said, leaning forward.

Ruby saw Terry knocked out and bleeding, the twins after Bobby had finished with them, hoped nothing like that ever happened to Pinky and Perky, smiling at the nicknames, never using it in front of people. They'd given Terry an injection and stitched him up, and next day he was semi-conscious, couldn't get out of bed and didn't know where he was, going on about being an engine driver when he grew up, like Casey Jones, and she held his willy for the bottle, helped him with something bigger. She smiled now, looking deep into his eyes, and it was like he could see what she was thinking and went purple, a big man like

Boxer, except Boxer didn't have the same pressure and could live a different sort of life. She felt sorry for all of them, everyone in the world, didn't blame anyone for anything, at the same time feeling good about life, knew there were jagged edges but that they just made it better, added flavour, made all the good things stand out.

She couldn't stop herself reaching up and kissing him thank you on the side of his head, right on the scar, smelling his aftershave, she wanted to run her tongue along the skin and make everything better, all the people with scars on their faces and in their minds, but she didn't, followed the others over and paid her money, then went inside.

She stood with Paula as Pinky and Perky went to the bar, feeling ripples off the music and hearing the fizz of smoke, warm air churning in her ears, this happiness she felt when she was out with her friends, no cares in the world, as if she'd earned the right to enjoy herself, to do anything she wanted, she'd contributed something to the world with all those hours of tender-loving care, coaxing people back to health, fetching and carrying, a shoulder to lean on when times were tough, and now it was payback time, if anyone deserved a laugh it was her and Dawn and Sally and Davinda and Boxer and Maureen and all the rest of them, and she laughed thinking about their Christmas party and how Boxer got drunk and Dawn took advantage, she was sex mad that girl, Boxer wasn't used to drinking, pissed on a couple of cans, Dawn taking him into the Ladies' where they made love in one of the cubicles, Ruby didn't know what had happened till the next day when Dawn told her, and Dawn was laying it on, maybe feeling bad but not about to admit it, said nobody did it better than a dummy, and it wasn't a nice thing to say but it was like that sometimes when you were dealing with amputations and cancer of the colon and brain tumours and heart disease, a way round it was this humour that made fun of everything, like nothing was sacred any more, that was the way Dawn was, drunk like Boxer, she loved him the same as the rest of the nurses, and Dawn called him a dummy because of this wanker they'd had in once, a moaner and a groaner who didn't like the food and didn't like the Paddies and didn't like the Pakis and didn't like the poofs caring for him, didn't like anything or anyone, and Ruby had tried her best, reckoned he just didn't like life, started fresh every time she spoke to him, but when he called Boxer a dummy that was it, because Maureen and Davinda and Clive could handle it, but not Boxer, and once Boxer had left she'd gone in and slapped the patient's face as hard as she could, told him what she thought of him in front of everyone.

He reported her as well. She got in trouble, Maureen saving her job by telling a white lie about him swinging first, and Dawn saw to him, a massive dose of laxative that had him on the toilet for a week. She wished Dawn was with them, that they could all be together right now, and the funny thing was that Boxer was more concerned about hurting Dawn's feelings after the party, said he preferred her teaching him to read and write.

– Mind out, Don said, slipping on the floor, almost going over.

Ruby saw the people around her, fit and healthy and not realising how lucky they were, the excitement stretching from one end of the room to the other.

– It was murder getting served, Des said, handing her a bottle.

A man in a Ben Sherman got up on a table and started doing a striptease, undoing one button at a time with exaggerated movements, flicking his wrists and tempting the ladies as his mates chanted WHO ATE ALL THE PIES, stretching his arms back and pulling the shirt off, twirling it around his head seductively and lobbing it into the crowd, to one of his mates really, a chorus of YOU FAT BASTARD, YOU FAT BAS-TARD directed at his shimmering gut, the blubber blue in the light, and he was happy taking the piss out of himself, saying look boys and girls I'm a big fat bubba who needs to lose six stone otherwise one day my heart is going to explode, and I smoke too many fags and drink more in a day than I should do in a week, I eat a greasy breakfast every morning of my life and chips and batter at night, and my face is battered and bruised and I'll never walk down the catwalk with the anorexics, but the thing is, I don't fucking care, just don't give a toss, I'm too busy living to waste time worrying and waiting for a miracle pill that'll mean I can last till a hundred, why waste the best years of your life planning ahead, and Ruby could see that two of the bouncers were on their way, the belly dancer knocking over a table full of glasses, and he was undoing his flies, pulling his jeans down an inch, back up, down two inches, back up, down three inches, finally they were around his ankles and he was showing off a pair of Union Jack shorts, and he wasn't finished, was going for the full monty, didn't want to let the girls down, but he was having trouble getting his jeans over his shoes, hopping up on to one foot and swaying for a second as the table tilted and sent him crashing forward where his fall was broken by his mates, and he still ended up on the floor, another table going as the bouncers arrived, Terry first, on the dance floor where he belonged, shaping up, and it wasn't necessary, they were only having a laugh, and the bouncers were having a word and shaking hands, everyone knew each other, and it was calm and sweet and happy and she watched this guy who moved so easy as he danced you'd never guess he was carrying all those bones inside him, that there was thousands of miles of nerves threading through gallons of water, you had to keep drinking, you didn't want to get dehydrated, and she was watching the lava bubbling in Perky's pint, people coming and saying hello, some she knew and others she didn't, their lips moving silently, and she danced like she always danced, felt happy like she always felt happy, the music nice and smooth with no surprises, she just loved dancing, didn't want to think, what was real was what she could see and touch and hear, and she loved this place because they did visuals with the music, someone had raided the Cartoon Channel with a VCR, and this meant she could dance with Mickey Mouse and Donald Duck, cheer as Top Cat dodged Officer Dibble, with Popeye on the door flexing his muscles, and best of all she could hug Pinky and Perky and feel glad they were in a different league and weren't being chased by the big bad wolf who'd huff and puff and blow their house down, and the lights were popping, extending things she saw every day, and when you worked with bodies you could go two ways, she'd seen how some student nurses couldn't cope and gave up, but she'd taken straight to it, for her it was the biggest miracle going seeing how the body worked, how complex it was, from the brain and heart to something like a fingernail regenerating after it had been chewed off, the way the blood flowed and was pumped by this muscle that had become a symbol for the soul, she liked that, cynics said it was just an organ, part of a machine that would rust and fail, but to her it was magic, part of what you were, your feelings came out in the way you looked and moved, and she did her work and went home, had her tea and went out again, maybe she was selfish feeling good about herself, thinking she made a difference, but she believed it, not in a grand way like she was important, she wasn't, she was one of the little people, but it was good being ordinary, she didn't want to be famous, that was another world, she got on with what was right here, right now, it was how she was, part of her genetic make-up, laughing, genetic fingerprints, laughing, Fred Flintstone and Barney Rubble grinning, the arm of a record player lifted and the beak of a prehistoric bird lowered on to a slate record, Fred and Barney had a laugh the same as Pinky and Perky and Scooby Doo, she loved *The Flintstones*, wanted to live in Bedrock, have children like Bam Bam and Pebbles, talk to Wilma and Betty and lift rocks with dinosaurs instead of cranes, it was a dream town all right, Bedrock was where the men were manly and the women glamorous, and Fred and Barney were arguing on the screen, like they did, you only argued with the ones you loved, and then it was smoothed over, and they were going out for a late-night burger at a drive-in, the night had flashed past in seconds, cartoon time, and Ruby couldn't believe it, she was in the cartoon and saying goodbye to the nightclub staff – to the bouncers on the door – a glitzy affair built into solid rock so it would last for ever – breeze blocks and quality speakers – getting into Fred's car – Des's car – his trotters never got tired – Des was starving – and they were all four of them packed in now – Fred, Barney, Wilma, Betty – Des, Don, Ruby, Paula – the cartoon cutting off as they drove through English streets, finally parking up and going into the takeaway on the roundabout for something to eat, served quickly and back out into the car, all of them starving now like Des.

Ruby and Paula balanced the foam plates on their knees, spilling beans and rice, the blow was calming her down now, the twins in the front digging into kebabs, Ruby counting her beans, red and green jelly babies, losing track and going back to the beginning when she reached twenty-three. She shifted the rice around with a fork, thinking of her mum a million years ago sitting at a table showing her how to hold her knife and fork properly, like a big girl, and when you were little you wanted to be all grown up and adult and then when you were all grown up and adult you wished you could be small again.

The radio played quietly and Don tuned into a police frequency, the voice of an excited man saying that the raid had been a success. Three men were in custody. Hundreds of pills had been confiscated. Crack cocaine had also been found. It was time to put the kettle on and break out the biscuits. They'd soon be back at the station. Better call a doctor as well. One of the prisoners had a head wound. Another voice cut in and asked if he needed hospital attention. The first voice saying no. Crackle blanking the rest of the message.

Don flicked through again, German voices, then French, announcing an accordion, and he moved on, through a sitar, ragga vocals, garage, an Arabic song that sounded like a prayer, and finally the sound of a choir cutting out and a preacher launching into a sermon about sin and retribution and the power of the Lord that was truly awesome to behold.

He would soon unleash His wrath upon the world, the lesson dealt to Sodom and Gomorrah would be repeated on a far greater scale, the ice caps would melt and floods devour the wretched, the four of them stopping to listen as specks of rain hit the car, they rolled their windows up and Ruby saw this short fat man in a sweat-stained suit tap-dancing down the aisle lost in the sheer bliss of revelation, feet moving fast as his trunk stayed still, like a more righteous Barney Rubble, water pouring off his skull, and he was talking about fire and brimstone and eternal damnation, only by turning their backs on the sins of the flesh could they enjoy His reward of everlasting life, because the Earth was a battleground for the fight between Good and Evil, and demons were lurking in the dark recesses waiting to strike, God had made man in His own image and expected him to do His work, and Ruby snapped out of it and thought of Terry guarding the Pearly Gates, St Peter at the bar selling whizz, trips, charlie, E, and she understood that this was the sort of sermon that could go either way, turn really vicious and dark when they were open to suggestion like this, Don reading her thoughts and changing the station, sticking with a country and western song.

– Thanks, she said, and Don knew exactly what she meant.

When they finished eating Des drove Paula home, Ruby going in with her. It was three o'clock and Paula went to check the kids, her mum babysitting, asleep in Paula's bed. She came back down with a blanket and went into the kitchen for a can of Coke, shared it with Ruby in silence, then went back up. Ruby turned the light off and rolled over, lay there for ages unwinding things, cartoons stuck in her mind, finally falling asleep.

Mr Jeffreys was a romantic, but level-headed enough to understand the nature of hardship. Not from personal experience of course, but through a profound sense of empathy. He felt that this awareness was more genuine. A man of means was not expected to fight for the welfare of those less fortunate than himself, yet this was the path he had chosen. Public service was more important to him than the pursuit of wealth.

A factory worker or clerk joined a trades union and struck for higher wages and less hours while the self-employed evaded taxation and cheated the system. No matter the consequences to society. Trades unionism smacked of jealousy. The politics of envy a curse on the national interest. He knew that for the majority life was a struggle, but sacrifices had to be made. It was natural for people to try to better themselves. This he accepted, however insignificant their victories when compared to the victories of heroes. While he wished humanity could be free from suffering, he was a realist. Struggle was the way of the world. Natural selection a basic law. It was a cliché, but true, that life was not fair. No number of revolutions would ever change this fact. There would always be leaders and there would always be those who were grateful to be led. Without educated men being prepared to make sacrifices civilisation would crumble.

This same inevitability applied to life itself. Which without exception ended in death. He now understood that death conditioned life. What was harder to accept were the diseases than plagued humanity. He was not unique in feeling this way of course, but felt it more strongly than most. The decay of the body and mind depressed him. The way in which people passed through life blindly helping themselves to God's rich bounty was shameful. Too few stopped to consider their fellow travellers. Wasted their energy on trivial matters while the broader picture was ignored.

Despite being raised as a Christian, and one who had studied the Bible and attended church during his youth, he could not help but question a God who allowed a disease such as cancer to kill small children. A creator who watched as men and women who had worked hard all their lives were ravaged by senile dementia in their retirement years. They had nothing to show for their prudence. Their descendants ran riot. Drinking and taking drugs. Laughing when there was nothing to laugh about. Where was the justice when a selfless man ended up in heaven with a selfish brute, both enjoying everlasting bliss? This unfairness left the bitterest of tastes.

He clicked his mouse and conjured up a list of cases arriving in Accident & Emergency over the last year. Those needing instant attention and those able to wait. He pictured the waiting room. A grim affair with a children's playpen and various second-hand toys. A flickering television set that pumped out soap-opera inanities. Red plastic chairs and the general grime of a railway station. People dropped their sweet wrappers on the floor and spent cigarettes on the pavement outside, too stupid to realise that the build-up of rubbish had a negative effect on doctors and patients alike. That somebody had to be employed to clean up the mess. A small point. Perhaps he was being pedantic, yet felt this reflected the general lack of respect shown by far too many people. He felt such frustration at this basic lack of cooperation.

But never mind. He began working his way through the list. An elderly woman with breathing problems. A sprained foot. A car accident. A small boy who had swallowed bleach. Pneumonia. A severe headache. A pub fight. Burns from a spilt saucepan of boiling water. A heart attack. Throughout, Mr Jeffreys cross-referenced the time and nature of the admission, building a pattern. Seeing what could be avoided and what could not. This absorbed his attention for the next hour. Until he saved the document and leant back in his chair, giving his eyes a break from the screen. He was in a good mood.

Mr Jeffreys preferred to work at night, when the hospital was at rest and the corridors empty. His office was centrally located yet quiet. Removed from the main thoroughfares. But once outside it was a very different story. It was difficult to move freely. Staff were busy and he did not want to be in their way. He spent one day each week in the hospital, to remain in touch, but found he achieved far more at night. He was able to think clearly and his conversations with staff proved fruitful. People were less busy and far more relaxed. Welcomed him rather than tolerated his presence. His job involved the collection of first-hand information and opinion. It was essential that he listen before acting. The night nurses were dedicated and astute. He respected their observations. Theirs was a tough job. He found them more than happy to talk. It was not all work either. They conversed in a friendly way, about generalities. He was comfortable with the staff and believed the feeling was mutual. He never interfered, of course. He watched. Listened. Learned.

When he had started at the hospital his first task had been to learn its layout off by heart. He studied the plans for several days before setting out to match the various wards, theatres, laboratories and storerooms to these drawings. There was no point in rushing this work. He had to know every corridor, cupboard and WC. It was a period of discovery and reflection that lasted for the first month. It was also a time to gently introduce himself to his fellow workers.

He fully understood the potential for problems. Those who spent their lives caring for the sick did not readily accept an outsider whom they suspected of promoting spending cuts. This was not his role and he had patiently explained that the nature of his work was to ensure things ran more smoothly. He made the effort of introducing himself as an individual rather than as a job title. The personal touch made his work so much easier. At the end of this month he felt he knew the hospital and had been accepted by his colleagues. He was not arrogant enough to believe he could ever stop learning though, and was forever discovering new corners. Short cuts. Links. But he was thorough in his work.

The sounds of the hospital became familiar. The building was new compared to his last place of work, so the atmosphere differed. The floors were quieter and he generally moved in near silence. Any echo was softer than in older hospitals built in an age of acceptance and military-like regimentation. Many sounds were the same. The human element. The sound of suffering. But this hospital had been designed for the modern age, some twenty years ago. Ease of access had been a major consideration for the architects. A great deal of money had been spent in the search for efficiency.

From the outside the hospital was bland, some would say depressing, and obviously did not stand comparison with the great brick constructions of a hundred years before in terms of architectural design. Jeffreys preferred the grand entrances of the older establishments but understood the need to concentrate on practicalities. Money was more important than ever. Health care had evolved. Huge wards with long rows of beds did not exist here. Privacy and a sense of individuality had been attempted, beds clustered in small groups. The atmosphere was more personal and this made his job easier.

Now he was fully accepted. One of the gang, so to speak. He quite obviously did not pose a threat and was on particularly good terms with the night nurses. They shared a bond. He was part of the furniture and knew the routine. The rounds, habits, problems that arose. He knew what time Nurse Hopkins had her second cup of coffee, even the fact that she took milk and three sugars. A large woman in her forties, she was buxom and generous. He himself had made her coffee on a couple of occasions. This she had found charming. He also knew that Nurse McKenna lacked such a routine. If he was in a rush he could pass without disturbing her, such was her love of cheap romantic fiction. She should not really be reading while on duty, but the patients were asleep and it made no real difference. They joked about this love of romance. Nurse Daliwal had been harder to get to know. Perhaps due to a difference in culture. She was more reticent, but he had eventually won her over.

The alarm on his computer sounded. The sweet chimes of Mozart. He had achieved a lot in the last hour. He shut down and stood up, turned off the light and left his office. His legs were stiff and his back ached. His head suddenly heavy. A brisk walk would cure this. The corridors were stark and empty. The pressure eased a little. Muscles stretched and his mind began to clear. He was free to walk for miles if he so wished. There was a reassuring smell of disinfectant, a vital weapon in the continuing war against infection. But it was a never-ending task. As soon as one disease was cured, another erupted. During the day the voices of the sick were constant. The necessities of life demanded attention. Food was consumed and expelled, bodies washed and wounds tended, beds changed and sheets washed, symptoms considered and diagnoses given. Medication administered. There were so many things to consider. His work was pressurised, there was no question about that, yet he coped. The long list of admissions he had been working on began to fade. Everyone deserved a break.

He was certainly no paper shuffler. No desk-tied theorist. A glorified time-and-motions expert pontificating from afar. There were no ivory towers for Mr Jeffreys. Oh no. That was the easy option, both unacceptable and dull. The human touch was what made his work so enjoyable. He could flex his administrative muscle if need be, but did not. He was more than satisfied with the way things were going. Progress was being made. Everyone within the hospital was working for a common cause and even unskilled workers deserved to be heard. The porters, cleaners, volunteers. Consensus was all-important. Goodwill half the battle. He had the power to assist in their efforts but sought no special treatment. His office was small yet adequate. Just as long as he had privacy. The central location allowed easy access to every area of the hospital. He was hands-on. The problem with too many men in positions of power was that they were complacent and out of touch. Their position, salary and prestige was enough. Their decisions became tainted. He himself was already a wealthy man and the salary he received made no difference to his life. Position and prestige were easily obtained. Only fools craved a job title. Embraced arrogance. His work was a vocation.

Mr Jeffreys walked towards the west side of the hospital, turned left before he reached Pathology and began the return leg of a loop that generally took him thirteen minutes to complete. His circulation was restored now, mind stilled. He veered right before reaching the first of the children's wards and found himself facing a barefoot man dressed in striped pyjamas. They stood staring at each other for several seconds. The face of the man was drawn tight over the skull while the pyjamas reminded Jeffreys of a concentration-camp inmate. The eyes seemed too large for the sockets, the skull clearly visible under taut flesh. Bone pressed through bloodless skin devoid of life. The poor man was aged anywhere between forty and sixty years old. He did not know what to say to this walking skeleton, felt sick just looking at him. The man was grotesque, his odour foul, yet it was the eyes that unnerved Jeffreys the most. There was an unnatural glint that made a mockery of his weak and rotting body. A smirk covered the face.

– Are you all right? Jeffreys finally asked. You look as though you are lost.

The skeleton did not reply. The eyes scanned Jeffreys from head to toe. It was a long, malicious inspection.

– God sees everything that happens in here, the man said at last. He's everywhere, watching and waiting.

The voice was vindictive and Mr Jeffreys was chilled by its intensity. A skeletal hand shot out and gripped his arm. The man was strong and he was strangely scared. He could easily resist this patient if need be, but detested violence. The man was obviously confused, medication highlighting an evil side to his nature.

– Don't think you can fool me. I see everything that happens in this place. God gave me eyes. I know what you're up to, creeping around at night spying on women, stealing their panties and sniffing them in the bogs. You dirty cunt. I bet you wank in them as well, or do you go all the way and molest the women? Chop them up and flush them down the toilet? What's your game? Why do you do it?

Mr Jeffreys was embarrassed. His legs felt weak and he didn't know what to do. The man was senile, obviously demented and dredging the basest horrors from the depths of a decaying mind. The nurse on his ward must have let him slip away. This was unacceptable. He wondered which ward the man was on and cleared his throat to speak, aware of the horrendous glint in the eyes. Jeffreys did not want to cause a commotion. He was a gentle man and this patient obviously was not.

– Come on now. You are confused. What ward are you on?

– Ooooh, the man minced. La–di–da. But I can see through you. The fancy accent doesn't impress me. God treats everyone equal. I'm His worker and I've got your number. You're ripping the guts out of poor working girls and hanging their insides all over the room. You've got the surgeon's skill and think you can use it how you want, eating livers and drinking blood. Well, you can't, you fucking wanker. I'll fucking stop you ripping. Even whores have families. You're Lucifer in disguise.

Mr Jeffreys brushed the man's hand away. He felt nothing but disgust now. To be compared to a murderer. A fiend who inflicted pain when he had dedicated his life to its relief. His own father had been a surgeon. This was the basest behaviour imaginable. He saw a nurse at the end of the corridor, behind the skeleton. This man was more monster than innocent victim, the putrid smell of his body and clothing all-embracing, swamping the senses.

– Andrew!

Mr Jeffreys saw that it was Nurse McKenna. The man turned at her shout and watched as she walked towards them. Her head bowed. No doubt embarrassed for allowing the patient to wander off. Not to mention the fact that Jeffreys knew all about the romantic fiction.

– Wait there, Andrew.

Mr Jeffreys wished she would hurry. The corridor was very long and she seemed to be hardly moving. Yet her footsteps were getting louder. She could not arrive quickly enough despite the fact that he felt sorrow for this man, who had lost his dignity and been reduced to a blubbering shell. It was a terrible way to end one's life, walking about in dazed confusion. It was odd how those with mental problems so often turned to religious symbolism. This was obviously conditioned, whether consciously or subconsciously, in a church, school assembly or perhaps these days through television. But even so. It was amazing that anyone took this imagery seriously in the modern age. Lucifer was an amusing enough creation, but myth nonetheless. Did these people not understand that it was a story? Jeffreys was a rational man and had no time for superstition. He dealt in hard facts and clear figures.

– Come on, love, Nurse McKenna said, when she reached them. It's time to get back to bed.

She was careful to avoid looking Mr Jeffreys in the eye.

– He snuck out while I was answering a call.

Mr Jeffreys smiled. Nodded. Showed that it was okay. He understood that romantic fiction was not to blame. She was doing her best in difficult circumstances. A little lax perhaps but her heart was in the right place. Inefficiency was nothing more than a human frailty.

– It's quite all right.

– The drugs confuse him, but he's wonderful really, aren't you, Andrew?

Mr Jeffreys smiled and prepared to leave. It had been an unfortunate encounter. The smell of the man seemed to be getting worse.

– They want me dead, don't they? I know they want me dead.

– We're here to help you, Nurse McKenna said. We only want to help you. Come on, let's get back to the ward. I can't spend all my time chasing you up and down the corridors. What about the other patients?

The skeleton turned and stared at the wall. Jeffreys marvelled at the patience of the nurse. She was humouring him as if he were a child.

– Do you think me or any of the other nurses want to hurt you? Do you?

– No. But someone does. The bad people don't like me because I can see what they're doing. They want to cut me up into tiny pieces. They hate me.

Nurse McKenna turned to Mr Jeffreys.

– He'll settle down when I get him back to bed.

He's confused. A couple of days and he'll be back to normal.

Mr Jeffreys wondered what exactly normal was in this case. The man was obviously in a bad way. He would check his details later, but right now wanted to move on. Nausea was creeping up. He kept smiling, drawn now to the skeleton's bare feet. The nails were either broken or in-grown. What was left of the skin was covered in dirt. Below that would be all sorts of abrasions and growths. The bones were even more obvious in the man's feet than in his face. The smell was disgusting. Swelling over the odour of his breath. Clothes. Body.

– Hurry up, Nurse McKenna said to the skeleton. You're trouble, you are. Trying to get me told off.

She smiled at Mr Jeffreys. A good worker. A basic type but with enough sensitivity to humour a smelly, senile old man who, if he had been living in a more natural environment, or as little as twenty years before, would be in his grave instead of on a ward. Scientists had worked hard to prolong life, but, sad to say, too often at the cost of dignity. This nurse was willing to lie and tell her patient that everything was all right when it very obviously was not. She was a carer easing the suffering of a dead man. A skeleton. Hers was a tough job and Jeffreys was full of admiration.

– I'm hungry, nurse.

She tutted and shook her head. A little boy.

– You'll have to wait for breakfast, like everyone else.

The man suddenly turned towards Mr Jeffreys, pushing his face forward.

– You cold-blooded murdering bastard. They'll catch you and hang you. I hope you rot in hell.

A hell inhabited by a horned devil and full of raging fires no doubt. Red lizards with forked tails. Imps and sodomites. He was shocked by the outburst, even a little hurt. It was certainly not nice being abused in front of Nurse McKenna. But he remained professional. The man was sick. His sympathy returned.

– I'm sorry. He doesn't mean it. It's the drugs.

He watched the skeleton walk along the corridor with the nurse scolding him. She was slightly taller, wider, though not fat. Even when they disappeared from his sight the smell of the man lingered. Organs were decaying inside the body and the brain had turned rotten. It was so sad. He considered this encounter for several minutes.

Finally Mr Jeffreys continued on his way. He now realised that the fear he had felt was merely shock at the depths to which a human being could sink. He had seen this sort of disorientation many times before of course, but had never been abused in such a way. He laughed. He was not as tough as he liked to think. Working in a hospital steeled a man to the harsh realities of life, yet this incident had reminded him of his own vulnerability. There was always a surprise around the corner.

He walked fast and was soon back at his office. He locked the door and put the kettle on. He made himself a cup of tea and settled down to work, wondering for a short moment whether certain men did in fact steal women's underclothes in order to masturbate. Did they sniff the material? As a romantic he hoped that it was just the ravings of a lunatic. It seemed highly unlikely but you could never tell in a town such as this. It was not the most cultured place in the world and perhaps such perversion was rife. He did not want to think about such things, and immersed himself once more in his work.

R uby didn't stir when Paula gave the girls their breakfast, nagging at them to hurry up, get dressed, brush their teeth, tie their laces, walking them round the corner to school. Ruby didn't move till the blanket was pulled off her face and the sun shocked her eyes, a couple of seconds later the rich smell of coffee pounding her nose, opening up to see Paula kneeling by the couch holding out a mug with this mad green dragon spitting bright red flames at her, steam off the coffee blowing forward as Paula moved the mug, smoke off the fire, and the thing was, this griffin was three-dimensional and hologram-looking, like it was alive or something, a shock that lasted two seconds and then was gone.

She sat up quickly when she saw the hurt on Paula's face, heat burning her hand, the handle broken so she was holding the mug around the middle. You had to have tough skin, Ruby's mum had been like that, could handle anything, never seemed to feel the heat, and Ruby was reaching out and taking the coffee before it dropped on the carpet, another colour adding to the food and mud, dirty shoes the girls forgot to take off when they came in, it didn't matter how many times they were told, Ruby nearly spilling this rich-looking tar on the sofa, not ready for the heat either, leaning forward and putting the mug on the floor, blood rushing into her head as she went, wincing when she felt the stiffness in her neck. It was the angle she'd been sleeping on the couch, snapping her fingers till they cooled down.

As the blood flowed one way she imagined anti-freeze in her spine racing the other, right down her back to where wood pressed out of the couch. She'd been moving all night long, tossing and turning and trying to get comfortable. The sofa had seen better days, but it was Paula's mum who'd given it to her and she was lucky having her mum around, Irene did a lot for her children.

– You look like I feel, Paula said, moving away and sitting on the edge of a chair opposite. Out of it.

– I am, Ruby smiled, rubbing sleep from her eyes. My head's killing me and I feel like my blood needs a wash.

– Can you do that then, have your blood washed? Paula asked, laughing.

– Not for a hangover. That coffee smells strong.

– It is, I got it special offer as well, you should smell it when you grind the beans down. You know what, don't you, I only went and forgot those tins I got last night. I left them in Des's car.

– He'll bring them round when he sees them.

– It was a good night, wasn't it, specially walking in like that, straight to the head of the queue, special guests of the bouncers. Don't think everyone else waiting was too pleased.

– It wasn't fair, was it. I never thought about it at the time.

– So what, I don't mind a bit of preferential treatment. Do you remember that time we went out with Jerry's cousin Gary? When he took us over to The Honey Pot as his guests, on my birthday?

Ruby remembered all right. Gary was a crook with a stake in an out-of-town nightclub, a big flashy effort near the reservoir. It was plush inside, and even the bouncers seemed better dressed somehow, but there was a nasty edge to the place and the music was shit, the worst sort of jazz-funk and shitty disco. They'd been treated like royalty by Gary, and while it was a novelty Ruby felt funny sitting on a platform with free drinks coming over all night with a waitress, everything on the house, a ready supply of drugs, if they wanted it, and they weren't the sort of women to look a gift-horse in the mouth, her, Paula and Dawn from work done in by the end of the night, though fair play to Gary he made sure they got home, even when Dawn, worse than the others and only half joking, offered to give him a blow job as thanks for the night. He just laughed and patted her on the head and said not to worry about all that, as a respectable business-man he had easy access to all the oral sex he required thanks very much, and that was one of the things that stood out about Gary, his manners, and he made an effort to use new words he found in the dictionary, a self-educated spiv with diamonds in his collar, another sort of dress sense she didn't have a clue about.

– You were sick down the side of the car, remember?

Ruby nodded and groaned from the dull pain stuck in her head, a leftover she didn't want, teeth fuzzy from not brushing them last night when she got in, she hadn't brought her toothbrush along, forgot, usually she would've tucked it in her handbag, or if she wasn't taking a handbag she'd put it in a pocket, or if she didn't have a pocket she'd slip it in her waist, remembering a time she was dancing, well and truly nutted, and her toothbrush went spinning off under hundreds of feet and she was crawling around trying to find it, a pink brush she'd bought the day before, and eventually she grabbed it, when they were back at the bar Dawn took it off her and stirred her drink, laughing, big-shot cocktails when they were only drinking vodka, and next day when she woke up her pink toothbrush was packed with dirt, and the worst thing was she'd cleaned her teeth with it when she got back to Dawn's, the thought of it almost made her throw up, so she thought of something else instead, saw them sitting in the back of Des's car last night, eating, with that preacher on the radio, a Bible-bashing voice straight from Dixie tormenting the speakers and praising God, doing his best to conjure up the devil as he dished out public health warnings, eternal damnation and the tormenting fires of a dodgy nightclub down near the core of the Earth, deep in the cellar where the walls were hot like coals, rock glowing behind the turntable as this tricky little geezer spun his wax and had the horn something rotten, two of them sticking out of his head, radio waves on the surface hijacked by a fundamentalist with no sense of humour.

With the sun out and about, the idea of hell didn't mean much, a joke to match with Gary the star-spangled gangster, Paula sipping from her Pokémon mug, she knew all the names as well, big gangs of computer-generated mythology. Ruby rubbed her eyes and sipped the coffee. It was thick and muddy and just what she needed. Her legs were stiff as she sat cross-legged, her and Paula sitting in silence for a long time, enjoying the drink.

– The girls had to wake me up this morning, Paula said, at last. I was sick when I got up, but I made their breakfast and got them to school in time, like a good mum. My mum left early and left me to it.

She laughed and emptied her mug.

– I'm going back to bed, Rube. You don't mind, do you? You'll be all right, won't you? Make yourself some toast if you want, there's bread on the counter and jam in the fridge, cornflakes in the cupboard.

– Don't worry about me.

Paula went back upstairs and Ruby went into the kitchen, where she made herself four slices of toast, because she was a greedy cow, smothering them in honey she found in the fridge next to the jam, then went out into the garden. It was a beautiful day and she was feeling better, the stiffness more or less gone. There was a deckchair by the back door and she set it up, eased back, ate her toast in the sun, long strands of honey dripping on to the plate, chewing it well and appreciating the texture.

A crow landed on the roof of the house behind Paula's, so big it could've been a raven, claws gripping slates as it peered at a paddling pool down below, the plastic sagging and slowly leaking air, long plastic tubes full of someone's breath, and she'd done it enough times, blown up balloons and had an aching jaw for hours afterwards. There was a rabbit hutch back against the house, out of sight of the crow, straw scattered over grass that needed a cut, a lot different to the one next door where it was shorn close to the ground, and she could see all the houses and gardens from where she was sitting, the fences made out of wire. Paula could do more with her garden if she wanted, but she wasn't green-fingered, had tried with a curry plant her mum gave her but then forgot to water it.

Ruby watched the crow for a long time, its body so beautiful and strong, oily feathers gleaming in the light, water off a duck's back was the expression, except the crow was a tougher bird. She used to feed ducks with her mum, in the park, the drakes the pretty boys, stale bread scattered over the water and pulling in coots, sometimes flocks of seagulls so Mum said there was a storm brewing at sea, the ducks quacking as the bread went soggy and swelled to twice its size.

When she'd finished her toast Ruby hauled herself up and went inside for her handbag, sitting back on the deckchair and rolling a nice chunky spliff, the crow turning its head left and right, maybe it had a predator, she couldn't think what sort of bird would go after a crow, not round here anyway, there were no eagles or hawks cruising the skies, and she knew what they said about crows, that they had a nasty streak and pecked the heads off other birds, robbed nests and decapitated chicks. They lurked on the moors, bleak landscapes that were only bleak if you were an outsider looking at them and expecting the worst, it was the same as a city or a town, anywhere really, it was there inside the observer. Ruby knew that well enough. It was a way of seeing things. There were no moors here, but maybe there had been once, a hundred years ago, you couldn't tell, generations of crows too stuck to move away, adjusting to changing times, dustbins spilling food. The foxes liked it round here as well, she'd seen them, didn't want to think of pecking devil birds, admired the shape and colour of the crow instead, the gold fur of a vixen.

Ruby lit up and sucked the smoke in, easing further into the chair, the sun on her face, at just the right angle, hitting her arms and legs. She was feeling mellow, the leftovers of last night gone, coffee melting the fuzz on her teeth, and Paula bought good coffee, it was a luxury but well worth the extra pound or so, and that toast had filled the hole in her belly nicely, everything was beginning to simmer, the clouds thin, air sweet, the crow launching itself, wings swaying with a lazy swagger, flapping and squawking its way across the houses and off to the flats with their blue railings and white wood panels, disappearing behind the roofs.

That bird was strong and slow and on the move, but Ruby wasn't going anywhere. She was knackered and, stretching her legs out, could easily sit here for the next ten years. She stubbed out on the grass, imagining the soil below as her eyelids dipped and she drifted in and out of sleep through long tunnels full of worms and moles, under the earth towards the devil's nightclub with its Wurlitzer jukebox and decadent sounds, happy songs that for some reason were called evil, the walls of this cave moving and the coals of an electric fireplace flashing, a remix of her earlier thinking, Ruby turning her face sideways, enjoying the warmth, glad she didn't have to go to work today, seeing furnaces in a crematorium deep inside the hospital, amputated arms and legs that made her back away from the light, plastic dolls from a shop display, and she was climbing the steps again, didn't like sitting on a platform with a man in diamond cufflinks, chunks of rubble and broken planks in the soil, glue and plaster strung together with gold wire, the garden slanting where the bulldozers packed up early, the housing association concerned short of cash, it was Paula's mum who'd bought her the turf six months after she'd moved in, six-inch nails in the gravel, stabbing one of her grandchildren in the foot, Ruby skipping in the playground a million years ago sinking her head down into the fountain for a mouthful of water, hot summer days, the best days.

Everything was blank for a while, no cares in the world as the shouting of her school playtimes shot through the years from the school where Paula's girls went, a few houses away, the playground on the other side of a wooden fence. She could hear cheering and laughing from boys and girls and the bang of a ball on the panels. Two more days and they'd be breaking up for their summer holidays. Paula was looking forward to having her kids at home but at the same time scared of the energy they were going to let loose on her, laughing when she told Ruby that last night, sipping her lager, water in her eyes thinking of her children, family values as strong as ever, the sound of shouting, another thump on the fence, Ruby floating away, a football flying over and bouncing a few feet in front of her.

She looked towards the school and saw a small blond head appear, eight-year-old fingers holding on to the wood, a pumpkin face with short hair and a wide grin, a pound coin under his pillow, and Ruby stood up and got the ball, threw it in the air and tried to volley it back, missed, the boy laughing, and now his head was multiplying, three more cropped pumpkins sticking up, grinning, one of the boys wolf-whistling, Ruby connecting with the ball second go and kicking it back over the fence. She was proud of the kick, to be honest it could've gone anywhere. She bowed.

– Thanks, they shouted.

The heads dropping down, out of sight.

– You've got sexy tits.

– Horny baby, horny.

– Shagadelic.

Ruby laughed at small boys and words they didn't know the meaning of, the thump of the ball on the fence again, drifting, talk about leisure, she was thirsty and would go get a glass of water in a minute, when she could be bothered to move, later hearing a bell ring, the sound of shouting fading away, the fence silent, and there was peace again, a car engine reaching her every now and then, a radio somewhere, and she heard the bell again except it sounded more like a phone, heard a click and the sound of Paula's mum's voice in the machine asking where she was, if she'd gone down the shops and if not, maybe she was in the garden hanging up the washing, the volume turned up so the voice came into the garden, into Ruby's head where it turned into the voice of her own mum, a woman raising a child, she thought about the responsibility involved, Ruby had nothing like that, she was free, okay she had to work and earn enough to pay the rent, buy food, and she did this okay, could pay for herself going out so she wasn't one of these women who looked at men as if they were walking wallets, and those sort did exist, she just wasn't one of them, equal meant equal in her book.

Paula's situation was different to Ruby's, she understood that, harder, but at least she had her mother to help, as well as her dad, Ruby floating over yellow grass and the passing years and imagining her own mum putting her doll's clothes on the line, shirts and dresses and jeans and socks and underpants and knickers and everything else. Her mum and dad's clothes pulled the line down with the weight of the water, Ruby a small girl watching her mum, handing her pegs, trying to see the water evaporate. Mum told her how it melted away in the heat, right there in front of her eyes, except you only saw a bit of steam, the temperature rising, a hot day and then a nice breeze gave the clothes a special fresh smell. She wished she could smell her mum's clothes now, hold a jumper to her nose and suck in the woman's warmth, and there were bright plastic pegs with the wooden ones and they fell out of the split plastic bag and were trodden into the soil, sunk deeper and deeper until one day they'd be a relic in a museum, seen as a work of art, a contraption, something from a bygone age.

Someone else lived in their house now. It had been the same as this one, more or less, but Ruby didn't want to be back there with the memories, she wanted to stay happy.

– Yeah, all right, Mum.

Paula's voice was indoors, she was talking loud, moving out of range, a door shutting for privacy, one of those phones you could walk around with, pushing buttons and trying to find a frequency, all mod cons that didn't work, Ruby minding her own business.

– Here you go, Paula said, coming out ten minutes later, handing over a cold drink, orange squash with a squiggly straw.

– Mum woke me up phoning. It was a good job she did, I'd have kept sleeping. You don't want to waste this sort of weather stuck inside.

– You're lucky having someone who cares about you so much.

– Suppose so.

– You do, you just don't know it.

– No, I do, of course I know it, I'd do the same for my kids. People help out, don't they?

Paula was sitting on the grass, an ant biting her leg. She jumped up and looked at the ground.

– It bit me. Look.

The skin was coming up. Ruby smiled.

– It'll be okay.

Paula went over and got a plastic chair, sat with her feet tucked up. She looked better, and Ruby felt sorry for her, Jerry running off with a secretary from work, a teenager who wore stockings and a short skirt every day and turned his head. Paula had a go at her, scratched her face and wanted to scratch her eyes out. She blamed herself for not wanting sex for a long time after her second child was born, for taking things for granted thinking it didn't matter if she slobbed around playing mummies and daddies. At other times she blamed the girl at work. Ruby had never seen her but been told what an evil, scheming slag she was, and just nodded. Jerry was to blame really, but there was nothing she could do but stay loyal to her friend.

– Sneaky little bastard, hanging around in the grass and nipping me like that, then it goes and gets lost again. Does the damage and doesn't own up.

Paula was laughing, and Ruby started skinning up, Paula looking nervous.

– There's a drug dealer lives in that house over there, she said, laughing, and a copper in that one there, a real nasty bit of work who buys his gear off the other guy, but would probably nick me if he smelt that stuff. They'd probably take the kids away and put them in a home.

Ruby felt guilty and stopped what she was doing.

– Sorry, you have to think about these things when you've got kids. His car's there so he's in.

Paula went inside and five minutes later reappeared with a tray filled with food, Mickey Mouse on the plastic, Goofy grinning ear to ear, all that Disney magic of last night revived. She put the tray down on the ground, flicking an ant away and lifted it on to the chair she'd been sitting on, a pile of cheese sandwiches on a plate, the MiniRolls cold from the fridge when Ruby reached out for one. They'd have to eat them fast otherwise they were going to melt in the sun. Paula went back in and came out with a blanket, in her bikini now, two cans of cider in her hands. Paula waved and the copper's curtains moved.

– He's probably having a wank right now, watching us through binoculars, she laughed.

Ruby hoped not, didn't think so somehow, and this was the life all right, having a picnic on your day off. It didn't matter that she'd been sweating and hadn't brushed her teeth. They were a couple of slobs all right. Ruby covered in dry sweat from dancing and sleeping and sunbathing, going red on her arms. The sun was high in the sky as they drank their cider and ate their sandwiches, jam in the sponge inside the chocolate rolls, Ruby and Paula enjoying the best sort of day.

The sun was high in the sky when Mr Jeffreys awoke from his slumber. He had remained at the hospital until 5am, wearily climbing into his bed at precisely six. His taxi had been waiting when he walked through the hospital doors and, with the streets devoid of traffic, he had reached his hotel within fifteen minutes. The skinhead driving was a genial chap, clearly sympathetic when he saw the weary state of his passenger. They shared the bond of two night-shift workers. Jeffreys felt confident enough to ask that the radio be switched from the barely audible country and western to some mellow jazz. This the skinhead had done with a friendly smile. If he had been listening to the hillbilly station Jeffreys would not have done so, but it was clear that his driver had forgotten the radio was even on.

Cruising through the empty streets with a gentle saxophone playing in the background was a fitting reward for a hard night's work. It took time to come down after such a prolonged and intensive burst of activity, yet to a certain extent this was achieved on the journey. He tipped the driver generously when the trip was complete and collected his key from the man on reception. The elevator was ready and he was whisked away. Mr Jeffreys studied his face in the

99

mirror opposite the door. It was polished and clear. His reflection was fed into further mirrors on either side of the elevator. It was as if the lift was full of carbon copies. As if he had been successfully cloned. He laughed, but his face looked so tired. The doors soon opened and he padded towards his room, soft carpet even in the hallways. On returning to his room he had felt rather peckish and immediately ordered a club sandwich and two bottles of cold American beer in an ice bucket. The man who promptly delivered this was very polite and Jeffreys tipped him.

Left alone with his thoughts, Mr Jeffreys had cracked the first beer using the supplied opener and guzzled greedily. He had achieved a great deal and needed time to unwind before retiring. He was not a big beer drinker, but enjoyed this particular brand, which was especially imported for the hotel's American guests. The beer did not have a high alcohol content and was very refreshing. He finished the bottle and bit into his sandwich. It was delicious. He took his time. In keeping with the high standards of the hotel, the club sandwich had been lovingly prepared and presented. He liked the crusts removed and this had been done with precision. He sat and admired the sandwich, the contents as well as the shape. He savoured the taste in between sips from the second beer. When he had finished he brushed the crumbs into a small pile. These he ate. He inspected the plate. Emptied the second bottle. Looked at the clock and saw that there were another three minutes to go until six o'clock. He waited. On the stroke of six he had rolled over and buried his head in the pillow.

Now, eight hours later, he felt groggy at first, then refreshed as he recalled the amount of work completed. There was nothing better than an arduous task achieved to set a man up for the coming day. It was the same in any walk of life, he was not blowing his own trumpet. Not at all. It was similar with, for instance, a commando unit sent out on a difficult mission. Success hung in the balance. Nerves were taut. Yet the sense of achievement once the task had been completed was immense. Of course, he was a man of peace rather than war, and, if he cared to admit the fact, perhaps a little too sensitive at times. That encounter with the raving lunatic in the corridors of the hospital had disturbed him, but with the work he had done and the good relations he had enjoyed since, from the nurses to his hotel employees via the jazz-friendly taxi driver, he felt very much back to his old self. Normal service had been resumed.

He hopped out of bed and strolled into the bathroom where he urinated, defecated, washed his hands, brushed his teeth and then took a shower. He dried and put on his swimming trunks. Did some stretching exercises in front of the mirror, loosening various muscles in his arms and legs. He moved his head in a slow circle, easing the vertebrae in his neck. He tidied certain of his personal belongings and removed a video from the VCR. Added this to his collection of television documentaries. He had several hours' worth of material but was in no great rush to view these programmes. It was work-related and not urgent, although he never allowed more than six hours' worth of footage to accumulate at one time. He preferred well-informed, socially aware documentaries to garish movies and soap operas. This programme was educational and would further help him to understand the world. He wanted to know everything there was to know and above all keep pace with the changes taking place within society.

He dressed and gathered his sports bag, put the sign on his door requesting urgent maid service, and strode purposefully to the lift. The elevator arrived in seconds and he took it to the ground floor. He skirted reception with a cheery wave to the girls who were busy with a crowd of newly arrived Japanese tourists, passed along the hall leading to the sports centre, his destinations the swimming pool and gymnasium. There were two squash courts available, and although he enjoyed the sport he was short of a regular partner. On occasion he knocked up alone on one of the courts, while at other times, having fallen into conversation with a fellow guest and broached the subject, he had arranged a game. It was a fun sport, not particularly good for the knees, but a game now and then would not hurt. The facilities within the hotel were, naturally, first class, and he made the most of the pool, weights machines and sauna.

The man at the desk returned Mr Jeffreys's smile and they exchanged pleasantries as he collected his towel. He proceeded to the changing room nearest the pool. Sunlight shone through large windows. He walked to the pool and lowered himself beneath the surface. Put on and adjusted his goggles. Began to swim. He was soon lost in the steady motion of his strokes, working the heart and lungs. He stuck to crawl which was, he felt, more beneficial to his metabolism than the more leisurely breaststroke. He swam well, always had done, appearing in galas for his school. He would swim for half an hour today. No more. Swimming was an aerobic exercise and very good for his health. Most professionals were aware that a sedentary working environment demanded they make an effort to stay fit. The brain was forever being pushed and challenged to achieve greater and greater feats, but the body was not. It was ignored at the peril of the person concerned. Without a certain level of physical fitness Jeffreys knew that he could not function at maximum capacity. His keen mind would be brought down by lethargy and illness. He might even make mistakes. Compromise his professionalism.

He thought briefly of the community swimming pool and those lovable dive-bombers he had encountered on his one and only visit. He almost laughed and swallowed water. Found his rhythm again. What amazed him most about these boys was the anaemic whiteness of their skin. It was as if they had been drained of blood and colour. Never had a suntan in their lives. He knew that as soon as the sun shone the masses would strip off their shirts and burn, unaware that sunblock and a moisturising cream were essential. Not only for a lasting tan but for the good of their skin. With the ozone depleted they were at risk as never before. The dive-bombers would turn red, then strip off their skin to reveal the white of their bones. He saw their blond, ginger and black hair cut to the skull. Gap-toothed grins and brittle ribs. Trying to be tough in front of their chums, they larked around and took chances on the diving board. Until the lifeguards gruffly warned them to behave. Fat boys strolled by the pool without shame. The guts of huge men wobbled under the lights. It was the same with the women. Rolls of fat appalled him. The thinner women smacked of anorexia. It was a question of education and self-discipline. He was looking at this from a professional viewpoint of course. The sort of man who could never leave his work at the office. The heart was a muscle that had to work for its supper. So to speak. It had a job to do and had to be maintained. Nourished and respected.

His visit to the local pool had been an experience in itself. He had to admit that he had been left shell-shocked. He had no problem with the people, but the sports centre embodied the sort of machismo the British had to abandon if they were ever to successfully integrate with the more cultivated cultures of the European continent. The weights room played loud music while men lifted enormous weights and whistled at any unfortunate young woman who wandered into their view. These men displayed their muscles and tattoos through a full-length window opening on to the pool. There, water spilt on to the tiles and the screams of children and teenagers reverberated under a brightly illuminated roof. People ran about with no thought for their safety. Or that of others. There had been a powerful smell of frying food coming from the front of the building. In the changing rooms, lockers had been vandalised and graffiti scratched into rela-tively new walls. Youths pushed each other and swore, their language crude and often sexual in nature. Chaos reigned. He had left with his head spinning. It was very different to the calm of the hotel pool. Here he was not disturbed. His physical health and mental well-being were maintained with a steady completion of dive-bomber-free lengths.

When his time was up he showered and lathered his body. Washed his hair with an anti-chlorine shampoo. He did not mind the smell in the least. There was nobody else in the pool, and he doubted whether the sort of people who constituted the hotel's clientele would ever urinate in the water, yet the chlorine was vital to stop any chance of infection. There was something reassuring about the odour of cleansing chemicals, be they chlorine, bleach or the various solutions used at the hospital. He hated to imagine what the dive-bombers added to the pool they used, never mind the dirt and disease that accumulated within the sports centre itself. He remained in the shower for ten minutes. The shower gel was easy on his body and the water hot. He was washing away any sins he might have inadvertently committed. He laughed at this idea. Imagined Pontius Pilate showering after a cleansing swim. He dried himself and quickly dressed.

Mr Jeffreys had booked a massage and arrived a minute early. The woman who ran the health suite was glamorous but with a rough accent that she tried, without success, to modify. She was very informal, but he did not find this offensive in the least. The hotel offered a wide range of services for both its male and female guests. There was a beauty parlour to one side and he noticed a plump woman having her nails manicured. His masseuse was slightly late, which while an irritation was not worth making a fuss over. She was a friendly enough young woman from southern Spain, the daughter of a fairly well-known painter who had moved to London and set up as a freelance. He sat down and found nothing worth reading on the table before him. The woman at the desk offered to make a cup of coffee but he declined. Smiled to show it was not her fault his masseuse was late. He waited. Checked the clock on the wall. Then his watch. Marking each minute. He hated it when people were not punctual. But he controlled himself. Nine minutes after his massage was due to commence the woman concerned appeared, out of breath. A traffic jam no less. He smiled and told her not to worry.

Mr Jeffreys went into the room and stripped down to his boxer shorts. Lay face down on the table, his head staring through the gap in the head rest at the carpet below. He noticed a long strand of blonde hair. Whoever vacuumed the room had missed this hair, unless of course the table had already been used today. That was the probable explanation. He thought of the dead cells that would have fallen from whoever was here earlier. The hair was that of a woman. She would be clean and healthy. Of that there could be no doubt. Otherwise she would not be staying at the hotel. He wondered from which country the woman originated. The purpose of her visit. Scandinavian perhaps. A photojournalist for an upmarket fashion magazine? Or American. The wife of a high-ranking financier? Or even a Brazilian. The wife of a vacationing politician?

It was all conjecture and he pushed the gentle image of a glossy, naked blonde away, conscious that his penis was beginning to swell. Certain low-class men might go to a massage parlour for sexual favours but he found the idea repugnant, not to mention disrespectful to his own masseuse and the skill she had spent so many years acquiring. It was a pity that so many things in society had to be degraded by the selfish few. He allowed his arms to hang down and surrendered to the professional fingers of the Spaniard. She was an excellent masseuse.

They generally talked for a few minutes at the beginning and a few minutes at the end of each session. More when he had first met her, but then less as they were easy in each other's company. The bulk of each session was now conducted in relaxed silence. She was a professional who did not witter on about minor matters. She understood the true benefit of a good massage. He was now able to escape the world for a short time. The swimming pool permitted something similar, yet he had to work hard to become lost in the movement, the mind forever wandering. With a good massage he did not have to do a thing. This was in welcome contrast to the hectic schedule of his everyday working life, where the pressures were enormous. There was so much to do and so many variables to consider. The lives of human beings rested in his hands. His masseuse worked on his muscles, finally turned and stretched his limbs. She sprinkled oil on his skin and worked it in. At the end of his half-hour Mr Jeffreys was completely relaxed. He dressed and paid, and gave her a tip.

He returned to his room and quickly changed, took the elevator back to the ground floor and proceeded to the hotel coffee shop. He ordered a cappuccino. It arrived with a flourish and he savoured the coffee. Truly superb. He looked around the tables with appreciation. Men and women sat in couples and alone. The mood was sedate. The pleasant aroma of coffee beans prevailed. The chair he sat on was wicker, the table a fashionable design of wrought iron and glass. In with the distinctly Italian atmosphere the hotel had cleverly mixed a sharp Japanese element. It was there in the lampshades and ornaments. Very subtle, but impressive.

With his coffee consumed, Mr Jeffreys moved next door to the restaurant. It was rather early to eat, but he was on a treadmill, returning to the hospital this evening. He requested a seat by the window and settled down to study the menu. The lobster took his fancy. This he ordered with a starter of sun-dried tomatoes on bruschetta. A bottle of Perrier would quench his thirst. There were other people in the restaurant, but it was quiet. He could hear organ music in the distance, and looking towards the Piano Bar was not surprised to see the lid of the baby grand firmly shut. He could see people in the bar but the pianist would not strike up until later. His tomatoes arrived and he settled down to a well-earned meal.

By the time Mr Jeffreys returned to his room, he was as content as any man could wish. His breathing was steady and his muscles tingled. He went to the bathroom and reluctantly brushed away the lingering taste of the lobster. It had been beautifully cooked. A fine meal in a fine hotel. It was a fine life that he enjoyed. He was very fortunate. He undressed and stretched out on the bed. Set the alarm for four hours' time.

*S*teve was a family man who worked hard for everything he owned . . . from the car he drove for a living to the house he lived in with his wife and little girl . . . and with Steve his home really was his castle . . . his wife a queen . . . his daughter a princess . . . they were the only things that mattered . . . the house a place where his family was safe . . . and warm . . . and happy . . . and it used to make him feel good inside when he was out at night . . . driving . . . dealing with drunks . . . who didn't want to pay their fare . . . or were looking for a fight . . . he carried a cosh for self-protection . . . after he was robbed and beaten up one night . . . when he first started minicabbing . . . he wasn't going to get caught out again . . . but it was okay . . . he could look after himself . . . he was no fool . . . and people liked him . . . he had plenty of friends . . . a gentle giant . . . and the thing you noticed most was how content he was . . . all he ever wanted out of life was to marry Carole and live happily ever after . . . that was his only ambition . . . he didn't mind admitting it either . . . and even though they'd been going out with each other since they were fifteen . . . he was still shaking when he proposed . . . six years later . . . scared in case she said no . . . he looked the part so you wouldn't think he'd get nervous about something like that . . . and he took Carole to the pictures . . . asked her to marry him in the pub after . . . the ring more than he could

afford . . . but he wasn't bothered about the debt . . . Carole
was worth every penny . . . and what he did was wrap the
ring up and slip it in the packet when she offered him a crisp
. . . then sat there waiting for her to find it . . . she was a
slow drinker . . . he always ended up having two pints to
every one of her drinks . . . she only drank shorts as well . . .
and Carole was the same with the crisps . . . took them out
one by one . . . she was a lady . . . you wouldn't catch her
scoffing her food down . . . or chewing with her mouth open
. . . and when she found the ring he leant over . . . waited
till she'd unwrapped it . . . then asked her . . . his dream
come true when she said yes . . . Carole loved telling the story
. . . and Steve would look embarrassed . . . at the same time
. . . pleased . . . the ring and the crisps . . . it was so
romantic . . . and the look on his face . . . she'd never forget
the look on his face when she said yes . . . she would marry
him . . . and he'd always treated her special . . . nothing was
ever too much trouble . . . he held doors open for her . . .
listened to every single thing she had to say . . . felt what she
felt . . . and the first time they'd ever gone out together it was
to the same cinema . . . so it was nice he proposed like that
. . . six years later . . . to the day . . . he'd only ever been
out with her . . . and it worked both ways . . . she loved
Steve like nothing else . . . he was everything to her . . . her
life . . . it was one of those marriages made in heaven . . .
true love . . . they never argued . . . were meant for each
other . . . it was perfect . . . and Steve was even happier
when she fell pregnant . . . he couldn't believe it was
happening to him . . . that he was going to be a dad . . . put
his hand on her belly and left it there for ages as they ran
through all sorts of names . . . tiny legs kicking inside . . .
tossing and turning . . . he could tell the baby wanted to

hurry up and be born . . . and his hands were massive so he could feel everything . . . and now their lives were even better than before . . . till the water started building up and Carole was in and out of hospital . . . complications during the delivery that could have killed them both . . . Carole needed blood transfusions and Steve spent as much time as he could in the hospital . . . waiting . . . only going home to wash and sleep . . . he stopped going to work . . . and if he didn't work he didn't get paid . . . they needed the money for when the baby came but he didn't want to be away from Carole in case something happened . . . and he was scared . . . one night stretching his legs . . . walking through the corridors . . . he passed a chapel . . . went inside and sat down . . . started to pray . . . it happened just like that . . . he didn't even think about it . . . he was the only one there . . . sat forward in his chair . . . looked up at the bloody thorns digging into the plastic head of Jesus . . . red rivers flowing out of matted hair . . . down over pure white skin . . . the plastic looked more like china . . . porcelain . . . something you'd find in a junk shop . . . a lost heirloom . . . the light catching it . . . a spooky glow coming off the ribcage . . . and Steve never went to church . . . he couldn't remember praying before . . . but things came back to him from his religious-education class at school . . . he was thinking of the ribs of man . . . the rib woman grew from . . . the Garden of Eden and the forbidden fruit . . . and he thought of the thieves next to Jesus . . . their legs broken by soldiers so their weight crushed down on their hearts and lungs . . . a slow torture for the sadists to enjoy . . . he didn't understand why people were cruel like that . . . their hate and perversion was beyond him . . . and Jesus was calling to God and having his faith tested . . . wanted to know why he was being forsaken . . . Jesus didn't condemn prostitutes and criminals . . . he loved everyone . . . saw the good in everybody . . . after all . . . they were all made by God . . . how could God let a baby die before it had a chance to breathe in air . . . Jesus laid his hands on the lame and made them walk . . . made the blind see . . . he performed all sorts of miracles . . . Jesus didn't turn his back on lepers . . . he steamed into the synagogue and turned their tables over . . . for charging an entrance fee . . . it was easier for a camel to go through the eye of a needle than for a rich man to enter the kingdom of God . . . he remembered that one all right . . . you had to think about it . . . and it all came back to Steve as he sat in the chapel . . . Jesus was having a dig at the system . . . big time . . . putting people first . . . nowadays they'd shut him up in a loony bin . . . say he was mad . . . Jesus screaming in the night waiting for God to come and carry him home . . . you had to have a heaven to look forward to . . . Steve knew that much . . . and Jesus was saved . . . rewarded . . . he was right and the hypocrites and judges were wrong . . . simple as that . . . and that's why they built churches . . . the chapel a warm place to go . . . there was a reassuring atmosphere that made Steve strong for Carole and their baby . . . and he prayed hard . . . for an hour . . . glad there was no one around . . . but fuck it anyway . . . he didn't care who saw him . . . not here . . . it was the same as when he was at home . . . he could relax once the front door was closed . . . could tell Carole things . . . some of his fears . . . that was a bit like praying . . . except he wasn't asking for anything . . . and there were some things you couldn't talk about . . . you had to stay strong . . . dependable . . . he told Carole about praying in the chapel . . . when she was home again . . . but he was staunch . . . said that his prayers had been answered . . . he really did believe that God had done him a favour . . . his wife and daughter were fine . . . and even though his little girl was strong and healthy he didn't turn into a churchgoer . . . nothing like that . . . but he was the sort of man who never forgot his family and friends . . . always remembered a kindness . . . honest as the day was long . . . a grafter . . . proud of his achievements . . . a house and family . . . so he didn't forget . . . would never be rude to the religious people who came knocking on his door trying to save him . . . he respected their beliefs . . . and now he was a father as well as a husband . . . he took this extra role so seriously his mates used to take the piss . . . but he didn't care . . . it was all good-natured . . . and the thing was he could look after himself . . . nobody mucked him about . . . and if Steve was happy he showed it . . . he had a daughter . . . a defenceless little girl who relied on him one hundred per cent . . . it was a big responsibility but he could handle it . . . knew some people were weak but he was strong . . . felt sorry for the weaklings but looked after his own . . . worked harder than ever . . . did all the hours going . . . he really worshipped his daughter . . . was gentle with her and played any game she wanted . . . took her for walks and to the pub . . . sitting on his shoulders . . . listened to everything she said . . . when she was old enough to talk . . . just like he listened to her mother . . . and he worried about her . . . they swore that if their daughter ever died then they would kill themselves . . . together . . . but first they'd have to make sure there was a heaven . . . somehow they'd have to know . . . and if there wasn't they'd make the most of their time together before one of them died . . . it was impossible to imagine life without the other . . . but there had to be a heaven . . . and they pushed the fear away . . . for a while . . . and Steve wanted his daughter to have everything . . . it *was like her coming along sent him on a mission . . . they'd wanted lots of kids . . . five or six . . . boys and girls . . . cats and dogs . . . the more the merrier . . . but it just wasn't possible after the first one . . . Carole couldn't have any more now . . . it was a shame but it just made their little girl extra special . . . five or six times as special . . . one child was a million times better than none . . . and they poured all their love into her . . . never let her go without . . . and an outsider would look at Steve and see tattoos and a shaved head . . . maybe label him . . . but he was a good man . . . one of the best . . . and before she started school he used to take his girl to the swings and slides during the day . . . doing more of his work at night so he could see her while she was awake . . . watch her growing up . . . and he'd sit her on the roundabout and spin her round for as long as she wanted . . . then soon as she was fed up he'd grab the roundabout and pull it to a stop . . . like every second counted . . . and he'd be remembering what his wife said as they were going out . . . not to make her dizzy or she'd get sick . . . like last time . . . he'd bought her too many sweets . . . he mustn't spoil her . . . and he watched her every second . . . going up the steps to the slide with her till she got the hang of it . . . keeping an eye on the bigger kids . . . pushing and shoving and not knowing their own strength . . . you had to watch the swings . . . a kid could easy run out in front of one and get hurt . . . Carole was nervous when he took her out . . . you have to watch her, Steve . . . don't let her out of your sight . . . it only takes a second and a pervert will grab her and take her away . . . do sick things to her then dump her in a lay-by . . . he'll throw her off a cliff and she'll be washed out to sea and never found . . . he'll chop her up and put her in dustbins . . . and his face would change as he imagined the bad things that happened . . . and if he got hold of someone trying to grab her he'd kill him . . . the fucking cunt . . . not in front of her, Steve . . . you'll scare her . . . she knows not to go with strangers . . . but I would . . . I'd fucking kill him . . . dirty fucking child-molesting scum . . . plus the ones who don't fiddle with kids but kill them anyway . . . men who go out and rape women . . . rape other men . . . scum who mug old dears . . . break in and beat up old men in their own homes . . . steal their pension money . . . torture animals and hurt people who can't call for help . . . you know . . . anyone who can't defend themselves . . . I fucking hate all that, Carole . . . I fucking hate it . . . it cunts me right off . . . and she'd agree and calm him down so the horror passed and he was all right again . . . sorry, love . . . it just gets me going . . . what's wrong with people anyway? . . . and Steve was a family man . . . a drink with his mates once or twice a week . . . he went to work and paid the bills . . . did the normal things . . . but his family was what really made him what he was . . . his wife and daughter and all the rest of them . . . their parents . . . brothers and sisters . . . cousins . . . nieces . . . nephews . . . neighbours . . . he never wanted to do anything else . . . he really was content . . . I'm not lying . . . he didn't bother anyone and didn't expect anyone to bother him . . . Steve was a happy man . . . simple as that.*

Ruby was washing sick off one of her new shoes when Sally leant over and told her about Ron Dawes. She blanked the words at first, nodded and kept rubbing. Twenty-five pounds and the first time she wore them a patient did the dirty on her, Papa splattering the leather with a collection of carrots and peas. She couldn't believe it. She'd only been at work two minutes. Papa wasn't well, and she knew puking up was extra painful with those stitches in his belly, an exploratory operation with the threat of more to come. She couldn't be angry with him, plus one of his sons hadn't charged her for last night's meal, recognising her from his visits to the hospital. She'd tried to pay, didn't like owing people, but ended up with a free kebab and a nutty little pastry dripping in honey. Papa did his best but hadn't made it to the toilet in time. It wasn't his fault. Uneasy on his legs, he needed a helping hand, and as he disappeared into the WC she knew he felt ashamed. She called after him not to worry, she'd seen it all before. And how many times did she say that a day? She left Papa to it, going over to a sink, grabbing a towel and a bottle of disinfectant.

She was buzzing anyway, with a tune in her head and a spring in her step, stuck with this idea that the whole world was sound, the vibration right there in her head, the stem of her brain feeling like it was being twanged, DJ Chromo talking to her last night as she lay on her bed with the lights off, knackered, the window open and radio rolling, going on about how nothing was solid and it was just a case of being able to see the truth.

Did she know, and it was like he was sitting in the corner the signal was so clear, that once upon a time the scientists swore blind atoms were the building blocks of life, rock-hard solid, at least till they looked inside and found that every one of them was made up of vibrating energy, and sitting in a secret location he was emphasising the point for the benefit of the DTI who couldn't wait to confiscate his aerial again, that last raid had cost Satellite dear, and the point he was making was everything around Ruby wasn't how it seemed, it was vibrating faster and faster, and it was music, vibration, sound that made up the world, like that chest of drawers with the woodworm dots in front of her eyes, and she could see beyond the shapes, knew it broke down into smaller units, so many zillions of options you could never ever count them, and it was inside her already, Johnny Chromozone's take on life, it came from working in the hospital where there was no end to the job, at the worst times it was a conveyor belt that never switched off, viruses you couldn't even see wiping out the strongest people, that amateur fighter they'd had in, killed by microbes, twenty-five and all his muscle couldn't save him, there was no happy ending, but if you looked at things individually then there was, most patients got well again, so when

Chromo said the world around them was breathing in and out and working to a different agenda she understood, could see it was true, watching the walls move, ripples gliding along next to Paula the other night as she stood with a bottle stuck in her mouth, rubbing her teeth on the glass, froth crashing along the neck, wet paper towels finally getting rid of the sick on her shoe after five minutes of rubbing, Dawn coming over and spraying them with perfume. Ruby held the shoe up to her nose, couldn't smell the sick, went over to the WC and knocked for Papa.

– You all right in there?

There was a muffled sound and she stood back. She couldn't think about Ron, Mr Dawes, right now, anything but that, concentrating on DJ Chromo as if she could still hear him, and if nothing was solid then nothing mattered, not really, none of it was real, tears weren't needed, nor the flapping butterflies in her belly, the nausea she had to control.

The door opened and Papa was holding the frame, looking at the floor. She helped him back to his bed. His head was hung so low with shame she wished he could see everything moving around them, those protons whizzing back and forward, and she wished he could understand that smells and colours weren't always how they seemed, it was only carrots and peas, nothing to worry about, energy-giving food, and she almost laughed thinking about it, tucked him up in bed instead. He reached for his beads and started clicking them, the steady tick of Papa's worry.

– Thank you, nurse, he said.

Now the job was done she thought about Ron.

Hurrying out of the ward she heard Sally saying he was eighty-four years old and that was a good age, Ruby's tears stuck inside her. There was silence. Just her breathing, heavy like a scared old man behind an oxygen mask gasping for breath. Nobody died of old age, not really. Ruby knew what Sally meant, he'd lived longer than most people, but so what? It just didn't seem like it was his time yet. You got a feeling about these things.

Ron was so fresh and interested in everything, even though he'd done more than anyone she'd ever met, geography and history rolled into one, a glimpse into another dimension that was more wacky than life in the Chromo Zone, and when Ron got going, Ruby sitting in the TV room with him drinking tea, it was almost trance-like, same as waking up to *On The Parish*. He could listen as well, interested in everyone and everything. She liked that about him. That's how she felt. When you were old, memories were more important than lots of money. Those were his words and they struck a chord. She knew what he meant. It was personal, and she loved him for it, had only met him three weeks ago but felt like she'd known him all her life. You had to hang on to the memories. The worst thing was having them stolen after you'd worked so hard, ending up tired but with no reward. She thought of her mum and felt the cold trip across her body, her skin nearly frozen even though the hospital was hot, fans clanking on the wards she passed.

Ruby ducked into one of the toilets on the corridor, for visitors and passers-by, locked herself inside a cubicle and burst into tears, washing the grit away. She was sobbing, tried to control herself. It was like her granddad had died or something. It was so sad. Ron was happy, more alert than a lot of people her age, and he was healthy enough, was almost ready to go home. She'd never seen his house, but knew how he spent his time. It wasn't like he was alone, bored, depressed.

.She sat there for a good ten minutes, wiped her face with paper and flushed, went back into the corridor. Sally was waiting for her.

– I saw you go in, she said. Are you okay?

– Suppose so. It's silly really, I hardly knew him. It's just, I don't know . . .

– Maureen said you should go and have a cup of tea. She knew how much you liked him, sitting in the TV room on your breaks. It was like he was your granddad. He had a long run. You have to remember that.

– I know, but it doesn't seem right. I know he was old, but you get a feeling after a while. I don't care what anyone says. What did he die of?

– Seems like his heart gave up. It was weak, you know that. He died in his sleep. Didn't suffer.

– That's something, but I can't get my head round it. You think you know what's coming. Some patients aren't going home from the moment they come in. Do you know what I mean?

Sally nodded, thoughtfully. She was always trying to smooth things over, at least between the people she knew, but was tough when it came to union affairs. She'd had a few conversations with Ron herself, about the trades union movement in the old days, while Ruby preferred hearing about the places he'd been in the navy. Sally was more of a fighter than her, didn't like a lot of the doctors on two scores, class and sexism. Ruby kept out of all that, knew that too many of the doctors looked down on the nurses, but believed in giving everyone a chance.

– Come on, Rube, he didn't suffer or go senile. He had his wits about him right to the end. He had his day and now he's gone to a better place. It would be worse if he'd suffered, wouldn't it? He died in the best possible way, at peace with the world, no fear or panic. Come on . . .

Ruby started crying again and Sally hugged her. She knew she should be rational and agree he'd reached a ripe old age, but for some reason it wasn't working. She tried to be tough, but couldn't. She knew she was being silly.

– Go and sit down, Sally said, once she'd stopped.

Dawn was suddenly there as well, ruffling Ruby's hair.

– Here, let me clean you up.

She took out a tissue and started dabbing at Ruby's eyes and cheeks.

– Mr Dawes? Dawn asked Sally, who nodded.

Ruby looked away.

– You silly cow, Dawn laughed, but in a friendly way. He lived longer than most people do. He died in his sleep as well.

Ruby was fed up with hearing he was old so his death was expected. There'd been a lot of talk about the elderly receiving second-class treatment in the NHS, files marked so there was no attempt at resuscitation, things like that. It was as if slipping away in their sleep was seen as a nice end to a life that had outlived its usefulness. She knew Sally and Dawn didn't think like that, they were only trying to make her feel better, but what they were saying reminded her of that. There was nothing to say or do, so she thanked them and walked down to the cafeteria, keeping away from the staff canteen.

She stood behind a middle-aged woman and a boy of twelve or thirteen, who moved awkwardly, a problem with his hip, space-hopper trainers on his feet, waiting for his mum to pay Peggy on the till. He stood back from his mum, turning from a boy to a teenager, and Ruby couldn't help smiling remembering how she was at that age, thinking of her mum again. She bought herself a can of Coke and a cream egg, sat at a table sucking the drink up through a straw, peeling away the foil and biting the top off, the yellow blob in white cream, noticing sugar on the table and brushing it on to the floor, and that's what little girls were made of, sugar and spice and all things nice, looking at the boy arguing with his mum, thinking of slugs and snails and puppy-dog tails. It depended on your mood. She made a decision.

She wasn't going to pity Ron, treat him like someone who'd done nothing with his life, and she was thinking of those funerals where the relatives did their best to turn a sad occasion into a celebration of life, thanking God for the good times, that was all you could do, so instead of a dead man in a hospital morgue she was watching a cocky young Jack-the-Lad sailor swagger along a Shanghai street and turn down a rickety alleyway, following a shoeless kid to a blank door, paying the boy and entering a hidden opium den, walls lined with carved panels and glass cabinets, flame-tongued dragons and framed ancestors, painted china girls sitting on a platform covered with a mountain of silk cushions, an ornate pipe passing his way.

Sitting on foam chairs in the TV room he'd taken Ruby back and told her how he'd smoked opium fresh from the poppy fields, squeezed her hand and said it was pure opium, not heroin, and he'd done the same in Hong Kong and Canton, before moving up to Shanghai, later on he visited opium dens in San Francisco and New York, the East End of London, but Shanghai stood out, real opulence buried away out of sight of the world, he could smell it to this day, sniffing his tea. He was young and took risks, spent most of his spare time in ports when he was in the navy, after months of doing nothing at sea they were bursting at the seams when they docked, and these places knew how to look after sailors, there were bars and girls most places they went, but you had to watch yourself, he'd been in some rough old holes, sheer poverty you'd never see back in England.

They'd lost one of their boys in Calcutta, dragged down a backstreet and his throat cut, but other seamen had been to this place in Shanghai and said it was kosher, he wasn't a drug fiend, just visited a few dens and forgot about it when he was in another part of the world, and she could feel his fingers right now, gentle on her hand, and she was tripping across the globe with Shanghai Express, running at Epsom, because Ron liked a flutter, had this special system he used where if the name of the horse connected with something in his life he'd put a few bob on it, he never looked at the form, it could be something connected to his navy days like Shanghai Express, a place and memory, or from his years at work in England, when he settled down, Hard Labour at Aintree, or a son or daughter, one of his grandkids, a favourite drink or a pub, anything he had a feel for, and from Shanghai Express she went to a horse called Burmese Days, Ron telling her how they'd got stuck in Burma for a month, the air heavy with water building up for the monsoon, so humid he was soaked twenty-four hours a day, massive insects dive-bombing them, mosquitoes everywhere, the food beautiful like nothing he'd ever tasted before, this was a long time ago, before curries took over in England, and he laughed remembering how the boys off the ship were chewing betel nut that turned their mouths red like they'd been fighting, but the Burmese were good as gold, Buddhist monks parading past with their bowls first thing in the morning, and because they had to wait around he was able to get out of Rangoon and travel upcountry, Rangoon a decent enough town with this massive gold dome in its main temple complex he'd read years later could be seen from space, and Burma had some of the most beautiful women he'd ever set his eyes on, along with the Persians, Brazilians, the girls on the Ivory Coast, but that was something else, him and his best friend Fred took the train north to Mandalay then travelled on to Pagan, a temple city next to the Irrawaddy River, and it was one of those experiences you only ever have once in a lifetime, surrounded by thousands of forgotten stupas and pagodas, temples staggering to the horizon, he was told there was near enough ten thousand of them, and so many years later Ruby had watched his eyes light up with the memory, and Fred and Ron walked into this deserted city late in the afternoon and climbed one of the tallest pagodas, sat and watched the sun sink down beyond the river, and in the East the sun really did look like a fireball, you were nearer the equator so closer to the sun, and they slept the night on the temple, it was cold but well worth it because in the morning they'd seen the sun rise again, light shooting out over the stone and sand, abandoned temples a red he'd never seen since, a fantastic sight he would never ever forget, and if he died next week he'd know he'd been lucky enough to see something most people never even guessed could exist, it gave him goose pimples thinking about it now the image was so clear in his mind, a magical place in a magical country, he'd felt so alive seeing the sunrise, as if he knew all there was to know about life in a split second.

Ruby loved Ron when he talked like that. He had the innocence of a little boy, still wide-eyed and open to everything, there was no cynicism or bitterness, no cruel edge to his character. He kept going, remembering the good times, Lima Girl a dead cert, she couldn't remember where the horse was running, he never told her about that one, so instead she imagined him in Peru, falling in love, a one-night romance that lasted a lifetime, and she knew Ron had been a bit of a boy, running away to see the world, he'd been everywhere, probably done everything, yes, he'd seen some beauties in his time, the Siamese before it became Thailand, the girls of South America and Africa, those ports on the Mediterranean, and he loved those Burmese girls in Rangoon, what a place that was, the girls in Manila and Hong Kong, the list went on and on, and he'd realised who he was talking to and looked embarrassed, told Ruby instead how he did his best to find out about the places he saw, the customs and religions. He'd seen the pyramids in Egypt as well as the temples of Pagan, told her that because the Egyptians believed the soul returned to the body after death they preserved it with chemicals and wrapped it up for when it was needed again, and it wasn't just the pharaohs, though those were the ones you heard about, there were millions of mummies over there, just waiting. And he'd laughed at the look on her face.

He'd been to New Orleans, said there was voodoo over there, all those zombies waiting to come back to life and terrorise the locals, and Ruby didn't like horror stories, pushed it away, he was only playing with her, and now she was thinking of death and religion, Ron telling her about a huge mosque in Istanbul, the Hindu temples in Bombay, and she laughed remembering how he'd impressed Davinda by knowing the names of the three main Hindu gods, talking about another god who was half-man and half-elephant, and he'd been to Palestine before it became Israel, went to Jerusalem, saw an old Crusader castle, and those places were hot, ten times worse than the hottest day in England, flies and dysentery had an effect, mosquitoes tapping away at your skin, beggars pulling at your legs, and he'd been up to Scandinavia, the girls in Oslo and Stockholm were among the most beautiful he'd ever seen, he kept saying that about everywhere, and there were women from all over working as nurses right here, from England, Ireland, Jamaica, Trinidad, India, Pakistan, Bangladesh, Sri Lanka, the Philippines, Australia, New Zealand, the world was full of beautiful girls but none of them were as beautiful as Ruby, and she'd blushed and told him he was an old charmer, thinking now how there was so much more she wished she'd heard, so many stories that had died with him, she loved his sense of humour when he told her about these places, always playing himself down, but there were more than his navy and work tips, this content look on his face when he circled Hurry Up Harry or Chantelle or Jimmy Jimmy, these were his grandchildren, and he had a few of them as well, and he'd look so happy, say something about a PlayStation game or school team, shake his head, they'd be grown-up soon, time passed so quickly, mumbling for a few seconds, shaking his head, then smiling at Ruby.

She was doing her best but it wasn't working. The stories were mashing together. The night he spent in Pagan was the way she wanted to remember him. On top of the world, on top of a temple, watching the sun set, then rise again the next day. She finished her cream egg and sucked at the straw stuck in her drink, biting into the plastic. She felt more tears and was looking for a tissue when a hand reached out offering her a hanky. She looked up and saw Mr Jeffreys, someone she'd only spoken to once before.

– Go on, he said, smiling. Plenty more where that came from.

She took the handkerchief and wiped her eyes. She wanted to blow her nose but couldn't, not in his hanky, with him right there. He sat down and waited. She would take it home and clean it before she gave it back.

– Are you okay? he asked.

Mr Jeffreys had a nice smile, a calmness about him that set her at ease. His skin was very clear, hair neatly groomed. He was a gentleman. It was in his accent and the way he moved, holding back in case he offended her, picking his words very carefully. She could see he was thinking about the meaning, doing his best not to upset her. She liked him.

– I hope I am not intruding . . . his voice drifted off.

She dabbed at her nose.

– One of the patients on my ward died last night and I'd got to know him a bit. He had this way of looking at things that I loved. For some reason I felt close to him. I don't know why, I only knew him for three weeks. He was the past in a way, and now he's gone. My grandparents died when I was young so maybe that's it. Sometimes you can skip generations, get to like people a lot older.

Mr Jeffreys nodded. She didn't expect him to be interested, after all he'd never met Ron, but he was genuinely sympathetic.

– What was wrong with him? he asked.

– He had water on his lungs, but was getting better. He was confused when he first came in, rambling away, but he turned round quickly and was going home in a few days. He had a weak heart.

– Was he old?

– Eighty-four.

Mr Jeffreys nodded. He was solemn and respectful, like he didn't expect someone to die for that reason alone, though it was obvious enough, something she knew and had to accept.

– I know you probably don't want to hear it, but he did have a good innings. Far better than most people. It may be of little comfort now, but it is well worth remembering. Sometimes in old age death is a release.

She knew all that but it just wasn't his time, she really believed he was going to go home, and yet what Mr Jeffreys was saying was right, the same as Sally and Dawn were right, it was just her being stupid, getting too attached when she should protect herself. She had to get on with things, life continued and there was always work to do, jobs that would make her think about something else till the reality settled in and she was able to accept what had happened.

Mr Jeffreys sipped at his drink and made a face, the drink too hot. He looked embarrassed, as if he shouldn't have sat down, but it was nice of him, he didn't have to do that, it was obvious he was shy, humble like Ron.

– It isn't wrong to feel upset, you know. Everyone working here is a carer and we would be hardly human if we did not feel sad sometimes. It is just a case of getting it out of your system. If someone is in pain or distress death can be a relief. Or if they are lonely sometimes they welcome death. I have always tried to look at the positive aspects, even if I do not really believe them myself. If you can control the way the mind works then you can create something positive from the negative. Think of all the hundreds of thousands of people doing their best to help others. You can go right back to ancient Egypt and Greece and find the same desire. We have made enormous strides and continue to do so. The one thing we can say for sure is that your patient had the best possible care and attention. Nothing more could have been done for him. That has to be of some consolation.

Ruby nodded, smiled. That's exactly what she was trying to do, look on the bright side, doing her best to turn a sad occasion into a celebration, that's all you could do, that's what she and Mum tried to do when Dad died, and the harder they tried the worse it was, he didn't live as long as Ron did, died young, when she was a kid, so she hardly knew him, and sitting with Ron was like sitting with a dad she never had, older, but still telling her stories, she'd missed that, and she could remember them crying and crying after the service, Dad was so young, it wasn't fair, everything coming too early, the clock ticking away, then stopping.

– I best be off. I hope you feel better soon.

She watched Mr Jeffreys move over to another table, sit down with his drink. She felt better than when she'd arrived in the cafeteria and decided to get back to work, and she smiled at Mr Jeffreys as she passed, it was nice how he was sad on her behalf, a thoughtful man, and she walked along listening to what he'd said and forcing herself to look on the bright side and remember how many good people there were around who cared about their fellow human beings, went all the way and dedicated their lives to helping them.

When it came to health everyone was in the same boat. The country invested billions of pounds in care and research, and the scientists kept going, never stood still or gave up, pushed ahead all the time, there was no more chewing on bits of leather as a saw cut through your arm, and parasites didn't run wild like they did in the past. Illness wasn't looked on as a punishment from God, that's what they used to think, that any illness you had you deserved, and the treatment was a bit more sophisticated than astrology, magic and potions, these days surgeons had laser scalpels and ultrasound blasters and micro-forceps, there was nobody chipping at skulls with bits of sharpened stone to release evil spirits, no Great Plague or Black Death, and she tried to imagine swollen buboes in her neck and under her arms, the door to her flat marked with a cross, and then there was smallpox with its sores and ulcers spreading down the windpipe, this suffocating death wiped out with vaccination, tuberculosis attacking the lungs, that one still existed abroad with occasional outbreaks at home, but nothing like the old days, measles was an illness kids caught but which used to kill millions, and there'd been no outbreak of flu like the one after the First World War when twenty-five million died, though there were always predictions of something stirring in the Far East, getting ready to unleash a whirlwind that would spread across the planet, carried on the wind, and she thought of Ron in

Shanghai and Hong Kong, all the sickness he could've caught as a young man, when there was no cure, and she was singing ring-a-ring o' roses, under her breath, a pocket full of posies, thinking of the plague, a-tishoo, a-tishoo, all fall down, and bandages and clean water had replaced boiling oil to treat wounds, and she thought of Alexander Fleming discovering penicillin, how mould had landed on his bacteria and killed it, and she thought about Joseph Lister and antiseptic, Edward Jenner and vaccinations, Marie Curie and Antoine-Henri Becquerel and their part in radiotherapy, attacking cancer cells, and she thought of the scanners and imagers, something simple like an X-ray and how it could pass through muscles and nerves, and she thought of the highly trained professionals who spent years becoming experts in their field, the neurologists, obstetricians, geriatricians, cardiologists, paediatricians, they were all here, the hospital full of learning and caring, and she was racing back up again thinking of the chemicals and techniques that had been developed over the years, the antibiotics and disinfectants, irradiation, so many things she took for granted, she was pushing herself, appreciating running water and electricity and toilets, and to even see a germ someone had to invent a microscope, and they'd planned immunisation programmes, fought back against polio, tetanus, measles, and even something as rare as SCID got attention, kids stuck in a germ-free room when in the old days they'd have died right away, and she could go on and on, but the point was things were always getting better, they were winning, and she felt proud, she really did, it was strange but her spirit soaring.

Ruby wanted to go out and get drunk, celebrate and mourn at the same time, smells reaching her from a passing trolley, apple pie and custard, and the corridor was this massive artery pumping white blood cells along with the heart in the middle, refreshing the parts other beers never reached, she had drink on the brain now, crayon drawings on the walls, getting nearer the ward and fixing a smile to her face, slowing down behind a family carrying flowers, the petals of the roses with a velvet texture, opium-den cushions, and she thought of white doves flapping their wings, thousands of feathers that broke down into smaller units, down and down, Ruby on an up, another trolley stacked with plates, DJ Chromo in her head, him and that Mr Jeffreys, two very different characters but with a similar message, leftover food and green plants lining the short hallway leading on to the ward where Ron had died, dust settled on a windowsill, Sally and Dawn up ahead in their starched uniforms, watches on their chests, ticking, on and on, small chains and long hands, plasma packs and a stethoscope on the reception counter, seeing every pulsating dot of a child's red-crayon drawing of a sailing ship next to an old man's empty bed.

Nurse James was a diligent worker and an earnest young woman. She was showing sadness at the death of a patient, but Mr Jeffreys felt that this was excusable. So long as it did not become a habit. She was obviously an emotional person. Perhaps even a little unstable. Yet such lapses had to be expected. She would soon forget the death of Mr Dawes. The acceptance of death was essential to efficient hospital care. If members of staff became attached to every single patient with whom they dealt then the system was doomed. Emotions were natural of course, but a luxury when dealing with sickness on such a large scale. Staff had to remain detached. Had to be strong for the sake of the patients. Yet despite the tears he sensed an air of responsibility about Nurse James and felt that she would quickly come to terms with the loss of Dawes.

Professionalism was required at all levels. Every single job was important. Those less skilled workers such as nurses had to strive for the same efficiency as, say, a surgeon. It was no use cleaners resting on their laurels or porters dithering. What would happen if a consultant allowed emotion to cloud his decisions? Or if he himself let sentiment influence his work. He tapped on the table and watched Nurse James get up to leave the cafeteria. The sound of her shoes was loud as she started on her way back to work, his handkerchief still in her hand. She smiled her thanks as she passed and he felt warm inside, pleased that he could help and offer some sort of comfort.

In a strange way Nurse James was attractive. More so than Nurse Cook for instance, whom he believed was promiscuous. James possessed a modesty too often lacking these days. On the downside was her accent, which, to be blunt, he found a little common, but it did not matter. If he was searching for a partner he would certainly not look within the nursing staff. Different customs and expectations were bound to cause friction. He was not being a snob, merely realistic.

He thought briefly of Mimi, his former partner. They had enjoyed a decade of ordered bliss, two people so well matched that their relationship could almost have been arranged. Ten years was a long time to spend with one person and, perhaps inevitably given their busy work schedules, they had drifted apart. He was the first to admit that his dedication to the health service had been partially to blame, but she was equally culpable with her long hours in the City. Yet the split had been amicable, especially considering the fact that she had left him for one of her colleagues. He had no regrets, although occasionally he missed the companionship, both intellectual and physical. Even so, he had welcomed his new-found freedom. Work was more important to him than anything, even Mimi. Thank God there had been no children involved.

A mother and son sat nearby. The boy in his early

teens. He was big for his age, with huge feet. Plastic white training shoes protruded from beneath their table. The lad was sulking. Stuffing chips into his mouth. A fly landed on the table where Mr Jeffreys was sitting and he brushed it away. It flew off, transporting sewage to the fat boy's plate. Depositing faeces on the crusty ridge of his pie no doubt. He shivered. Felt germs in the air and heard the hacking cough of a man. Nothing was free. Neither dust, nor soil, nor water. The men and women around him carried billions of germs on their skin. The potted plants were breeding grounds for bacteria. Neither animate nor inanimate, viruses were the scum of God's creation, flooding the planet with measles and influenza. The fly returned to buzz around his head.

He imagined he was in the Maldives. The fly a mosquito, sucking blood and transporting disease, infecting innocent people with malaria and sleeping sickness. He saw fleas. Lice in the hair of babies. Epidemics stirred by freak weather conditions. Germs waiting for their chance to cause havoc. Always waiting. To live. Grow. Reproduce. Die. The same as human beings of course. Yet humans lingered. Measured their lives in years rather minutes. The boy was chubby-cheeked. Growing. Jeffreys thought of the suffering children. Of rubella. Mumps. Asthma. Chickenpox. Cystic fibrosis. Measles. Tonsillitis. Diphtheria. Their trials were endless, the war unwinnable.

He pictured a GP feeding the boy sugar lumps, the chubby mouth chomping away, stuffing more chips on the fork. He imagined he was looking into the boy's eye with an ophthalmoscope and watching the blood vessels pump. Heart beating. The pressure of the blood in his veins. The boy developing into a man with so many problems to face. He thought of the doctors studying sputum. Urine. Pus. Taking blood. Body fluids. So many new diseases lurking. Life an ordeal.

Yet the coffee served here really was appalling. He understood that many people drank instant coffee, but how about those who preferred freshly ground beans? He considered the food on offer. Chips. Reheated pies. White-bread sandwiches. Crisps. Sweets. Nutritionless fizzy drinks that were consumed in vast quantities. This was supposed to be a hospital, for God's sake. It followed that the food should be full of goodness. A balanced diet would save the health service so much unnecessary work. Instead of carbonated chemicals the children should be drinking freshly squeezed orange juice. Snacking on apples rather than crisps. Instead of pies and chips the masses should be forced to eat grilled fish and lightly cooked leafy green vegetables. Their tastes would soon change. A fresh side salad was far better than a stodgy pudding.

He smiled to himself. He was not such a fool that he actually believed this was possible. While such a diet would benefit both the individuals concerned and the state, most people ate for pleasure rather than nourishment, slaves to their taste buds. They were unable to make even the simplest of sacrifices. It was the same with cigarettes and alcohol. It was a problem, the messages of health workers and corporate interests clashing full on. It was very frustrating, but a part of the challenge he so enjoyed.

He forgot the fat boy and thought instead of Ronald Dawes. Talking to Nurse James, he pretended he had never heard of the man, yet this was not strictly true. He did not know the patient personally, of course, but was aware of his existence and death. He had told a white lie but with the best of motives. As far as James was concerned, a sympathetic ear was more productive than a stark observation. Dawes was elderly and his heart weak, a build-up of fluid on his lungs the cause of his being admitted to hospital. It was not an unusual case, yet the man was very elderly and in his twilight years. It was a harsh fact that his life was coming to an end and this could not have been easy for him to accept.

Depression was common among men of his age, their joints painful from arthritis and organs struggling to cope with the most basic of bodily functions. A tiny patch of garden constituted their outside world, if they were fortunate. He envisioned the old man sitting alone day after day in a badly maintained house, money short and his contemporaries dead, his wife long deceased. It was such an undignified way to pick through one's final years. He saw the man trembling with fear, frightened by the young hoodlums throwing stones at his windows and pushing dog excrement through his letter box. Neighbours looked the other way for fear of confrontation. Rubbish heaped high in the kitchen and the sink filled with dirty dishes. His meals were basic, clothes in need of a wash. Gradually he would give up on the essentials such as shaving and washing. His family were too busy with their own lives and forgot the old man. Left his welfare to the state.

To strangers who nevertheless did their best in difficult circumstances. This was how he saw Mr Dawes, while Nurse James did not want to confront the sadness of the situation, nor the inevitable consequences of old age.

Nurse James saw good in every situation. Perhaps this was because she so feared the terrible nature of life. Yet he admired her optimism. She convinced herself there was hope when there was none. She was not a realist in the same way as he, but she meant well. The patients needed a positive outlook from those dealing with their everyday care, while behind the scenes, at the higher end of the scale, cold facts were the order of the day.

He could not criticise the nurses. Indeed, would not. They had to deal with the nitty-gritty of hospital life and this was a thankless task. His role was more delicate, albeit equally thankless. Each needed the other. Without his expertise the hospital would soon be overwhelmed and sink into chaos. The same applied to the nursing staff. He did not want her to be sad at Mr Dawes's death. The man had lived a long life and made his choices along the way, no doubt enjoying many good times. After a few days the sorrow would fade and this patient would be forgotten. Nurse James would find other people to help. Life went on.

He sipped at the coffee. Forced the muck down. It was so different to the blends he was used to drinking, yet the caffeine would help him stay awake when last night's lack of sleep caught up with him. It was difficult to adjust to working during the day and he had spent much of last night studying, finally watching the documentaries he had been recording. This was a vital part of his work, although sometimes rather depressing. But it was important to know his patients inside out, to be aware of changing trends.

He had watched the entire six hours of footage, starting with a one-hour programme on holidaymakers in Ibiza, a current favourite holiday destination with the young. The film was shot on a bouncing hand-held camcorder and had given him an inside look at the behaviour of a section of today's youth. For an hour he had listened to drunken teenagers talking utter rubbish, but refused to judge people, although he had found them both crude and boring. Obsessed with trivia, they screamed and giggled for the camera, one girl in particular turning his stomach. Sleeping with men she did not know and boasting about it in front of the whole nation. Had she never heard of venereal disease? Aids? He could imagine Nurse Cook behaving the same way, perhaps even sleeping with two men at the same time as the girl on the documentary had done. Even animals behaved with more dignity.

He had been glad when the programme ended. Had called room service and ordered a plate of pasta with basil sauce and a glass of wine to wash it down. The standard of the food and service in the hotel was so very different to the cafeteria in which he now sat. There had been a knock at his door and a woman delivered his food. She was well turned out and with different coloured hair to the girl on the video. Her skin was untanned, but he could not help but match the two. He studied her as she set the tray down on his desk, carefully moving his papers to one side. He imagined her on all fours in Ibiza with a man penetrating her from the rear in rapid thrusts while she performed fellatio on his friend. The men were rough types and covered in tattoos. First they were white. Then black. Finally a combination of the two colours.

Many of the disc jockeys on the documentary were black, hence this imagery. It really was disgusting. Not the racial element of course, but the animalistic mating with strangers. There was a violence there that unnerved him and he wished the girl had never mentioned the episode on camera. When the maid put his tray down he tipped her generously, giving no hint of these craven thoughts. It was not nice projecting such things on to an innocent member of staff. She thanked him and blushed a little. Perhaps she found him attractive. For a split second he had thought about engaging her in conversation, but resisted.

When she left his room Mr Jeffreys had collected his plate from the desk and taken it to an easy chair. He was going to eat on his lap. This was a bit like ordering beans on toast in a good restaurant. Ironic. If the beans and toast were cheap and served in a cafe full of common men they would taste revolting, yet decent surroundings elevated the experience. In this particular case he was experimenting with something he had seen on his television set. Whole families balanced plates on their knees as they watched their favourite pro-grammes. Some did not even own tables, or so it seemed. He had seen pensioners next to small children, parents stretching for bottles of sauce, shaking salt over food that already had an unhealthily high salt content. They splashed fried breadcrumbs and pieces of boiled potato down the front of their clothes as they ate. So he had tried this custom for himself. It was not so difficult. At least not at first. But he soon tired of the experience and wanted to move to his desk.

The flavour of the polish was so strong and attractive that he could almost smell it now, sitting at a barren vinyl table in the hospital. It was a nice desk, busy with his laptop, reference books, CDs, a lamp, and unused envelopes bearing the mark of the hotel. He had laughed and resisted the temptation, cut into his food and seen the thing through. He recalled the basil on his tongue, in among the instant coffee.

He thought back once more to last night's recordings, closing out his immediate surroundings. Following the hedonism of Ibiza an authorative voice had introduced life on an inner-city housing estate. The place was similar to a bomb site and not a single person featured had any interest in working for a living. Five youthful individuals were the focus of the documentary and he found each one a disgrace, either drunk or on drugs. They were inarticulate and self-obsessed, but he had learnt about burglary, heroin and under-age sex. There was a violent assault outside a youth club and a teenager sustained minor head injuries. As the camera team arrived with a police unit he was able to observe the boy's cut head first hand. The hair was blond and smeared with blood, skin white and pale. His friend had a bruised eye and ginger hair, and was interviewed by a member of the production team. He shouted and blasphemed and blamed everyone but himself. His sentences were broken by bleeps. Hundreds of obscenities had been painstakingly edited out.

Mr Jeffreys's sympathy was with these television professionals. It could not have been much fun working in such an environment. Yet as an honest look at the country at large, it was invaluable. It was easy to match the faces to those he saw within the hospital.

So it had continued through the night. Another documentary showed the work of the police force in combating crime. There was frightening footage of football thugs in London. High-street violence from all over the land gripped him with its viciousness. Flickering images of shaven-headed thugs kicking at each other in drunken rage. This was followed by a programme highlighting the use of CCTV and other surveillance equipment in policing a notorious red-light district. Prostitutes were spoken to with their faces digitally masked. This he found dull, albeit informative.

Next was a visit to the United States where forensic experts convicted killers with the smallest of DNA samples. This he found fascinating, a glimpse of the future. Finally he watched a documentary on teenage mothers, but by this time he was dozing off. Everything he had seen blended together. The theft and drug abuse of the estate merged with violence on the country's high streets, the prostitution and lapsed morals. A lack of family values. It really was a vicious circle. Education was the key, of course. A long haul back towards civilisation, but that was another argument. These documentaries were vital, a slice of real life expertly presented.

He returned to the present and left the cafeteria.

Once safely ensconced in his office he prepared a cup of tea and drank it eagerly. This quickly replaced the lingering taste of the coffee. Refreshed, he settled down and was soon absorbed in his work. The outside world no longer existing. Documented horrors erased. His mind moved smoothly as he studied data and focused on his monthly report.

He needed to urinate, but instead of leaving his office and walking to the nearest WC, took out a bottle. This was hospital issue and saved valuable minutes. Plus the corridors were busy, crowded with the sick and dying, the sad and lonely. The WC was basic in the extreme and used by visitors and passing staff. On one occasion he had heard a man defecating. It was disgusting and he had felt sick. He placed the bottle in his cupboard. Before he left he would empty and clean the vessel. He went straight back to work.

It was hot in the office and he opened the window. Switched on the fan. He had brought sandwiches with him and ate these at his desk as he worked. The hotel had made them up. He wanted to finish his report. His legs were stiff and he knew he should walk the corridors, but they would be noisy and disrupt his concentration. Instead he paced the narrow width of his office. He returned to his report. Urinated several more times. Drank more tea.

At one point he thought of that documentary footage. Were there no hard-working, community-spirited people left? Then he settled back down to work. Kept going. The temperature finally dipping and the light outside fading. There was no view from his window, only a small concrete square and brick wall. There was plenty of light though, and he kept the blinds half-closed. The worst of the day was over and soon the hospital would begin to quieten. The last visitors would leave and the patients find rest. They would have their final cups of tea and any medication prescribed. They would be at ease. The majority of staff at home taking a deserved rest. The world would be at peace.

His bottle was full and he decided to empty it, put on the white coat he wore in the hospital and walked to the WC. A couple of people passed but did not see the hidden bottle. It was nine o'clock now. He reached the toilet and relieved his bladder inside the cubicle. Tipped the contents of the bottle away. Someone had drawn a picture of a penis on the wall. A woman was positioned in front of it with her mouth open. He thought of the girl in Ibiza. Someone else, or perhaps the same person, had written a plea for gay sex. He flushed the chain. The WC needed a clean but he was not going to complain. Everyone was working flat out. He understood that. He washed his hands in the sink and imagined the hundreds of hands that had touched the soap. Thought of the bacteria. He steeled himself and left quickly. Became immersed in his report. A near religious experience.

Another three hours passed and the alarm on his computer sounded midnight. Long ago people called it the witching hour. A time of superstition before science made sense of life. The masses had believed in magic, witches, warlocks. The supernatural. He smiled to himself. It was almost unimaginable now. His report was more or less complete. Another hour at the most.

He could do no more right now. The corridors would be deserted and he had earned his exercise. How many people worked as hard as he did?

Mr Jeffreys strolled along the corridors. He did not dwell at corners but passed the sleeping wards and empty operating theatres with the satisfaction of someone who had completed a difficult task. The machines were silent. Life-saving drugs awaited the call. There was no noise. No confusion. Just blissful silence. The raving maniac of the other night had been a fluke. He knew that. Walked steadily for the next half an hour before gravitating towards Accident & Emergency. He thought of little Daisy in the children's ward when he passed. One of the nurses had told him her story last week and he knew there would be a happy ending. The hospital specialised in happy endings. He thought of the women who came in to keep the little ones amused. They were called play specialists. Told stories and helped out generally. Imagine that. It showed how the system had developed. He looked into the cafeteria where he had sat earlier in the day. He could not now imagine the gloom he had felt. There was a dead fly on the ledge in front of him, on the other side of the glass. He did not know if it was the same fly as the one he had brushed away. How could he? But it was dead.

He soon reached A&E. It was here that, sadly, many of those documentaries came to life. Car accidents. Drug overdoses. Street fights. He had seen these things many times over the years. The waiting area was empty but he could hear voices. He followed the sound. Nodded at the staff on duty but did not interfere. He stood by the wall and observed the three men being attended to. One was covered in blood and it took Mr Jeffreys a while to separate their characters. He saw them outside a nightclub on the high street swinging their arms at other young men. Someone fell to the ground and was set upon. The head used as a trampoline. That image had shocked him the most. The street was unnamed and could have been anywhere. Of course, this was a separate case and these men were different. They just seemed the same. There was little difference.

– Fucking hell, Chas. You all right, mate? one of the men said.

He was a chunky fellow with a thick ring on his middle finger. A yellow shirt hung out over his jeans and was tagged with the letters YSL. Whatever that meant. When Mr Jeffreys looked closely at the man's hands he could see that the ring, a circular gold monstrosity, was caked with dried blood. His hair was close-cut, as was that of his two friends. The man next to him was shorter. A silver chain hung out of the collar of a polo shirt. He was squat and stern. Shook his skull slowly from side to side but remained silent. The shoes were flat, with tassels. He wore white socks. There was a mobile phone protruding from his back pocket. A thick wallet filled the other. Mr Jeffreys was reminded of that television comedy about cockneys in Peckham. He forgot its name. He had never found it funny.

– Course he's not, you plum, the squat man said, half laughing.

It was the first time he had spoken. Mr Jeffreys

watched. Fascinated by the sheer brutal tribalism of these people. He sounded like a cockney yet lived in a new town outside London.

– That cunt is fucking dead, I tell you. Him and his fucking mates. We nearly had them as well. That skinny geezer got a proper slap before he legged it out the door. We'll have them, don't you worry.

Mr Jeffreys wondered if he should report these comments to the police. Murder was obviously in their minds. As a medical man he recoiled from this notion. Any sort of violence sickened him.

– Go and wait over there, will you, a nurse said.

The two thugs wobbled on their feet. Blinking.

– Come on, hurry up, or you'll have to go and sit in the waiting room.

It was the first time Mr Jeffreys had properly noticed the doctor and nurse tending the injured man. The nurse was a thin little thing, skin and bones under her uniform. Her hair was in a small bun and her lips were without lipstick. Her watch seemed artificially large on a flat chest. She could not have weighed more than eight stone and was far from imposing. The thugs towered above her yet to his surprise did exactly as they were told. Perhaps it was the threat of the security guard at the far end of the room, but he did not think so. It was hard to understand this sort of obedience. He had expected harsh words and a threat of physical assault. Obscene suggestions of a sexual nature. They were almost meek.

– Does that hurt? the doctor asked.

He was Asian. In his early thirties. Probing the patient. Mr Jeffreys looked more closely and tried to see something beyond the blood and short hair. It was hard to make out features. There was a nasty gash across the face. The nurse seemed friendly with the injured man, smiling and nodding. He could not hear what was being said. They spoke quietly. The two thugs leant against a wall opposite though he doubted they did so for support. More likely it was a display of cockiness. If so, then it was unseen. The short bulldog gazed into space, his brain pickled by drink. The YSL yob looked around blankly for a while before staring at his injured friend, then the doctor and nurse. Mr Jeffreys tried to follow the line of his gaze but it was very difficult. It seemed as if he was staring at her buttocks. He hated to think what was going on in his head. Felt as if he knew these men. Much as he believed he understood Ronald Dawes.

In many ways Dawes had represented the past. An industrial age of petty class politics. He had lived through momentous times, but those days were gone. The West had settled down and made great strides. Britain was more streamlined and less wasteful than ever before. Organised rebellion was no longer an option. He knew that Dawes had been active in the trades union movement, and even though the unions had been broken for more than a decade he still felt that these men and women had a case to answer. Unions had forced the nation to its knees. Of course, he respected the right of every man and woman to hold their own opinions. They lived in a democratic society and the right of the individual was paramount. But this democracy had to be respected by the Left as well as the Right.

Dawes was a minor figure within the trades unions, of course. Unimportant. No doubt a decent enough individual who had worked towards a generous retirement. The state did its bit by providing a pension but it was up to those around him to lend a helping hand. Had he bothered to invest in a private pension, for instance? Expectations were changing. Something of the past had died with Mr Dawes. He mourned the individual as he did all individuals, yet not the notion of the nanny state.

If Dawes represented the past then these thugs standing in front of Mr Jeffreys were the present. Their offspring would embody the future. A cultureless rabble who consumed with no regard for their fellow citizens. They had never had it so good yet still fought pitched battles. They used illegal drugs and battered defenceless women to a pulp. This was the direct result of years of undisciplined liberalism. These were the sort of mindless hooligans who would have knocked Mr Dawes off the pavement and into the gutter. They would not notice his pain, the fact that he was alone and unloved. What sort of life was that?

In a curious way these thugs represented a natural progression from the trades union movement, even if they lived in a time of political apathy. They were rabble, yes, but highly dangerous and organised rabble. He thought again of that documentary detailing the use of surveillance equipment in tackling street crime. These men before him no doubt gathered in football gangs and organised confrontations via mobile phones and the Internet. Union thugs had embraced violence and fought the police, who were merely attempting to enforce the will of the people. Today's organised gangs would fight about anything. Drugs a source of income.

Mr Jeffreys's remit did not of course stretch to the running of society at large, but as an individual he held certain views. His interest lay in improving the quality of hospital treatment. Meaningless confrontations such as this one cost the hospital dear. It was wastage pure and simple. If only they could control themselves.

It was not just the thugs either, but the junkies, prostitutes, heavy drinkers and smokers. Everyone had to take responsibility for their actions. This did not mean he was reactionary. Far from it in fact. The nature of his work meant he had to deal with these realities. For instance, he had nothing but sympathy for the victims of Aids. Too many people were disparaging about Aids sufferers. Of course, if people could only control their sexual behaviour, their use of needles, then the problem would vanish. But for some reason they could not. This was frustrating but did not mean that he hated homosexuals and drug addicts. People fought among themselves. Paranoid and hysterical. He did not understand.

– No, he's had a jab and going to be stitched up in a minute, the bulldog was saying, talking into his mobile phone.

Mr Jeffreys looked over at the doctor and nurse. An empty syringe lay next to the doctor. He wondered if the injured man was a drug user himself. He could not tell. These people blended together. A terrible thing to think let alone say, but he was tired. He had been working all day.

–You all right, Charlie? the bulldog called out.

The man seemed concussed. Merely nodded. The nurse had her arm around his shoulder now. There was no condemnation in her gaze. She was easy with him and he seemed to respond. It was obviously an attempt on her part to diffuse any lingering violence. She was trying to encourage the man to fight back against his injuries, a mirror of Nurse James and her approach to Mr Dawes. Just as long as it did not turn into attachment. He watched the nurse more closely and could not detect any personal motive.

– He's going to have to stay in overnight. We'll wait till he's had his stitches and tuck him in. It's not pretty, but the doctor said he'll survive. He'll have a scar and that, but it could've been worse.

– Let me talk to him, the YSL thug said.

– Hold on. No, come down if you want but he's a bit dopey. Just had an injection as well. It's up to you, the bulldog continued.

Mr Jeffreys faded the conversation out as nothing of value was being said. He watched the stitches being administered. The two thugs soon sitting on chairs. Silent. Tired most likely. The nurse was busy bandaging the wounded man when a woman was rushed in with a suspected heart attack. The doctor moved on and the thugs looked up. They seemed upset seeing the woman's face and panicking husband. The man and his wife were in their sixties, the victim wrapped in blankets.

Mr Jeffreys made his exit. For a moment he was nervous as he thought of the raving skeleton of the other night. That had been the worst abuse he had ever suffered at work. Otherwise things had gone well.

He walked at a steady rate and allowed the silence to engulf him. The thugs were forgotten, locked into a video cassette. Sometimes he felt he could take his remote control and click the scenes back and forth. From the VCR to real life, and back again. He knew the situations that arose in A&E and was able to sum up the people. The trick was not to become cynical. To stay alert. The corridors were empty and safe and his annoyance subsided. He would work for one more hour and then leave.

By the time he reached his office, Jonathan Jeffreys was fully relaxed. He was only human. He closed and double-locked the door, sat at his desk and stared at the blank screen of his computer. All around him men, women and children were on the mend. Safe in the knowledge that they were being watched over and monitored by dedicated staff. He thought of Nurse James and the handkerchief he had lent her to dry her tears. That was a nice touch. She had felt such sorrow at the death of a patient, an old man at the end of his life. Mr Jeffreys forgot the name, albeit momentarily. Dawes. Of course.

He pushed the relevant button and waited as a trail of symbols trickled across the base of the computer screen. He remembered something and unlocked a drawer. He thought of his father and matched him to Mr Dawes for a moment. His father was a good man who had died four days short of his seventieth birthday. He had set high standards and his son believed that he was following in his footsteps. He recalled the funeral service and the tributes paid to his father by men of standing within the profession. His father had been a surgeon and saved many lives during the course of his own. He was very proud of his father's achievements. These had been rewarded during his lifetime and acknowledged upon his retirement.

Mr Jeffreys opened the drawer and took out a pocket watch. He opened the front and watched the second hand snap its way through sixty seconds, causing the minute arm to move. The numerals were Roman and the hands tipped with squat arrowheads. Provided it remained wound the watch would count out the centuries. Perhaps one day it would jam or a cog break. The mechanism might wear out. Time would remain rooted until an old-fashioned clockmaker could be found. He wondered if such men would exist in two hundred years' time. The constant drive of consumerism meant that everyday items were no long built to last. It could not be helped. Time was constant, whether measured or not. Only death could stop its flow. After death he firmly believed there was no more time. Just infinity and eternal bliss for the righteous, although he would not describe it in such biblical terms.

The computer was ready but Mr Jeffreys sat for a long time staring at the watch. He thought of his father and pondered the ways of the world. Finally he clicked the cover of the watch shut and returned it to the drawer. He locked this and returned the key to his wallet. He appreciated antiques, yet the value of this particular timepiece was not monetary. It was personal, a keepsake, and something to treasure.

*S*teve was lucky . . . he married Carole and settled down . . . while for Pearl things worked out differently . . . but as for those lies about her being a bitter woman . . . a frustrated . . . sadistic . . . lesbian . . . all twisted inside . . . well . . . that's just spite . . . says more about the person saying it than Pearl . . . nothing could be further from the truth . . . she was a diamond . . . a pearl . . . and I laugh . . . almost cry . . . she was dedicated to her work . . . a teacher who was so passionate about education she never wanted to retire . . . she really worked hard to make school fun for the kids in her care . . . saw it as their big chance to learn and develop . . . to channel their energy in a positive way . . . and when a scared child arrived for the first time Pearl was waiting with a smile . . . she was firm . . . but friendly . . . and fair . . . she had so much to give . . . felt close to her little boys and girls . . . and it didn't matter if they were good or bad . . . she cared about the troublemakers as well as the weaklings . . . loved the bullies and the bullied . . . believed in discipline but was warm at the same time . . . it was just finding what they were interested in . . . if it was reading . . . writing . . . drawing . . . football . . . netball . . . anything . . . it didn't matter . . . and with the difficult ones she really had to coax them . . . everything crossed over . . . interrelated was the word she used . . . telling me about her children . . . her work . . . and for the little boy who loved football it was a way of pulling him towards his reading and writing . . . he wanted to know what was happening in his football comics . . . and she'd get him drawing his favourite players . . . writing about a game in the playground . . . one he'd seen on TV . . . and just as important was the way the kids got on with each other . . . school was where they learnt to make friends . . . and Pearl tried to encourage friendships as well as interests . . . if a girl was all alone in the playground she sat different girls next to her in class . . . till they clicked and she had a friend . . . and they started playing with each other outside . . . she really loved children . . . their wide-eyed innocence . . . the good ones and the naughty ones . . . there were angels and little monsters . . . and she studied their mums and dads when they came in for parents' evening . . . most cared about their kids but some didn't . . . she didn't understand that . . . she looked at the ones who didn't and wondered what was wrong with them . . . hated the way they ruined something that was precious . . . and she put herself out for the boys and girls from broken homes . . . a few times over the years children who were battered . . . that really upset her . . . she had tears in her eyes telling me . . . told me about one girl who was being abused by her dad . . . too scared to say anything . . . social services mucking about with their committees . . . not doing anything . . . so Pearl changed after work and went round to the man's house and knocked on the door and when he answered she punched him as hard as she could in the face . . . caused a commotion on his doorstep . . . and when a crowd quickly gathered she told his neighbours what was going on . . . made his life a misery . . . stronger people took over . . . and she went home and had her tea . . . soon after the girl was taken into care and ended up with foster parents who raised her . . . Pearl talked

to them over the years and the girl grew up and got married
and was happy . . . Pearl was always willing to take people
on . . . that was an extreme case but she made her mark . . .
Pearl was dedicated . . . and just because she never married
that didn't make her a lesbian . . . that's a stereotype . . . the
spinster dyke . . . stud bachelor . . . and being anaemic
didn't make her twisted . . . she was just a good woman . . .
she liked a laugh . . . away from school with her friends . . .
she had a good sense of humour . . . a few glasses of whisky
at night as she sat marking books . . . the endless hours of
unpaid overtime . . . work that was unrecognised but expected
. . . her basic wage wasn't brilliant either . . . specially
considering the importance of education . . . those who earned
the biggest salaries were the ones who least deserved it . . . the
takers . . . and teaching had always been a hard profession
. . . politicians sticking their oar in over the decades . . . and
now you had inspectors coming in harder than ever . . .
causing havoc with their stopwatches . . . looking at everything in terms of cost . . . she said it was the same with
medicine and the police . . . you needed those three services
more than anything . . . not that she thought about these
things when she was younger . . . no . . . she hated school
and had never been to hospital . . . she thought she was
invincible just like Charlie . . . and as for the police . . . well
. . . they spent most of their time dodging them when they
were teenagers . . . specially the ones from Wembley who
hassled them at the Ace Cafe on the North Circular . . . this
was in the fifties when it all began . . . when Britain woke up
and started in on the American Dream . . . when rock 'n' roll
came over with Billy Haley . . . when 'Rock Around the
Clock' was first shown at the pictures and the seats were
being slashed and ripped out . . . she'd never been the stay-

at-home type . . . this was when the country started speeding up . . . the Ace Cafe was the centre of her life when she was a girl . . . this was where she met Charlie . . . he was one of the original rockers . . . a ton-up boy in his Levis and leathers . . . grease in his hair . . . and the rockers were just taking things on from the Teds who were more flashy . . . Pearl could tell you all about the Lambeth Boys and the corner boys of Notting Hill . . . she'd grown up hearing about this hooligan menace to society . . . but she preferred the new style . . . the rockers with their Triumphs and Nortons . . . she loved the smell of petrol . . . the power of the bikes revving up outside the Ace . . . Elvis on the jukebox . . . her skin used to tingle sitting inside drinking coffee with her friends . . . tingled thinking about it now . . . watching the boys and the bikes . . . and she was so alive sitting there watching them race past . . . the speed and power got to her . . . everything was moving . . . and she fell in love with Charlie soon as she saw him . . . he was cocky all right . . . a hard nut . . . always in trouble . . . racing with the devil . . . taking chances . . . and he had a Triton . . . a customised mix of the Triumph and Norton . . . was always working on that bike . . . the grease in his hair dripped into the Triton . . . and back again . . . Pearl laughing . . . yes . . . she really loved him . . . wanted to get married but he wasn't ready yet . . . but one day . . . it was agreed . . . and he used to take her out on the back of his bike and they could go anywhere they wanted . . . she felt so free . . . they both did . . . and there was this time he took her round a blind corner doing a ton . . . both of them leaning into the machine and sparks spitting up from the road the bike was leaning so far over . . . and she could feel his leathers on her face and smell them deep inside . . . it was a smell that was always with her . . . raw and

alive . . . the wind was rushing past burning her ears . . .
Charlie always pushing things to the limit . . . and he'd done
blind bends a couple of times . . . she argued with him about
it . . . but he said it was special and she shouted in his ear
and he opened up the accelerator and they were right there
staring death in the face . . . taking it on . . . it was the
biggest rush you could get outside of a war . . . it wasn't like
she hadn't done a ton before . . . she had . . . but doing the
bend like that was different . . . brilliant . . . and they used
to go all over . . . through London . . . have a cup of tea on
Chelsea Bridge . . . the roar of bikes in the traffic . . . fifty or
sixty of them feeling like no one could touch you . . . she
loved it . . . and when Gene Vincent and Eddie Cochrane
came over she saw them . . . one of her favourite songs was
Vince Taylor's 'Jet Black Machine' . . . she asked me if I'd
ever heard it . . . but I never had . . . and there were other
places over the years . . . Ted's Cafe . . . the Cellar Bar . . .
the Busy Bee . . . and she used to go to the 59 Club in
Hackney as well . . . they all did . . . then to Paddington
when it moved . . . and Charlie was never going to grow up
. . . he was the sort who stayed young forever . . . and they
were really in love like nobody else could ever be in love . . .
he didn't want the normal things in life . . . the house and car
. . . but he wanted her . . . Pearl was his girl . . . they just
lived for the moment . . . there were no plans . . . he was
more into burn-ups and punch-ups than kids . . . she could
never control him . . . that's one of the things she loved about
Charlie . . . but when she turned twenty-one she knew she
wanted a family . . . and he still wasn't ready . . . they had
plenty of time . . . they were young with the rest of their lives
in front of them . . . and Charlie had a temper but wasn't a
bully . . . she couldn't have been in love with a bully . . .

*and she could look after herself as well . . . she was a teacher
now but wild when she was a girl . . . and she laughed so you
could see it . . . and I thought about the pervert and how she
punched him in the face . . . you never know what's behind
the appearance . . . and maybe Charlie had a death wish . . .
she said this with a dark look suddenly on her face . . . but
she loved him for all his faults . . . Charlie was one of the
originals . . . they were young . . . so young . . . and there
was a game the boys played at the Ace . . . and Charlie was
one of the boys all right . . . a lot of the others looked up to
him because he never backed down from a fight . . . or a
challenge . . . and one night he put Gene Vincent's 'Race
With The Devil' on the jukebox and ran out and jumped on
his Triton and roared off down the road to the roundabout
. . . he had to get down and back before the record ended . . .
and when she was telling me this I was imagining Pearl all
dolled up in her beehive . . . eating a sausage-and-liver
sandwich . . . finishing it off and running outside . . . waving
as he drove away . . . like something from a song . . . nice
and romantic . . . and Pearl waited for him to come back and
beat the record . . . she called it a death disc . . . a real death
disc . . . none of your latter-day bubblegum girl-group love
songs . . . she loved Gene Vincent up till then . . . never felt
the same way again . . . and the thing was the 45 ended and
Charlie was nowhere to be seen . . . she never thought of him
crashing . . . he'd come off a couple of times before . . .
broken a few bones . . . but they thought they were immortal
. . . and then someone came back and said Charlie was in a
bad way . . . and one of the boys took her down . . . and
there was her Charlie lying on the North Orbital with his
brains splattered all over the road . . . she held him in her
arms and cried and cried and didn't stop crying for two or*

three years . . . she was a mess . . . her life was finished now
. . . and her pals were good to her . . . the boys as well as the
girls . . . the funeral was another story . . . and she stopped
then . . . didn't want to go into that . . . but she recovered
. . . you do . . . it doesn't matter what happens in life you
always go on . . . you have to . . . and Pearl never believed
in heaven . . . this was it right here . . . and Charlie was in
her . . . she'd been with him for years and his soul was inside
her . . . she thought about him every single day . . . and
eventually she got on with her life . . . she trained to be a
teacher and her classes were her children . . . in a way . . . it
wasn't the same as having them yourself . . . but good enough
. . . and she was happy . . . in school she was the well-
turned-out . . . respected teacher . . . turned sixty and still
working . . . she was the deputy head . . . had turned down
the headmistress's job . . . Charlie would've been glad . . .
she wanted to concentrate on teaching rather than administra-
tion . . . and she never cried now . . . she'd done all her
crying years ago . . . and she had her interests . . . never gave
up dancing . . . her and Charlie used to drive and drink and
dance the nights away . . . she danced slower now . . . went
to biker events . . . she'd kept most of her friends . . . lots of
the old faces turned out once or twice a year . . . she was at
that Rockers' Reunion in Battersea a couple of years ago
when the two boys died . . . that was such a shame . . . and
that's where the grannies were these days . . . she was
laughing again . . . listening to Joe Brown & the Bruvvers
. . . teaching was what got her life going again . . . she'd had
boyfriends over the years . . . but it was never the same . . .
she never wanted to get married again . . . Charlie was the
love of her life . . . and she reached round her neck and pulled
out a locket . . . a small silver heart with a lid . . . opened it

and held it over to me . . . showed off the face of a young man
with specks of dark black hair hanging over his forehead . . .
the sides combed back . . . and this was Charlie . . . tough
on the outside and tender in . . . she smiled and asked me if I
thought he was handsome . . . and I said yes . . . he honestly
was . . . and if I'd been her I would've fallen in love with
him as well . . . danced with him to rock 'n' roll . . . and she
looked into the locket for ages . . . she kept Charlie's picture
with her all the time . . . she never went to his grave . . . you
had to move on . . . and he was so gentle when they were
together . . . treated her right . . . like a lady . . . and then
she was back on the Triton . . . talking about one night she'd
never forget . . . a few months after she'd done her first ton
. . . and they used to go down to the coast sometimes . . . but
this one night was special . . . the best of all . . . it was
summer and they headed out at midnight . . . got down to
the south coast in time to see the sun rise . . . sat on the cliffs
together with Charlie's jacket around her shoulders . . .
keeping her warm . . . and then the first little pricks of orange
appeared over the sea and the sun began to rise and they
watched it swell and finally form a ball . . . lighting the world
. . . a gentle breeze shifting the tall grass . . . and they made
love on the cliff . . . and it was perfect . . . she wished she'd
fallen pregnant at that moment . . . had his baby in her belly
when he died six months later . . . and maybe that would
have calmed him down . . . stopped him racing with the devil
. . . but those were maybes . . . and she said that in the years
they had together she bet she lived more than most people . . .
she looked at some of the young people today and they were
lost . . . where was the speed and power and rush of adrenalin
you could only feel when you were out on the road . . . going
down to the coast . . . into the West End . . . off round the

North Circular . . . out into the West Country . . . they used to go to Wiltshire . . . on a Sunday . . . had picnics out there . . . and she clipped the locket shut . . . slipped it back between her breasts . . . and no way was Pearl a sad character . . . she had her life and a man she saw regularly . . . she said she would never live with him . . . Charlie was the love of her life and she was lucky . . . most people never got that . . . she was married to Charlie . . . in sickness and in health . . . just think of a young Elvis . . . the grease and smile . . . he used to ride a bike then got rich and famous and started collecting Cadillacs . . . and she often wondered what it was about Charlie and her that made them take those risks . . . all that energy had to go somewhere she supposed . . . she'd learnt from that and channelled it into teaching . . . that made her feel her life was worth something . . . and it was never ever boring . . . and she laughed and said that it had all worked out for the best . . . at least her and Charlie hadn't grown old and angry and bored with each other . . . and I didn't really believe her when she said that . . . but I sort of knew what she meant.

It was early, too early, but Ruby was so wide awake she couldn't wait the extra half-hour till the baker's opened. She skipped downstairs in her bare feet and the T-shirt she'd been sleeping in, peeped into the street to make sure nobody was around before going out and spotting Mick and Dilly through the window, knocking on the glass for some preferential treatment.

Mick came over and opened the door with the clang of a bolt and the rattle of glass, and she went inside, hungry with the smell of bloomers strong in her flat, all that yeast and flour, ten times better down here, and she always left the window open at night, as wide as it would go, never worried about prowlers. She was over the shops and felt safe, knew her neighbours and would've screamed her head off if someone got in.

She loved the breeze blowing over her skin in the summer, when heat rippled off the hot tar, burning barrels, red coals, roasting spuds, that black asphalt smell of baking bread, somewhere between the petrol drifting off the motorway and the fresh loaves and buns, her mouth watering like mad and her brain skimming away from her across the airwaves.

– Hello, Dilly said, yawning. You're up early today. Couldn't sleep?

Her eyes focused properly and saw that Ruby was

only wearing a T-shirt, didn't seem bothered, kept talking.

– Can I have a coffee and a cheese roll please. And a jam doughnut.

Dilly did the honours, talking over her shoulder.

– You know Norma, who lives on the corner, next to Eileen? The chubby woman with the little girl who lost a finger? Well, she's only gone and won a thousand pounds on the lottery. She told me yesterday. They're going to go on holiday with the kids to Bognor.

Ruby took her breakfast back up when it was ready and moved the switch on her radio, sat on the chair and ate her roll, the bread so fresh it was hot, the sugar on the doughnut sparkling like a million specks of glitter, and she was buzzing, really shifting, skinned up and had a smoke to level things out, the long, long track Charlie Boy had been playing coming to an end, cranking down at the end with the gears in her brain, surprised when DJ Chromo came out through the speakers.

For a second she thought she'd mucked up the time, checked the clock and remembered the baker's wasn't open yet, they were busy cooking, realised she was right but wondered what had happened, all this in a split second guessing that even DJs went on holiday, a week away sitting on a beach drinking cold lager, just what the doctor ordered, she could do with a holiday, hadn't been away since she didn't know when, only thinking about it now because of Norma's win.

DJ Chromo's voice had an ugly edge that made her jump.

– Last night someone cut up our good mate Charlie. You know who you are, boys, and the message I'm giving you right now is you better be careful. You have to understand there's nowhere to hide. You're the cause and we're the effect. Your time is coming, so you better watch your backs. We know who you are and you were lucky, on your toes before the boys with him had a chance to do you some real damage. We know where you live. You ran last night when the odds were evened up, but this is only the start. Just so you know . . .

Ruby didn't like her DJs talking rough, preferred happy music, seeing as there was enough misery in the world without the TV and radio adding more layers on top, but she was upset about Charlie. She knew it would be his face. That usually was, thinking about Terry the bouncer. She remembered another time these guys had tried to scalp a man. It was just plain evil. She avoided trouble, had always been a peace-maker, even in the playground.

She rolled out of her chair and went into the kitchen, opened the fridge door and felt the cold, took the orange-juice carton out and poured herself a glass. Vitamin C would get her working properly. She drank long and deep, and then used the toilet and had a shower, the electric light in the windowless bathroom sparkling along the metal towel rail. The water was refreshing. The spray from the nozzle even and her body tingled, each drop filling with light and explod-ing as it bounced down her and into the drain, spinning away in a soapy whirlpool. A beautiful thing to see.

She brushed her teeth carefully, rinsing her mouth with mint-flavoured wash and dabbing cherry-scented deodorant under her arms. The pores stung and the smell tickled her nose. She could see the scent rising. It floated up quickly, then flattened out in front of her face, so she stood and watched, waiting for the vision to fade away, a cloud from the hot water hovering and mixing together, colours sparking same as when there was a thunderstorm, and she couldn't hang around all day thinking life was brilliant, went back into her bedroom.

– Charlie is our mate and he's going to carry a scar for the rest of his life. He's lost blood and . . .

She turned the radio off, felt she was closer to Charlie Boy than a lot of people she knew, he was often the last person she heard before she went to sleep and the first when she woke up, almost like he was sleeping next to her, not in a sexual way, she didn't even think of him as a man, he didn't have a face with a scar for her to see, and while she slept he was playing records, it was like he was in a factory stuck on the night shift, he probably wouldn't see it that way, it was love that made him do it, and she wondered if there was any money in a pirate station, saw him dossing all day, knew that wasn't the case, he worked, she knew that, it was just a hobby. But it was bad him getting hurt. She hoped he was going to be okay.

Ruby got dressed quickly and left the flat, taking a different route to the hospital, one of two options, today passing the brick hall where the evangelists preached, spreading the word, walls covered in thick graffiti, a maze of laser guns and alien faces, massive trainers on skanking white kids, and she was caught by the criss-cross pattern of bricks and mortar, the way it sectioned the figures, same as the human body with its cells and packs of muscle, the currents that kept it going, and the faces on the wall were happy, smiling with rays of light coming off silver teeth, the windows of the block wired with a touch of stained glass behind the grime, nothing like you got in abbeys and cathedrals, the older churches, but still it was colour, and there was a football pitch to one side, houses to the other, a row of cars gleaming in the early light.

There weren't many people around yet, those she saw either hurrying to work or too tired to notice her, one old man enjoying things the same way as she was, retired, walking over to a bench, there was no rush, soon he'd buy a paper and have a cup of tea, when the cafe opened, and she had time as well, wondering if Ron Dawes went out early like that pensioner, didn't want to think about him right now and make herself sad, didn't want to hear about the slashing of Charlie Boy, just wanted to see the good in people, that's all she asked for. People lived and loved so when something bad happened, a murder or train crash, it was unusual, a big story that sold papers, that's the way she saw things, you could listen to the stories and worry about leaving your window open thinking a rapist was coming or a murderer was lurking in an alleyway, but it was rare.

– Good morning, a man said, as she passed the shutters of a cash and carry.

She nodded and smiled, didn't know who he was, but guessed it was an old patient, and that happened a lot, normally she remembered, but over the years the numbers built up, and it was nice they remembered, Ruby cutting across to the hospital grounds, going and sitting on one of the benches near the psychiatric wing, and it was good over there, like the bushes and flowers were supposed to ease the mental pressure, and she sat in the sun for a while lapping it up, pretending she was on a beach in Bognor, just listening to the birds singing, insects buzzing, breathing fresh air before she started work.

When it was nearly time she went in and was soon busy, dealing with the men she was caring for, making them laugh with her jokes, weighing up the sort of people they were, if they were confident or scared, and they loved their newspapers, she couldn't begrudge them their reading, it gave them something to moan about, and that's what the politicians were really, figures of fun, dollies to stick pins in and slag off, they had their friendly arguments but none of the men on the ward were that far away from each other, and she had a fag with Dawn outside in the sun. Lost in her work. The same as always.

A bit after eleven Ruby recognised a familiar face, a youth in his mid-teens who was one of Ron's regular visitors. She could see he'd been crying from the state of his eyes. He was trying to be strong, and she could see Ron in him all right, a small youth with a spring in his step, even if she didn't know it was his grandson Eddie she'd have been able to guess. He was carrying a bunch of white carnations with long rich stems and extra frilly heads.

— Just came in to say thanks for everything you did

for Granddad, Eddie said. I brought these in for everyone, and to get his belongings. My dad was going to come in but I said I'd do it. He was too upset, to be honest. We all thought he was going to come home in a few days.

Ruby smelt the flowers. They had a powerful scent. Sally would be back in a minute and she could sort out a vase, and then they'd go to someone who never got flowers given to them, subtly done, in a nearby corner that needed a splash of colour and a fresh smell. You never knew how long the petals would last. Sometimes they started to wilt after a day or two and nothing you did could get them going again, even changing the water and moving them into the sun, back into the shade, had no effect, then other times they'd last for weeks, go on and on like they never wanted to give up, flowers that looked so delicate you thought a gust of air could blow them apart, and yet they were strong and determined and not ready to die. Finally, though, they did fade, lost their strength, the colour siphoned away and the leaves curling, rotting, it happened every single time, and you could see it coming, could usually see it coming.

— Why don't you sit in the TV room for a minute, Ruby said. I'll get his things for you. Go on, there's nobody in there right now.

Eddie sat on a chair, leaning back and looking at the ceiling, then shifting forward and stared at the floor. Ron's belongings were in a plain fabric bag his family had brought in when he arrived. There were home-made cards of a man and a house, horses running along a road, more flowers and a yellow sun like it was sinking down into the horizon. Ruby took the bag into the television room and sensed the boy wanted to say something. She sat down opposite him, various celebrities flat on their backs facing the ceiling, scattered over a cheap coffee table.

– I can't believe he's dead, Eddie said. I mean, I know he couldn't walk far, he got puffy and that, but he didn't need to die yet, did he? He had everything he wanted. He liked the garden, always waited for the crocuses to come up in spring, went down the bookies most days, round the shops and that. He still had mates. Watched telly at home. He wasn't an invalid. Dad got him satellite TV. Someone went and saw him every day, and he was always in and out, we only lived across the road. He came round every Sunday for dinner. He could have had all his meals cooked if he wanted. He was fit. I can't understand him dying like that. They said it was his heart. I mean, I know it happens, when you get old, but it's a shock. He wasn't the sort of person who dies.

Ruby just smiled and nodded, because she'd had the same feelings when she heard the news, but now she was thinking that he was eighty-four after all, and was tempted to repeat what Sally and Dawn had said to her at the time, but she didn't, it was just like Eddie said, his granddad was the sort of person who was never going to die, was going to live for ever, but he didn't, he lasted a long time and stayed sharp, beautiful, then died, same as the flowers.

– My sister dusted for him, and I did the lawn, it only took five minutes. He was going to live to be a hundred. That's what he said. I believed him as well. It was like he'd set his mind on it so it was going to happen.

Ruby watched a family pass by in the corridor. Most people had someone to love them. Family and friends to help out. That's how real life worked. That was the reality.

– I can remember when I was little he used to tell me stories all the time, and they were better stories than the ones in books. I never knew they were real till a couple of years ago, he never told me, so I got him to tell me again so at least I know that much. It's like time ran out. It's just good I got to hear some of the things he'd done. I wish I'd written them down, so I got them right. I don't want to forget.

– You could still write them down, Ruby said. That way they'll stay fresh.

She sat with him for a while, listening, and then said goodbye. She watched Eddie walk along the hall with his head bowed. It was nice of him to bring the flowers in, so soon after Ron died as well. She supposed he wanted to talk to someone. Normally it was a week or so later when they got cards, sometimes flowers. She could see he was upset and close to his granddad.

When Ruby went back on the ward the carnations were in a vase and sitting on a windowsill next to Mr Davies, a man of fifty-seven whose wife came in every day but only ever brought cream crackers.

– That was Ron Dawes's grandson, wasn't it? Sally asked when she came round the corner. Has he gone?

– Yes, he just came in for the clothes and cards, the stuff in his locker. I gave him the bag.

– It's a shame, I was going to sit down with Ron

and talk about when he was in the union. Properly. He invited me to go round for a cup of tea when he went home. You never learn, do you? You always think there's a tomorrow, and there isn't.

– I know.

– You okay now?

– Have to be, don't I. Thanks. I was being stupid before.

– Come on, don't be silly. We all get attached to someone now and then. Wouldn't be normal if we didn't.

Ruby smiled and squeezed Sally's hand.

– Who's in his bed?

– A Mr Parish. He was in a fight and got slashed across the face. He's had stitches, but was kicked in the head as well, so that's why he's being kept in, as a precaution. He's asleep at the moment.

It took a while or so for the information to register, and then Ruby was remembering DJ Chromo on the radio and his announcement that Charlie Boy had been cut up. She wondered if it was the same Mr Parish, seeing as his show was called *On The Parish*. It was probably a coincidence, but she'd check, went over to the bed and unhooked his chart, saw that his first name was Charlie. He was cheeky, that's for sure, but there again, who was going to put two and two together and realise they had the real name of the pirate waiting to be deciphered, certainly not the DTI. The fun squad would be kicking themselves if they ever found out, and she stood at the bottom of his bed for another minute looking at what she could see of his head, a bandage over the side facing her while the other was buried in the pillow, the hair short and body still under the blankets.

She knew it was only a radio show, and most of the time he was playing music, but Charlie talked as well so it was like she really knew him, she'd thought it many times before, not like who his family were, his friends and that, where he drank and socialised, but she knew some of his opinions and definitely his taste in music. It was as if he was her long-lost brother or something, the brother she never had, and how many mornings had she woken up and flicked the switch that shut out the police sirens with the sound of his voice. It really was a small world, minute if she was honest. Straight into the bed where Ron Dawes had died. If only it had been another bed, and though she was actually excited to see what Charlie Parish looked like, she felt disrespectful to Ron that she could feel any sort of excitement while he was waiting to be buried.

She looked around at the other men and saw they were upset, brooding. They would've known Ron as well as her, probably better, he was one of their gang, even if they'd only been together a short time. She went back over to the desk.

– Do you know him? Sally asked.

– No, not really. I just recognised the name.

– You look like you do.

– All right? Dawn said, strolling past, licking her lips as she flashed a bottle of urine.

Ruby and Sally laughed and went their separate ways. Ruby would always remember them, never forget the old man in the TV room with the thin body and wagging tongue, but even so, she couldn't help smiling to herself and thinking it was mad how the world just kept on going, no sooner had one man been carted out than another was wheeled in, Charlie Parish off the radio, Satellite FM's top DJ who spun records for a couple of hundred locals, a celebrity in her eyes, the man without a face cut across the cheek, and when they said life was for living she knew what they meant, Dawn passing back down the corridor and wiggling her bum, holding the piss bottle up again, like it was a fine wine or something.

– What a fucking job, she said, leaning over and whispering in Ruby's ear. We must be mad.

Mr Jeffreys decided to drive to work. For a change. It was said that variety was the spice of life and who was he to disagree? He could fully relax on his own and escape the primitive beat of a skinhead in a checked shirt. Instead of the motorway he decided on a series of local roads. He preferred the major route, but traversing these grim tunnels was another aspect of his studies. The town in which he worked was not the sort of place he would normally stop, and if he used the motorway he might be tempted to keep on driving until he reached the countryside. A green and pleasant land no less. Those dark satanic mills had only ever existed within the warped mind of the revolutionary Blake. Imagine seeing angels in Peckham. He thought of cream teas and sprawling farms, roast dinners and elegant mansions. It was wishful thinking, of course. He was dedicated to his work and could not abscond willy-nilly. He was content to serve the people, yet these streets were so empty of culture it made him despair.

Endless houses butted the tarmac as if they were blank walls. He passed parades of shops, service stations, pubs, yards, fast-food outlets, a snooker hall, patches of wasteland. The burnt-out remains of a car sat in a lay-by. There was no individuality and very little colour to stir the spirit. The roads were a continuation of the hospital's deadening corridors, the dullness of the town reflected in its wards and waiting rooms. The staff did their best, but were from the same root.

Even so, Mr Jeffreys's mood was good and matched the smooth hum of his newly serviced BMW engine. German automobiles were most definitely built to please. Teutonic efficiency and American free enterprise represented the ideal combination. Add a good French meal and he was more than content. Passing a bus he glanced left. Jolted at the sight of so many bodies packed inside. His sense of well-being exploded as he saw himself destitute and forced to travel with the masses. Incarcerated within the bus. Pressed against the rancid clothes of men and women who stared straight ahead and said nothing. Surrounded by juvenile delinquents who said too much. School-age yobs spitting and swearing. Mocking his manners. He felt his lungs crushed by a herd of witch-like women. Their hair matted and teeth broken. Foul breath turned his stomach. He could feel threadbare coats on his skin, the fabric soaked in vats of sweat. These hags were straight from the pages of Shakespeare. Babbling harlots clasping plastic toys to sagging breasts. Presents for snotty-nosed grandchildren who repaid them with violent crime and loose morals. Dolls for the girls and guns for the boys. When they reached their teens the boys would steal cars and rob pensioners, the girls stab each other with knitting needles. High on drugs as they flitted from one sexual partner to another. Passing on syphilis and herpes with a nonchalance he found obscene.

This documentary-inspired vision continued as he pictured a young mother clattering a plastic bag against his right leg. The sharp edge of a tin stabbed into his kneecap. A retarded brat tugged at his arm and begged for fifty pence. Fingernails bitten. Nose running. A smile on its face. It was so degrading. He dare not imagine what went on inside the child's home. No doubt the father was a bully with tattoos surrounding his navel. The sort of man who stood outside bars on foreign street corners throwing beer bottles at peaceable locals. A user of amphetamines and strong lager. The mother little more than a common whore, a Dickensian slut with bloodless skin and grey eyes. Quite prepared to sleep with any man who took her fancy. Totally without shame. Hollow cheeks and a love of crack cocaine. Her brother another drunken skinhead who stared at him across the bus. Hate etched into redneck features. A swastika tattoo on his forehead and a knife in his hand. Mr Jeffreys fought the unfurling film footage, and recovering from the shock accelerated away. The bus stopped for a mob of howling peasants who surged forward with their plastic bags swinging, frothing at the mouth. It was a glimpse of hell and of no consequence. He was a man of reason.

Public transport made sense of course. If every single person was to drive a car then the roads would soon be at a standstill. A brave new transport policy was essential. An intelligent strategy where only those whose jobs were vital to the welfare of society were allowed a vehicle. If this rule was implemented he would be able to cut as much as ten minutes off his journey to work. When he arrived he would not have to waste valuable minutes searching for a parking space. Other employees had bays reserved for them yet he was left to fend for himself. He had a permit, but felt it was unfair as he was forced to park with the visitors. The attendant was a fool, of course, with a gormless smile and constantly shrugging shoulders. This man was at home with anarchy, cars filled with skinheads and bleached blondes. Their children exact replicas. The attendant allowed cars to rest on yellow-lined kerbs rather than banish them to the street.

Mr Jeffreys kept his dignity. He was not angry for himself, not at all, it was just the inefficiency involved. Instead of driving up and down he should be in his office working. He did not hold this favouritism against other members of staff. No, it was the system that was at fault. The staff car park needed extending, thereby increasing efficiency. It was common sense. He often worried that his car would be scraped.

Some of the vehicles on the road were an absolute disgrace. They polluted the atmosphere and threatened other motorists. Worn-out automobiles driven by lazy thinkers. Men such as the thug hunched over the wheel of the van he was passing. The bodywork was filthy and the wheel arches lined with rust, engine struggling to cope with the fifty miles per hour it was doing. The driver's face was unshaven and his expression fierce. A Neanderthal head turned to look Mr Jeffreys straight in the eye. The thug raised a dirty hand in a gesture that implied masturbation. The mouth curved in a sneer, lips forming an obscenity. Mr Jeffreys felt his buttocks quiver with fear and accelerated away, wondering about the odour of the thug's mouth, the state of those teeth. Worst of all guessing that the lips were infected with herpes. Sores oozing pus. He considered recording the licence plate and passing it to the police via his mobile phone but was too far ahead now to see clearly. He did not want to slow down and invite a road-rage assault. He might be wounded. Murdered even. This was a very common occurrence these days and a sign of the times. He was putting distance between the two vehicles and able to relax once he had passed through a set of changing traffic lights, neatly dismissing the thug from his mind. He refused to lower himself to the man's level by even thinking about him. Film of petty thieves and brawlers replayed in his mind's eye. Conmen and robbers who risked prison for insignificant returns. Honesty and decency qualities they could never comprehend.

Mr Jeffreys was in a bullish mood. He was sympathetic to other motorists yet frustrated by the lack of organisation. Hard decisions were needed. It was not just the health service and public byways that cried out for reform, but the whole of society. It was one of his pet topics. Something to mull over when he was not working. The justice system was an area that needed immediate attention. Sentences had to be stiffened for a start. A policy of zero tolerance adopted towards offenders, be they murderers, shoplifters bad mannered children. If this meant more prisons had to be built, then so be it. The malaise was deep-rooted and sometimes it was necessary to be cruel to be kind. Firm but fair. Of course, these were expressions, but the truth could not be denied, however loud liberal do-gooders bleated. He was not a cruel man, saw himself as both kind and considerate, perhaps even too amenable at times, not speaking out enough as he did his best to maintain good relations. It was his education. His background. A highly civilised and cultured way of behaving.

He saw the junction he wanted and indicated right. Waited for the traffic to subside before crossing towards the maisonettes. He parked in a side street and walked back, rang a doorbell and waited. There was the sound of footsteps. Candy kept the chain in place until she recognised it was Jonathan. He smiled and followed her up the stairs.

He had found her through an advert in a local newspaper and visited once a week. She was in her thirties with blonde hair. He did not know if she was a natural blonde as naturally he had never seen her naked. She provided him with an insight into the nature of the women of this godforsaken town. He had to play the role of 'punter' to glean information yet considered this essential research. She wore an apron covered with pictures from the seaside. Shells and suchlike. She took this off and hung it over the back of a chair. He doubted Candy was her real name, that she used it to express some sort of American glamour. He believed her real name was Carole, but it did not matter. It was a professional exchange. The procedure always the same. Simple yet effective. Soon she would offer him a cup of tea and they would talk. Maybe she would make him some toast. That would be nice.

Candy was dressed plainly, in the sort of cheap blouse and slacks he saw so often in the hospital. She knelt on the carpet and bowed her head. Mr Jeffreys walked over and stood inches away from her face. He stroked her hair. There was bacteria there but he did not care. He felt the dirt on his palm. Stood stroking her head for two minutes. When he had finished he raised his hand to his nose and smelt the odour. He looked around the room and unzipped his trousers. Withdrew his penis. His bladder was full from the tea he had drunk in the hotel before leaving. It was a very nice Darjeeling blend. Soon he would drink PG Tips. Candy opened her mouth and he moved forward. Held his penis at the correct angle. The urine burst forth from his loins yet she managed to catch and swallow it without spillage. She must not mess her clothes, no doubt bought on the high street. He looked down at the hair. The blonde strands and white skin below. But he was not a beast. Every so often he squeezed his penis to stem the flow. This allowed her to catch up. He leant sideways to observe the swallowing motion. He continued. In control. There certainly was a lot today. He smiled generously although Candy could not see. He controlled the sexual urge and he controlled the working of his bladder. She was under his spell. Bewitched. Under his control.

Once he had finished he shook himself dry and tucked his penis back inside his underpants. At no point did he touch Candy's mouth. Neither did he have an erection. He rezipped his trousers and stood for a few moments surveying the room and its cheap furnishings. It was a natural act and he felt better. Candy stood up. Her breath was truly wretched. Disgusting in fact. It was as if someone had urinated in her mouth. She retired to the bathroom and he heard the tap running. Two minutes later she returned and stood before him again. He leant forward and breathed in. Her breath smelt sweet now. Toothpaste and the strongest mouthwash available had done wonders. He went to the sofa and sat down.

– Would you like like a nice cuppa? Candy asked, exaggerating her accent so that she sounded like a chirpy cockney in a Dick Van Dyke film.

He loved it when she talked like this.

– That would be nice.

She went to the kitchen to put the kettle on. As he awaited her return Jonathan pondered her collection of cheap ornaments. The Queen's face adorned several mugs. Cheap trinkets stretched in a long line along the windowsill. Shells had been glued together in the form of a horse which sat on top of an electric fire. He almost expected to see a half-eaten stick of rock there, fluffy with dust. It really was preposterous. But an experience. Irony was the key word here. He did not make a habit of slumming it yet this was purely business. There was very definitely no sexual thrill involved. The woman left him cold in that respect. She had apparently worked in a massage parlour but been pushed aside by several younger girls. According to Candy these girls were teenage slags prepared to do anything for money. It amused him how she made such comparisons. As if she had higher standards. But never mind. He was not making judgements. She was a human being with feelings, which he respected.

— I'll make you some toast, she sang, popping her head into the room. You like your toast, don't you?

It was unfortunate that he had been caught short. It was lucky he had a friend such as Candy. She offered what she had once jokingly referred to as a piss stop. A crude comment in fact. But just what he would expect. At first she had been unwilling to allow him this form of relief, but eventually he had managed to convince her. He had been surprised at first, a little irritated even. One hundred and fifty pounds was a hell of a lot of money for urinating in the mouth of a common tart, yet it proved that there was no honour in the rancid sprawl of this awful town. It had taken three visits to strike a deal. On their first two meetings they had talked. He had broached the subject and been rebuffed. At the third attempt an agreement had been reached. The routine was the same each time. He did not seek variation. There was a pattern. The world was rotten. It was rotten to the core. A failing heart that had swollen through abuse and no longer pumped efficiently. It was very sad. But he had to know. He was one of the few men in the country who could not be bought. He was as honest as the day was long. His soul was truly his own property.

— Here you are. Would you like some Marmite?

— No thank you. This is fine.

He ate the toast. It was cheap white bread. The texture reminded him of cardboard. It was soaked in margarine.

— Fancy a bicky?

He took a biscuit and dipped it in his tea. It was milky and the biscuit was bland. How people ate such rubbish was beyond him.

– Perfect, he said, forcing the goo down.

Jonathan stayed with Candy for exactly half an hour. When it was time to continue his journey to work he briefly used the WC so as to spare her any inconvenience. He pecked her on the cheek and slipped the envelope containing her wages into her hand. He knew that she had a daughter to look after, the girl's face big and grinning in a silver frame, the rest of the photographs in the room stuck in plastic. He *assumed* it was her daughter. He had never seen the child himself. Maybe he was wrong. But he did not care. He did know that Candy's nerves were not good and she lacked confidence. This she told him as they sat drinking tea. He did not want to hear this. It was not what ordinary people spoke about. They talked about football matches and their betters. He did not care a jot for Candy and her problems. One hundred and fifty pounds was damn good money. But she was appreciative. Looked forward to his visits. He knew that she was rubbish and without standards, but he had to confirm the fact. It was her resistance he was paying to break. Proving a point. They were two consenting adults and both prospered from the arrangement. He smiled and she smiled back. He felt warm inside. He was helping her with his money. The simple act an excuse for him to give generously. He did not want her to feel as if she was begging. Hand held out and dignity lost.

He walked across the street feeling happy. As if

treading on air. A gang of hooligans stood outside a chip shop talking. They were no doubt up to no good, but such was life. They did not even look his way. His role within society was centred on the hospital. He was not a police officer. He was grateful his car was parked out of their sight. They would remove the wheels given half a chance. Break a window and steal his stereo system. The alarm would sound and off they would run.

He started the engine and moved away from this squalid little corner of the world, tuning into a radio discussion on a famous miscarriage of justice. So-called. He did not believe that the police had fabricated the evidence. Perhaps they had skirted certain procedures but it would not have been intentional. The judge would have offered an independent perspective. Of course, many of these so-called mistrials were merely justice by other means. These people came from criminal backgrounds. Bleated on about how they had fallen into bad company at a young age. Everybody knew they were guilty of something, even if this could not be proven. The legal system was designed for the benefit of criminals. The jury itself a weak area. In a very small number of cases he had to admit that mistakes may, possibly, have occurred, yet no malice was intended and that was a fact that was well worth remembering.

In his own field he was both judge and jury combined, albeit in a far less confrontational way. The judicial system was based on firm ideals. A man was innocent until proven guilty. It was easy to tell the criminal type, but the judiciary was forced to go through the motions, wasting resources on long and expensive trials. A necessary evil of course. He was certainly no fascist, nor communist. However, a major problem was that jurors were chosen at random from the general population. This meant that virtually anyone could sit in judgement of their fellow citizens. The one saving grace was the judge, a trained and neutral professional. He was able to guide the jury in the right direction. Even so, the concept was flawed. There were certain people who believed in curtailing the right to trial by jury, which in his humble opinion seemed a fine idea.

Having a dozen sentimental oiks pontificating on every decision was quite clearly out of the question with regard to Mr Jeffreys's work. Nothing would ever be achieved. He weighed up the evidence and made a decision, the responsibility his and his alone. At all times he remained impartial and judged according to facts. There was no room for mistakes and he made none. The pressure, however, was sometimes unbearable. His judgements had to be spot on or people would suffer.

When he arrived at the hospital it was nearly seven o'clock and he had no problem parking. A group of Asian youths kicked a tennis ball against a wall. He found this annoying but said nothing, not wanting to be accused of racial intolerance. The subcontinent had supplied the NHS with many fine doctors and nurses over the years. He did find their customs odd, and their food was revolting, the garlic and spices oozing from their skin foul. Yet as a professional man he respected these people for their work ethic. Their ability to endure the behaviour of low-intelligence whites was quite amazing. West Indians fulfilled lower-caste jobs along with their English counterparts. These people were closer to nature, more spontaneous and less hard-working than Pakistanis, Indians and Bangladeshis. Then there were the Irish of course. Many Irish girls came to England to work as nurses. They toiled next to the Asians and Caribbeans. A large number had been absorbed into the indigenous population, as indeed had Asians and West Indians. The Irish had been here longer and their DNA had filtered into the gene pool. Many were unrecognisable now. The same was beginning to happen with these brown- and black-skinned peoples. This was no doubt a good thing in terms of stability, and while he did not possess an ounce of prejudice, it nevertheless reflected the low morals of the common whites. It revealed a distinct lack of self-respect. While more educated whites preached racial tolerance he was fully aware that they maintained segregation, although they would obviously never admit this fact.

Mr Jeffreys passed through reception and smiled at members of staff, aware of differences but accepting everyone as an equal. No matter what their ethnicity or social background. He despised bigotry in all its forms. Loathed crass prejudices based on colour and culture. Too many of these white men and women lacked this awareness and revelled in a false sense of racial superiority. The men shaved their hair close to the bone, thereby erasing individuality. This custom crossed the boundaries of age. From old men to young boys they accepted the fact that they were little more than robots. The women wore cheap clothes that were far too tight for their bloated bodies. Make-up swamped their features, layers of powder forming crass masks which they believed could hide their inherent ugliness. There was no point being dishonest about the facts.

These were common people. Ordinary. Prone to sentimentality and outbursts of anger and joy. They lived and they loved and that seemed to be enough. Where was their ambition? Real ambition. Not small-scale hopes but full-blown dreams. He understood that these people had dreams of a sort, but they were so small as to be meaningless. They spent their lives working to own a modest home as if this set them apart from those who rented. They lived in flats. Terraced houses. Made distinctions between manual and office work when they came from the same streets. This snobbery was amusing of course, but quite ridiculous. The masses had no power yet were so stupid that they fought over the crumbs thrown to them from on high. This narrow thinking filled him with loathing.

The canvas of his life was far larger than that of the ordinary man and woman in the street. Ah yes, the street, its imagery captured by cameras rather than the palette. The street flooded with uncollected litter and discarded refrigerators. Lined with takeaways and greasy spoons. Soaked in the stench of fried batter and roasted chicken. Tender ears assaulted by the constant boom of bass and treble. Fear stirred by gangs of mindless hooligans. The skinhead element. Everywhere he looked there were bloody skinheads. It was as if every male in this horrible town had a shaven head. Scars and nicks from electric razors. The stench of aftershave. The smell of a black man with dreadlocks standing with a gang of skinheads sipping a carton of fruit juice. Tossing it to the ground and crushing the cardboard with his heel. Streets packed with drug dealers and pimps. Gutters trimmed by torn newspapers. Shutters fastened. Protecting the sort of garish jewellery he would not accept from a Christmas cracker. In winter there was no colour. During summer the reds and blues merely washed out and faded.

No, the streets he was forced to view were grim and uninviting for a civilised man such as himself. His dreams were far grander. He did not have to worry about money, of course. He was rich beyond their wildest hopes. No, that was not true. The dreams of these people had been stretched by the National Lottery. They had become totally unrealistic. He was amazed at the importance the National Lottery had assumed in their lives. Patients became terrified they would lose out on a fortune as they lay dying in one of his wards. They had favoured numbers and feared that these would be selected at the very moment they were in hospital. This fear consumed them. Visitors were quickly pressed into service. They recorded the sacred numbers and bought the relevant tickets. Until these lottery numbers were safely in their hands his patients were anxious. It applied to both men and women and across all the age groups. He had witnessed this himself and had spoken to one of the night nurses about this phenomenon. It honestly amazed him. Those who could ill afford to waste even a pound spent as much as ten at one time. The eyes of the unemployed shone at the thought of winning millions. The elderly waited eagerly for news. It was too late for them, but they wanted so much to leave a fortune to their children and grandchildren. It was absolutely pathetic. Relying on a lucky dip. It was so demeaning.

One of the nurses had explained that it was all many people had to keep them going. The lottery offered hope. That word again. She had taken out her purse and shown him her own ticket. If she won the jackpot she would never have to worry about money again. Everything would suddenly be possible. He had nodded to show that he understood as he did not want to appear out of touch. But it was beyond him. Any one of these people could win a million and it would not change what they were. The root of their being would remain the same. They would still be dull and faceless, sudden bursts of emotion leading them to trouble. They would feel sad hearing hard-luck stories. Cry at a ridiculous drama swamped with sentiment. They would spoil each other if they won a few pounds. Fritter the cash away on a takeaway meal. A visit to the cinema. It was impossible to buy breeding. It was not for sale. At any price. It really was not about money at all. That was the problem with the small people who imagined they could work themselves up out of the gutter. He saw them in the hospital. Puffed-up and proud. He hated them more than the failures. They fooled themselves. Did not understand that money was not the issue.

On the day he was born he had been worth more

192

than these fools were after a lifetime of hard work. Wealth gave a man a degree of power, but it was of a crude form. The nature of his work gave Mr Jeffreys the greatest power of all. He had the power of life and death. At the same time he was able to serve the community and help those less fortunate than himself.

He despised many of the people within the community for their lack of control, for their ignorance and selfishness, yet at the same time loved them as you would a foolish child. A soldier had the power of life and death, but was a lackey. A moron who killed according to orders. The soldier did not think about who he exterminated. Did not care. He was a coward, a destroyer of life. Mr Jeffreys had no respect for the military. He had dedicated his life to helping society rather than being a part of its destruction. His father had been the same and had saved thousands of lives during a lengthy career. Jonathan Jeffreys was merely following in his esteemed footsteps.

*T*he Green Man was Danny's local . . . opposite the milk depo . . . a car park away from the Latter-Day Church Of St John The Baptist . . . a yellow-brick pub with fruit machines and pool tables by the function room and a handful of tables and chairs down the other end . . . most of the space there for standing and drinking . . . the TV screen showing everything from Brentford–Millwall on a Friday night to the Old Firm game Sunday dinner time . . . regular European trips during the week . . . and there was always a session going on in the Green Man . . . Danny sticking to lemonade . . . the pub a two-minute walk from his flat . . . so he knew everyone . . . was well liked . . . on the brink of life looking at a future that stretched over another half-century . . . fingers crossed . . . juggling oranges and lemons on the fruit machine . . . chalking his nickname Wax Cap on the board between Bubba and Paul P . . . silver on the table . . . waiting his turn . . . choosing a hole and potting the black . . . next game up slaughtered by Gal . . . he looked over at me and shrugged his shoulders . . . handed his cue to Steve with the glass eye . . . going over to the pinball machine and rolling a big chunky spliff on the glass . . . Wax Cap's nightcap . . . going out front to smoke his motorway draw on one of the benches . . . leaning back and thinking about the ways of the world . . . how things had panned out . . . a green man watching from the pub sign . . .

blue eyes peeking out of green moss and brown leaves . . .
Bubba inside raising a pint to his mouth . . . performing the
ritual . . . celebrating life . . . licking his lips . . . draining
the glass . . . and the pub had these massive windows that
showed everything . . . there was no hiding in dark corners
. . . the lights bright . . . the bottom of the windows lined
with all sorts of specials . . . Sunday roast for the Old Firm
game and a regular beef curry during the week . . . extra chips
if you ordered before kick-off . . . faded England fixtures on a
newspaper pull-out . . . flyers for Thursday's garage night at
Jubbly's . . . and then there was the once-a-year circus with
photos of elephants and lions that didn't travel any more . . .
sharp letters on smooth paper . . . the tape yellow and peeling
. . . Bubba lifting a fresh pint to his lips . . . Danny Wax
Cap looking down the street now towards the Karachi Kebab
. . . Billy's Fish Shop . . . and he loved sitting outside at
night and kicking back . . . the best time was after it had been
raining and the tarmac was glistening . . . summer when it
stayed light till ten . . . the streets quiet by eight . . . he just
sat there watching . . . a pensioner walking his dog . . . three
boys doing wheelies . . . a woman eating a pasty . . . the
smell of batter frying . . . chips . . . petrol . . . a family
crossing the road and the little boy stroking the old man's dog
. . . it went on and on . . . never stopped . . . and Danny
sat there for ages before going back in for another glass of
lemonade . . . putting Wax Cap on the board . . . twenty-
three years old but teetotal for two . . . he laughed when he
told you that . . . it made him sound like a prissy woman in
a biscuit-tin village . . . all dentures and sponge cake . . .
sipping tea at the village fête . . . and he liked his tea all right
. . . PG Tips plus those herbal flavours . . . ginger for zest
. . . bags of the stuff . . . they were expensive but easy to slip

*in his pocket . . . those supermarkets were making billions
every year . . . they didn't notice a few tea bags . . .
camomile was good before he went to bed . . . helped him
sleep . . . though to be honest by the time he got in at eleven
after a smoke he was on his way . . . then on Saturday he
had his special cuppa . . . something to look forward to . . . a
treat at the end of the week . . . another ritual . . . he wasn't
working but still looked forward to the weekend . . . it was
there from when you were at school . . . and he did odd jobs
. . . when he could get them . . . but he got by signing on
. . . didn't need much to live . . . the corporations were
pumping out cheap food . . . own-brand . . . pasta . . .
butter beans . . . bread . . . baked beans . . . spices that
lasted for years . . . and his rent was paid by housing benefit
. . . the bills were low . . . his membership for the sports
centre subsidised . . . he didn't drink a lot . . . a couple of
glasses of lemonade at night . . . didn't buy clothes . . . more
interested in living than working . . . what did you get for
fifty years of yes-sir no-sir . . . a plasterboard house and
subsistence pension . . . if you were lucky . . . by the time
you retired you were knackered . . . all your strength sucked
out by the banks . . . even if you managed to save a few
grand you were too worn out to use it . . . no . . . it was a
load of bollocks . . . he was saving his strength . . . any one
of us could die tomorrow . . . and on Saturday mornings he
had a fry-up and read the paper . . . finished off with a nice
mug of liberty-cap tea . . . the name summed it up . . . magic
mushrooms sounded better as liberty caps . . . it was all to do
with freedom . . . and they weren't addictive . . . that was
important . . . he knew the technical terms as well . . . this
was his only drug these days . . . the skunk didn't count . . .
Danny was fighting back . . . the law had given him six*

months in prison for thinking too much and fucked him up big time . . . done for ecstasy then introduced to heroin . . . from E to H in six long . . . short . . . months . . . it was wrong sending him to prison . . . he'd never hurt anyone in his life . . . wasn't even a small-time dealer supplying friends . . . like the police said . . . it was just that Danny was intense . . . did more Es than was normal . . . gulped the MDMA down like it was sweets . . . he was dedicated . . . that's all . . . looking for answers to all those questions most of us bury away . . . but as well as the E he was sent to prison for being scruffy . . . for having a ponytail . . . that was part of it . . . Danny tried to explain the way he saw things to the magistrates . . . that he was a spiritual man . . . but they didn't know what he was talking about . . . didn't have a clue . . . their faces blank . . . he tried harder . . . went into one about how the drugs and music matched . . . a ceremony . . . lifted him up so he saw life in a better . . . cleaner way . . . but they wouldn't believe him . . . it was beyond them . . . and the thing with Danny was that this addictive personality made him what he was . . . no doubt about that . . . his enthusiasm rubbed off . . . an exciting edge to his nature . . . but it caused him problems as well . . . it didn't matter if it was drink . . . drugs . . . music . . . a place . . . a girl . . . he had to have it all . . . right now . . . he was so glad to be alive he wanted the girl till his head swelled up with love and exploded . . . everything magnified . . . or if it was a pub he'd be in there every night . . . or with a drug he'd be sucking it down and snorting it up till he was done in . . . big time . . . moderation didn't come into it . . . he was out of control . . . did what he wanted . . . when he wanted . . . all the time the questions nagging at him . . . why was he him and not someone else . . . why was he born and why

197

did he have to die . . . it was all there in his head . . . a child's questions he couldn't silence . . . and he kept on at the magistrates . . . about wine being used in religious ceremonies for years . . . matching a rave to a Christian service . . . the hymns and blood of Christ . . . he was looking for the same euphoria . . . where everything made sense . . . he was trying to appeal to their own experiences but didn't realise till after that they didn't have any . . . these were people without knowledge . . . or imagination . . . they hugged the Bible because they were scared . . . it was written in stone all right . . . they did what they thought they'd been told . . . reckoned Danny was trying to hide a sick way of life . . . saw him as immoral . . . a hedonist . . . to them hedonism was a crime . . . and they believed in sacrifice . . . as long as it was someone else being sacrificed . . . Christ was the perfect example . . . and Danny said they were the sort of people who believed in hoarding their money and controlling their feelings because deep down they were afraid . . . and this made them bitter . . . they wanted revenge for feeling this way . . . for never feeling drunk . . . and he was another mug to punish for their frustration . . . jealousy . . . they were wasting their lives waiting for a better time that was never going to come because it was already here and they were missing out . . . they were the exact same people who'd sit in judgement and crucify Christ . . . so they gave Danny six months . . . and then he laughed and told me to forget all that . . . they just didn't like scruffy young herberts . . . their reasons meant nothing really . . . it was prejudice . . . repression . . . with this belief that the spiritual was separate from the physical tagged on for good luck . . . if something like ecstasy could give him insights it meant their sacrifices were a waste . . . and he came to feel sorry for them . . .

before he knew the effect switching to smack had on him . . . then he just forgot about them . . . Danny believed in living life to the full and when he came out of prison he was worse than ever . . . a junky now . . . racing downhill with no brakes . . . and it was like the stuff was being shipped into prison specially to mess everyone up . . . the authorities knocking prisoners out for the duration of their sentences then sending the likes of Danny home with a habit that would eventually kill him . . . and he said it was like someone had dreamt up an extermination plan that couldn't be done out in the open but was working in the shadows . . . shifting the blame to the inmates . . . how could you ever prove it was a state policy . . . no one would believe you . . . it was mixed up with blame and retribution . . . and a year or so after he came out he was diagnosed as HIV-positive . . . the next six months the worst of his life . . . he was dying . . . and life was shit . . . he had no hope . . . no future . . . till one day he just woke up and his personality had swung again . . . he got out of bed early and walked through the empty streets . . . could smell the world and feel the wind on his face . . . saw the sun come up over the houses . . . knew that the odds were stacked high against him but wanted to live . . . he was going to fight the virus . . . and his brain clicked . . . he went through withdrawal and kicked the habit . . . alone . . . by sheer will power . . . it was his addictive personality did it . . . switched him from a fucked-up junky to this hardcore straight-edge life . . . he started looking after himself because weak he didn't have a chance . . . but strong he might survive . . . and he worked out a fitness regime . . . lifted weights and went swimming . . . bought the right food to eat . . . read up on it . . . the drink and drugs were out and fruit juice was in . . . beetroot for his blood . . . carrots for the carotene

. . . celery for iron . . . he could run through a long list of the stuff . . . he was up early and out jogging . . . a year later seriously fit . . . and it was hard work but he had the inner strength . . . said exercise was the key to happiness . . . released endorphines into the blood and gave you a natural high . . . how many unhappy sprinters did you see . . . laughing . . . one day they were going to discover a cure for HIV and he wanted to be around to enjoy it . . . and anyway . . . not everyone who was HIV-positive developed Aids . . . if he took care of himself he had a chance . . . if he'd kept on the way he was going he'd be dead . . . imagine dying from a cold . . . a skinny wreck of a man withering away . . . he had the will to live . . . it was going to save him . . . Danny knew it for a fact . . . had it sorted . . . as much fizzy drink as he wanted and one smoke a day . . . to quieten him down at night . . . he'd always had trouble sleeping . . . up late with insomnia . . . and he was doing his living during the day now . . . in bed by eleven . . . he was a spiritual man . . . always emphasised the point . . . a spiritual man . . . so the magic mushrooms were vital . . . gave him another view . . . made the world softer . . . opened things right up . . . he never stopped thinking about life . . . women loved him for that . . . flocked to him . . . he never had a bad word to say about anyone . . . stayed positive . . . a quiet man with everything in its place . . . he was the fundamentalist now . . . a spoonful of olive oil in the morning . . . the virgin stuff . . . expensive . . . but the mushrooms were free and how much had he spent on smack? . . . thinking back for a second . . . he knew it was too late to change what had happened . . . he hated thinking about the needle that infected him . . . sliding the poison into his bloodstream . . . what did a man condemned to death feel when he was strapped down and sedated . . . the executioner stepping forward and giving him a lethal injection . . . Danny asked me that and I didn't know what to say . . . that was pure evil dressed up as civilisation . . . it was planned and worse than something that happened in an instant . . . an argument and murder . . . it was the same as a serial killer tracking his victim . . . a paedophile in an orphanage . . . it was warped . . . but Danny was thinking long term . . . getting into the regular motion of the breaststroke . . . breathing in and out as he sunk deeper into the swimming pool . . . chlorine in his hair . . . scrubbing his skin as the jets in the shower drilled in . . . imagining the virus being sand-blasted out . . . or if he was doing weights he pushed his muscles to the limit . . . sweating the virus away . . . and either way he was going to win the battle . . . all the things he used to worry about were sideshows now . . . every second ten times more precious than before . . . and he'd always tried to grab as much of life as he could . . . feared death and how it was always going to end in tears . . . he was planning ahead . . . reading hard . . . sitting in the library for hours on end . . . every day . . . feeding his brain . . . concentrating . . . his life rich . . . just breathing was enough . . . and he talked about the way hardcore Christians impose their heavy manners on a pagan country where people drink and fight and kiss and make up . . . and he hated being told how to behave . . . limits set on what he could . . . and could not . . . do . . . this was supposed to be a country where eccentrics were welcome . . . part of the tradition . . . and the major problem was the way these Christians separated body and soul . . . inflicted harsh Judaic desert laws on a land that was wet and green and fermenting all sorts of magic potions . . . spores floating through the trees and across fields . . . rotting fruit and hops melting into alcohol . . . a place where the boys drank in the Green Man and the girls rented the function room for their hen nights . . . strippers dressed as Vikings . . . and that's how he saw things . . . the magic mushrooms had opened his eyes . . . given him a natural take on life . . . they weren't manufactured . . . concocted in a test tube . . . there were no military chemists involved . . . no pharmaceutical companies . . . no CIA . . . the spores rode the winds same as a good DJ . . . and once Danny started on this track he was off . . . an expert on the subject . . . loved talking about fungus . . . and it wasn't just the magic variety either . . . he picked all sorts . . . ate more than his fair share . . . he knew his stuff . . . could tell a grey knight-cap from a cornflower bolete . . . he had to . . . some made you sick . . . others you could eat . . . and he'd tell you about the gills and everything . . . the colours and textures . . . where they grew . . . on open land or in forests . . . so they called him Wax Cap in the Green Man . . . it was a type of mushroom . . . and they were only interested in the magic variety in the pub . . . didn't care about the ones you could eat . . . why bother? . . . there was plenty of food around . . . Danny laughing at Bubba and the rest of the boys . . . going into one about how he gently heated some oil and added a fresh puffball . . . the common variety . . . crushed a few cloves of garlic . . . he was Danny the chanterelle hunter . . . an earthstar man . . . a stinkhorn gatherer . . . the fungus chef . . . he was feeding his mind and feeding his body . . . and mushrooms were expensive . . . why waste good money when you could pick your own . . . get them fresh . . . and he looked forward to spring and autumn when there was a glut . . . went out to the woods on the edge of town . . . on his bike . . . chained it to the fence lining the main road and was soon lost in among the pines . . . the steady hum of the motorway in the distance . . . and there was a lake where people went to swim in summer . . . a tea shop selling ice creams . . . the burger van doing a roaring trade in bacon rolls . . . but that was in the car park and it wasn't hard to get lost in the trees and ferns . . . specially when summer was over . . . nobody went into the woods in the autumn and winter . . . least not where he walked . . . he knew the small tracks and new plantations . . . older trees shutting out the light . . . a pit where they buried rubbish . . . and he went there more and more . . . for a walk when there was frost or a bit of snow . . . all alone in the wood . . . he never saw the tramps who built the lean-tos . . . he loved it there . . . the shades of black . . . grey . . . brown . . . the white of the frost . . . it was lonely but good . . . healthy . . . the tracks hard under his feet . . . sheets of glass covering puddles . . . sometimes he'd smash the ice and lift out big chunks of broken window . . . and because there were so many pine trees there was lots of boletes growing . . . so when the time was right he'd be looking through stacks of needles and ferns . . . the smell of the earth heavy . . . rich . . . rotting logs and tree trunks sprouting all sorts of fungus . . . big brain-like shapes and multicoloured killers . . . the thing with fungus was it could be good or bad . . . could rot timber or make bread rise . . . create antibiotics such as penicillin or rot potatoes and cause the Irish potato famine . . . the mushrooms themselves were there to spread . . . to reproduce . . . the main fungus underground . . . out of sight . . . he was feeding off the messengers . . . the spores in tubes under the cap . . . once he told me he'd seen goblins in the woods . . . another time witches . . . another time an imp . . . that was a bad trip . . . sometimes in summer he'd spend the whole day in this clearing he'd found . . . it was in the middle of a plantation . . . there was no path and you had to get through a wire fence . . . and he always went home at night . . . there was no way he would ever sleep in there . . . but the clearing had long rich grass . . . a tree trunk to lean on . . . sunlight reaching in . . . and he was happy . . . away from the concrete of the town . . . on holiday . . . day-tripping . . . Danny laughing . . . and the trees were tight and blocked out the sound of the motorway . . . he was in another world where there were no roads or factories . . . cars . . . lorries . . . he knew all the players . . . Jack Frost . . . Hern the Hunter . . . Will o' the Wisp . . . and he was just interested . . . you wouldn't call him a hippy or anything . . . when he went into something it was right to the limit . . . but most days were planned . . . trying to keep healthy . . . Saturday his reward . . . what Danny saw depending on his environment . . . he understood how to guide things . . . there was no point putting yourself in a dark corner where Death was waiting . . . holding up a syringe laced with dirty blood . . . Death laughing at Danny who couldn't move a muscle . . . sedated . . . a death-row case . . . and when it was grim outside he stayed indoors with his videos . . . watched happy films . . . comedies . . . his tapes worked out in advance so he followed a course . . . and he took the mickey out of himself . . . knew who to talk to about certain things . . . he'd never tell Bubba or Paul P or any of the boys in the Green Man about the clearing in the wood . . . the witches . . . but he was spiritual . . . a stupid word that didn't tell the whole story . . . stunk of wankers . . . hypocrites . . . he made a joke of it . . . knew what was what . . . and then his mood would shift for a second and he shook his head sadly . . . one fucking syringe . . . it had to be that one . . . sitting in a cell . . . and most inmates stuck to dope

. . . knocking themselves out . . . but he had to go further . . . he called himself a stupid cunt . . . but then he was strong and was going to win . . . addicted to being moderate . . . doing the right thing . . . he was sorted . . . knew he was going to live to see a cure . . . was going to die of old age . . . live a full life . . . he could see things clearly . . . like Bubba lifting that pint to his mouth . . . Paul P with a pool cue in his hand . . . the sights and sounds . . . these days he didn't wonder so much why he was here . . . why he was who he was . . . he just wanted things to stay how they were . . . and on Sunday he'd be sitting there outside the Green Man with a roast dinner in his belly and a spliff in his hand . . . the Cross of St George flying off the roof of the pub next to the Skull & Crossbones . . . the roar of the boys inside as the ball hit the back of the net . . . miles away in Glasgow . . . a contest none of them cared about but offer a few drinks were happy to go along with . . . enjoying the excitement for a couple of hours . . . bar heaving . . . bodies pressed against the windows . . . Bubba holding his pint in the air and balancing it on his head . . . doing a dance for the lads . . . who were laughing . . . cheering . . . Steve Rollins next to him . . . maybe . . . grinning from ear to ear and looking out of the pub to check his wife and daughter were okay and didn't need a refill . . . the two of them with another woman and two boys . . . Carole waving to Steve and then smiling over at Danny who nodded back and turned to look down the street . . . a police car cruising past the pub . . . the driver looking into the Green Man while his mate sat with his head down . . . busy tucking into a Big Mac . . . window open . . . the smell of the burger hiding the scent of the dope.

R uby tilted Aggie forward and puffed up her
pillows, balancing the woman's weight with
one arm as she used the other to smooth the
sheet and tuck it under the mattress, easing her back so
she could feel the angle, Ruby's arms thin but strong.
Aggie wasn't comfortable so she had another two goes,
shifting the weight back and forward, seeing a trapeze
artist high up in the roof of a circus tent, leotard
catching the light, spangles sparkling, sequins and
diamonds, the clowns below mesmerised by the glitter,
talcum powder dusting Aggie's nightie, sad chemotherapy smiles you could see from the top of the tent,
greasepaint and morphine injections easing the pain.

Aggie was fussy, had a sharp tongue on her, but
she'd be sitting there for hours so Ruby didn't mind,
stayed in the circus with the ballerinas and lion-tamers,
smiling, nodding, sitting next to her mum, holding her
hand, excited by the costumes and jungle animals,
sniffing the talc, loving the way it turned the woman's
skin white same as a geisha, and she'd told her mum
she wanted to be a geisha girl one day, watching the
clowns and wishing she had a white face and bound
feet, but when she was older the clowns made her
want to cry they were so sad, tattooed teardrops on a
sad man's face, Aggie's skin pink and creased where

she'd been sleeping, cuts that faded, freckles along the ridge of her nose and small pearls in her ears.

Not that Aggie took liberties. Ruby wouldn't let that happen. Once a patient started bossing you around you might as well give up. This was a lesson she'd learnt early, realising that deep down they wanted you to run their lives. Like a child they needed to feel secure, had to believe you were going to see them through their illness and pack them off home healthy. They'd try it on, but once you laid down the law they relaxed. They were testing you, and when you were trusted that was a great feeling, the biggest compliment you could have. It was give and take, the same as life, easing the worries that could weigh a person down. Kindness didn't cost, but if a patient was rude, like Aggie could be, then Ruby knew enough to see it as fear, or a deeper sadness, but she was no fool, setting a limit and sticking to it, adjusting the bottom of the bed as this woman with cancer threatening her organs looked out of the window towards the sky.

– When I was a little girl, Aggie said, her voice different suddenly, soft so it made Ruby jump, I had a friend called Doris, and we used to lie on our backs in the summer and look up at the sky and watch the clouds move along. Doris said that when you die your soul turns into a cloud and you float around the world for ever, so you can see heaven right there above us. My dad died when I was a baby so I never knew him, but Doris, her dad died when she was six or seven, and she did know him. I just saw my dad's face in photographs. It was harder for her, I suppose. With me, I was always wondering.

Ruby stood next to her and wanted to cry, reach out and hug this woman like she was a small child, as if she was her own mother.

– I didn't know if I believed her at first, but then I started thinking about it and it seemed a good idea, better than being stuck underground in a coffin. I liked the idea and we used to lie on the grass together, and I could see my dad's face. He was always there, high above, watching me when I was walking to school, sailing off over the horizon at night and coming back the next day. He was always with me, keeping an eye on me, and one day I'd be a cloud as well, float along next to him, the two of us tangling together.

Ruby made herself strong instead of sad, thinking it was a nice idea, making up your own heaven like that, the power of positive thinking, and she saw Aggie on the grass, the sun shining, dreaming her dreams.

– I never wanted to be a star. Some kids said you turned into a star but it's too far away, just a dot of twinkling light. They looked too small. At least a cloud is moving and changing shape and colour, like a person. My dad died of TB. If he'd been born later he would have lived and I'd have known him.

Aggie hated being in hospital and Ruby didn't blame her. She'd had two operations and chemotherapy, been in and out for a couple of years now. She could be fussy and bossy but if someone was suffering like that, with a good chance that they would die, you could forgive them most things.

– I don't like storms, all that thunder and lightning, and then the roof starts leaking so you have to put a bucket out. I worry it's going to get into the electrics and the house will burn down. Tommy takes care of it, never worries about that sort of thing, goes up on the roof and has a go, but I suppose you get used to it if you're a cloud.

Maybe Aggie didn't have long to live. Nothing was for sure right now except that she was going home soon, and it was like that with cancer, you had to wait and see, if it was malignant or benign, and it was the way they defined these things, all the terminology that broke sickness down and stuck it in categories – congenital or newly acquired, chemical or mechanical, genetic or environmental. Everything had a reason. At least she had Tommy and her family.

– Cheer up, Aggie said, the hard edge coming back, but in a jokey way. You'll be no good to us crying.

Ruby could hear the dinner trolley coming, a highlight for most of the patients at the end of a busy morning, every meal an event, and she knew Vicky was humming a calypso even though she couldn't see or hear her yet, she'd been on the same tune ever since she went to Trinidad for the first time to see her gran, making everyone jealous going on about the beaches and carnival, and Ruby would love to go on holiday but couldn't afford it this year, she'd said that last summer as well, and the calypso was in her head, went with the clanking plates and cutlery, Vicky's own steel band serving pastry, potatoes, peas.

Ruby looked back at Aggie and hoped she could fight back, beat the cancer, and she thought of her mum again, near enough the same age as Aggie and nowhere near as healthy, saw birthday candles and tissue hats, and her mum would live to be a hundred even though she wouldn't understand what the cake was for. Ruby hoped she wouldn't live that long, that she'd break out and float away, up into the sky where she'd be pulled into a current of warm air and circle the globe, following the sun, come back and smile through the window every morning, her soul free of the disease that rotted her brain and churned out all that spite, turned her tongue vicious when she'd always been so gentle, confused her personality and let in the monsters, her memory destroyed, and Aggie had it worked out right, blowing with the wind.

– It's apple pie today, Aggie said, licking her lips, like a different person now that she'd stopped being bossy and opened herself up.

Ruby smiled, felt so guilty now wishing her mum was dead like that, it was a terrible thing to think, she was ashamed of herself, just hated seeing Mum in the nursing home. She knew what they said, that the Alzheimer's meant she didn't know where she was, that she wasn't worrying about the past or the future because she didn't know they even existed, that it was worse for Ruby seeing her mum go senile in front of her, and Ruby tried to use this but it didn't really work. She was being selfish, and if it was physical she could nurse her mum, even if it was something terminal, at least she could look after her till she passed away, like Tommy with Aggie, if things turned out for the worst, and she'd tried, had really done her best, the outbursts and tantrums taking over, the constant criticism eating into her till Mum started smashing things up and calling her every name under the sun. Ruby didn't want to go back and think about the memory lapses that had slowly got worse, the anger, and considering the facts did nothing for her either, nerve cells failing in the brain cortex, what did that mean? She was hurt seeing her mum lose her personality and memories, so she didn't even remember Ruby was her daughter.

– Is old misery guts sitting comfortably? Vicky asked, out of hearing range.

– She's all right, Ruby said. I like her. She's just scared of dying. You can't blame her, can you?

– It's her favourite today, apple pie for dessert.

Ruby walked down the hall to one of the ward toilets and went inside, sat on the lowered seat. Her mum was always there in the background, fixing jigsaws together with women older than her, a picture of Big Ben without the clock, pieces hidden for a joke that the comedian forgot in seconds, so they didn't know if it was humour or a nasty streak coming out.

Mum was shining bright, fiddling with the same jigsaw Ruby helped with last time, a month ago now, she was down for days after every visit, didn't see the point if Mum didn't know who she was, she was going for herself and hurting herself, Big Ben replaced by a stone bridge humping over a country stream that babbled around greasy black rocks, Ruby could feel them on her hands sitting in this sterilised world of kidney failure, calcification, strokes, blue water talking in tongues, whispering sweet nothings that weren't sweet at all, licks of white froth that didn't last, under pressure from the sort of bloody flow you could never escape, everything going downhill towards the sea, and they never finished the jigsaw, her mum losing interest and turning from a child into an old witch with a bitter stream of abuse, slagging off Ruby's dress, shoes, hair, getting more and more personal, at least till one of the nurses came and calmed her down, knowing what to say, firm with a little child, another skill, and Ruby just sat on the toilet and cried, braced herself, stood and washed her face, checked she looked okay in the mirror, going to Maureen and telling her she was off now.

She left the hospital and walked to the bus stop, paid and sat at the back with the sweet wrappers and bent cans, next to the emergency exit with its danger signs and penalty warnings, trapping a bottle under her foot third time it rolled back with the motion of the bus, picking it up, wiping sticky glucose off her hand with a tissue. The bus crawled along, stopping and starting, Ruby stuck inside her head making herself think about Charlie Boy, Mr Parish on the ward, and she'd grabbed her chance and persuaded Sally to let her change his bandages, glad to meet the man behind the voice, better than a famous name on the radio because he invented his own playlists and didn't have to answer to a controller. There was no money involved and that was the secret. Once it came into the equation everything was ruined.

She had no interest in getting off with him, the thought never crossed her mind, it was the voice and music that made her go over, and Charlie was chuffed when she told him she listened to his show, mostly early in the morning but sometimes when she couldn't sleep, it depended, normally she was tired, on her feet all day, and she loved the records he played, the combinations, and she liked him right off, felt a tingle in her tummy standing next to his bed, asking if he'd tried the hospital radio, it was run by volunteers and played lots of pop and easy listening. He said he'd been listening to Dolly Parton and gone a bit nutty, groggy still, and he was quiet but sharp at the same time, least that's how she saw him, and Charlie said he was surprised anyone he didn't know actually tuned-in, he was being modest, said he thought he was playing records to himself half the time, firing songs out into the night like rockets, and she thought of Bonfire Night in the car park, roast potatoes in foil, down the rec with her mum and dad when she was small, two kinds of bangers, burnt sausages and exploding gunpowder, Guy Fawkes smiling in the flames, sitting by the shops, rockets shooting into the night, lighting up the sky, the clouds, all those spirits passing over Bali and Burma, and Charlie's eyes lit up as he told her there was nothing better than sitting over his decks as the sun came up in the summer, drinking coffee and playing records.

He told her how the sun flickered through the buildings, slabs of grey and white concrete turning orange and yellow and red, each sunrise different depending on the clouds, the location, the people watching it, the time the sun broke over the rooftops, shaping aerials and antennas like they were long stems of grass, skinny saplings, and he'd sit there just feeling how good life was, glad he didn't have to go to work today. It was something special. Most people never saw the sun come up. Ruby loved him for saying that, well, almost loved him, understood what he meant at least, more butterflies in her stomach.

She dabbed at his stitches as gently as she could, feeling him wince, sensing someone watching her so she turned her head and saw Dawn standing where Charlie couldn't see her, raising her hand and pretending she was giving someone a blow job, rolling her eyes and fluttering long black eyelids so Ruby felt herself going red same as Boxer, it really was tongue-in-cheek with Dawn, and suddenly she turned and walked off, seconds later Maureen marching past.

Charlie was settled and she had time to spare so she asked him what he'd done to get the stitches, heard how he'd been DJing at what he thought was an easy night when these men had started mucking about with his records, and when he told them to leave it out one of them had cut him, another punched him so he toppled over, then he'd been kicked in the head. Simple as that. His mates had jumped in and saved him. It was a feud that had been simmering. Stupid stuff. She could see his mood changing and pulled him back, asked him about the other DJs, the music he played.

Back on the bus she jolted as her subconscious told her the stop was coming up, and she was thanking the driver and walking down the street with the hum of the door's suction in her ears. She went into the sweet shop and bought a packet of mints, carried on to the nursing home. It was an old building with a lawn in front, not classic Victorian, more like something from the war years, and round the back there was another bigger lawn with a small pond where she sat with her mum when the weather was warm and her mind alert enough to cope with this funny girl pretending she was her daughter. Ruby felt the zinc in her pocket and hoped her mum had taken the last lot of tablets she'd given to one of the nurses. She'd read that Alzheimer's might be due to a lack of zinc. She'd also read that it could be due to a lack of folic acid, and that's why you had to eat your greens. There were all sorts of theories, and she'd seen enough patients in the hospital clutching at remedies, looking for answers to mysteries, and she did it herself, waiting for the scientists to come along and save all the people stuck in limbo, and as she went through the front doors she made herself strong just like she did at work. Ruby had to be brave for Mum same as she'd been told when she was a child going into the playground, swallowing her medicine, having an injection. She was strong as she went into reception, then along the corridor, said hello to the nurses, pointed in the right direction, into the TV room where the screen was showing *Scooby Doo*. She sat down next to her mum and stroked her arm.

– Yes, dear, are you lost?

– It's me, Mum, it's Ruby.

She was only fifty-six but looked much older, her crinkly black hair combed over and over till it had turned straight and fine, the curve tracing the sides of her face. Ruby hated her hair looking like that because when she was three and four and five, ever since she could remember, her mum had had hair that stuck out like she'd been electrocuted, and she jumped inside, that wasn't funny, electric shock therapy they called it, she didn't mean that, it was just the way the hair fizzed like it was full of static same as when Dad rubbed a balloon on his jumper and stuck it to the ceiling when she was having her birthday party, and when she rolled around playing with her mum it stuck in all sorts of funny shapes, the tears welling up.

Ruby was a girl bouncing on a bed, pulled down and tickled under her arms, and when she was tired and her face had turned red, gasping for air because she was laughing so much they lay on their backs and Mum held her arm in the air then let it go floppy so it fell this way and that way and her job was to grab the arm and stop it hitting the bed, push it so it stood up again, and Mum kept it there for a few seconds before it started to sway and move in small circles that slowly got bigger and bigger looping down towards the bed, fast for a second then hardly moving, one second it didn't weigh a thing and the next it was a tower ready to crash down, and when it finally did come tumbling down most times Ruby stopped it, for a split second it was too heavy and then it was easy to hold up, it made her feel like she was strong but really she knew Mum was in control, making it easy for her, and they played till they were tired and their arms were aching and then she'd rest her head on Mum's shoulder and Mum would sing a song, Ruby had to think about the words, giving her love a cherry, without a stone, she wished she could remember the rest, she wanted to ask but didn't want Mum to look at her blank like she was mad and kill the good memory, it was Ruby's memory and she wasn't having it spoiled. They were only words anyway. It was the smell of the sheets and

blankets that counted, the talc and her mum's shampoo.

– Have you come to mend the telly? she asked
Ruby. We can't get the satellite channels. They say we
have to pay for them but I think it's the set. They
don't want to spend any money, do they? My husband
will be here in a minute. We're going shopping.

Ruby smiled and felt the mints in her pocket.
Alzheimer's wasn't fair. If you were evicted from your
home, kicked out on the street and lost your way
somehow, at least you had the memories, that's what
made you alive, but without memories you didn't
exist. She played the game and told herself you never
missed what you never had, all the usual stuff, and
what she really wanted was for Mum to mess her hair
up like she used to wear it, the endless combing made
her face look pointed, like a witch with a broomstick,
in the cartoons, in *Scooby Doo*, made her look prim and
proper and evil-minded, too in control and stripped of
emotion, she'd always been warm and laughing, it was
emotion that made you feel alive, and it was like the
groomed hair was the opposite of her illness and its
debilitating confusion, and thank God she had been
like that, thank God for the memories Ruby had inside
her head.

– Did you see the meteors last night? Is that why
you've come?

– I never saw the meteors, Mum. I bought you
these though.

Ruby gave her the mints. Her mum had always
loved mints.

– That's kind of you, but I don't like mints. You

weren't to know though. Shall I share them round? Maybe later when you're not here any more.

There was a man and a woman near them watching the TV.

– Shall we go and sit outside, Mum? It's sunny out there. Let's go and sit by the pond like last time.

Her mum looked at her funny, shook her head slowly, as if Ruby was mad, and it was obvious she didn't remember, had probably already forgotten the meteors and the satellite channels, that's how it was, but at least she wasn't angry, slagging off her clothes like part of her knew enough to be insulting, and she placed her hand in her mum's and sat with her while she watched Scooby running from a ghost, which was really a professor in a sheet, and she wondered if they should be seeing things like that, but nobody was scared of the cartoons, and a nurse came in with a drink for her while her mum kept watching *Scooby Doo*, and the nurse gave her a sympathetic smile, and *Scooby Doo* moved straight into a Laurel and Hardy film where Stan and Ollie fell over and got wet because it was raining, the cars big and tacked together, and every so often Mum looked sideways at Ruby, then down at her hand.

– Why don't we sit outside? Ruby said after a while.

– No, dear, Mum said, looking at the screen and squeezing Ruby's hand. It's raining outside. Let's watch the film, like we used to. I'll make us some crumpets in a minute. You know, like we always do.

Ruby was a child sitting on the couch on Saturday afternoon with her mum right next to her and the television was on and it was raining outside and the wind was blowing against the windows and there was sleet and snow and thunder and lightning and Dad was working or had gone to football with his friends and her and Mum had a plate each with hot crumpets and Mum had a mug of tea on the floor next to her and Ruby was drinking orange squash and had to remember not to knock it over if she stood up and the crumpets were crisp around the edges and the holes had turned brown where they'd been cooked and the margarine was put on as soon as they came out from under the grill so it melted quickly and smothered the crumpets and sometimes she had strawberry jam on top either that or lemon curd but usually she left them buttery and they used to sit there for hours watching old black-and-white films most of the time they were musicals and Gene Kelly was singing in the rain dancing in the rain and she leant against her mum when she was full up and her head was on the thick brown cardigan she always wore around the house the one her own mum had knitted her with the thick black buttons and they were warm indoors and Ben was in his basket while they ate and then he climbed up next to them and sometimes if it was really cold they used to put a blanket over them to keep warm a fluffy blanket with dog hairs in with the blobs of wool and it was so warm and she was so happy snuggled up with Mum and Ben she wished the film would go on and on so she could stay there forever.

– Goodbye, was the next thing her mum said, when Ruby left at the end of Laurel and Hardy, surprised by Ruby when she hugged her, like she'd only just arrived, but it didn't matter.

Ruby walked back to the bus stop with her head up. It had been a good visit, the best for ages, she was glad she'd come now, didn't like going to the nursing home, specially remembering those visits when her mum had turned on her. For a while it really had been like old times, for Mum it was a second or two, but for Ruby it was the whole time sitting there holding her hand.

According to the timetable there was another twenty minutes till her bus arrived. She needed a drink, and though she never usually went into pubs on her own she made an exception and headed towards the one across the road. It was musty inside, with a damp smell coming off the carpet, either beer that had flooded the floor or sick that had been soaked in disinfectant. The place was nearly empty, two old codgers sitting by the door laughing at a joke, all gums and bony jaws, three postmen at the far end of the bar still in their work shirts, heads down discussing something that seemed important, odd words floating down that meant nothing on their own.

Ruby bought a pint of lager off the woman serving, a tired smile on a face that was starting to age, her looks changing, giving her another sort of appeal. She took her drink and went over by the window, looked out to the bus stop and the home further down the street.

She was smiling and remembering how they used to go shopping together first thing on Saturday morning, out early come rain or shine, and it was a treat even though shopping was a job that had to be done, and she could smell the food trapped under the iron roof of the market, the mugs of tea and cigarette smoke, the seaside flavour of the fish stall, she loved the cockles and mussels Mum bought her, the feel of the polystyrene teacup on her lips and the marshmallow crush against her teeth, listening to the grown-ups around her talking about mackerel as she shovelled the cockles down, so salty on her tongue, and then there were the colours of the fruit-and-veg stalls and the sound of bacon sizzling, the memories so powerful they shut out the must of the pub, and she was leaving the market and walking into the precinct with its fancy displays and panelled ceiling letting in more light than the older market, Mum looking in the windows and telling her the dresses she was going to buy one day, when Dad won the pools, and the stalls had creeped into the precinct selling football towels and glitzy knickers, compilation albums and heart-trimmed picture frames, teddy bears and tinsel, Mum pulling her out of the way as a gang of boys came running past chased by older men from the shops, and they used to go into the big shops and flick through endless racks of clothes, Ruby running her hands over the material, once or twice a year going into a shoe shop and sitting down so the assistant could measure her feet, she was always getting holes in her shoes, some things never changed, and she couldn't wait to be the same size as Mum, to dress like her, sometimes her mum let her borrow her lipstick, for dressing up, and Ruby used to ruffle her hair to make it stick out but it never had the same electric fizz, and she loved going shopping, they bought the food and Ruby got to carry two of the bags, one in each hand, she never said when her arms ached, there were lots of things they did, like playing games and sitting on the couch together, Mum washing her hair in the sink, Ruby closing her eyes tight so they didn't sting from the shampoo, Mum drying it with a towel and tying it up in a big knot so she looked like she was wearing a turban, and then Mum brushed her hair, combed it, over and over, ran her fingers through Ruby's hair and told her about the Prince Charming she was going to meet one day, and Ruby made a face because she hated boys, thought they were silly, and Mum said Ruby would have babies and she'd be a granny, and they were good times, Ruby had those days to look back on, and those few seconds today were enough, Mum saying it was just like the old days, and it was, no matter what they said it was still in her, somewhere, the good times, and she finished her drink and put the glass on the bar, went back to the bus stop, happy.

Standing at the window of his hotel room, Jonathan Jeffreys poured himself a glass of champagne and viewed the scenery. To his left sprawled the airport with its endless terminals and warehouses, a mess of brick bunkers and potholed yards saturated with spent gasoline. Worker ants toiled through day and night squabbling over petty differences. The flesh was weak, but the mind weaker still.

Machines dwarfed these fools, luxury airlines passing over their heads spewing waste. Cables transported voltage to lost corners of the complex where bone-idle men hid beneath flat caps drinking endless mugs of tea. These work-shy loafers played cards and told filthy jokes about female workers who whiled away the hours painting their nails. Vacuum cleaners and mops remained unused as the filthy state of the multi-storey car parks shocked visitors, the stench of ground-in engine oil and leaking pipes turning stomachs.

Mr Jeffreys had viewed this first hand. Carbon monoxide trapped between car-park levels was bad enough, but the unscrubbed urine stains and piled rubbish made him ashamed to be British. This was not a town-centre bus station, for God's sake, it was an international airport.

What would foreign businessmen and holiday-makers think? It did not create a good impression. In between the car parks holes scarred the road and diggers sat unused behind rows of dented cones. Barriers slowed the traffic and created jams. Tens of thousands of people worked in the airport, yet they could not even tend the lifts, let alone organise efficient baggage collection. The only oases of dignity were the departure lounges, where duty-free shops sold luxury goods. Here he was able to relax in a hospitality lounge while contemplating an impending trip to New York or Rome, the golden beaches of the Caribbean or Maldives.

He allowed himself to be transported back to his most recent vacation, waylaid momentarily with memories of the short break he had enjoyed in New York since. Four days in which to attend Broadway productions and visit old friends in Manhattan. There was a cut-throat vitality about the city which he appreciated. The best people were not afraid of consumption and held a healthy disdain for those prepared to fester in the poorer zones, wallowing in their own misery. There was none of that peculiarly British hypocrisy with which he himself, unfortunately, complied. A trip to New York had also meant he was able to see Donna, whom he had met during his three weeks in the Maldives. How he had needed that holiday. To not only recharge his batteries but regain his composure. He had allowed himself to become overworked and this had affected his concentration. He had pushed himself far too hard, forgetting that the constant quest for perfection carried a hidden toll. Everything had become too much and he had teetered on the edge of the abyss. He had made mistakes and put his career at risk.

The accommodation had been perfect on this Maldives jaunt. Simple yet very comfortable. Screens protected him from insects and air-conditioning from the heat. The coral island on which he stayed was minute. Remote and peaceful. Within hours of his arrival the heavy weight of responsibility began to lift.

The swimming pool was cool and refreshing after the probing heat of the sun and his skin quickly tanned. Muscles stretched with regular swimming. The food was superb, and he enjoyed some of the best fish he had ever tasted. He drank in moderation. Ventured to various lagoons in chartered boats. The resort was exclusive and he was spoilt by the staff. Palm trees masked the deck outside his bungalow, from where he could scan the sea, all very different to the last seafront he had viewed on the south coast of England.

He was distracted from these pleasant memories of the Maldives as he recalled those two years spent on the south coast working in that godforsaken hospital, forced to live in a decaying resort filled to the brim with pensioners, shabby locals and the dregs of London sent down to rot by desperate councils who could no longer cope. He could not walk along the street without seeing failure, be it the flaking paint of empty hotels and hostels or the unemployable with their plastic bags and specially reduced, out-of-date food. He had stayed in the town's best hotel, but this was not saying a great deal. Summer was a little better, but the rest of the year dire.

The hospital had suffered vicious epidemics during his two winters there. It was quite ridiculous, and he had been under pressure from his very first day. Not that he was complaining, or not up to the task. It was just that under such circumstances he had to be more concentrated than ever. The hospital was hard-pressed and with staff working overtime his decisions were even more vital than usual. Resources were stretched to the limit and he had to work faster than he liked. He did not feel comfortable and believed that his standards risked being compromised. Of course, he had done his best, and knew that he had helped ease the congestion. He had definitely made a difference, and that was some consolation.

He sipped his bubbly and returned to the Maldives, recalled his holiday romance with Donna, the poor thing in equal need of a break from a hectic schedule. Jonathan greatly respected American values within the workplace. Much of the culture he found shallow, based on quantity rather than quality, yet the American dedication to a free-market ethos more than made up for the crassness. This lack of quality was to be expected. There could not be consumer freedom without a compromising of standards. The masses had to express themselves through their consumption and business merely supplied the means, interpreting and repackaging their cheap tastes. It was no good feeding caviar to a pig as the beast would not appreciate such a delicacy. People were similar to pigs. Why feed the common man quail's eggs when he would crack them into a greasy frying pan and plaster the resulting mess over a slice of toasted bread?

Donna herself was an intelligent, and beautiful, woman. She admitted on the night they met that she made movies for morons. Those were her exact words. The people dictated her product and she was their servant. Jonathan found her easy to speak with and very cheerful. As the only two people holidaying alone it was perhaps natural that they should find each other. They swam together in the pool and ate lunch in the shade. Went on a fishing trip and caught a baby shark. Snorkelled in among the coral of a lagoon. Made love in Donna's room.

It had been a romantic interlude to both their lives, but he did not see the relationship developing into something long-lasting. Naturally he looked forward to their rendezvous in New York yet did not pine for the woman. They had enjoyed each other's company and that was enough. He appreciated her achievements and vitality while she was impressed by the fact that he reminded her of the actor Hugh Grant. It was a typically American thing to say of course. She appreci-ated his restraint and modesty, plus the fact that he was articulate and toned, soon to be tanned. She knew that as an American he had the one thing her own wealth could never buy. If he was to fall on hard times, gamble his fortune away or give it to charity, he would still have breeding. Being wealthy was icing on the cake, so to speak. He laughed and ran his tongue along the rim of his glass.

Donna was a fine-looking woman who also kept to a fitness regime despite her workload, but it was her vitality that he most admired. There was a lack of tradition that freed her to make hard decisions with barely a second's thought. This was something that he found near enough impossible, bogged down as he was by history and precedent. She was from a good New York family and had been educated at the best schools and universities, yet she still possessed the pioneering spirit.

He turned away from the airport and looked to his right. Here lay the outer reaches of London and the town in which he worked, a monstrous carbuncle on the edge of a great capital. Another tangle of confusion, it had none of the romance of the airport, which at least offered a gateway to New York, Rome, Paris, cultural centres on a par with central London. In the town where he plied his trade, the scent of Chanel and cappuccino was replaced by the stink of cheese-and-onion crisps and barrelled lager, a stomach-churning stench of batter and curry powder etched into the very brickwork. This was a sordid world with no meaning or will to change on the part of dull people who walked in never-ending circles, too stupid to understand that their lives were futile. That they amounted to nothing, however much they tried to delude themselves.

These things were determined at birth. Had they read the classics, he wondered. The texts of Socrates, Sade and Nietzsche? If by some miracle they had, was there a brilliant professional mind by their side to guide them towards the true meaning of the words? Did they listen to the great composers being interpreted by the world's finest orchestras? Did they view the masters? Take tea at the Ritz? Venture to the theatres of the West End and boutiques of Knightsbridge? No, they drank Coca-Cola in McDonald's and watched football matches and searched for cut-price pints and shopped in cheap bazaars. It was the difference between high and low culture, the latter term assuming a quality that did not actually exist. There was no culture there, just an energy-sapping mediocrity dressed up in garish sentiment.

Jonathan Jeffreys was in reflective mood. He lifted his glass once more, fully appreciating the year. But he was feeling generous of spirit. The lights twitching in the distance masked so many ordinary lives that he was almost humbled by a sense of scale, the sheer size and complexity of the universe, the eternal battle between Man and Nature, the constant struggle for perfection.

His face was held in the window, his reflection merging with the airport and the town, depending on the angle of his head. It was a curious effect and best enjoyed with a casual glance, both outer and inner worlds visible. He held his glass high and toasted his success. Life had been good and long might it continue. He allowed his mind to wander once more.

When he was a boy his parents had given him a pet. A puppy dog that immediately wet the carpet. His mother had beaten it with a stick in order to show that such an action was unacceptable. She was being cruel to be kind. Even now he could recall the crack of wood on bone. He had laughed at the time, but nervously, unsure how to react. The sound of the puppy's skull vibrating from the blow remained with him, its squeal high-pitched and primitive, slightly disconcerting. He had comforted the creature after-wards, amazed by the affection it displayed. The creature soon forgot its punishment, but did not mess the carpet again. This was during the holidays and one of the maids looked after his pet when he returned to school. He had tolerated the animal, but never felt particularly close to it, never allowed it to sleep in his room and did not stroke the fur. He was uneasy remembering a period a couple of years later when he had actually hit the animal to cause fear, then comforted it and rebuilt its trust. All children went through a stage in their lives when they displayed such cruelty and he now regretted his actions, but had been interested by this idea of trust, how it could be built so quickly.

At a later date, when he became interested in science, he had used the poor dog for his childish experiments. On a couple of occasions his potions had made the animal vomit and roll its eyes. He realised secrecy was required and this was easily achieved. It was the crying that put him in danger of punishment, not silent contortions. Then there were the electric currents that made its body twitch. He winced thinking of this now. It had been so unnecessary and he had been so unaware. The dog would have howled the house down given the chance, but he had bound its mouth so only faint whimpering was audible. The dog became terrified of him for a while, yet it was very stupid and could always be tricked back. This notion of trust came to fascinate him. A natural childish interest in science could be misinterpreted as cruelty of course, but he knew for a fact that this was not the case.

The masses were ignorant and therefore critical of such things as vivisection. Animals were objects that did not experience pain in the same way as human beings. Imposing human feelings on animals was ridiculous. The sentimental hordes held similar reactionary views about genetically modified crops, abortion, genetics, even the use of pesticides. For this reason the powers that made society work employed a great deal of tact. It was a shame, but the price of a society as yet unable to control its emotions. Sentimentalism angered Jonathan Jeffreys. Even as a teenager he had found it embarrassing. Those opposed to abortion and vivisection really did annoy him. Slaughterhouses were screened from view and guarantees given that the killing was humane, as if that was not an obvious contradiction in terms. The hypocrisy and easy self-deception of the people was truly amazing. Multinational companies understood this and employed public-relations agencies, then carried on regardless. Likewise the state. Misfits who dedicated their life to protest were arrested and sent to prison, the will of the people obeyed and its conscience massaged.

As a teenager he had been interested in chemistry and physics, yet it was medicine, and later economics, that he had studied until his mid-twenties. He had also been intensely interested in the spiritual world. His parents were religious and he was raised to believe in God. Even so, from an early age he had started to ask questions. Was there an afterlife, for instance? Did consciousness end with death? If there was a heaven then how did anyone know what it was like? The Bible was not believable, his parents decent people who accepted it without question, yet he could not.

He had a restless, enquiring mind. If there was only endless nothingness to look forward to then that would be unbearable. There had to be a life after death, there just had to be, yet the more he thought about the existence of heaven the more scared he became. What if he hated it there? Why should he be forced to stay for ever in a place he detested? The Bible had been written by men and they had created God in their own image. From fire and brimstone to socialism, the messages were confused. The same applied to the official view of heaven. These men did not know. As a teenager he was determined to control his own destiny.

It was this desire for self-determination that separated man from the beasts, the intelligent man from the fool. He had never liked his pet, never felt emotion towards the animal, merely forgotten it as he grew older and let the maid dote on the creature. Pets were a sentimental attachment and this sort of thinking held back the higher minds. Dumb emotion curtailed the work of vivisectionists and geneticists, and stopped scientists experimenting on human beings. Why waste millions treating the mentally ill and physically disabled when they could serve the greater good? Of course they would have to be willing, he was not proposing enforced vivisection, but he felt these people would be happy to assist. It was all very well pumping rabbits full of chemicals and watching the response, recording blood-sugar levels and the growth of created cancers and tumours, but how much more efficient it would be if these tests were carried out on humans.

Another source of ready labour was the truly poor.

A mass of men and women who could be chosen according to their lack of importance to society. A dole-queue sponger who took and took and gave nothing back could be gainfully employed. They would receive payment of course. He was not advocating slavery. Was no Nazi or communist. He laughed at this ridiculous idea and admired his face in the glass. Knew that women found him attractive.

When he turned eighteen his pals had given him a woman as a present. He was a virgin and had no sexual experience whatsoever. They had referred to this young woman as a lady of the night, chuckling and egging him on. They had been drinking wine in an Italian bar in Covent Garden and then walked over to Soho, which was a rough-and-ready area in those days. The memory made him wince. The girl herself had been low class. This was no discerning call girl with a luxury apartment and select list of clients but a common tart waiting at the top of a neon-lit stairwell, the original gateway to hell. Her name was next to a buzzer and when he had ascended the stairs he found her door wide open. She was sluttishly glamorous with a childish voice, the skin powdered and eyes dull, no doubt from some sort of narcotic. She had performed oral sex on him in a seedy room above a striptease parlour and he had felt humiliation throughout. After he had ejaculated and withdrawn, he was over-whelmed with shame. The girl was disgusting and the room foul. He became angry at her for forcing him to lose control and refused to hand over the agreed fee. He attempted to leave the building but a large man had cornered him in the hall. Jonathan had been punched hard in the stomach and he was sick. This thug then forced him to pay the money, plus an extra five pounds to clean up the mess. The girl had come on to the landing and spat in his face. Called him all sorts of foul names. The man then struck him in the face and kicked him down the stairs. He could have died. Broken his neck perhaps. As he lay at the foot of the stairs their howls of laughter echoed in his ears. He stumbled into the street and vomited in the gutter.

Fortunately nothing had been broken, but he had been sore for a week afterwards. It was a terrifying thing to happen to a sensitive young man. His friends had disappeared by the time he reached the street, and he found them in the restaurant where they had agreed to meet if they became separated. But not before he had been forced to run the gauntlet of the lowlife crowding the area. It had been an experience, but not one he ever wished to repeat. Thankfully his friends were not there to see him grovelling on the pavement, though outrage was expressed at his injuries. The result they believed of a mindless attack by a gang of football yobs.

How Jonathan hated that prostitute. For spitting in his face as much as the oral sex and his own loss of control. He hated the man who had belittled him so easily. He thought about returning and finding the girl. Telling her what he thought of her. But he was not stupid. He knew that it was far too dangerous. He held no sway in that twilight world. Things had quickly spiralled out of his control and he had found himself at their mercy. He shuddered even now, sipping his champagne so many years after. The man could have stabbed him, slashed his throat, kicked him to death. He could have jumped up and down on his skull or castrated him like a dog. Anything. Jonathan had been completely powerless for the first time in his life and it had been a sobering lesson.

It was largely his own fault of course. A mistake he attributed to youthful naïvety. Yes, he had experienced life in its darkest corners, and if there was a lesson to be learnt it was that such physical violence was the preserve of the ignorant. Hurting the tart would have meant lowering himself to her level, and he was anyway incapable of such violence. He was an intellectual, not a brute. He hoped that the prostitute and the thug found peace in heaven despite sins that would inevitably send them to hell. They did not possess the awareness to control their destiny.

When Jonathan Jeffreys turned twenty-one he did not repeat his earlier mistake and allow himself to be led to another prostitute. By now he was engrossed in his studies and had no time for such debauchery. A meal had sufficed, his friends also busy studying for their coming examinations and therefore glad to eat early and avoid a drunken binge. He was lost in thought remembering this birthday, walking through the West End crowds after dinner, sober and alert.

She was a common girl, as they all were. Unloved and unwashed, a bundle of smelly rags in a Strand doorway. A souvenir shop as he recalled. Selling Swiss penknives and china models of the Tower of London, framed photographs of royalty and mounds of sleeping bags. It was very close to the Savoy in fact, where he had met his mother the previous day for tea. It was easy to say that the girl sleeping rough was the fault of others, an example of the weak-thinking afflicting society in general. Liberalism had gone mad while socialism was busy ripping at the guts of the nation. He was a tolerant young man but sometimes decisions had to be made for the greater good. No, she had to shoulder her share of the blame for causing such an eyesore. Theatregoers and tourists were disturbed by her presence. Barristers coming along from the Inns of Court appalled. He knew only too well that an evening out could so easily be ruined by the sight, smell and sound of a street urchin begging, as if London was no better than Cairo or Calcutta. The South Bank had suffered for many years, with beggars and drunks terrorising gentler souls. Rough-sleepers were selfish and lacked self-respect, let alone respect for others. They needed a helping hand and the sense to stand on their own two feet once that hand was withdrawn.

He had squatted down next to the girl and quickly earned her trust. He was sympathetic to her plight, her initial aggression quickly fading as he switched on the charm. He allowed her to speak, in a strange accent. Northern, he imagined. She was alone and scared and wanted to tell him her life story. A flood of family tales burst forth. The death of a father followed by the alcoholism of a heartbroken mother. The subsequent loss of the family home. It was a depressing story, but so, so familiar. He did not know if it was true of course, but gave the girl the benefit of the doubt. He remained on his haunches for perhaps five minutes as she poured out her emotions. Inwardly he found this embarrassing yet outwardly was sympathetic.

He smiled. Then and now. Remembering how he had nodded in time with the breaks in her speech, not listening to the words after a while. The basics of the story were death and drink. Everything after was window dressing. Swiss knives and the Tower of London. Sexual abuse at the hands of her headmaster. He did not believe that for one moment. His knees began to ache.

It was funny how he could recall the pain in his knees all these years later, as champagne bubbles tickled his tongue. He had offered to take the girl for a meal and she had accepted. He could still see the smile on her face. Her choice of restaurant was an American-style diner that sold hamburgers and French fries. Milkshakes were brought by a young woman in a short skirt. He relived the smell of frying food and the sound of Elvis Presley's voice in the background. It was very tacky, even twenty years ago, before the globalisation of McDonald's. He hated Presley as much as he hated the new punk rockers. Rock and roll was a blend of British folk music and black slave rhythms. The common people of America had accepted this abomination and danced to the tune of Satan. Naturally, this was all imagery. He did not believe it was literally the Devil's music, it was merely the language of the Southern states of the world's greatest democracy, a land of achievement with a continual war between the forces of civilisation and barbarism. Rock and roll was a cheap mixture of popular cultures and without meaning. Presley was its representative, a hillbilly with greasy black hair and a loud taste in clothes.

The diner seemed to be frequented by young shop assistants and older couples. A man with a quiff and a woman with red lipstick sat nearby while a gang of youths were huddled near the door. The prices were very cheap and he felt uncomfortable with the endless parade of hamburgers, gherkins, melted cheese and ketchup. When they ate, he found the ingredients tasted artificial. The lights were too bright and the colours fluorescent. It was different to the dimly lit Soho staircase in which he had almost lost his life, yet strangely similar. It was the tackiness that linked the two. But the girl seemed to like the place. She was easily pleased, no doubt slow at school. Perhaps her headmaster had pointed out this fact and she had concocted outrageous accusations out of sheer spite. She smiled a lot and was very appreciative of the meal, seemed to find great enjoyment in the hamburger bun and was profuse in her thanks. She was obviously happy and this in turn pleased Jonathan, yet he was nagged by the notion that she was lying about the death of her father and the alcoholism of her mother. If she was prepared to lie about something such as sexual abuse then she would lie about anything. It was part of a greater malaise, a tendency towards dependency and the seeking of sympathy, a strain on the government purse, a burden to society.

As she had no accommodation it would be difficult for her to claim benefit, but then her age was also against her. She was only fifteen, yet was begging from cautious people who preferred to invest their money rather than waste it on alcohol and drugs. She had nothing to contribute and there was a good chance she would never be able to fend for herself, forever inventing problems and excuses. Even the simplest tasks beyond her. She seemed so content just sitting in the diner, accepting a second hamburger when he offered, along with a further bowl of French fries. She added big dollops of tomato sauce which dripped on to the table when she bit into the hamburger. She also made a noise with her straw when she finished her milkshake. He felt embarrassed at such crudity but nobody seemed to notice. At the tender age of twenty-one he realised that this was an experience from which he could learn. It was a glimpse of the world at large, an early vision of that prostitute in Soho three years before. But he hoped not. He did not want this girl to end up in the same situation. He was determined to help her.

Even as a young man he had inspired trust, so when the girl complained of tiredness and he offered her a bed for the night she accepted. He stressed that nothing was expected in return. He was a decent man who understood her plight and because of her unfortunate experience with the headmaster should not suspect all men of ulterior motives. Empathy was the word he should have used, yet was aware that her vocabulary would not stretch that far. He paid the bill and left a generous tip, explaining to the young girl that the waitress did not receive much in the way of a salary. She was a decent sort and should be rewarded for her efforts. This impressed the girl, as indeed he knew it would.

The girl was stunned by his apartment. The same three-bedroom affair overlooking the Thames that he owned to this day. North bank of course. She stood by the window, mesmerised by the partially lit water below, south London stretching into the distance. He had to admit that it was a decent location in which to live, it would be churlish to deny the fact, yet felt she went a little overboard in her praise. He did not think she was mocking him, merely gushing, another out-burst of emotion. She marvelled at the decor, running her hands over the wood panelling and cool marble of the fireplace. He had already noticed that her nails were bitten and lined with dirt, all but one nail longer than the rest. It was on the small finger of her left hand and very curious. He asked her about this and she explained that it was a sort of keepsake, a memory of better times. She used to have beautiful nails, before her father died each one had been over an inch long. She had a collection of varnish and wore a different colour every day, and chose bright red on the weekend. Her father would not allow her to wear that colour to school. Her mother loved her nails. Every girl had to have a special memory of her mother. She told Jonathan that now she bit her nails because she was scared, but always kept this one as it used to be. As a reminder.

She walked slowly around the apartment and he was slightly irritated when he noticed her running a hand along the back of the couch. It was made of expensive fabric and he did not want her leaving paw prints. He urged her to bathe and promised to buy her new clothes in the morning. She would then be able to find a job, and a place of her own in which to live. He would lend her the rent and she could repay him when she was older and had had time to save. Tears filled her eyes. She was undoubtedly a simpleton, but she told him he was very kind, that there were not many decent people in the world. He feigned awkwardness but was nevertheless pleased. He was by nature humble and this further moved her. It was all highly awkward, but he wanted to do something for those less fortunate than himself.

He pointed the girl in the direction of the bathroom and offered her a clean towel, a flannel and dressing gown. It was quite strange how, when he opened the door to the bathroom, she actually gasped. It was also odd that she did not smell worse. He was usually very conscious of a person's aroma. She was musty, and not exactly fragrant, but did not pong like some of the older tramps he passed. He smiled and left her to enjoy her bath.

He returned to the living room and mixed himself a cocktail, sat on the sofa and allowed his mind to rest. So many new impressions had been gathered in so short a time. The diner meal rested heavily in his stomach. It was as if he had swallowed a ball of molten metal and it had solidified in his gut. The meat in the hamburger was probably rotten. Mayonnaise had been added to his hamburger by the chef and although this had annoyed him at the time he had kept quiet, not wishing to spoil the girl's treat. He leant his head back and concentrated. The mind was all-powerful. He had believed that even as a twenty-one-year-old. Mind over matter was his motto from the earliest days. If he believed something then it was so. The food would not affect him so it would not. There was always a faint doubt but this did not matter. It could be controlled. Things were going well, certainly better than three years previously. He thought of the prostitute and felt her phlegm on his face. Disgusting. He wondered where she was at this moment. Eating a hamburger or performing oral sex in the same dirty hovel. How he had hated the flow of customers in the street below, the laughter and sound of music from amusement arcades, the mean streets of the city, the exploitation of innocents.

Half an hour later, once the girl had washed the filth from her body and shampooed her hair, she walked into the living room wearing the gown. Jeffreys was surprised by the change in her appearance. She was no longer a scruffy urchin fit only for Fagin's notorious gang of pickpockets. He saw her face properly for the first time and it was far prettier than he could have imagined. Her hair was lighter, brown rather than black, with flecks of blonde. This realisation was tempered by her lack of modesty. Parading around a stranger's home with just the width of the linen preventing him from seeing her naked. Yet it was not her fault. She was a child. Or was she? Perhaps she would do anything he asked of her, perform fellatio on him or allow herself to be sodomised, if he was so inclined. But he had no sexual designs on her. He was helping a victim in distress. Nothing more.

She did not wait to be invited and sat down on the sofa. She rested her head against the upholstery. For a moment he worried but then remembered that she had washed her hair. It seemed dry. She was very much at ease and he felt a great deal of pride that he was trusted. It was important to be liked. The face was mere decoration and should not reflect a man's deeper thoughts. The masses did not know how to control their facial expressions. They tried but betrayed their emotions, shed tears and opened themselves up to ridicule. Jonathan had separated the physical from the intellectual. His mind followed one course while his expressions set the outside world at ease. Nobody knew what he really thought, the questions he considered, the worries he had concerning concepts such as truth and justice. This ability was etched into his genes. Some were chosen, most were not. This girl was most definitely not. She spoke about the diner they had visited, the awful food busy rotting his intestines. She was so happy it actually made him sad.

He handed her the drink he had prepared, a mixture of fruit juice and sedative to help her sleep. She smiled at him. It was a meeting of two very separate worlds and he understood this perfectly, hers physical and prone to passion, his intellectual and quietly understanding. She sipped her drink and said that he was the most generous person she had met since arriving in London and that she would never forget his generosity. She had hesitated to go for the meal because she thought he might be after sex. Even coming back here she had been a little nervous in case she had misjudged him. But her instinct had been right. He was a decent man. Her friends said she was too trusting, and she told him a story about a boy she had known, who wanted to have sex with her and would not respect the fact that she was a virgin. She wanted to marry before she made love to a man. She blushed and Jonathan was very uncomfortable. He smiled and nodded and looked towards the bathroom. He hoped that she had washed the scum from the bath. She was quiet for a while, then he realised that she had fallen asleep. She was breathing deeply. He was surprised the sedative had worked so quickly, but what she needed most now was rest.

He sat next to her for a long time looking at the young face and thinking about the horrors awaiting her in life. He felt so sorry for the girl, her circumstances, but he would help her. When he was a boy he had been unaware of suffering, while at eighteen he had been naïve and misled, exploited even, but now he was twenty-one he was a man and set on his course, ready to dedicate his working life to the relief of suffering in all its forms. His career pattern was mapped out. Helping this rough-sleeper was merely a beginning, a celebration of where his professional life would lead.

He lifted her up and carried her to one of the spare bedrooms. She was very light. He eased her out of the dressing gown and returned it to the bathroom. He hung it up and neatly folded the towel she had used to dry herself. This he placed on the electric rail. The flannel was draped over the hot-water tap. This was silver-plated and he wondered if she had noticed. The bath was clean, a pleasant surprise. She was a good girl, a victim of society's selfishness. That and the failure of her mother to cope with death. He checked the drain and found several hairs. These he held up in front of his face before dropping them into the toilet bowl and flushing. He noticed a wet outline on the seat where she had sat. He ran a piece of toilet paper along it, washed his hands and dried them, made to leave the bathroom. He stopped and returned to the sink. Scrubbed at his hands once more. He looked at the bath and imagined the germs she would have been carrying. He went to a cupboard and took out a bottle of disinfectant. Slipped into a pair of rubber gloves and squirted the bottle around the bath tub. He took a brush and worked at the marble. He covered every corner and finally rinsed it away with hot water. He flushed the toilet to be sure it was clean and switched off the light.

He returned to the girl. He left the door open so that light from the living room entered the bedroom. He glanced at her, noting the way her adolescent breasts pointed towards the ceiling, the shape of her small body and the extra pinkness of the flesh between her legs. A thin matting of pubic hair. He wondered whether she was telling the truth about her virginity. But it was no business of his. Temptation lay on the bed, and if he was an evil man he would take advantage of this innocent, sexually abuse her as she lay naked and defenceless and at his mercy. But he was not. He quickly dressed her in a pair of pyjamas and eased her beneath the covers. Her breathing was strong and rhythmic as she enjoyed the first decent sleep she would have had for many months.

He left the bedroom and closed the door. Went to the refrigerator and poured himself a glass of champagne, before taking out his book and studying for a couple of hours. He then retired for the night. When she awoke the next day he would do as he had promised and provide the girl with a new start in life. He felt good about himself.

Jonathan Jeffreys emptied his glass and noted how the lights of the airport twinkled. Electricity guided the aeroplanes home. Supersonic jets that brought in the finest minds from around the globe. At their head the best the United States had to offer. Corporate generals. International bankers. Free-market philosophers dedicated to the spread of opportunity and wealth. The airliners also brought tourists whose welcome dollars and yen and marks helped boost the economy. These were wealthy men and women fully appreciative of the real Britain. The London of Shakespeare, Buckingham Palace and the Houses of Parliament. Of course, there were spongers who tried to creep in, there always had been and always would. The authorities would control the situation, no matter what the media claimed. He had no fear there. Was an educated man who did not pander to prejudice and hysteria.

Jonathan did not want to, but could not help but remember the morning after his twenty-first birthday. He had allowed the girl to sleep, but by midday decided to wake her. He would make her breakfast and then find her a place to live. He would help her start a new life. She was still deeply asleep when he went in, and when he opened the curtains and gently shook her shoulder he had received one hell of shock. The girl was dead. He could not believe it. She was only fifteen.

Without an autopsy he had no way of knowing

what had happened, coming to the conclusion that she had either a weak heart or a fatal disease. Apart from the despair he felt at the loss of such a young life, he realised that he was in an awkward situation. Would anyone believe that his actions had been purely honourable and that he had not expected, or taken, any favours in return for his kindness. There was also the small matter of the sedative, which he had administered to help her sleep. This could not have killed her, but questions would be asked and the evil nature of mankind would look for dark motives where none existed.

He regretted his generosity and spent the next few months lost in regret, which soon turned to depression. In the immediate aftermath of the discovery he had sat on his couch and cried. Actually cried. That night he had disposed of the body. He woke in the early hours depressed and confused. Threw himself back into his studies and gradually softened a little of the horror. At least she had died happy, that much he knew, and as small a comfort as it was, it was still something. He worked on this idea until he believed it to be true, admitting that her life would have been one of endless misery. She would never now end up at the top of a stairwell forced to service strangers, or as a wandering old woman with a brain destroyed by alcoholism.

From that day on he had channelled all his energy into making amends, even though he was guilty of no crime, his resolution to help those less fortunate than himself stronger than ever. He had made mistakes. With his treatment of the pet and his visit to the prostitute, but the girl had been an act of charity that had gone horribly wrong. All these years later the memory saddened Jonathan Jeffreys and he did not dwell on the unfortunate death, returning instead to his view of the airport, sipping champagne and smiling back at his reflection.

Standing in front of the pet-shop window, Ruby was able to switch from a reflected view of the street behind her to the display in front, diving into a heap of plastic bones and bouncy balls, a wicker basket full of studded leather collars, blank name tags and clockwork mice, jellied chunks of meat for cats and dogs, blankets and packs of catnip, a glass tank with a cardboard star offering it at half-price, bags of sunflower seeds and wood shavings. She looked back into the reflection and saw a woman loaded down with bags, a little girl next to her, helping.

There was no familiar face so she went back to the pet shop, further in to a stack of silver cages, plastic wheels for gerbils and hamsters, a wall of goldfish swimming in and out of wrecked galleons, star of the show this kennel where a black puppy was sitting, huge paws too big for his body, tufts of white around claws she couldn't see, a rubber nose and eyes that focused on her, and he stood up and wagged his tail, licked his lips with a massive pink tongue, and she wondered what he saw, what he thought, if he remembered another life, and she was tempted to find a brick and smash the window so she could take him home with her, noticed the kittens now, piled on top of each other, fast asleep, and she'd take the lot, the puppy and the kittens and the gerbils and hamsters, knew she wouldn't get far, the tap of a policeman on her shoulder, Charlie Parish standing behind her like he'd come up out of the pavement, through a manhole cover, she'd been watching for him, clicking back and forward, in and out of focus, expected him but still jumped, more butterflies in her tummy, Charlie twice his normal size, the glass blowing things up out of proportion.

– Gotcha, he laughed, moving forward so he was standing next to her.

– You made me jump. You came from nowhere.

– I thought you saw me in the window. You looked like you'd recognised someone. Smiling and that.

– I was looking at the puppy, see, next to the shelves.

They stood with their faces pressed against the window so the world behind was shut out.

– He's wagging his tail he's so excited, Ruby said. I wish he was mine, that I could take him home with me. He's beautiful, isn't he? I had a dog when I was little and he looked like that, it could almost be him when he was younger. He can't be more than a month or two old. He's so small and cuddly. But it wouldn't be fair keeping him locked up in the flat all day, when I'm at work, he'd get lonely. It's not like I've got a garden either.

– You should buy him. As long as you love him he won't mind.

– No, it wouldn't be fair. He'll get a better home with somebody else.

– Suppose so. Someone will have him. He'll be all right.

They stood looking at the puppy for a minute.

– Come on, I've got to pick something up in the pub. We can have a quick drink then go out.

She waved goodbye to the dog and felt so sad for a second, but then it was gone and they were walking down the high street. Charlie had taken the bandage off his face too soon, he needed to keep the wound covered so it stayed clean, and the stitches turned heads, blood congealed and black, bruises turning yellow. All the time the skin was healing, and the scar wouldn't look so bad, would fade and become part of him, and she was looking at the colours again, past the muck of the stitches to the shades of red that were going to blend in, and she was always amazed how the body repaired itself, skin growing and melting together. After years of working in the hospital she still reckoned it was a miracle how people recovered from their injuries, both skin and bones mended, it was magic, and they could transplant organs that would settle in and thrive, the body a fantastic thing, some people called it the temple of the soul, and she could see that easy enough.

– How does your face feel? she asked.

– Sore, you know. It could've been worse. That's the way I'm looking at it. They could've had an eye out, or stabbed me through the heart.

Ruby saw his chest being opened up and a replacement heart slipped in, a beautiful operation performed by miracle workers, the surgeons who saved lives on a daily basis, and she thought of that instead of the trauma the victim went through, happy endings all the way.

– It will look better when the stitches are out and it starts healing, she said. You'll be fine.

– I'll look like Action Man.

Ruby slipped her arm through his, and she'd known he fancied her within a few minutes of talking to him in the hospital, felt the same way herself, and she wasn't going to miss out, life was too short, so when she knew he was being discharged she went and saw him, asked how he was feeling and got him to ask her out, made it seem like it was his idea, guessed Charlie was shy, even though he was on the radio, it was probably easier talking into thin air than to a live person.

– I thought you might be on the radio this morning, but it was dead.

– I wasn't in the mood, to be honest, but it was coming to an end for a while anyway. I was working evenings so it was easy going in after, then sleeping through till three or so, but I've got a lot of days coming up. I need the cash.

– We all need money.

– You have to live, don't you? Work comes first. The radio's a laugh. I've got a month solid at the airport, delivering round the M25 mostly. We used to do a lot of gigs, but cut down with the radio. The other night was the first one for a while.

They walked past the multiplex and the entrance to the shopping centre, the underground pub there full of junkies and alcoholics, a half-lit zone with velvet seats and no windows where the only music ever played was Jimi Hendrix and Led Zeppelin, she'd only been in there once but it was well known, three girls mucking about on their skateboards up ahead, doing flips off a concrete slope, dry plants burnt in the sun perking up with the first pricks of a summer shower that in seconds was a flood of thick blobs from the ocean, raindrops lined with oil, drips off the end of a needle, Ruby standing in the shelter of a shop doorway leaning on the grille, china horses and Mickey Mouse clocks through the slats, gypsy ponies and field mice on the edge of town, towards the airport, and a puddle was forming, oil slicks washing out, catching the light and creating vinegary patterns, the faces of her mum and the puppy swishing around in the water, Mum stroking Ben's tired old head, opening a tin of chicken chunks and him going mad, whining and wagging his tail, gobbling it down in seconds, climbing up on the couch with them, snuggling under the blanket, Gene Kelly stuck in the rain, clicking his heels, the shower over, the puddle still, little girls back out on their skateboards, foam-padding kneecaps, scabs on their elbows.

– What do you want to do? Charlie asked.

– I don't mind.

– Come on, anything you want.

She thought for a minute.

– Take me on holiday. A day will do. A few hours on a Spanish beach.

He laughed and they turned the corner, Charlie guiding her into the pub, the place busy, full mostly of men on the piss, in straight after work, and there were a few women with their husbands and boyfriends, a noisy group of five dressed-up blondes sitting at a table pulling a lot of looks, faces pretty but puffing up now they were into middle age, chubby but making up for it with their confidence.

Up the back was a platform with a row of pool tables where Charlie's mates were sitting, calling him over, a skinny man in a shell suit with a cue in his hand, the handle resting on his right foot. She waited for her drink and recognised one or two faces. Bob from the end of her street, a short fat man with a bald head and sense of humour, he'd had a heart attack the year before and shouldn't be drinking that pint of bitter, the cigarette in his hand, and there was one of the skinhead dustmen she saw in the morning sometimes, the one who was always whistling at her, he was at the bar with his arm wrapped around the waist of a ginger girl who was stunning, really fantastic-looking, and he saw Ruby, nodded, no wolf whistles now, trying to impress, and he was in the prime of life, no health worries, a pint of lager on the bar.

– Here you go, Charlie said, passing her a bottle.

She followed him over to the platform.

– This is Del Boy, he said, as they sat down. And this is Johnny, better known as Johnny Chromozone, also known as DJ Chromo.

– Special AKA.

– It's Derek, not Del Boy, the guy with the silver chain said.

– No, it's Del Boy. If you want to buy some good whizz or dodgy porn, he's your man.

– Fuck off, he said, laughing. Only fools and horses work.

– This isn't fucking Peckham though, is it? said the skinny man, leaning over. None of your bushwhacker bollocks over here.

– Call me Derek, the Trotter version said, leaning over and smiling at Ruby.

She nodded and sipped her drink. She felt like she was with people she'd known for years, hearing Charlie and Chromo's voices so often, and they sounded more or less the same in real life, maybe calmer, but then you probably had to pump yourself up to perform, and she wondered about the other DJ, Punch, who played the punk and reggae and mixed it in with Tricky and the Prodigy and Beenie Man, not her usual listening but okay, with her it was the sound, the worries of the world right in front of her every single day so she needed to escape, had enough to think about dealing with cancer and comas, never mind the party-political squabbling, that's why they had a union, so they didn't have to listen to the career broadcasts, and Sally took care of union affairs, argued the toss, Ruby wanted a laugh, happy sitting with Charlie and waiting for DJ Chromo to play a record, launch into a speech about space and time, how life was all about motion, vibration, energy, nothing solid, he was the philosopher, and that's what you got when you entered the Chromo Zone, she was in his presence now, had stepped through the curtain into an eternal present where there no past and no future, nothing to worry about because nothing was how it seemed, and she wanted it to be like that for her mum, they said that was what happened to you, when you had Alzheimer's you lost the plot but you lost your worries as well, nothing to regret and nothing to fear, and she grabbed the straw and held on, grabbed and held on to life, went out as much as she could, lived in the present, didn't believe in planning ahead.

– I remember seeing you in the hospital, Johnny said, and she was thinking how he didn't look anything how she would've imagined.

– You had your uniform on, but I remember your face. Did Charlie have to use a bedpan when he was in there?

– He was all right to walk, a bit drugged up at first, but he was okay.

– I tell you what, Johnny Chromozone said, pissed. Nurses are the fucking business in my book. Anyone'll tell you the same, whether it's a crook like Del Boy or a man of reading like myself. We all know the score.

– It's Derek.

– You do a hard job well, in my opinion. For not much reward either. Fair play to you.

He leant forward.

– I'm not patronising you either, he slurred. I'm a bit pissed, that's all. Been in here since five.

DJ Chromo tapped his pint against her bottle, made Charlie do the same, and he was toasting Ruby, making a big song and dance about raising his glass in the air, wiping a fluorescent tongue over purple lips, battered and bruised from too much drink, too much something, she felt embarrassed but saw he was one of those bubbly characters who spout off at twice the normal speed, three times the volume, a beatbox on legs, barrel chest plugged into the mains, but there was a racket going on in the pub so it was only her and

Charlie and Derek who could really hear what he was saying, and it was all right watching his face pulling shapes, she would've had him down as thinner and with glasses, not this drinker, but it made sense, a pub philosopher who was busy with the ideas, books and music, anything that worked.

– To the nurses, who do the hard work while pop stars and actors get all the wonga. Them and footballers. It shows what a shit society we're living in when it's the pretty boys who pull all the girls. What happens to an ugly fucker like Del?

– Derek.

– Ugly bastards like me and Del Boy.

– Derek.

– They're just the ones they take pictures of, the man in the shell suit said, leaning in for his pint, taking a sip off the top as he held his cue over his shoulder, Charlie forgetting to introduce him.

– You don't see the real money-spinners, do you? They keep you wound up on footballers and what have you so you won't do your homework and find where the real money goes. They're the ones who've come from what you've come from, done well, so they slag them off so you don't worry about the silver-spoon brigade.

– They're all a bunch of cunts, Johnny Chromozone said. It's just, I don't know, you expect it from that lot, you know, the rich and that, but when someone gets in a position to say something from your world you'd think they'd tell it how it is.

– They wouldn't get the publicity if they started moaning, would they? It's the price you pay for fame and fortune. As long as you know your place and don't rock the boat you can have it all.

– All I know . . . Chromo said, lowering his voice.

– All I know is that when it comes down to it nurses are the heroes. They lend a helping hand and get sweet FA in return. It's not about money with them, is it? Doctors and nurses do it because they want to help people. Them and teachers dealing with all those snotty-nosed little hooligans trying to wreck their lives.

– Fuck off, said the pool player. You upset enough teachers when you were at school.

– I know I did, and I was wrong, wasn't I? A right little toerag. I wish I could go back and change things, but I can't, can I? What's done is done. I wasn't interested in learning then, but I am now.

Ruby could see Chromo sitting down with Sally and being serious about life, and she was thinking about how she'd have pictured him again, an older version of the kids on the hard shoulder, talk about flavour, that skunk blew your head off it had so much petrol in it, rocket weed they should call it, and this was weird putting faces to names, voices, ideas, and as for Charlie, well, she was into his music, didn't feel like she had to talk about life, they both knew what it was about, he could've looked like anything, three eyes and one leg, she'd never cared about the glossy world of beautiful people in shiny clothes, what you were was more than skin-deep, it was there in the organs, but things moved fast, shifting so no day was ever the same, people having their ups and downs, every single person busy doing something, even if you couldn't see what, every brain was charging, millions of electrical impulses firing off opinions, visions, she loved all that, the drink on her tongue and the click of pool balls a few feet away, the smell of the pub and its clientele, paint off the overalls of a man nearby, the smell of chips piled next to a hamburger, next to an ashtray full of fag ends, embers of a bonfire, bangers and mash and jumping jacks.

– You're on, Del, someone called.

– Derek. It's Derek, you piss-taking cunt. I'll fucking nut you in a minute.

– Sorry, Del.

Ruby watched him walk to the rack and take a cue, guessed he liked the attention, and he was searching for the chalk and polishing the end, giving it the professional touch, flamboyant now, so she could understand why the others were calling him Del Boy, wondering if the whizz was as good as Charlie said, what sort of porn he was selling, Derek raising his eyebrows and giving up because the chalk was worn out. He approached the table and leant forward, scattering the balls, the special crack that went with breaking. Chromo got up and took his pint over so he could watch, leaving Ruby alone with Charlie, being discreet, and someone else who'd just arrived came over and handed Charlie a set of keys, whispered something in his ear, patting him on the back, walked off.

She'd finished her drink.

– Same again? she asked.

– No, come on, we'll go somewhere else where we

can talk. You wanted to go on holiday so we'll run away together.

She laughed and waved goodbye to the others, following him through the pub with her hand in his, the dustman kissing his model, Bob knocking back a chaser, laughing his head off.

– Hello, Ruby, I never saw you come in.

It was humid outside, water hanging in the air, and she followed Charlie across the road to a van, imagining a beach in the sun, wanting to know where they were going. He opened the door and got in, leant over and opened the passenger side, Ruby climbing into a sauna, one that needed a good clean, Charlie reaching down and lobbing the plastic cups and cartons into the back, flicking a chip on to the floor, and she was weighing up the front of the van now, a mess of fag ends and cassettes, a couple of green bottles he must've drunk on the way back from Calais, gulp-size Stella, and even though it was stuffy with dirt and grime in the carpet, gravel in the ridges of the mats, Charlie's smell was in here, same as she noticed when he was laid up in hospital, Charlie Parish coming through the disinfectant, and it was a smell that made her think of trees for some reason, wholesome, with a sweet note, his deodorant maybe, and he was just a boy grown up who didn't put his toys away, had a hobby with his music, he didn't deserve the cut face, at the same time knowing his attackers were boys grown up as well, they'd lost the thread somewhere and gone too far, spoilt the game, and it was all a game, the chopper coppers and the DTI and the riot squad barrelling down the hard shoulder, everyone playing a role.

– Where are we going? she asked.

– I'm taking you on holiday, that's what you wanted.

– No, really, what are we doing?

– Wait and see.

Ruby shrugged her shoulders and looked back at the pub as they drove past, small windows she couldn't see through, the door wedged open.

– I want to show you this Cadillac.

She looked blank.

– There's a Cadillac I'm going to buy.

Ruby nodded.

– It's not far. I've got a loan sorted out but I'm still a grand short. The bloke wants six thousand, but he'll take five and a half. That's what he said. It doesn't do good mileage, seven to the gallon, but it's the sort of car you take out on special occasions, you know, drive up to Heston or down the Embankment.

– It's a lot of money.

– It's going to be for work. What I reckon is you get people hiring Rolls-Royces and Daimlers, you know, for weddings and funerals, special occasions, like I said, but when have you ever seen a bride come out of an old Norman church and jump straight into a pink Cadillac.

– It's pink?

– Has to be, doesn't it. Anyway, people go to a wedding and everything turns formal. They buy, borrow or rent suits that they would never think of wearing normally, then ponce around waiting for cars none of them have ever ridden in before, and the reason they've never been in a Rolls or a Daimler is they can't afford one, and that's it basically, they have to taste the good life to make the day stand out, drink champagne when they'd prefer a pint. They listen to middle-of-the-road music when they'd prefer something a bit more lively. Least till everyone's drunk and then it's over to the bar for a pint, and they get the music cranked up, everyone asking for their favourites, and it turns into a party.

– What's that got to do with a pink Cadillac?

– Well, my idea is why not use a Cadillac instead? People would love that. Imagine coming out in your suit and wedding dress and jumping into a classic pink Yankee, big silver fins and polished chrome, playing Love Me Tender as you drive them to the reception, and then when you take them to their honeymoon night you could play Great Balls Of Fire.

Ruby laughed, like he was joking.

– Really, you think about it. Would you like a vintage Rolls, all stiff and proper and boring, or would you rather get into a Cadillac that's big and flash and more of a laugh, not taking yourself too seriously? What would you choose? Be honest.

– A Cadillac. I'd choose a Cadillac.

Charlie turned down a side street, did a right.

– There it is, in front of that end house.

She didn't need him to point it out, the car was pretty obvious, like it was the wrong size model for the houses. Kids did that, played with cars that were out of scale, where one would fit in the boot of another, toy soldiers where the German could crush the Englishman with the click of a jackboot. It was a beauty all right, no doubt about it, parked at an angle as it rested on the pavement, the black cab behind it looking like a miniature. The Cadillac was clean, gleaming in the fading sunlight, the fins massive, everything about it big and flash, like Charlie said, and she didn't have him down as a show-off or anything, it was a different sort of class, but where was he going to get another thousand from? It was a dream, something to aim for, she supposed.

– I got the idea for a Cadillac service when we went to Las Vegas. My mate got married and he wanted Elvis to conduct the service. Twenty of us went. It worked out cheap and we loved it, stayed in this smart hotel, and you go through the casinos and they lead into each other so it's hard to get out again, and all the time they're giving you free drinks to get you pissed. We stayed five days and had a blinding time.

– So your mate got married by Elvis Presley?

– It was an impersonator.

– I didn't think it was the real one.

– It was the older Elvis, he was wearing a cape and sideburns, then the bride and groom went off in a Cadillac. It's not my own idea, but everything's recycled, isn't it? I would've had the young Elvis, not some fat old boy with a stick-on chest and medallion. That got me into the rockabilly records I play with the other stuff. It was a good laugh.

– Where will you get the extra thousand? she asked.

– Don't have a clue. I just hope he doesn't sell it in the meantime. He's not getting a lot of interest, but he won't drop the price any further. Maybe it'll go before I get the money. I'm pushed to the limit as it is. Fingers crossed though.

They sat in the front of the van looking at the car for five minutes, then Charlie turned round and moved off.

– Where are we going?

– On a magical mystery tour. Wait and see.

Ruby sat talking with Charlie, watching the streets pass, fields where the china horses had come to life, the sun sinking down, and she was wondering if he was taking her into London, and then they were turning, past the airport boundary and down a dip, into the tunnel leading into the airport, and she was sitting up now, wondering, and it didn't take long to come out the other side, Charlie veering towards Terminal 3, pulling up at the barriers of the multi-storey. He stopped and stretched for his ticket.

– We used to come here when we were kids, sit on top of the car park and watch the planes taking off, guessing where they were going, pretending we were on board.

The light was dim inside the car park, the sweet smell of petrol swelling in through the window, the bays almost full on the ground, and they bounced up the ramp leading to the first floor, rocking on the angle, slowing down at the top for the blind spot, turning right and following the arrows through the grey columns and colourless shapes of Fords and Datsuns, a man with a suitcase marching towards the stairs with a woman in a red coat, and Ruby loved the smell of the petrol, going up the next ramp, following the arrows, looking out at the buildings, on and on till bang, they were up on the roof, an explosion of fresh air hitting Ruby same as an oxygen mask, they were the only ones there and Charlie let the van drift to the edge, the sky fantastic in front of them.

Charlie stopped by the wall and turned the engine and lights off. A plane rose up, past the terminals, coming off the runway and into the air, a boom reaching them against the breeze.

– It's the next best thing to going on holiday, Charlie laughed.

He took out some Rizlas and looked at Ruby, knowing what she'd say, and it was like they were the only people in the world now, so near and yet so far away from the terminals, the people who worked in the airport, most of all the jets roaring into the air and heading off across the world. It was magic, better than sitting in a pub with DJ Chromo and the others, not that she didn't like them, she did, but it was her first time out with Charlie and this made it special somehow, better than the dark of a cinema, and she was thinking how she loved watching the traffic pass by from the banks of the motorway, everyone hurrying somewhere else while she could sit back and enjoy the show, that's what it was like now, and maybe they were made for each other, you couldn't say this early, but it was as if Charlie liked the same things, felt the same way, and she stopped that one dead, wasn't thinking ahead, savouring the moment as they had a smoke and watched the night sky, the blinking of lights and motion of planes building up speed and shrinking into the dark, sitting in silence.

– That's a new sign, Charlie said after what seemed like ages but was probably only five minutes.

Ruby looked at the board nearby, a warning that parking was banned on the roof of the car park and anyone who did so would be arrested and fined.

– It's so they don't get terrorists coming up here with rockets to shoot down planes, I suppose, Charlie said.

– A sign's not going to stop them, is it? You know, 'Please Don't Fire Your Anti-Aircraft Missiles Here'. That's not going to work.

They sat for a while.

– It would be a good place to put up an aerial, Charlie laughed. They'd get it right away though. They're probably watching us now. Definitely, I'd say. They're not going to put up a sign like that and not have the roof under surveillance. Wouldn't be surprised if there wasn't a camera on us, filming.

– Do you think so?

– They must have, he said, sitting forward over the wheel. They're not going to muck about with something like an airport. It's big time when it comes to terrorism and shooting down planes. If you had the gear you could set it up in a minute and knock out a jet, kill hundreds.

Ruby looked out into the dark but couldn't see anything suspicious, just the tops of other blocks, terminals and offices, dark outlines with some stray light coming off the road below.

– They've probably got a sniper out there looking at us through the sights of his rifle.

– We shouldn't hang around if they're watching us. I can't see where they could be, can you?

– Could be anywhere, one of those buildings over there. They're not going to put a neon light up, are they? They work in the background, pick their targets out with special sights then get you when you don't expect it. As long as it's got the official stamp it's legal and they can get away with anything. There's some nutter out there with a high-powered rifle with an invisible dot on our faces, a cross or something, his finger itching, moving slowly from me to you, back again, zeroing in ready to pump a round into each one of us, blow our heads to pieces.

– Don't, Ruby said, shivering, looking into the shadows.

– I'm serious. Wouldn't be surprised. Some official killer sitting there weighing up the odds, wondering if he can get away with it, seeing us having a smoke and getting all righteous. Probably thinks we're scum even though he knows we're not terrorists, just looking for an excuse to tap the trigger and wipe us out. There'd be no sound, and he'd come over and cart the bodies away, no questions asked.

She didn't know whether to believe it or not, couldn't see that happening to be honest, but it was possible, shooting down airliners was big league and maybe they didn't take any chances, but no, what would be the point, what would they get out of it? The sign was loud and clear and even if the sniper and his mates weren't going to shoot them they'd be watching, no doubt about that, and you sort of got used to the spy cameras, walking down the high street, through the precinct, anywhere the shops might get robbed, even some clubs had CCTV, and it didn't matter because you were in a crowd of people and could merge in with everyone else, but up here, out in the open and separated from everything, that gave them strength, and what made it good being up on the roof was also the danger. They were on their own and she felt scared, the fear growing, just the two of them trusting in someone they didn't know, putting their lives in the hands of an executioner, and any second he could squeeze the trigger and end it all.

– Why don't we go? I don't like it up here.

– It's all right. I was only thinking out loud.

– No, they'll come hassle us and do us for the dope. It's spooky up here now. It's all changed. I don't like thinking about the sniper.

Charlie laughed and started the engine, and she knew he wanted to move as much as she did, but like all men had to put on a brave face, pretend he didn't care, and he did a circle of the roof first, doing his bit swerving side to side, and then they were going down, floor by floor, and the fear was gone, it was irrational she knew, a touch of paranoia, and she was glad Charlie had brought her here, it was an exciting place. He paid and they left the car park, lost in traffic.

– Shall we have a coffee?

Ruby nodded, happy again, the lights of the cars spread out, picking up the motorway and then pulling into the services. It was quiet and she could hear the hum of a generator, the machines showing silent space rangers on their screens, heroes exterminating aliens, joysticks carrying thousands of fingerprints from thousands of players, and Ruby thought of all the DNA evidence gathered in one little spot, none of it admissible in court because it had all merged together, and they went into the cafeteria and bought two coffees and a cake each, sat by the glass wall, looking at the motorway, and Ruby leant over and breathed in the coffee fumes, felt the heat on her face.

– I hope I get that Cadillac one day, Charlie said, talking quietly, so the few people around them couldn't hear, a family near the door, a couple of lorry drivers, a teenage couple sitting in silence.

– I could chauffeur you around in style if I had it.

Ruby didn't know if she fancied that, everyone turning to look at them as they passed, and anyway, it was a dream, it was like the puppy in the shop, it wasn't really going to come true, but it was good to pretend. She stroked his hand on the table.

– We wouldn't have been able to go on to the roof of the car park if you'd been driving the Cadillac. It wouldn't have got through the barrier. We'd still be there now, stuck, with the paint scratched, ruining the car's good looks.

– I never thought of that.

He looked sad suddenly, the first time since she'd known him. Even when he was in hospital having his wound cleaned he'd been upbeat, it wasn't in his nature to be unhappy, another reason why she felt they were the same, both of them looking for the positive rather than the negative. She knew he was thinking he'd never own that car, same as she knew she'd never have the puppy, and it was like she didn't have to even speak to him, could read his mind, and she looked into his eyes so he laughed and smiled and finished his drink, the roar of bikes turning everyone's heads as three Hell's Angels rolled in. The Angels bought three teas and sat near the door, keeping an eye on three shining Harleys parked outside. Ruby couldn't help thinking how quiet the place was, really silent like a library or something, the family getting up and leaving, Charlie holding her hand now and maybe wondering if she wanted another coffee, getting ready to speak.

Mr Jeffreys checked his watch and pushed away the file he had been studying. He unlocked a drawer and took out his special box, running his fingers over the teak. He rubbed at a small smear. It was a stubborn mark so he wet his thumb and pressed harder, using his handkerchief to polish the wood. When it was spotless he straightened the box on his desk. It was a gift from his father, an antique, and while this in itself meant a great deal, Mr Jeffreys loved the box more for what it contained.

He opened the lid and appreciated the way the light caught the barrel of the syringe inside, a classic instrument from a bygone age. The hypodermic rested in a velvet mould. He enjoyed the manner in which the syringe fitted his hand and became an extension of his body. Plastic syringes were toys in comparison. Cheap and disposable, they matched the age. Everywhere standards were being eroded and it was up to him to make a stand for traditional values. This hypodermic harked back to a time when the social order was rigid, medicine a brave experiment rather than a human right.

He lifted the instrument from the box and wrapped it in a new chamois leather he had bought from one of the valets who cleaned his car. The shop was convenient to his hotel and specialised in prestigious automobiles. It was a curious business run by a Sikh who employed numerous young skinheads in blue overalls. The shammy had taken his fancy and he now bound it with a length of cord, specially measured and cut for the purpose. He slipped the package into the left pocket of his coat, the thickness offering protection from the needle which he naturally pointed away from his body. He returned to the box and took out a phial. Placed this in the right pocket. He returned the box to its drawer and turned the key, picked up his clipboard and left the office, ensuring that the door was secure. He was doing his best to remain calm yet could not help but feel excited. He stopped and counted to twenty before continuing.

As he headed towards his destination Mr Jeffreys managed to strike a calming rhythm. His feet moved easily and his breathing was steady. The next few minutes would see the practical aspect of his work, the reason for his presence within the hospital. It was also the act that gave his life its deeper meaning. This was his chance to truly serve the community and make a difference, yet he was nothing if not honest, fully aware of the primitive instincts lurking inside every man, even educated and sensitive individuals such as himself. He was an expert at controlling emotion, but even after all these years there was a degree of exhilaration. It was a balancing act of course. This energy must be channelled in the right direction, the end result was all. Professionalism was essential and he prided himself on the manner in which he carried out the most crucial element of his work. There was no room for mistakes and he made none. His success was earned and the same would be true if he ever failed.

As ever, the walls of the corridors were blank and bereft of character. Occasionally he noticed clusters of official notices, posters and leaflets, then drawings and paintings, none of it worth a second glance. These sheets of paper were lost in the plaster much the same as the windows of the surrounding houses merged with the concrete. His journey via local roads always emphasised the importance of his work as the corridors of the hospital and the streets of the town mirrored one another. Too many things had been left to slowly rot and decay, decisions ignored because they were either too painful or required a modicum of effort. Too many people sat around pontificating, delaying the inevitable. Choices had to be made and decisive action taken, no matter that these decisions were hard and laced with regret. He was a realist and believed this with his whole heart. Would have been unable to continue if he did not.

Mr Jeffreys noticed a smudge of what appeared to be paint on the tip of his right shoe. Despite the importance of his task he could not stop himself bending down to inspect the blemish. Yes, it was some sort of paint. He rubbed at the mark and most of it came off, but some lingered. It seemed a mixture of paint and plaster. It was on his fingers now. There was a WC around the corner so he decided to stop briefly. He had time. Entered the room and wetted a paper towel, then scrubbed at the mark. Eventually it was clean. The smell of the WC struck him as he washed his hands. The soap was in a dispenser and he had to press a button. The thought of the germs present on this button disturbed Mr Jeffreys. He filled his palm with the gel, ensured his hands were clean and dried them with towels, ignoring the hot-air machine as he did not want to dirty himself switching it on. He imagined the room crawling with germs and disease. Why oh why could these people not live as he lived? The odour within the WC was foul and he dare not look inside the cubicle. It was a disgrace. It did not take a lot of effort to scrub a damned toilet once a day. He knew that he was allowing himself to become distracted. Breathed deeply and left the WC, continued on his way, shoes spotless once more. He soon felt at ease. Turning right past Pathology, then left, back in his initial rhythm. Time was on his side and he was confident. He would not have stopped otherwise.

The ward was still when Mr Jeffreys arrived. The gentle spin of a fan the only sound. He savoured the moment. The calm before the storm, except there would be no storm. Nothing so crass. A distant snore reached him as a man dreamt of beauty and innocence and no doubt a win on the National Lottery. He smiled at the thought. Wished the gambler well. The sound of the fan increased a little. He was inside the machine now. At its very heart. This appreciation lasted a few seconds, no more, and he moved forward to the relevant section, only feet away. He inspected the four sleeping men. Two had been given sleeping tablets and the third was heavily sedated. The fourth man was very sick and nearest the exit through which

Mr Jeffreys had appeared. Each customer was considered in relation to those nearby, the health of neighbouring patients, whether they would be conscious or otherwise. The position of his client was also vital. This section at the back of the divided ward.

The world was at peace. The night nurse a friendly girl out of sight at the front of the ward. He had spoken to her on many occasions and they got on well. There was a mutual respect there that made him feel good inside. If she changed her routine she would wonder what he was doing here, yet he was nothing if not prepared. His clipboard at the ready, explanation honed. If you could not trust a colleague, a professional, then who could you trust? He was secure but far from complacent. She rarely moved from her desk, but there was always the possibility. He looked around the corner to check she was where she should be, could just make out one of the woman's shoulders. The only real period of danger lasted a matter of seconds. As long as he was not seen with a syringe in his hand he was in the clear. The actual injection was a tense time, yet he was experienced. A quick and gentle operative.

Living in a civilised culture that had not yet embraced the ideal of truly free capitalism, Mr Jeffreys looked to the United States for some sort of guidance. He believed in private medicine as a matter of course, but accepted that a transfer from the old state system would take time. Misplaced idealism was a problem and tradition a heavy burden. The Americans were free from this sentimentalism and able to make brave decisions. Hard work was rewarded, laziness was not.

Crime, meanwhile, was severely punished. A policy of zero tolerance had been adopted for the lawless element and he fully supported humane execution for the most depraved murderers and sexual molesters, carrying as it did a guarantee of dignity in death for even the cruellest of men. Hanging was savage, the electric chair barbaric, but death by lethal injection eased the conscience of all right-thinking men and women. It offered a compromise and some sort of consensus.

But he stopped himself. His own work could never be compared with that of the law-enforcement agencies. It was up to him to help the innocent rather than punish the wicked. He was operating in a completely different arena, ending lives that cried out to be aborted. He was an angel of mercy, easing the agony of old age and terminal disease. His patients were customers and he was providing a service. The state and the individual were in perfect harmony, although this service was kept under wraps. There was no violence involved, and no regret on the part of his clients. He was a carer dedicated to making the health service work for all concerned.

Mr Jeffreys glided over to Mr Webster. His muscles taut and mind keen as he pulled the curtain the few feet needed to mask them from the other patients in the section. Webster stirred, his face gaunt from the cancer and hair close-cropped behind an oxygen mask. On a superficial level he represented the regular flow of yobs brought into A&E, yet the haircut was due to his treatment. Despite the worthiness of the cause, hospital terminations such as this were dangerous affairs. Restraint and imagination were the keys to success. The state could not be expected to support Mr Jeffreys if he was exposed. He understood this well enough. For a few seconds he saw in Webster the thug in the YSL shirt, the smaller bulldog, the man who had attacked him in Soho many years before, a succession of minicab drivers and any number of hooligans with whom he had been forced to deal over the years. He saw the skeleton who had insulted him. Webster, though, was being assisted for other reasons, for the sickness that was slowly killing him through no fault of his own.

Mr Jeffreys took out his hypodermic and inserted the needle in his phial. Withdrew the plunger and filled the barrel. He lifted the man's arm and found a vein. Fed him the cleansing fluid. Mr Jeffreys withdrew the needle and replaced his antique within the shammy. He did not bother binding it with the cord. He hurried the package into his pocket and relaxed. He was in a secure position now. The magic potion was flowing through Mr Webster's veins with the heart assisting in its own demise. Soon the poor man would be at peace. He felt a very professional sense of achievement in with myriad other emotions. He was helping a fellow human being escape the misery of his predicament.

If challenged now, Mr Jeffreys would say that he had heard a patient cry out and rushed to his assistance. He had never been in this situation, but was confident he would not be revealed. It was ludicrous to have to be concerned with such matters, yet that was the way things stood at the moment. Webster's eyes opened and Mr Jeffreys moved forward to comfort the dying man.

It took him several seconds to realise where he was and Mr Jeffreys was quick to reassure him that everything was all right. The expression on the patient's face flickered for a few seconds, showing uncertainty, perhaps even fear. Mr Jeffreys leant forward and spoke softly into Webster's ear, guiding him in the correct direction. A well-delivered message always found root, be the recipient conscious or otherwise. Even with a coma victim his words found a way in. At least he hoped so. He held Webster's hand in his own. Talking him through the death experience.

As his clients gently passed away, Mr Jeffreys helped create the eternity into which the departing soul would rest. He believed that Man formed his own heaven or hell on Earth, and thus the afterlife could also be created. He merely offered a helping hand. Webster was struggling to sit up but was very weak. Mr Jeffreys stayed with him as he entered the eternal realm, tears in his eyes as he nursed this sad diseased man in his final seconds, talking softly, smelling the wax from his ear and fighting the foul odour, dedicated to his task. He knew his life was afflicted with pain and misery and felt as one with the dying man.

Webster's heartbeat soon ceased and he was no more. Mr Jeffreys remained with the dead man he had helped for a short time, gently arranging his head on the pillow. The eyes were open and these he closed. He touched the forehead momentarily and prepared to leave. Death was as important as birth and he was privileged to be present. It was hard on Mr Jeffreys, a great strain that tugged all sorts of strings within his being, yet he knew that his work was worthwhile and he steeled himself against the sadness involved. The decision had to be made and he had done so, then carried it out. He had no regrets. Webster was grateful for his assistance. He knew that for a fact.

He looked at the locker next to Webster's bed and finally took a packet of mints from among the other debris. He popped these in his pocket, stood and moved around the bed, easing the curtain back to its previous position. He checked the shapes of the other patients and saw that none had stirred. He looked along the hall and made sure it was clear, moved quickly to the emergency exit through which he had entered and crossed a small square of brick and grass. Within a matter of seconds he was walking along the corridors he knew so well. He was safe now and decided to take a long route back to his office. The adrenalin was racing and he needed to exercise in order to calm himself. He knew this feeling would not pass quickly, but motion would help. While he could always present himself as fully relaxed, he was throbbing inside. The office was too small for him at this moment.

So Mr Jeffreys walked. He could do this for hours if he wanted, and go nowhere. As he strolled along he swung his arms back and forth and moved his neck. Finally he took the mints from his pocket and popped one in his mouth. They were coated with some sort of powder and tasted awful. It was a sorry memento but he would still add it to his collection. These objects were a whim, and the habit had started many years before with the fingernail of a young girl he had found in a shop doorway. Nobody knew the meaning of the objects he collected, and he was the only one who had ever seen them together. There were times when he wished he could share his secret. Tell someone about his good work, the suffering individuals he had helped liberate.

Although a slip towards sentamentalism, these objects had a practical purpose. They acted as reminders of the good he had done and spurred him on when his spirit sagged under the weight of responsibility. There was a feeling of failure inherent in the objects but he collected them nonetheless. He did not keep them in his apartment, however. He had invested in a ware-house conversion on the south side of the Thames, a disused candle factory with a view of the river, and this is where he stored his mementos. Gates and security guards protected the premises from the local population and he could almost see his apartment on the north bank from this conversion. It had now become quite a little museum, a gallery of sorts. He displayed these objects in glass cabinets out of respect for the departed souls.

It was a drab collection in as much as the articles themselves were mundane, but the fact that they marked each passing made them worthwhile. It was personal to the work he had undertaken rather than his clients. Pieces of jewellery. Small items of clothing. Toothbrushes. Glasses. Even a snippet of hair. They

represented merciful acts, his own sacrifices. Sometimes it was difficult to find a token, hence the hair,
but these things represented an outlet for his imagina-
tive nature. The cleansing process itself was straightforward. An injection in the hospital. An injection,
accident or act of suffocation within the home. But
they were repetitive tasks and if he was to stay alert he
had to be allowed to exercise his mind. The intelligent
man needed stimulation.

Mr Jeffreys hated the taste of the mint in his mouth,
wrapped it in his handkerchief and put it in his pocket
until he could find a waste bin. This soon became a
necessity. He removed the mint from his pocket and
held it in his hand. He did not want the mess to drip
and dirty his hypodermic. He loved the syringe. It held
such power and was a quality instrument, fitting for
such a profound act. He stopped and thought. There
was a bin near to the X-ray department. He soon
reached this and rid himself of the mint. He felt better
now. Turned and passed the chapel. The door was
open and on a crazy whim he stopped and peeped
inside.

The chapel was empty, which was no surprise given
the hour. During the day he often saw people here,
sitting on plastic chairs with their heads in their hands,
gaze lowered towards the carpet. Some sat staring
blankly at the model of Christ nailed to his cross.
The chapel was merely a room with strong lighting
and twenty or so chairs. There was a small altar with
the cross above. There were no oak pews. No
atmosphere. The chapel resembled the cafeteria, a
sterile, functional room. Of course, he was not

complaining, merely observing. He was not about to recommend that the hospital waste funds redesigning the chapel. Those who sat here would not appreciate it being rebuilt.

Despite this, Mr Jeffreys went inside and sat down. The chair was so flimsy he thought it was about to buckle beneath his weight. It was not as if he was heavy either. He hated to think what happened when some of the fat men and women he saw strolling around the hospital stopped here for a rest. How they suffered, these ignorant fools, sitting in front of a Christ that was made of plastic and flaking around the calves. The thorns in the head were crudely painted, the blood streaming down the face more pink than red. It was stuck in blobs, watery elsewhere.

He stared into the eyes of the plastic doll and saw nothing but failure and acceptance. The altar had been built with the sort of cheap wood they sold in those terrible do-it-yourself stores. He hated the tackiness of the chapel. When he attended church, which was rarely, he walked to Westminster Abbey. The power of the place enthralled him. He visited the crypt and stood with the immortals of the British establishment. That was the worth of religion. The meaning of true power. When he walked out of Westminster Abbey he stopped and savoured Parliament, the root of the world's democracies. He felt awe in such a setting, in the presence of greatness, but here, in this godforsaken town?

In their deepest despair men and women came and sat in this pathetic cupboard and hoped God would know they were here. But God did not even know this room existed. He was busy elsewhere. Jonathan Jeffreys shook his head and laughed at the slobs, the junkies, drunks, tarts, yobs, brats and witches who prayed for mercy in their trainers and T-shirts and grubby hundred-pound suits. They sat in dressing gowns crying like emotional fools. Sobbing and asking for forgiveness and another chance to make things right. As if anyone was listening.

The chirping of sparrows pulled Ruby into the TV room, the set pumping out silent images, volume turned down, so she switched it off and went to the window, looked out into the small square, a patch of grass with a concrete border. She'd put a bowl of water on the bench, two birds perched on the back, one below drinking, eyes fluid in tiny heads, feet dancing and voices singing, knowing there was no danger here, no cats lurking in the middle of the hospital. She'd been rushed off her feet but had remembered to put the water out, always did when it was hot, carrying on from the winter when she bought nuts at the pet shop, helping the birds through the cold months when food was scarce.

It had been one of those days, but she didn't care, wasn't even bothered when a consultant had a go at her for nothing, some of them bossing the nurses around like they were the only people who counted. Sally was always going on about the sexism and snobbery but Ruby let it wash over her, she'd be going home soon and was starving, gone down the shops in her dinner break, thinking about Charlie as she walked through the precinct, looking for a new top, wishing she earned more and wondering whether she should get a part-time job in a pub, but then they tried to get you working Friday and Saturday, and that meant she would miss the best nights of the week, what was the point of that, and she skipped back to Charlie Parish, like a dream come true, meeting the voice on the radio. The sparrows kept looking around, still alert, cautious, and it was just the way they lived, survival of the fittest, Ruby glad it didn't work like that with humans.

– Who had a good bunk-up last night then? Dawn shouted, creeping up behind Ruby and grabbing her bum.

She blushed and the sparrows flew off. Dawn had been on at her all day, knew she got embarrassed easily, and Ruby shook her head and laughed, left the room, Dawn following her back down the hall, she loved exaggerating things, swearing, acting rude, a proper wind-up merchant.

– I can see it in your walk and in your eyes. Bet he's got a big dick as well.

Ruby turned on to the ward, walking by Maureen, Dawn quiet, at least until they where past.

– I saw him walking down the road with you this morning. He's nice. Pass him my way when you've finished, will you? I could do with a stud instead of some of these five-second wonders I end up with.

Boxer was ahead of them and Ruby looked at Dawn, who shut up. He turned red at anything, and Dawn liked to tease him, but not at Ruby's expense. She was only having a laugh, knew when to keep quiet.

– Hello, big boy, she said, patting Boxer's arm.

His face went beetroot.

– I hope you've been behaving yourself. Haven't been chasing the girls again.

Boxer was moving into a purple effect now, Ruby glad she could save him, pulling the man right as Dawn carried on straight ahead.

– She's funny, Boxer said, thoughtfully.

Ruby could almost hear the tick of his brain, a concentrated look on his face, and Ruby felt sorry for him suddenly, knew Dawn wouldn't be joking with Boxer if he wasn't different, she'd keep her distance if it was one of the other porters, a male nurse or doctor, at least when she was at work, sober, and Ruby had seen Dawn pissed enough times. Poor old Boxer just needed to settle down with someone who'd love him for his good nature, childlike ways, but instead he woke up alone with the radio for company, maybe the TV, tuning into his morning hosts as they flashed false smiles. If he found someone he'd live happily ever after, just like the stories, and Ruby smartened up and knew he was fine, that she was the one who believed in fairy tales, sat watching musicals for hours. She didn't mind living on her own, like the song said, you couldn't hurry love, but it would be nice, in a way, to find someone special. Two better than one.

– She's always acting sexy, pinching my bum. But she's not my sort of girl. I can't tell her because she'd be angry with me, or feel bad, think she's ugly, but she's not ugly, it's just I don't fancy her. Do you know what I mean? I wonder why she fancies me so much. Do you think it's because of Christmas?

– No, she's just being friendly, that's all. You know what she's like.

– I don't like it though, someone might think we're boyfriend and girlfriend. I like her, but she's rude. All that sexy stuff.

Ruby thought about the Christmas party. Poor old Boxer didn't know what hit him, thought he was drinking fruit juice when really it was Maureen's punch that she'd made specially, a lethal kick in the orange and pineapple. Dawn was bad getting off with Boxer but she'd always had a different approach. Boxer didn't seem worried and that's what counted. But she wondered about Dawn sometimes, was surprised but not shocked when she'd told her a month back that she'd been working at Melanie's Massage. Ruby asked Dawn how she could sell herself like that, Melanie specialising in the moodiest massages in town.

Ruby had ended up with a lecture, Dawn saying that if you thought about how much a nurse was paid and the sort of jobs they were expected to do, what was the difference between digging shit out of an old man's arse for pennies or earning a day's wage for wanking a young man off. She was helping people out both ways, and if nurses were valued more then she wouldn't be forced into part-time work. She could take it or leave it, unlike some of the girls, with kids to feed or drug habits, fallen on hard times. Dawn went on and on and Ruby wished she'd never opened her mouth. She came on all militant the same as Sally would, saying how prostitution was the oldest profession in the world and for a lot of women that's the only way they could make a living, and anyway, Melanie's was a decent place, discreet, no drunks allowed, no S&M or kinky stuff, it was a laugh, there were some funny girls working there, and besides, she was only doing a day here and there, a top-up for her wages, it wasn't as if she was going to pack in her job like a lot of nurses did, fed up having their noses rubbed in it all the time, treated like dirt and expected never to go on strike because their jobs were so important. Sally was right, everyone wanted health care but none of them wanted to pay the bill, expected people like them to do the work for fun.

– See you, Boxer said.

Ruby continued walking, on her way to collect some sheets, thinking about Charlie and how he dreamt of buying that Cadillac, the same old story holding him back, a shortage of money. It was never going to happen, but it was good to have a dream.

She saw Mr Jeffreys coming along in the opposite direction. He was looking tired. He worked hard, and she knew from other nurses that he usually went right through the night, and she was thinking what a nice man he was, everyone said so, and she remembered how he'd been sympathetic the other day, and she had the hanky on her, was just waiting for a chance to give it back. He was engrossed in his thoughts and didn't notice her.

– Mr Jeffreys, she said.

He jumped, startled, looked and tried to focus, so she waited till he was ready and could see who it was, his hair cut smart but very conservative, the white coat over a good suit, a stylish man who could've been anything he wanted. She took out the handkerchief and held it towards him.

– Nurse James. I am sorry. I was miles away. So rude of me.

– It's your hanky. It's washed and ironed.

– Handkerchief? Mine?

– You lent it to me the other day.

– Of course. It slipped my mind. You need not have gone to so much trouble though. There was no rush.

– Thanks for giving it to me, I was being silly, crying like that.

– Thank you. Plenty more where that came from. I always travel prepared.

He pulled out a hanky to show her and something clattered to the floor, Ruby bending down to pick up a pocket watch.

– That's a nice watch, she said. Lucky the glass didn't break.

He smiled at her, seemed really embarrassed, like he was going to faint or something. It was the heat, sweat on his forehead and cheeks.

– Thank you, he said, after a pause. So stupid of me. My father gave it to me. So stupid.

– It's funny, she said, handing it back so he slipped it into his pocket with the two handkerchiefs. Mr Dawes had a watch just like that, he showed me once, I must have him on the brain, but it was true what you said, time helps, even a few days.

He was looking at her strangely, as if he was seeing her for the first time, and she felt so sorry for Mr Jeffreys, it was like he was lonely, it couldn't be much fun working at night and doing a job that was so important, every department trying to get the best deal possible.

– Suppose it's standard, she said. A gold watch when you retire. Anyway, I better get going, thanks again for being so nice.

Ruby looked at her own watch, didn't have long to go before she could go home, and Ron was in her head for a while, a nice memory, someone worth meeting, and she got the sheets and finished her shift, waved goodbye to Boxer who was talking to one of the cleaners, Christine, hair so black and shiny, deep brown eyes and fluorescent plastic bracelets on her wrists, these pink and green and orange loops, and Boxer smiled back at Ruby, blushing now as he gave himself away, gently rocking foot to foot, and she was really hungry, wondering what she should have to eat, didn't fancy cooking, and she was soon walking through reception and passing Ted sitting with his CDs and books, yellow-page romances he sold in an empty unit, the paper looking like it had been dropped in the bath, big wads of brittle words, Ted in between the inner and outer doors, opposite a room where the porters stored the wheelchairs, and she smiled at him, redundant at fifty-five and after a year on the dole he'd started doing charity work to keep himself sane, Ruby knew his wife, she was working, and he was stretching his arms over his head, yawning, going back to his cardboard boxes and collapsible tables, and it had a good feel that room, musty because there were old books but alive like a jumble sale, like there was treasure in there waiting to be discovered, and maybe that's why it was always packed, half the people who came to visit seemed to stop for a look, so serious as they flicked through, making sure they checked every book and CD, guessing that it would be just their luck if they stopped short and missed a treat. Ruby knew, because she'd done it herself, hadn't been in for a week or two but would have a look tomorrow, she was hungry and couldn't stop.

She went out front past the taxis and a bus waiting behind an ambulance that was unloading a man with a cast on his left leg. She caught some of the words his friends must've signed, GET WELL SOON, ROY WOZ HERE, STEVE AND BEV, plus on the bottom of his foot where he couldn't see was I LIKE LITTLE BOYS, and she did her best not to laugh knowing it was probably his best friend who'd done that one, and she went down the ramp past two guys sitting on the railing talking about chemotherapy and cancer of the liver and life and death, and they looked like brothers, the same pattern that spread out across their eyes, and they were talking hushed and serious so it was maybe their mum or dad, maybe an uncle or aunt they were close to, and she started across the car park towards the path leading home, tired but bouncing along with a spring in her step, trying to remember if there was any food in the fridge, knew there wasn't, thought of Papa and the kebabs, didn't want to take advantage, knew she'd get another free meal if she went in, and maybe she'd stop and buy some bread, she had a tin of baked beans at home, or she could walk a bit further and go to the supermarket, no, she couldn't be bothered with all that, or she could do the easy thing and go down the chippy, that seemed the best option, mouth watering as Vinnie crossed her path.

– Night, Rube, he said, laughing.

He always called her Rube instead of Ruby, lots of people did, but he thought it was funny, just couldn't finish the word, and she was laughing as well because there was so much of that, the one that really got her was Ian, how it had to be one of the shortest names around and still it was cut down to E, so she always called him Vincent back, seeing the look on Vinnie's face, a good lad who had to stand in the car park all day directing traffic. It didn't matter what the weather was like, he was stuck on the kerb getting slagged off by drivers who had a lot on their minds, moaning about the lack of places, like it was his fault, but he took it in his stride, the weather toughening him up, he had the wind and rain to think about, the smell of the exhausts, he liked being outside, did his own thing.

– Did you listen to that tape I gave you? he asked.

– It's good, I'm doing you one back, she said, only slowing down.

He was all right, Vinnie, but if she stopped she'd be there for ten minutes, and she remembered that time she'd been in A&E and he'd come in with a black eye after someone had punched him, that wasn't fair, it wasn't nice, but she smiled remembering how he had this hurt look on his face, and how his best mate, Jerry from security, went running out looking for the man, but in summer it was payback time, he was out in the fresh air while the rest of them were stuck indoors, he was lapping up the sun, getting a tan, and she was thinking of the tape she was going to make him, so he could listen on his Walkman, and it wasn't a bad job, being a car-park attendant, she could think of worse things to do with your time.

– Don't forget, he said, moving his head in a circle.

So these spirals came off him, making her think of the patterns of a radio, the sort of thing you saw on adverts and posters, diagrams showing the way sound moved through the air in waves, great big ripples on a lake made of gas instead of liquid, the sound of a person's voice picked up by a receiver, translated back so you could hear what the broadcasters had to say, the music they wanted you to hear, sharing experiences, and she had to finish that tape for Vinnie, he was a good laugh, always smiling, with all that stubble on his face he never looked right in the uniform.

She'd never seen him out locally, knew he was living with a girl, and she turned again, noticed a bottle wedged under the tyre of a car, bent down to pick it up wondering if it was kids mucking about or if it had just rolled and got stuck. As soon as the car moved it would smash and maybe burst the tyre, so she carried it in her hand feeling the stickiness of the sugar left behind after the drink had gone, a wasp chasing the bottle for a few seconds then catching a whiff of something better and disappearing, Ruby thinking of the bus ride to see her mum, there was always a tin or a can rolling along, a fizzy drink, sweet wrappers dancing in the wind in winter, she loved it, loved everything, everyone, on a real high, seeing all those bottles melted back down and reused, billions of cans crushed and turned into big blocks of gleaming silver, it was almost like she was in love.

– Hello there.

A voice caught her unaware so she jumped.

She was getting ready to cut through the fence, stopped and turned round.

– Are you in a hurry?

She didn't need to worry, it was only Mr Jeffreys. He was standing next to a silver BMW, not that she knew much about cars but could see the initials, and he was very smart in his suit, the white coat hanging in his office probably, back in the hospital, and he was an interesting man, exotic, from a different world basically, hesitant in the way he spoke to you like he was so shy it hurt. She didn't fancy him or anything like that, no chance, it was just he seemed like a genuinely nice person, Ruby relaxing and smiling back.

The twenty years Ron Dawes spent in the navy was only one part of his life . . . what made him stand out was how he used the experiences . . . the sort of man they made him . . . everything he saw had an effect . . . shaped his thinking . . . not just the beauty but the ugliness as well . . . the lepers . . . child prostitutes . . . cruelty . . . the extremes of wealth and poverty . . . it was all there inside him . . . and he made it plain as well . . . so you could see the link . . . and I can remember this time he put a tenner on Caped Crusader to win . . . that was a lot of money . . . normally he never bet more than a pound . . . but he explained that this horse was extra special . . . then told me about the day he rounded Cape Horn . . . at the tip of South America . . . and the Cape was notorious for its rough seas . . . the weather fine at first . . . then suddenly it turned . . . and soon he was stuck in the middle of the worst storm he'd ever known . . . and for the first time in his life he was sure he was going to die . . . the waves really were like mountains . . . they shut out the sky . . . freezing spray killed the feeling in his face . . . huge swells lifting the ship up and sending it crashing down . . . a rollercoaster ride straight to the seabed . . . and he used to dream about that storm for years afterwards . . . usually nothing upset him . . . it was following the war as well . . . he'd been on convoys . . . but this was different . . . he was different . . . he'd changed as *he got older and never realised . . . he was right there when two of his pals were washed overboard . . . skidding across the deck and hitting the side and disappearing in an explosion of water . . . bang . . . they were gone . . . lost at sea . . . he hoped they died quickly . . . didn't see the ship moving away from them . . . time to think about what was happening . . . one was a Glaswegian lad . . . Tommy . . . the other a man of fifty . . . Ernie . . . from Penzance . . . good lads . . . he would never forget them . . . the sight of their bodies tumbling over the deck . . . vanishing . . . and once they were round the Cape and the storm was over the crew had a service for Tommy and Ernie . . . he said it was horrible standing there . . . mouthing prayers . . . with no corpses to focus on . . . and by the time they reached Buenos Aires he knew that storm had changed his life . . . he'd seen enough . . . didn't want to end up like those two lads . . . scattered bones at the bottom of the South Atlantic . . . the Falklands War brought it back years later . . . started him dreaming about that storm again . . . about the ocean . . . how the spray could turn to ice before it hit the deck . . . the swell that ripped into your stomach . . . those boys going off to fight probably didn't think about all that . . . didn't worry too much . . . that's how he'd been . . . didn't worry about anything . . . it had taken him decades to get the wanderlust out of his system . . . he was lucky to survive that long really . . . after the scrapes he'd been in . . . even backing Caped Crusader was light-hearted . . . but now he was serious . . . telling his story . . . transporting you to another time and place . . . it wasn't just about romance . . . roaming the world like that . . . the exotic sights and a carefree life on the ocean waves . . . no . . . he'd been a bugger . . . had to be honest . . . drinking and brawling from Liverpool to San Francisco . . . to Buenos*

*Aires . . . specially Buenos Aires . . . after the storm . . . the
crew drinking away the loss of their pals . . . going at it worse
than usual . . . and they had a big fight with the locals . . .
Ron shook his head remembering . . . it started in a bar and
spilt into the street . . . more and more Argentinians coming
for them . . . and he was stabbed in the chest . . . a couple of
inches lower and it would've pierced his heart . . . he took it
as a sign . . . a double warning . . . the storm and the
stabbing . . . and it looked worse than it was . . . the blade
only went in an inch or so . . . if the Argentinian had been
closer and got it in to the hilt . . . who knows . . . he could
easily have been washed overboard . . . stabbed to death in
the street . . . and when he was back at sea and heading for
Rio he decided he was going to leave the navy when they got
back to England . . . he'd had his fill . . . wanted a place of
his own . . . a pub he could call a local . . . women around
him . . . children playing in streets he walked through to work
. . . and dying at sea became a real fear . . . it lasted for the
rest of his life . . . he didn't want to be stabbed to death where
nobody knew his name . . . hacked to pieces . . . by a
machete . . . in a brothel . . . in Mombasa . . . a good ten
years before Buenos Aires . . . he was laughing about it an
hour later . . . in a bar . . . drunk . . . he had choices where
he could settle down . . . there were opportunities for men like
him . . . Australia . . . New Zealand . . . America . . .
Canada . . . South Africa . . . or he could try India . . .
Hong Kong . . . the Middle East . . . it would be harder
there . . . but the more he thought about it the more he
wanted to go home . . . and from never thinking about
England he was suddenly homesick . . . England was
recovering from the war . . . it would be hard . . . and now he
was excited . . . the world was changing . . . for the better*

. . . *the war had seen the country run according to socialist principles . . . the profit motive outlawed . . . people worked for the common good . . . big business was sidelined . . . and he was going home a socialist . . . a self-educated man who'd seen a thing or two . . . when he wasn't working there wasn't much to do at sea . . . so he'd read everything from 'Das Kapital' to 'Mein Kampf' . . . could tell you all about Lenin . . . Trotsky . . . Hitler . . . Mussolini . . . Kropotkin . . . Mao . . . Churchill . . . people who'd shaped the world . . . he laughed . . . told me Ronald McDonald was more important now . . . and he didn't settle in Shepherd's Bush when he got back . . . that's where he'd grown up . . . he moved out to find work . . . a fresh start . . . the new-town factories crying out for labour . . . booming . . . all sorts of people moving in . . . building a brave new Britain . . . and he loved every minute of it . . . the room he rented . . . the pubs . . . streets . . . shops . . . people . . . everything . . . and a couple of years later he met Anne and they got married . . . moved into a house . . . had four children in the next seven years . . . and Ron stayed at that factory until he retired . . . spent more time there than at sea . . . and he was a staunch union man . . . a hardcore socialist . . . he was keen to tell people there was no shame in socialism . . . it had nothing to do with communism . . . he couldn't believe how quickly things were forgotten . . . and this upset him . . . he'd seen Bolshevism in the East . . . the Nazis in the West . . . the fall of the old imperialism and the arrival of a new more efficient version . . . he fretted about the changes of the last twenty years . . . how most people didn't know their benefits had been fought for . . . maybe they thought they were a generous gift . . . from the Queen . . . or big business . . . how many of them even knew the name of someone like*

Bevin . . . but Ron wasn't bitter . . . capitalism had won . . . and was busy tightening its grip . . . there was nothing he could do . . . but he'd enjoyed himself slowing them down . . . he had to move on . . . same as when he was in the navy . . . and so he enjoyed his retirement . . . couldn't understand people who didn't know what to do with themselves . . . and he could tell a good story about the factory . . . for those who were interested . . . characters like Irish Dave . . . the time he knocked out one of the bosses . . . how the whole factory came out in support . . . Dave was going to get sacked . . . as well as charged with assault . . . but production was going to be lost . . . money counted . . . the union was strong and management backed off . . . maybe they even knew that Dave was right . . . had responded to a personal insult . . . no man had to put up with that . . . not then . . . maybe now it was different . . . there wasn't the same job security any more . . . and Ron's best mate after the navy was Wally . . . Fred moved to New Zealand . . . lived near a volcano in the North Island . . . and they wrote to each other for years . . . till Fred died . . . and Ron used to go drinking with Wally . . . a big man he said made Irish Dave look small . . . and even Ron admitted Wally loved a punch-up . . . there was plenty of fist fights . . . the way Ron told it you couldn't help but smile . . . and it was rose-tinted glasses time . . . he knew it as well as me . . . could run off a list of names . . . lost now . . . the town filling up with people spilling out of London . . . migrants from the West Country . . . Ireland . . . Wales . . . the North . . . everywhere really . . . Poles who stayed after the war . . . years later the Pakistanis . . . Bangladeshis . . . there was all sorts . . . and the accents melted down . . . there was no twang any more . . . the factories and warehouses spread . . .

it was still a boom town . . . still the future . . . and when Ron talked about England it was always the people . . . while in the navy it was places . . . events . . . and despite all the things he'd done with his life he was sad when he retired . . . they had a party for him and hundreds of people turned out . . . he never expected that . . . thought they'd have a drink in the bar . . . he was surprised by the spread laid on . . . young girls came up and hugged him . . . Anne watching . . . fuming she was so jealous . . . and he laughed about that . . . even when they got old she was jealous . . . but he liked that . . . it showed she cared . . . and it worked both ways . . . she was the most beautiful woman in the world . . . and a good mother . . . but with a temper . . . she could swear with the best of them . . . loved a drink as well . . . they were always rowing . . . she was looking forward to him retiring . . . she was younger . . . still at work . . . a good job with with the council . . . she said he could do all the housework now . . . and people were coming up and shaking his hand when he retired . . . this woman Sandra famous for her baking . . . she made a big cake . . . always called him Red Ron . . . and Wally stood on a chair and made a speech that went on and on . . . and then everyone called for Ron to say a few words . . . he'd had a bit to drink and luckily they laughed at the funny bits . . . and he had to hold back the tears at the end . . . from a drifter he was part of a community . . . that was the point of the story . . . why he told me . . . it was another realisation . . . a good night . . . lots of the younger ones came along . . . and stayed . . . he could understand them getting bored . . . boys and girls in their teens and twenties who you wouldn't think would want to give up their Friday night for an old man . . . there were punks . . . skinheads . . . Pakistanis drinking together . . .

and all they were getting was some out-of-date singalongs . . .
an old-fashioned knees-up . . . but they seemed happy . . .
he could remember looking across the room at the people
who'd turned out . . . he was really going to miss the place
. . . not the work so much as the people . . . and later on
there was quiet again . . . and he was presented with a box
. . . a big cardboard effort wrapped up in tape . . . he had to
use a knife to open it . . . and inside was another box . . .
and another . . . finally a present tied up with ribbon . . . he
unwrapped it and found a gold watch . . . he had tears in his
eyes . . . had to admit it . . . people joked about being given
a gold watch . . . but he really loved it . . . that watch meant
a lot . . . he always carried it with him . . . and Anne lived
for fifteen years after he retired . . . their life together was full
. . . they went on holiday every year . . . did the garden in
the summer . . . went to the pub a couple of times a week
with their friends . . . saw their children and played with the
grandkids . . . till Anne died . . . and he had his first real
depression . . . dreamt of drowning in the ocean . . . lost at
sea . . . but he was strong and pushed his way through it . . .
Wally was still around . . . and his family helped him . . .
the neighbours too . . . he had support . . . his grandchildren
were the most important thing to him now . . . he'd reached
that point where everything he wanted was within walking
distance . . . three of his kids . . . their children . . . the
garden . . . the satellite system his boy Micky had paid for
. . . and it was like a big circle really . . . that's how he
explained it . . . running around when you were a child but
never straying too far . . . then going off to see the world . . .
the one time he really said anything about his mum and dad
was then . . . how his parents always fought . . . money the
root of all evil . . . his dad had left and Ron was blamed . . .

just for being born . . . but he wanted to see the world . . . it wasn't just running away . . . he'd had a glimpse . . . that's all you got in twenty years . . . and then he wanted to settle down . . . and he did that . . . raised a family . . . did what he thought was right . . . had beliefs he did his best to stick to . . . and finally his working days were over and he was back to moving around a handful of streets . . . where he knew people . . . if he was knocked down he wouldn't die alone . . . this was home . . . where he belonged . . . and he was still interested in the world . . . but now he could see it all on the telly . . . go to the North Pole and swim around under the ice with polar bears . . . sit in the jungle with gorillas . . . he knew he shouldn't be watching Sky . . . seeing as it was owned by Murdoch . . . but he didn't care . . . Micky was generous . . . had him signed up for a decent package . . . but mostly it was the natural history he watched . . . some of the political documentaries . . . and with his grandchildren he watched the Cartoon Channel . . . he was eighty-four . . . and if he was old he had privileges . . . the right not to worry any more . . . he'd done his bit . . . now it was time for his reward . . . it was what he'd worked hard for . . . a pension . . . medical care . . . all the normal things . . . he always had one of his kids coming round . . . every single day . . . doing the cleaning even though he could do it himself . . . trying to cook for him . . . and on Sundays he had dinner with his family . . . now and then a pint with his boys . . . sometimes he didn't fancy it . . . he couldn't drink more than one or two these days . . . didn't really fancy it to be honest . . . and he could've gone round to eat in the week as well . . . if he wanted . . . but he preferred doing his own thing . . . he knew he was lucky . . . missed Anne but tried not to think about it too much . . . and he went down the bookies

most days . . . studied the form . . . saw Wally . . . they'd
started playing dominoes with this bloke Dennis in the cafe
. . . usually won . . . they drank a lot of tea there . . . but
Ron was getting better and would beat him one day . . .
Dennis had age on his side . . . a young seventy-one . . .
and Ron always had an opinion . . . could adjust to the
person he was talking to . . . his mind was extra sharp . . .
he wanted to live and see his grandchildren grow up . . . be
around when his first great-grandchild was born . . . and he
wouldn't stop there . . . maybe he was going to live to be
really ancient . . . and he laughed and went into a story about
this man he'd seen in Peru . . . the locals said he was 135
. . . he didn't know if it was true . . . there was no way of
knowing . . . but he didn't see why not . . . as long as you
could get around . . . still had your marbles . . . and he made
a face and shook his hands in the air . . . told me not to look
so sad.

Mr Jeffreys sat in his car drumming thin, elegant fingers on the steering wheel. His nails were clipped and filed and scrubbed clean. Knuckles squeezed dry with worry. Every so often he removed his hand from the wheel and clenched his fist, digging the nails into his palm.

He was waiting at the edge of the car park, discreetly positioned yet able to see the main entrance to his right and Accident & Emergency to his left. When an ambulance barrelled around the corner he could not help but watch its progress. It slowed for the bump then picked up speed, passed behind a Portakabin before coming back into view. It stopped. What load would it give up? What new strain would be placed on resources? For once, he did not care, quickly switched back to his view of the main entrance.

Mr Jeffreys was scared. Compromised. Under threat. That tart of a nurse had seen the old fool's watch. Yet it was his own fault. His foolishness had jeopardised everything. He had become cavalier. Overconfident. Throughout history this had led to the downfall of great men. Carrying the watch in his pocket instead of removing it from the hospital had been a stupid, stupid mistake. What had he been thinking? Nurse James had seen the watch and even compared it to that of Dawes. How long before she realised that it really was the old man's? Did she know the truth already and was holding her tongue as she plotted against him? That sort of woman possessed a primitive cunning. She would destroy him out of spite, because of his position and intellect. The politics of envy was about to rear its ugly head once more.

She was a cheap floozie. Brain-dead and ignorant. The state could not protect him against her evil spell. His work was so sensitive that he would lose everything if the police became involved. The state could do nothing for him. Nobody must know of the cleansing. He did not blame the authorities of course. He knew the score. Yet perhaps she did not know. Was she really so dumb and trusting that she did not see the significance of his mistake? He thought about this. He could not take a chance. He was not thinking of himself. Oh no. Nurse James was a danger to his mission. An evil, scheming tart. Common as muck. With her endless smiles and friendly manner, the fake humility. He hated her.

He took a deep breath and refocused his attention on the ambulance. With its paramedics running in circles. Add the nurses and porters and he doubted there was more than two brain cells between the whole sorry bunch. The trolley was loaded and rushed into A&E. He knew the routine. The concern. Diagnosis. Treatment. Recuperation. Forced a smile. The paramedics. The nurses. The doctors. The porters. The tea ladies. Every one of them acted as if it mattered whether these patients lived or died. Really, it did not. They were scum. White trash. The white niggers which infested every civilised nation. He despised them all.

But he had to remember his mission. He was employed to serve the interests of the state, just like the bankers and politicians, the artistic elite and media, the generals and senior civil servants. Yet he was restrained by ideology. If it was his decision, he would privatise the whole caboodle. Force those who could not pay for their health care to die where they fell. It was more honest that way and what God had intended. Why would He have invented cancer if it was not to control the population? Why should a person live beyond their allotted working life if they were only kept alive by expensive medication? What was the value of retirement to a dynamic economy? He firmly believed in the survival of the fittest, and not according to brute strength either. It was superior intellect that led to survival. He was God's trusty worker. Mr Jeffreys laughed. Tried to rein back his emotions.

Yet he could not help himself. He was a good man and wanted to help the people help themselves. If the state prospered then so would the masses. But he was frustrated in his efforts, the anger rising up when he considered the dole queues and all those who were out of work and living easy lives. He was paying for the drug addicts and prostitutes, the single parents and loafers, the criminals in their luxury prison cells, the whining pensioners and sponging asylum seekers. He could not remain strong every single second of every single day. He had to let off steam sometime. Did they not understand how hard it was for him to keep smiling at people he despised every second of his working life, surrounded as he was by dimwits, dealing with morons and hearing about their stupid prejudices, thinking they had inalienable rights? He wished he could just stamp DNR on every single file, be done with it, DO NOT RESUSCITATE, that would do the job, and Jeffreys tightened his grip on the steering wheel almost rocking it forward to his chest, a police car arriving now next to the ambulance so he knew that it was either a road accident or an assault, a drunk-driver or a knife-wielding maniac, he did not know for sure but could find out, if he wanted to, but he did not, watched the two policemen walk inside, lackeys of course, but necessary, puffed-up nobodies, and he was glad they were out of sight yet did not fear them, knew they were a part of the whole sorry mess, and he thought of the boy with the cut face, how he had escaped the needle, a certain Mr Parish had had a very lucky escape, on the receiving end but guilty by association, it was a basic rule, you did not get stabbed for nothing, not people like that anyway, it was the same with cheap tarts crying rape when all the time they were asking for it with their provocative clothing, although he did feel some sorrow for old folk mugged by hooligans, yet it was their fault for living in the wrong areas, for offering an easy target, for living too long, they were slackers basically, the sort of bone-idle spongers who held the country back, and oh how he would love to get hold of one of those muggers, the dirty little golliwogs made him sick, as sick as the scum who loved their jungle music and had sex with their men, the whoring majority and the smelly immigrant minority, and all together they jumped into the pot that spun in a whirlpool of mutant spawn, corrupted genes that moved faster and faster until they were absorbed and regurgitated as another wave of white trash, no, these people had no understanding of culture, of the finer arts that lasted for centuries and refused to change, the rigid lines of music, art, literature, architecture that stretched back through the centuries and were as pure now as they were then, so instead the common people craved novelty, as if excitement mattered, corrupted the language with their ever-changing slang, created a din for entertainment, laughed at jokes that were not funny, moaned and complained and then when they were offered a basic service did not want to pay their share of the cost, expected the state to nanny them, well, it was not happening in his hospital, he was running the show, distributing some long-overdue justice, and Jeffreys smiled now, imagined a future health system where he could work openly and reap the respect he deserved for a tough job well done, yet knew it was impossible in this day and age, looked back towards the main entrance and scolded himself for allowing his attention to stray, he had to stay in control, the ambulance a distraction, he was no better than those open-mouthed fools who gathered around road accidents, staring and not knowing what to do, gormless the lot of them, guttersnipes and urchins, and he squinted his eyes when he saw three nurses come out through the glass doors, a big black woman with two skinny whites, he thought one of them might be Nurse James, but no, she was not there, and they turned and were coming towards him so he reached over for his briefcase and took out a file, opened it and inspected a sheet of paper which he propped against his steering wheel, showing that he was busy, merely taking a breather in his car, still working, nose to the grindstone, right down on the surface, he put on a serious expression and raised his head as the nurses passed but they did not even notice him, how he hated them, especially the prettiest of the three, the one nearest his car with the brown hair pulled back in a tight bun, did he say pretty, that was the trouble with working in a place like this, God, how he hated the tackiness of these people, the place, longed to be in his hotel room, ringing room service and ordering a club sandwich, two bottles of American beer and a bucket of ice, or back in his apartment, or in his gallery. Anywhere but here.

He spotted Nurse James. She was strolling along with a smile on her face as if she was in control. She was a witch and he was not deceived. If she did not know about the nature of his work then she soon would. She slowed down to talk to the fool who passed for a car-park attendant. No doubt planning some seedy rendezvous, a sexual encounter up against the wall of the crematorium.

She continued walking. Bent down near a car. No doubt picking up cigarette butts. Swinging an arm and shaking her hand. Carefree and empty-headed. Selfish. Cheap. The car park quiet. Mr Jeffreys unobserved. The attendant disappeared around the corner and he popped the boot open and got out of his car. Called gently. Attracted Nurse James's attention so that she smiled and came over. So gullible. Trusting. A stupid bitch. She looked where he pointed. Turned her head so that he could smother her face with his handkerchief. A nice touch. The handkerchief she had returned that same day. Cleaned and ironed. No doubt hoping to impress. He held her firm as she struggled against the chloroform, then sunk into unconsciousness.

Very gently and with the utmost consideration Mr Jeffreys lifted Nurse James into the boot of his car. He covered her with a blanket and rested her head at a suitable angle. He did not want her to wake up with a stiff neck. He looked around but was in the clear. His confidence had returned. He shut the boot and got back into the car. Started the BMW engine and ambled through the car park with a friendly wave to the attendant. Who waved back. A nice touch. Between two men working for the common good. One a professional. The other a dedicated assistant. Doing menial yet important work. The directing of cars. Mr Jeffreys appreciated his efforts. Everyone had a role to play.

But he had a choice to make. There were three options. He could take Nurse James to his hotel. Security cameras, staff and a constant stream of guests made this indiscreet of course. He was not thinking of himself but the nurse. She was a sweet girl. Dreaming sweet dreams. Yet she had a reputation to uphold. The hotel staff would get the wrong idea. Or he could invite her to his apartment. For dinner. This would be too forward of him. Too personal. Or he could take her to his gallery. This appealed. No one had seen his exhibition before and it seemed a poetic solution to a delicate problem. Had she ever visited a gallery? He doubted whether she had so it would be an education. His mind made up, he drove carefully. Obeyed the speed limits. Ever the professional.

Mr Jeffreys shaved. Showered. Slipped into a fresh set of clothes. Poured himself a drink. Admired the decanters lining the drinks cabinet. So many shapes. Sizes. Cut crystal gleaming. He sipped his cognac. Walked over and sat in a chair opposite Nurse James, who was relaxing on the sofa. Dozing. Dreaming. There was no point standing on ceremony. He would call her by her Christian name from now on. Ruby. A precious gem. Much sought after. He laughed. Rolled the cognac around his mouth and savoured the warmth. He felt secure. At ease in the loft. His private gallery in the former factory beautifully refurbished to provide space for professionals and investors. His loft was the best unit within the development, in terms of both size and river view. The floorboards shone under layers of polish. The aroma incredible. It was hard to imagine the factory before the developers arrived. Derelict for years. A refuge for drug addicts and prostitutes. Before that a harsh industrial hell. Bedlam.

Every possible whim had been catered for during the development and he himself had employed an interior decorator once the deal was struck. To add a personal touch. His only stipulation the display cabinets and their positioning. These he had filled with his trophies. Which were subtly lit. Artistic touches meant the gallery remained vibrant. Forever expanding. Slowly but surely. Of course, the loft lacked the exclusivity of his apartment, yet as a gallery it was perfect. Ruby was indeed privileged. The first person he had invited to view his exhibition. Since buying the property. The development itself was secure. He came and went as he pleased. Rarely saw his neighbours. The ideal arrangement.

Ruby was beginning to stir. He had further sedated her on arrival but she would soon begin to regain consciousness. Very slowly. Disorientated yet pliable. Aware enough to understand what was happening but not to cause a scene. He did not want her distressed. Jonathan had worked hard while she slept. As a soft-hearted carer who broke down when an elderly stranger passed away she obviously needed toughening up. She was weak, in both mind and spirit. No doubt saw people as inherently good. She was the three monkeys in one. She spoke no evil. Which was acceptable. But neither did she hear or see evil. This was not. It was a flaw that needed correcting. It was time she grew up. She was a child in a woman's body. A simpleton.

After careful consideration he had identified four cases with which he knew she was familiar, having dealt with them personally. On the arm of the chair he had set down a ring. A locket. A dice. And a watch. He was ready. Safely tucked away in the loft he would be able to work without restraint. In the hospital terminations were rushed, while home visits were risky. The preserve of GPs. Ruby was an extraordinary case. A matter of self-preservation. Yet it had worked out well for both parties. She would learn about these four cases and come to understand the nature of his work. See the broader picture. The need to reallocate resources. To ensure fairness. Justice. God in need of assistance. Due to the weakness of the people. Fools such as Ruby. Sentimentalists. Emotional wrecks. He would allow her to savour the eternal damnation of each of these four leeches. To appreciate his work.

This was merely the prelude to her own punishment of course. How dare this lowly nurse put a man of his standing at risk. She was rotten to the core. His magic potion was inappropriate, a childish exit. In this special instance he would use the combat knife strapped to his calf to perform the termination. It was a purely professional decision of course. Her body would be found in the Thames. A senseless attack. He could not feed a young, healthy woman a barrel of morphine without arousing suspicion. A random attack was ideal. Its apparent sexual nature would throw off the hounds.

Her eternity would naturally involve sexual abuse. It was a hell he had conjured up on many occasions. Repetition inevitable but nevertheless effective. Sexual aggression was feared by every woman. A just dessert for a sluttish Lolita who posed such a typically feminine threat. Sweet on the outside, deadly within. Cunning. Devious. The VCR was loaded. The real world primed. Further documentary evidence of Man's cruelty to Man. Or in this case, Woman. It was merely a case of waiting. He was tempted to have another drink but determined to remain at his sharpest. Two cuts to the throat would suffice. A bowl was at the ready. Followed by a mock sexual attack. No more. Always the professional. The physical realm did not matter. It was the spiritual that interested Jonathan Jeffreys.

When Ruby appeared ready to begin he picked up his four keepsakes and sat next to her. Her eyes were misty. Vision blurred. She blinked and coughed. A weakling. He slid his right arm around her shoulders and dropped the objects in her lap with his left. The uniform coming in handy. He explained the relevance of the cabinets. How they contained keepsakes. Mementos. Trophies. Relics. She could choose her description. But what they really represented were the patients he had assisted over the years. Pathetic cases who were a burden to their loved ones. Not to mention the state. The sick and elderly whose time had run out. The system was on the verge of collapse due to a lack of realism. He believed in survival of the fittest. In the frugal use of resources. Decisions had to be taken. People were suffering. He was an angel of mercy who ended their misery. At the same time cleansing society of its unproductive element. Cutting costs in the best way possible. He talked for perhaps ten minutes. Repeating key points until he felt Ruby understood. There was no point bringing her to the gallery if she could not appreciate its significance. The work that he had been carrying out for so many years. Hidden from view. Operating in the shadows. Without recognition. He had dedicated his life to public service. Ruby must appreciate this fact.

She must also understand that the afterlife enjoyed by a departing soul depended on the individual. There were no absolutes. A man, or woman, could shape their own destiny if they possessed the necessary will. This was unfair of course, as those who had lived bad lives could achieve eternal bliss when what they really deserved was eternal damnation. Fortunately his work placed him in a position where he could right this basic injustice. He was able to guide people towards their just desserts, and this he did, shaping and creating their heavens and hells. His work was therefore both material and spiritual in nature. He smiled. He expanded on this topic until he felt Ruby was ready to begin her lesson.

The VCR's remote control was on hand and he began the documentary. There were no credits. Four men with shaved heads dragged a naked girl into an empty room. She was crying and doing her best to resist. But to no avail. She was screaming. Very loudly. He lowered the volume. The sound just audible. He did not want the roar of grunting men and a sobbing teenager to clash with his narrative. In the background teddy bears and fluffy toys lined makeshift shelves. The skinheads forced the girl on to a bed. She was spreadeagled. Vagina gaping for a professional cameraman forced to work in trying conditions. Searching for the truth. Providing a public service. Two skinheads held a leg each while the third pulled the girl's arms above her head. Their arms were covered in tattoos. The fourth stripped and moved into position. Applied lubricant to an erect penis and forced himself into the girl. She was a virgin and bucked her hips. Was punched in the face. Now semi-conscious. Like Ruby. Who tried to look away. He held her head in position and felt the terror rip into her gentle nature as the rapist ripped into his victim. He could barely watch the assault. It was a crass display of savagery illustrating the basic animal nature of the people. The man began to plunge into the teenager. Faster and harder. Jonathan Jeffreys reached for his combat knife. Held it to Ruby's jugular vein. Warned her that she must keep her eyes open throughout the documentary. Otherwise he would be forced to cut her throat. She had to understand that he was a civilised man who was trying to help her grow up and accept that the world was evil. That nobody could be trusted.

Mr Jeffreys reached into Ruby's lap. His hand lingered as he chose the ring. It was unpleasant but vital for Ruby to see the truth. The subtle intelligence and mental strength of Jeffreys versus the uncontrolled physical frenzy of the raping skinhead hordes. Wrapped in the Cross of St George. Moving to slave rhythms. She slowly focused on the ring. Which was made of plastic. String tied through the loop. He had taken it from a certain Steven Rollins two years before. Did she remember the man? He was sure she did. Whispering in Ruby's ear. Coaxing her along. He could reach out and lick her lobe if he wanted. But did not. Yes. She knew. There was recognition in her eyes. Followed by a quizzical expression. But he persisted. Until she mouthed the word yes. No sound emerging. Ruby fortunate she was under the control of an educated man such as Jeffreys who went on to explain how he had terminated the life of Rollins, a thug with a shaved head and tattoos, a probable rapist like those yobs on the screen, a macho fool who did not respect women, children, his fellow man, a drunken lager lout who was of course neo-Nazi in his political beliefs, a hooligan who drank in thug pubs and terrorised law-abiding immigrants, a self-centred white supremacist who patrolled the streets of the town armed with a baseball bat searching out defence-less Asians so that he could batter them to a bloody pulp, running off to hide into the dark shelter of night. Rollins was Nazi scum, a threat to national stability, an ignoramus following a spurious agenda, the swastika a mask for his basic criminal tendencies. What good was such a man to decent society? He caused havoc wherever he went. Quite prepared to physically assault his own mother. Wife. Children. He existed for the public house. For mindless brawls. Stanley knives. Cheap sex. Football hooliganism. Amphetamines. Cocaine. Razor blades. Merciless beatings of socialists and communists and Jews. The smashing of windows. Standing in the high street with his right hand in the air saluting Adolf Hitler. Himmler. Heydrich.

Ruby was trying to say something but he hushed her. She was naive. So he explained that as Rollins was dying, neatly injected with his magic potion, he had sent him East, to a Stalinist gulag where time stood still and malcontents such as Rollins were forcibly re-educated and shown the error of their ways by a harsh regime that did not care whether the individual lived or died, where every man's head was shaved to obliterate individuality. Rollins had done the same out of choice yet in the camp there was no choice, a frozen hell where a less civilised version of his own zero-tolerance approach had always applied. There was no hope, no chance of escape, only endless centuries of slave labour. First he would be transported across the icy expanses of Siberia, finally north towards the Arctic Circle, nearly dying on the way from dysentery, carrying his cancer with him forever, gnawing at his morale, and it was a long journey into oblivion, his fallen comrades buried along the line of the train track, cattle trucks used to transport this neo-Nazi to his celestial destiny, a reflection of his hero's treatment of the Jews, and on his eventual arrival he would be forced to work with the Slavic subhuman element he so despised, a rabble of cut-throat oiks, the cold with him at all times as he broke rocks, dug for salt, watched his fellow prisoners buried in slag heaps, bones filling the soil, death a welcome release that would never come, bitter winters and cold summers, and every so often he would be taken to the trucks and shipped to another camp, sitting in his own faeces, to another freezing hell.

The first rapist climaxed and withdrew from the traumatised girl. Made way for his fellow. Entry easier now. Mr Jeffreys moved Ruby's head back to the screen and noted the tears trickling down her face. The Rollins experience was allowed to sink in. He noted the cheap decor of the teenager's room. Pop stars adorned the walls. Taken from magazines. Taped to woodchip walls. It was all so tacky. Cheap and undisciplined. The edges jagged. Torn. There was another teddy bear next to a fluffy pillow. A plastic doll dressed like a tart. Mr Jeffreys placed the plastic ring on the arm of the couch and reached down into Ruby's lap. Picked up the locket. Smiled.

He held the locket up and turned Ruby's head. It was made of silver. He clicked it open. She started at this and he knew he did not have to tell her to whom it had once belonged. She fully understood what was happening now. But she also had to know that these terminations were more than the meting out of justice. Rollins was a thug, but also a costly thug. He was costing the hospital a great deal of money. His cancer would return. Of that Mr Jeffreys was certain. Why bother wasting resources on a no-hope situation? On someone who did not contribute to the common good. Each case was judged on medical grounds. The client's worth to society of secondary importance. Eternity an artistic twist. But he had moved on from the Nazi and explained how Pearl Hudson was nearing the end of her working life and was a typically frustrated, sadistic lesbian, twisted inside and unwilling to take her place in society, to marry and bear children, incapable of love, obsessed with disciplining small children who could not fight back.

To illustrate his power he had told Ms Hudson the story of Julie Drayton. A pupil of hers no less. The funniest thing had happened. Sitting in her living room on one of his home visits, with the teacher tied to her chair. Magic potion administered, she had actually cried as he described the death of Drayton. This had set him thinking. It was a little unorthodox yet he had decided to change his mind at the last minute. She was obviously tangled and perverted yet liked to be seen as a caring individual, a worthy addition to a society that secretly rejected her. Much like Ruby in fact. So he had included her in his vision of Drayton. Hudson became the wicked witch in the wood who tormented the little girl in her ramshackle home. Hudson doing her best to control her perverted feelings, tormented by this inner battle between good and evil. Which she invariably lost. Hudson was the lowest form of humanity, a child torturer, hated by everyone, who would drench her in phlegm if the Witchfinder General caught her. Paraded through the streets. Sins exposed to the world. All the time her mind would be in turmoil knowing that her brand of witchcraft was evil, the Witchfinder General moving through the woods ready to douse her in water. Build a bonfire where she would be burnt at the stake as the ignorant masses cheered and cursed her, only for Hudson to reappear in the woods and begin the cycle all over again.

There had been numerous framed photographs of the man in the locket in her front room. A brother he supposed. There were rows of books. Paintings and drawings. Batiks. There was the smell of a cat. It was really quite naughty of him to approach her at home. He remembered her face from the children's ward when she visited little Julie. The poor girl misled by a devious old hag. He had made enquiries. Felt the poetic side of his nature coming to the fore. Hudson reminded him of a teacher he had hated when he was young. But it was business. Ruby understood. It was not personal. He drew a line between work and pleasure. Not that he had derived pleasure from the woman's passing. She had no life to speak of, teaching in a pathetic little primary school, alone and without

interests, cold and bitter and redundant. It was easy
enough to banish the horrid woman to the woods and
then lift her into his arms and carry her to the top of
the stairs. Allow her to topple down and break her
neck. He had made sure of that. The accidental death
of a woman weak and dizzy after a spell in hospital.
Pearl was a gem. Just like Ruby in fact. Two gems
together. He laughed. Two witches pretending to
dedicate their lives to others but all the while plotting.
Did they really think he was fooled by their saintly
displays? Their pious concern for others? He wondered
if the two of them had engaged in devil worship
together. The old woman pleasuring the younger one
with a sex toy. Teachers and nurses. Public sector
whores. Agitating. Begging for funds.

Mr Jeffreys guided Ruby's head in the direction of
the television set once more. So that she could see
how the documentary was progressing. The second
rapist was finishing with a tirade of violent obscenities.
Rollins had deserved everything he got. Hudson a
danger to children. The rape victim was once more
aware of what was happening. Resisting. Struck again.
A knife was produced and held to her throat. The third
man stepped forward and plunged into the depths of
her depravity. Such was their passion they did not use
condoms. The masses were irresponsible even in sex.
Violent rather than tender. Aids a costly epidemic. He
placed the silver locket next to the plastic ring.
Reached down and took up the dice. It was home-
made. Cheap wood with smudged blue dots. It was
not even square. A childhood toy perhaps. He forced

Ruby to turn her face from the documentary. Yet she seemed fascinated, her face soaked with tears of joy.

Did she recall a certain Daniel Rafferty by any chance? She tried to nod her head but could not. Spit dribbled from her lips. Her face soaked. It was disgusting. Rafferty was a horrible specimen. A debauched young man. Not that he was prejudiced against homosexuals, not at all, many cultured and powerful people were homosexual and dignified in their conduct. What he found revolting was the likes of Rafferty, who had allowed himself to become infected with HIV and then expected the state to foot the bill. With his ponytail and casual manner about the ward perhaps he saw himself as a bohemian. An artistic rebel. Well. This was impossible in the town in which he lived. He was a faceless fool in a faceless environment. Not a Notting Hill rebel. He was even too stupid to practise safe sex. Claiming benefit. Trudging lost through grim streets. A meaningless existence. Cold concrete and depression. The poor lad. He was crying out for a helping hand and Jeffreys had been forced to oblige. His chance coming one night when the bed next to Rafferty was empty and he had a clear shot at the young deviant. Buggered in a public lavatory no doubt. By a succession of suppressed homos. Too scared to admit their tendencies in a vicious environment. This was one of his bugbears. The intolerance of the white scum who inhabited the terraces and flats and yet expected mollycoddling by the state.

Rafferty's hell was to stay where he was and be sent to work. Long hard shifts and monotonous, repetitive

tasks. Surrounded by macho males. The raping skinheads and football hooligans. Drug users and fornica-
tors. Rafferty would have to drink with these men
seven days a week. Endless lager, chips and burgers.
There would be no romance about his life, no
Bohemian finesse. His sexual preferences would have
to be suppressed and he would live in fear of his HIV
status being discovered. If he was found out he would
be attacked in the street. Bullied at work. Bricks
thrown through his windows. The torment would be
intolerable, yet there would be nowhere to run. He
knew that the people around him would turn on him.
Victimise Rafferty for the threat they thought that he
posed to their safety. They were ignorant. Rafferty
knew this. Mr Jeffreys leaning forward. Rafferty's face
unshaven. Passing away as he was sent packing to a
local pub. Without tradition. No fine decor to speak
of. Just ranks of hooligans. Pool players. Television
watchers. Mediocrity in all its bleached glory.

Ruby was laughing. Hysterical perhaps. But he did
not think so. It was almost as if she was mocking him.
As if she knew something he did not. No. It was the
onset of hysteria and to be expected. She had brought
all this upon herself. Picking up the old man's watch in
the hospital corridor and tormenting him with her
hidden knowledge. But the best was yet to come. The
old man and his watch. He could not wait. Moving
on. Turning Ruby's head towards the screen. He
thought he saw anger in her eyes. She really was evil.
The mute groan of the speakers. The naked masses.
Moving the dice to the arm of the sofa. Finally holding
up Mr Dawes's watch. Ruby's sugar daddy perhaps.

Was she having sexual relations with the fossil? The last skinhead mounted the girl as the others urinated on her torso. She breathed air but was dead. Ordinary men had destroyed an ordinary girl. The common people were no better than dogs. He smiled. Waiting for the documentary to reach its peak. The fourth rapist sliding into the gaping wound. Pumping faster and faster as the girl lay beneath him. Broken. All the while her mind ticking. Much the same as Ruby. No doubt planning a method of escape. Attempting to lull him into a false sense of security.

He licked Ruby's ear and felt her flinch, ever so slightly. He told her how he had leant in close to her beloved Mr Dawes and explained the situation. That he was old and alone and unloved and Mr Jeffreys was here to help him escape the mortal coil. Of course, as this was judgement day there was a price to pay. It was only fair. After all. So the old chap suffered from a fear of the ocean? One of the night staff had said as much. Well. The old sea dog had caused so much strife with his union activities that it was only right he should be buried at sea. Far from his homeland. Having helped bring the country to its knees with all those years of vindictive industrial action. Unwarranted strikes an assault on the very meaning of democracy. It was men such as Dawes who had destroyed the will of the people. Challenged a paternalistic system that had at one time ruled the world and cared for its subjects. Without union interference the health service would be privatised by now. How many man-hours had been lost to the petty prejudices of jumped-up communists? These men hated the people. Bullied and manipulated and exploited their basic ignorance. Refused to respect their betters, more educated men who had constructed a system that worked. It was impossible to quantify the damage the likes of Mr Dawes had inflicted on society. Thousands of cowardly clones in flat caps. Jugs of bitter. Chips and gherkins. Not an original thought among the lot of them. No experience of life away from the shop floor.

Dawes had turned towards Jeffreys and told him to fuck off. He had been shocked. Such language truly obscene in an elderly man. Who should have known better. Perhaps the dosage had not been strong enough. He took a handkerchief from his pocket and, leaning over the dying man, pushed it into mouth. Stretching the jaw. His customer resisted. Clenched his mouth as best he could. But Jonathan was far stronger. Something snapped and a tooth fell on to the man's chest. The tooth a surprise as Jeffreys assumed he was wearing dentures. He picked up the tooth and held it between thumb and middle finger. It was in fairly good condition. He thought about taking it for his collection but saw the watch and claimed that instead. Slid the broken tooth back into the mouth. He found swearing offensive. It was no way to treat a professional who was only trying to help. He had kept talking and seen the spirit die within Dawes's eyes. The man entering the tomb Jeffreys was so cleverly creating. Stuck in the hull of a sinking ship that came to rest on the ocean bed. Too deep for a rescue attempt. A dark world with a lack of oxygen. His fellow sailors dead. Rotting around him. Dawes forgotten. Claustrophobia gripping him as the ocean bore down on the creaking ship. Every second potentially his last. Waiting for the hull to crack and the sea to pour in. Mr Jeffreys's hand on Dawes's wrist. The slender fingers of the younger man encircling mature bone. The filed nail of his thumb pressed the tip of his index finger. He increased the pressure on old brittle bone. If he wanted he could snap the arm. But he was no sadist. Physical cruelty was crass. Violence repulsive. He was helping a communist, an atheist, a Bolshevik who bowed down to Vladimir Lenin. Trotsky. Stalin.

Mr Jeffreys looked over at the documentary and realised that the last skinhead had nearly completed his act of desecration. The girl unable to fight any more. Apparently. Another level of fear emerging as she saw something the viewer did not. He had seen the documentary before and knew that a dog was waiting in the wings. The ultimate degradation in a horrific display of callousness. Was nothing sacred to these men? He ran fingers over the blade of the knife as the fourth man finished with a barbaric roar. Withdrew. What sort of subhumans performed such acts? It was not pleasant viewing, but necessary. To understand what was happening behind the closed doors of the terraces through which he drove on his way to the hospital. These were the streets where Ruby lived. It was time Ruby realised the truth about her patients. Put childish things behind her. Understood that there was no goodness in the people she seemed to love. The neo-Nazi Steve Rollins. The lesbian witch Pearl Hudson. The deviant Daniel Rafferty. The communist Ron Dawes. Everything she held dear was rotten to the core.

He shared Ruby's disgust at the brutal rape and knew that the dog would tip her over the edge. She was soft and he was helping her to become strong. It was more honest this way. This was how terminations should be carried out. With the same drama as a court of law. A theatrical building of tension. The only ingredient missing was the gratitude of an appreciative audience. But Ruby was a fine physical specimen. Simple. Yet aware of her surroundings. She was no withered shell cursed with a barely functioning mind.

He adjusted the volume so that the documentary was clearly audible. Faced Ruby and prepared to terminate her life. Waited for the bark of the Alsatian. The beast roared out through the speakers and came on to the screen. It was frothing at the mouth. Confused. Moved into position. The girl in the documentary suddenly found the strength to resist, but held down she did not have a chance. She would soon be demeaned even further. It was the ultimate perversion and terrible to witness. He saw the panic in Ruby's eyes as the dog was forced forward. Girl and dog trying to escape.

He moved close. He would let Ruby witness some of the act and then neatly slit her throat. Hold her as she bled to death. She would take the memory into eternity. He peered into her tormented soul. Understood her sorrow. Raised the knife and felt his nose explode with pain, sight blurred from a vicious headbutt. The pain shot through his head and he was sure the tart had broken his nose. He was standing now and trying to regain his composure when the nurse's foot flashed into his groin, the base of her shoe making him bend forward, a second kick toppling him over on to the couch. He felt nauseous and vomited. Remained still for a few minutes as he waited for the pain to subside.

Nurse James had spent her energy. He knew that. Yet he was tired. Worn out. He could hear nothing. He clutched his chest for some reason. Noticed how the sofa was specked with blood. This was unacceptable. He was filled with indignation that the nurse had assaulted him. She would certainly pay for this impudence. The pain should ease but it did not. He felt weak. Blood began to soak the fabric. He tried to sit up and finish his work but was surprised to find that his body did not respond. He struggled for a minute before slumping back. Realised that the knife was embedded in his chest. Rather near to the heart.

It took Ruby time to realise where she was. There was no wake-up alarm, no easy rhythm stirring her blood, moving across a regular heartbeat, no sweet pillow talk from a tired DJ, just this vicious buzzing in her ears, temple, right between and behind her eyes, her whole head hurting like nothing she'd ever felt before, much too much drink, too many pills, a fine needle piercing the bone and sliding deep into her brain, injecting nasty thoughts like she'd never had before, real sick stuff from an insane asylum, physical perversion and mental cruelty, a vision of hell.

Everyone had nightmares, dreams that left you sad for days after, but this was different, sadistic and evil. She felt diseased, riddled with poison that was going to get stronger and turn into a giant tumour. When she tried to move her legs they were cramped worse than in winter when the blankets slipped off and the cold got in, she even listened for rain on the tiles, wind against her window, heard nothing but the static in her head, and she tried to curl up in the foetal position, tight as she could, rubbing her calves to get the circulation going, moving her hands down, everything about her aching, slow motion like she was inside and outside her body, a date-rape capsule in a glass of lager, being set up, seeing things happening now but unable to do anything to stop them.

When her back brushed something hard she imagined she was small again, Ben fast asleep on the bed, the feel of his fur as she stroked him, happy days she never wanted to end, and she could see his smiling face and twitching nose, he was always interested in what was happening, time mixed up, shot through with special medicine, all sorts of magic potions, black and white magic, good and bad trips, different doses. She knew she was older and Ben was in heaven running after a ball, Dad standing at the gates of a park, smiling, Ruby on a swing in the playground, and she missed her daddy, waved to him, but she was grown up so it had to be Charlie, and she was pleased, for a second, her neck bent at a funny angle, realised she was sleeping on the couch, A couch, the nightmare coming back and turning to reality as she looked towards the window of her flat but instead saw a wall and two framed pictures of flowers, and she sniffed for the smell of baking bread and cooking coffee but only smelt polish, and must, the room stuffy, listened for voices in the street down below and heard nothing, just an internal roar as her eardrums got ready to pop.

She pulled herself up and felt the pain race through her body, looked at the lump next to her and jumped as she saw the face of Mr Jeffreys staring right back, his eyes open, but empty, smooth featureless skin so white he looked like he was on his way out of the mortuary, his blood siphoned off, drained of colour and life, Ruby tumbling forward on to the floor, crawling away on all fours.

She tried to stand up but couldn't, afraid Jeffreys would grab her, all sorts of sickness in her mind, put there by a perverted mass murderer who wanted her dead, raped for ever and ever amen, he was a killer of the weak and defenceless, the majority of people who trusted each other, and the din in her head separated into mental confusion and fuzzy static off a TV set, she remembered the gang rape, choked, didn't understand how anyone could be like Jeffreys, leaning over her, leering, a knife in his hand, excited at the thought of a dog raping a girl, and she'd felt the strength slowly coming back into her as he told her his stories, and when she heard the dog barking she thought of Ben, stronger now, and there was no way he was ruining her memories, perverting every single thing in her life, ruining the goodness, butting and kicking Jeffreys before she blacked out.

Why hadn't Jeffreys killed her though? Why wasn't he on her now? She looked back and saw him properly, the handle of a knife sticking out of his chest, his skin so white and his shirt so red. She leant forward and puked up on the carpet, waited a minute, sobbing now, pulled herself upright using a chair and staggered away, found the kitchen, leant on the electric stove, new and unused, then went to the bathroom, leant over the sink and stuck two fingers down her throat, was sick again and again, taps running, filled a glass with water and drank it in one go, kept refilling it till she was full, spewing out water and bile.

She thought again and took no chances, locked the door and sat on the floor for a long time, leaning against the bath, shivering as she remembered everything he'd said, how he'd killed those four people she'd known, all the others she didn't know. His words were deep in her brain, pumping in and out of focus, mental rape like maybe she could never wash the filth out again.

She imagined herself pissing blood, the worst period pains she'd ever felt making her double forward, a great fire-engine flood of rich artery corpuscles that flooded the bowl and spilt over the sides, turning pink as it flecked the marble, and there was real marble in this bathroom, not the usual stuff, and she was standing and turning around and reaching for the handle, flushing it away best she could, so the toilet sparkled, like she did after a poor soul had finished shitting their lives away in the hospital, reduced to shit and vomit, rotting guts spewing the poison out of their bodies, the smell in her nostrils like it had been stored, she never knew she thought about all this, just saw the good in people, in situations, smelt the fragrant smells never mind if it was cheap air-freshener, like Jeffreys would say, and she was always looking on the bright side, every cloud had a silver lining, all the other sayings you picked up over the years, nursery rhymes that stuck in your head and songs off the TV commercials when you were a kid, pop tunes when you were a teenager and changing from a girl into a woman, and she felt the wet around her ankles, had kept on peeing on the bathroom floor and just didn't know what to do, where to run, who to turn to, there was no way out, the flood was right around her moving up from the floor, she was pissing everything away, her blood seeping under the door, clogging so the room was filling and she was going to drown in her own body fluids, couldn't understand where the blood was coming from, wished she was a little girl again, wanted her mummy and daddy.

Eventually Ruby stood up. Her head still ached but the nagging pain in her belly was easier. It was difficult to think straight but she was getting stronger, coming back fighting, and she stretched out her arms and legs, rotated her shoulders trying to loosen the muscles. She eased the door open and stood still looking across the room. It was massive, open-plan, with lots of furniture and big rugs scattered around, a four-poster bed, a steel kitchen with a dining table, the glass cases with the objects he'd talked about. It was a beautiful place, with so much space, but it was dead, like something out of a catalogue, a showroom with no character, no personality. She walked over to the cabinets and looked at the things set out like antiques in a museum, holy relics in a church. She was in a daze, staring at a toothbrush, a diary, a slipper. On and on. There were well over a hundred objects.

Jeffreys was a nutter, no doubt about it. She looked back over to the couch and saw that he hadn't moved, was well and truly dead. He'd said this place was a gallery, but the air was stale, more like a museum, but without the flavour of age. It was quiet, just the static on the TV in the background, and she went over and grabbed the remote control, turned it off so the buzzing stopped, but it kept going right there in her head, and she thought for a second and pushed rewind, had to see if the video was real or something she'd dreamt, drugged and confused, it was hard to believe any of this was true, clicking play for a glimpse of a screaming girl and a scared, rabid dog, Jeffreys had said it was a snuff movie, exaggerating the word snuff, like it was beneath him, and she supposed it was, her heart thumping, she turned it off, tears in her eyes, went over to the window.

She stood there looking out at the river, knew she was in London, the sound of traffic in the distance, outside what seemed like a compound when she went to another window and opened the blinds, then the glass. Light flooded the room, the sky blue, the sun on her skin telling Ruby she was still alive, and she breathed the fresh air deep into her lungs, feeling stronger all the time, realised it was early in the day, that she'd been in this place all night.

She went to the couch and looked at the body of Mr Jeffreys, wondering if he really was official, or a liar, some sort of split personality, and she could see that he was a manipulator all right, with no feelings or humanity, the only emotion he had was hate. She didn't know what was true and what wasn't any more, would never trust anyone again, but she couldn't think about it now, knew she had to get out and find a train station, head for home where she could buy some rolls and fill the hole in her belly, sit in a hot bath and scrub the evil off her skin, and she believed in evil now, there was no mistake about the things he'd said, the way he'd planned it, the pleasure he must've got from seeing people die, from having the power of life and death. He was a maniac. And she thought about how he'd wrapped his arm around her shoulders and held her head, pressing his fingers into the bone so a couple of times she thought her skull was going to crack, museum skulls in her mind, the bone fragile and pressing on her brain, she was going to buy a scrubbing brush and scrub and scrub at every part of her body, shave her head and scrub those fingerprints off her head, she hated him now, he was a fucking pervert, a gutless wanker preying on people who couldn't defend themselves, real slime. Ruby jumping as Jeffreys's eyes shifted and looked straight at her.

She moved back, to the window, waited, ready to fight, fists clenched, angry, but he didn't move and she guessed he was paralysed. When she was composed again she went over, ever so slow in case he was faking, conning her just like he'd conned so many people over the years, but she knew by the amount of blood and the paleness of his face that he was weak, finally reaching down and feeling his pulse. It was hardly there, and she knew he was almost dead, that this was his last minute on earth.

Ruby sat back down next to Jeffreys and thought about what he'd said, how heaven could be created, hell conjured up by a guide, and if he believed it then maybe it was true, for him, so then she could send him somewhere horrible if she wanted, but it was rubbish, he was playing God, bitter and twisted enough to get some sort of thrill out of imagining a person suffering, dying not enough for Jeffreys, the ultimate control freak, and for her dying was the worst thing, life was beautiful, every single second precious, and she knew at times she'd wished her mum would slip away in her sleep, maybe even wondered about euthanasia, but it was different, there was nothing merciful about what Jeffreys had done, and she looked at him and he was pathetic, there was nothing noble in this man, he had no class, he was alone and unloved, and maybe it was his choice and maybe it wasn't, was a person born wicked, she'd never believed that, she knew he was nearly gone, and all the evil things he'd said were suspended so she just saw a dying man, someone's baby newborn and gasping for breath, clinging to its mother, an innocent soul misled and moulded wrong, a child who was confused and unhappy and fading fast.

She cradled him in her arms the same as she would a man knocked down by a car and bleeding to death in the gutter, or a woman lying in the precinct after a heart attack. She didn't care about the blood rubbing off on her, would never forget what had happened and never be the same again, but she was a nurse, a professional, and all this talk about control and order was stupid. Jeffreys had no control. He was dying and right back where everyone started. She wasn't going to think about the horror, there was plenty of time for that later, and when she looked into his eyes she saw arrogance, then fear, mixing and swishing around in a puddle. She couldn't know for sure, not really, heaven and hell meant nothing to her as she did her best to reassure him in his final seconds.

Jonathan Jeffreys was slipping away. He understood that he was dying and that nothing could save him. He also knew that he had to maintain control and shape his destiny. He summoned up what strength remained and forced himself to imagine heaven. His own personal version. Death was his trade yet he had considered himself invincible and never planned ahead.

He was becoming a little confused. Fearful even. His heaven already existed on earth. His apartment. Gallery. Hotel room. His standing within the community. Most of all his work at the hospital. The power he wielded. He did not want to die and leave all this behind. He felt panic compress his lungs and found it hard to breathe. His investments would continue to grow after his passing and his property would be sold. There would be inheritance tax to pay. Many thousands of pounds would go to the government purse. His fortune could end up in the hands of the people he most despised, subsidising their misspent lives. He felt depressed. Intense, gut-wrenching depression.

Really, he would like to recreate what he had on earth. In heaven. Relief replaced despair. This then was how he would spend eternity. He would retain his power but move out of the shadows. This excited him.

There were no shadows in the celestial realm. He would glide through the corridors of the afterlife making decisions without the need for secrecy. The respect he received would increase a hundredfold when people understood his role and importance to the community. He would banish those he felt unworthy of a place in heaven to the dark horrors of whichever hell he deemed appropriate. He was firmly in control now and easing into the tunnel. The dull corridors of the hospital led to longer, illuminated corridors. Jonathan Jeffreys was at peace.

The woman cradling his head in her hands was a dumb angel. This plastic doll of popular culture was allowing him the calm he needed to shape his future. She was too stupid to take her revenge. She was soft and would never change. He was fortunate. Thought of the deaths he had arranged, the hells he had created over the years. Oh yes. He was very lucky to have fallen into the hands of a weakling such as Nurse James. It could have been much worse. Someone who was cruel and vindictive, a sadist who could not see the bigger picture. Nothing could stop Jonathan Jeffreys from reaping his just reward. Neither God nor His son Jesus Christ. He was in charge.

Mr Jeffreys could see ranks of citizens up ahead. He moved forward. Confident and at ease. He was laughing. Roaring with laughter as he entered paradise. There was a future and he was going to take full advantage of his opportunities. There was no limit to what he could achieve. He really was invincible and could do whatever he wanted. He had the power. Had always had the power. Now he would gain recognition. The crowd was bowing down. Paying homage.

Except they were not bowing down. Something was amiss. An old man was pointing at him and hurling insults. Such obscene language. Fuck. Cunt. It was disgusting. He had to remain in control. It was a mental exercise, an internal struggle. But the crowd was in focus now. There were no ordered ranks. No beautiful landscape. Thousands of heads turned and he was being sucked towards a howling mob of men and women, boys and girls, thousands of skinheads and peroxide blondes screaming at him, old men to the sides with greasy haircuts and cut-throat razors, and they were moving as one, stampeding, they were making accusations and shouting that he was a murderer who attacked defenceless old ladies in their own homes and family men and spiritual men and pensioners and anyone he could get his hands on pissed in the mouths of single mothers and the knives were out and there were flashes of faces he recognised they were out for revenge and he turned and ran along endless corridors his heart pounding he urinated with the sort of fear he had never experienced and they were going to catch him he could smell their breath on his neck they smelt of cheese-and-onion crisps dipped in amphetamine and flat cheap beer he could hear the snarling of dogs mad packs of pitbulls and bulldogs and homeless rabid mongrels snapping at his heels small jabs in the base of his back the steel blade of a knife the thuggish element jumping on his back pulling him down into the gutter, his head still in the hands of Ruby James but this caring nurse unable to save him.

*W*hen it's finished . . . when Mr Jeffreys is dead . . . I lower his head down on to the couch . . . looking at the expression on his face . . . and I see fear . . . panic . . . sheer terror frozen in his features . . . and the staring . . . blank . . . eyes . . . and for all his arrogance in life . . . when it came to dying he was gutless . . . a weakling . . . and there's some people who look proud in death . . . I've seen it enough times . . . they have this inner dignity so you know they've done their best and made the most of their lives . . . they die exactly how they lived . . . accept that their time is up . . . some have a belief in God . . . or are just tired . . . and they drift away . . . their deaths peaceful . . . a spiritual experience . . . and you get to learn about different beliefs . . . how death is treated . . . respected . . . a special time . . . and there's other people who are broken by the sadness . . . drugged against the pain . . . eased into a restful state . . . their time has come early . . . and it's not fair . . . and the thing is they love life . . . they want to keep going . . . and there's people who are terrified . . . and Jeffreys was one of those . . . maybe there is a hell waiting for the wicked . . . and if there is then that's where he is right now . . . I don't know . . . how can anyone know? . . . but I do know that his death was hard . . . and he lacked dignity . . . in death . . . in life . . . he fooled me . . . I suppose I'm not as good a judge of people as I thought . . .

but he fooled everyone . . . Dawn and Sally and the rest of the girls . . . they'll say it was his accent that conned people . . . the breeding . . . expensive clothes . . . but it wasn't . . . it was something simpler . . . it was his manners . . . he was humble and polite and hid his arrogance . . . and I reach down and close his eyelids . . . adjust his cheeks so he doesn't look so scared . . . try and give him some sort of dignity . . . and he's so white . . . the blood drained out of him and soaking the couch . . . and I look around the room . . . with the light coming in from outside I can appreciate how big this place is . . . and the polish on the floorboards makes me think of pine trees . . . Danny Wax Cap and his magic mushrooms . . . and it's a mausoleum . . . done up like a showroom but still a mausoleum . . . and I stand up . . . pull Jeffreys off the couch by his legs . . . his head banging on the floor so I wince . . . tell myself that he's dead and can't feel a thing . . . drag him over to this big carpet with all sorts of patterns . . . and he probably paid a bomb for it . . . I can see that it's expensive . . . it seems a shame to ruin something so beautiful . . . but I have to cover his body . . . he was a loony but still a human being . . . a long smear of blood trailing across the floor . . . lost in the darkness of the wood . . . I turn him on to his back and adjust his arms . . . lay the hands together . . . then roll up the carpet . . . and it's an effort . . . I'm aching all over . . . when it's done I walk back over to the glass cabinets . . . see one of those things you pluck a guitar with . . . Sun Studios written on yellow plastic . . . and I'll never know who it belonged to . . . I think of Charlie and wish he was here . . . and the funny thing is I feel calm . . . I should be screaming my head off but I'm not . . . it's shock . . . that's what it is . . . slowing my thinking down . . . and I don't want to tell anyone about what's happened

. . . not yet . . . I have to clear my head first . . . think it through . . . wait for those words to go away . . . move back a bit . . . and none of these people in the cabinets have a name . . . I turn off the spotlights and leave all those unknown victims in peace . . . go back and collect the things that matter . . . to me . . . sit on a chair . . . with the ring . . . locket . . . dice . . . watch . . . look at them one by one . . . taking my time . . . moving from plastic . . . to silver . . . to wood . . . to gold . . . and I'm shutting out the room and its cold designer atmosphere . . . closing the space down . . . concentrating . . . conjuring up the dead as I run my fingers over the string looping through a plastic ring . . . and it's something you'd find in a Christmas cracker . . . the snap of powder . . . a joke and a hat . . . a family occasion . . . or in a pound shop . . . the bazaar on the high street . . . next to the pliers and pads of paper . . . I pinch the knot between my thumb and middle finger . . . hard . . . squeeze till it hurts . . . and Steve Rollins tied this ring around his wrist and never took it off again . . . sweat and bath water turned it to stone . . . like a prehistoric fish that ends up a fossil in a museum cabinet . . . like it was never alive . . . and there's a new knot that's weak . . . it doesn't belong . . . this has to be where Jeffreys tied the string back together after cutting it off Steve's arm . . . once he'd injected him with whatever it was he used . . . his magic potion . . . on the children's ward they call antiseptic a magic cream . . . medicine a potion . . . a fairy-tale world . . . easing a kid's fear of something they don't understand . . . we all do it . . . and I think of the way Jeffreys murdered Steve and filled his head with poison . . . laughing at the man while he died . . . whispering like an obscene phone caller . . . Jeffreys a dirty old man . . . and I never spoke to Steve . . . only ever saw him on the ward but

knew about him from Dawn . . . she's friends with his wife
. . . Carole . . . and I saw his daughter as well . . . could tell
he was proud of her . . . and I suppose what I'm really seeing
is a younger version of my dad . . . a decent man with a
tattoo . . . a hard worker who liked a pint with his mates and
a night in front of the TV with his wife and child . . .
someone who loved his daughter like nothing else in the world
. . . and he carried me on his shoulders when I was little . . .
read me stories . . . played games . . . all the usual things
. . . and Steve's crime was having a shaved head and a flag
on his arm . . . that's enough for a tosser like Jeffreys . . . he
reckoned Steve was a Nazi who wanted to kill children . . .
knife men and women in the street . . . but Jeffreys didn't
have a clue . . . he goes on about his superior intellect then
does a parrot routine repeating everything he's been told by
the media . . . by outsiders who don't have a clue . . . the
same as him . . . outsiders . . . pedalling cheap stereotypes
. . . and he's taken their prejudices to the obvious conclusion
. . . he's their hitman . . . he works for the newspapers and
the politicians and the television . . . an assassin living out
their fantasies . . . dressing up murder and sadism as some
sort of public service . . . he was slow and calculated . . .
perverted . . . with Steve I suppose it was jealousy . . .
Jeffreys had the silver spoon but no strength . . . one punch
and Steve would've knocked him out . . . Jeffreys was a
wimp and Steve was a man . . . more than that he was
content . . . had everything he wanted . . . while Jeffreys was
restless . . . needed the sort of power money can't buy . . .
Steve was easy-going . . . living his life and not hurting
anyone . . . holding this ring tight I can feel how delicate it is
. . . so fragile that I just know it was given to him by his little
girl . . . an innocent present . . . money didn't come into it

. . . the ring too small for Steve's fingers so he tied it around his wrist . . . knotting the string tight as he could so he'd never lose it . . . and I wonder how Carole coped . . . imagine his daughter thinking about her daddy every day and waiting for him to come home . . . and this ring was precious and now it's worth nothing . . . I can see Steve's head on a pillow . . . in a hospital bed . . . hauling his big cancer-scarred body up and smiling . . . really grinning . . . turning to mush as his child hugs him . . . then sits up on the bed . . . Carole kissing him and trying to be strong . . . he's coming home soon . . . the worst is over . . . but it's been a worry . . . just as long as the cancer hasn't spread . . . he's weak but will get stronger . . . Carole's been going to the chapel to pray . . . she tells Dawn how Steve did that years before . . . how she copied him . . . and he's going to be all right . . . everything back to normal . . . a video to watch on TV . . . food . . . drink . . . warmth . . . that's all they want . . . as long as everyone's got their health . . . but she doesn't really believe it . . . not really . . . Carole gives Steve a cold drink from the machine . . . the freezing aluminium burns his mouth but the Coke on his tongue makes him feel alive . . . a drink with no goodness in it . . . just taste and sensation . . . and I close my eyes and run through his story . . . a version of Steve Rollins that's just as much my dad . . . putting things in their place . . . and I'm shaking imagining what I'd feel like if Dad had been murdered when I was small . . . that could've happened if Jeffreys was around . . . at least I had a few years . . . every day important . . . memories I'll keep for ever . . . and Dad could've been killed for having a tattoo and a belly . . . because he was happy . . . enjoyed his food . . . for being big instead of skinny . . . for having short hair . . . or he could've been committing

Danny's crimes . . . Wax Cap's hair was too long and his body was too thin and he kept off the drink and was watching what he ate . . . Steve and Danny couldn't win . . . it didn't matter what they did . . . Steve a character . . . a homeboy who loved the simple things . . . and I suppose Jeffreys killed family life when he murdered Steve . . . ruined the lives of a lot of other people as well . . . the rest of his family . . . his friends . . . a trail of misery that will run through the years . . . and Jeffreys was the sort of person who harps on about traditional values but practises something different . . . usually you can laugh these people off . . . big speeches and no action . . . but there's no way you could laugh off Jeffreys . . . and from killing a family man he killed Pearl . . . whose big sin was not having a family . . . and so he labelled her a spinster and a lesbian and a twisted old maid . . . bitter and vicious . . . but he never had a clue about her either . . . and I knew Pearl all right . . . I looked after her . . . talked to her . . . and she was a good woman and full of love . . . if Charlie hadn't died she'd have had kids . . . lots of them . . . but Charlie was the love of her life . . . no one could ever take his place . . . she was a romantic the same as Steve . . . different generation . . . different sex . . . but she did have children . . . hundreds of them over the years . . . and while she couldn't cuddle and hug them like a mother she was still giving . . . just didn't expect anything back in return . . . and no way was Pearl bitter . . . I put the ring down and pick up Pearl's locket . . . run my fingers over the silver . . . feel the texture . . . and the locket is older and chosen by a young woman who's grieving . . . she can't believe what's happened . . . doesn't know how to go on . . . if she even wants to . . . and there's little patterns on the edge of the locket . . . grooves . . . like flowers . . . and I click it open and look at the face *inside . . . see Charlie laughing . . . happy . . . maybe saying something for the camera . . . and the rest of his body has been cut away so his face fits . . . maybe he was on his bike when the photo was taken . . . and I lean my head back and feel the fabric on my head . . . Jeffreys had so much money . . . so much luxury . . . why couldn't he just be happy and leave us alone . . . and I run through Pearl's story . . . fitting it together . . . when Jeffreys murdered Pearl it was because she was a strong woman . . . who controlled her own life and really did put something back into society . . . she had a strength he couldn't handle . . . he was jealous of her independence . . . but really he was killing love when he killed Pearl . . . personal love but also the love that made her a teacher . . . a willingness to help others . . . she was honest and believed in the system . . . she was a giver while Jeffreys just believed in taking . . . doesn't matter how much he dressed it up . . . people like him grab everything they can . . . preach all sorts of high-minded morals but have none themselves . . . and Pearl had loads of visitors come to see her in hospital . . . more cards sent to her than I've ever seen . . . from the children she was still teaching to those who'd grown up . . . plus her friends . . . and other teachers . . . and I think of Jeffreys going into her house like that and I hate him . . . really hate him . . . I try and imagine the terror she must've felt . . . tormented in her last minutes . . . and like all of them I hope he was wrong about the effect of what he was saying . . . hearing all that filth as they were dying . . . in the presence of a nonce . . . the sort of man who should be locked up with child molesters . . . and what did she think when he was carrying her up the stairs? . . . then throwing her back down . . . I don't want to think about it . . . start crying . . . fight to keep back the tears . . . close the front of*

*the locket and pick up the dice . . . think of Danny now . . .
his life . . . situation . . . and as well as the way he looked
and how he spent his day Danny was killed for having HIV
. . . and Jeffreys thought he was gay when it was dirty
needles . . . and the funny thing is . . . if anything can be
called funny . . . is that he got Danny so wrong he set him
up in the sort of life he'd have liked . . . stuck him back in
the Green Man with Bubba and the rest of the lads . . .
playing pool . . . gave him a job and the knowledge that he
was never going to develop Aids . . . never going to die . . .
and I laugh despite everything . . . it was a shame Jeffreys
didn't know that Danny got HIV from using heroin . . . that
he was looking for answers to spiritual questions . . . that
would really have done Jeffreys's head in . . . he couldn't
have handled that one . . . and I talked to Danny a lot when
he was in hospital . . . I knew him from outside work . . . he
lived near me . . . drank in some of the same pubs . . . I
knew his views on life . . . what he was saying about the
mushrooms . . . a complicated character who did his own
thing . . . never thought he was better than anyone else . . .
he'd calmed down but still had this turmoil inside him . . .
something he was trying to control . . . for me things are more
straightforward . . . the drink and the drugs are for fun . . .
and I've never asked too many questions . . . just taken life
as it is . . . but Danny was different . . . I liked him . . . he
was a thinker . . . an intense person . . . spiritual . . . I've
never been like that . . . and there was a softness in there . . .
you have to be hard to brush all the worries away . . . to focus
on something to get you through . . . and I'm harder than he
ever was . . . I can keep going . . . like Pearl . . . push
myself through the bad times . . . I lose myself in my work
. . . the same as Pearl . . . block out the sad times . . . keep*

busy . . . moving . . . and with Danny you wanted to look after him . . . this tormented look on his face sometimes when he was trying to work something out . . . he was good to talk to . . . could point things out you wouldn't notice . . . he was definitely a character . . . same as the others . . . a spiritual man . . . and I laugh again . . . thinking of how Danny used the term . . . and the dice is rough on my skin . . . I let it settle in the palm of my hand . . . the gritty feel of rough wood . . . and I hold it up in front of me . . . for a split second seeing the paintings on the wall opposite . . . a maze of patterns that show me nothing . . . and I wonder how he cut the dice . . . maybe he made it in prison . . . I don't know . . . or someone gave it to him . . . I just don't know . . . the dice is a mystery . . . it could be anything . . . maybe it was made for him by his dad . . . his granddad . . . left over from a woodwork class at school . . . it meant something to Danny anyway . . . and he was an easy target for Jeffreys . . . bad blood that had to be eradicated . . . and the dice should have belonged to Ron really . . . he was the gambler . . . with his life . . . and then on the horses . . . and Ron was a threat to everything Jeffreys believed in . . . and I pick up the gold watch he was given by his workmates . . . think about his life . . . and out of them all I suppose I liked Ron the best . . . he was a lot older but had done so much . . . really used his life and never surrendered . . . he did what he wanted . . . was easy to talk to . . . he did most of the talking . . . telling me things I'd never have known if I hadn't met him . . . he'd seen and done so much . . . his life was rich . . . he could've lived to be a hundred . . . what a way for a proud man to die . . . murdered by a snivelling little shit like Jeffreys . . . a nobody . . . and I close my eyes for a long long time . . . feel so bad for them all . . . every one *of them loved life so much . . . that's what they had in common . . . and I think of the smug grin on Jeffreys's face as if he was something special . . . a big brave man instead of a mental case . . . a coward who bullied people when they couldn't protect themselves . . . with all these people he killed it was to do with innocence and trust . . . in his world none of his victims were worth their treatment . . . and he said it was official policy . . . that he worked for the government . . . and maybe he was telling the truth . . . it seems impossible . . . but maybe not . . . maybe not . . . and there's time to worry about that later . . . I have to move . . . get out of this place and think about what's happened . . . and I stand up . . . put the ring . . . locket . . . dice . . . watch . . . in my pocket . . . feel the plastic . . . silver . . . wood . . . gold . . . go over to the door and open it . . . taking a last look behind me . . . before I leave.*

The trip home was quick, a train and then a bus, Ruby locked inside her head the whole way so she didn't see the streets or people, heard nothing, she was in some sort of shock and handling it best she could, running over the same question again and again, whether Jeffreys had been telling the truth about the murders he'd committed, if it was true that money really was more important than anything else, even a human life.

Was Jeffreys really a social cleanser trained by the authorities? Was the government carrying out euthanasia according to the cost of treatment and a person's economic worth? If it *was* true, then she was in big trouble, and had to keep what she knew to herself. She followed this line of thought swinging into a nightmare vision of the world around her, where she was being recorded and evaluated by accountants, something as pure as medicine and public health infected with a deadly strain of cynicism, and then as quickly as she went that way she was snapping back in the other direction, saw Jeffreys as nothing more than a loner, a coward whose snobbery was out of control and meant he killed anyone he didn't like, whenever he got the chance. He was a control freak, power mad, the scum of the earth.

Walking out of the bus station, Ruby smelt the fumes of the dual carriageway and heard the roar of engines and it made her depressed, her normal joy at just being alive had been distorted, because usually the smell of the petrol was sweet in her nose, the thunder of cars and trucks a display of life, but things were different now, dark and sickening, her mind rocking, reeling, rabid as she was faced with the truth that euthanasia was being practised right across the country, in every hospital social cleansers ready and eager to carry out their orders, to implement policy, they were only carrying out commands and not taking any personal satisfaction from their actions, performing terminations, easing the pain and suffering of the sick and elderly and expensive-to-treat and anyone who took their fancy.

But she had to calm down and think properly, make a plan, fight the doom Jeffreys had created. Everything he'd said was in her head swishing in and out of the nightmare of that video, which was real enough, the stories he'd whispered into her ear, feeling like they'd been caught on film as well, endless reruns playing in her mind. She hated him, hated everything and everyone, felt so alone in the world she wished she was dead.

– Cheer up darling, a man said, as she waited for the lights to change and let her cross the road.

Normally she smiled at everyone, but now she was different, took no notice, her dreams horror shows, like the endless TV documentaries, there was nothing good she could think of, and she was seeing her mum in the hospital and her dad in his grave and she wished they'd had other children, that she had a brother or sister to turn to, they hadn't been able to have another child, and she thought about going round and seeing Paula, but she had her kids home from school, had enough to worry about, and Ruby thought about Dawn and the others, they'd be at work, Boxer couldn't handle that sort of thing, and anyway, she didn't want to go to the hospital, that was the last place she wanted to be right now, maybe she'd never go there again, anything could happen, and most of all she was thinking about Charlie, she hadn't known him long, but so what, he was special, she needed someone, everybody needed someone, there was no shame in that.

She crossed the road and went in a phone box, called his number, Charlie's voice right there on the other end in two rings, and it was like she was hearing him coming out of the radio, he was excited and said he'd been phoning her, he wanted to see her, she tried to talk but couldn't get a word in edgeways, he had a surprise for her, and she gave up, kept quiet, she'd tell him what had happened when he met her in the Brewer's, in ten minutes.

She only raised her head now to look at the traffic, then down at the pavement, ducking into the pub. It was the middle of the day and there were a few people in, but the Brewer's was big and there was plenty of space, she couldn't handle it packed, Ruby sitting by the window with a pint of cider, and she was thirsty, smelt the apples and swished it around her mouth, trying to wash away the sickness, wondering if the police were going to believe her, when she went and told them what had happened, and maybe they'd say she was mad, call a man in a white coat and hold her down as he injected her with special medicine, a magic potion to sedate her until she could be taken to an asylum, and there she'd pass away in her sleep, nobody would check the reasons if the doctor said it was okay, or if she jumped out of a window and broke her neck.

She wanted her mum but couldn't have her. Mum was nearby but out of reach. It wasn't fair, it just wasn't fair, she didn't understand what she'd done to deserve this, big tears in her eyes, dabbing at them with a tissue.

– Are you all right? the barmaid asked.

Ruby nodded and tried to smile.

– You forgot your change.

Ruby took the money and put the coins on the table, a handful of silver, looked through the window at the street and the shopping centre opposite, all sorts of people flowing into the precinct, and normally she loved this, the colour and noise and vitality, but now there was a fog over everything, all these people were doomed, they would live and die and that was it, there was no reward waiting, nobody was valued, it didn't matter how hard they tried, all they needed to do was get sick or have an accident and an ambulance would deliver them to the cleansers, civilised assassins armed with hypodermic syringes, full of controlled hatred, rational men leering at their sentimental, crying victims.

– Do you want another one? the barmaid asked, a few minutes later, as she passed by, emptying ashtrays. I'll bring it over if you want.

She was being kind, but one was enough, even though Ruby was tempted. She'd drunk it fast, watched the woman go back to the bar, then turned to look at the street.

A pink Cadillac made her start. It was right outside the window where she was sitting. It was just like the car Charlie wanted to buy, and it took her a few seconds before she realised that Charlie was sitting behind the steering wheel and waving at her, telling her to come on, and she blinked and stood up, left the pub and got in, it had a huge front seat, a black puppy sitting in the back on a blanket, and she didn't understand, the dog jumping forward so Charlie picked it up and plopped it in her lap, indicated right and pulled away, the suspension so smooth the Cadillac floated along, and she could see one or two people looking over but didn't care, and Charlie was talking a mile a minute so she couldn't get a word in edgeways, he was going into one, telling her how this bloke at the hospital had given him a tip, a horse called Ruby Murray, a 100–1 long shot, an old boy who'd passed away the day before he was admitted had given it to another patient, it was a shame he couldn't thank him, but anyway, he'd backed the horse and backed a winner, won enough to go and buy the Cadillac, it was his dream come true, and he'd had a bit left over, knew how much she liked the puppy in the pet shop, so he'd bought it for her as a present, there were no strings attached, she didn't have to marry him or anything, laughing, not yet anyway, and Ruby knew that she was going to call the puppy Ben, he was licking her face and she was hugging him and crying, really crying, so Charlie looked over at her all surprised, and she was happy, told him she was crying because she was happy, Charlie smiling, pleased, and Ruby loved the dog and loved Charlie and was so happy it was almost like she'd died and gone to heaven.

Also available in Vintage

John King

THE FOOTBALL FACTORY

'The best book I've ever read about football and working-class culture in Britain in the nineties'
Irvine Welsh

The Football Factory centres on Tom Johnson, a seasoned 'Chelsea hooligan' who represents a disaffected society operating by brutal rules. We are shown the realities of life – social degradation, unemployment, racism, casual violence, excessive drink and bad sex – and, perhaps more importantly, how they fall into a political context of surveillance, media manipulation and division.

Graphic and disturbing, occasionally very funny, and deeply affecting throughout, *The Football Factory* is a vertiginous rush of adrenaline – the most authentic book yet on the so-called English Disease.

'The most savagely authentic account of football hooliganism ever seen. The book's veins pulse with testosterone and bellicose rage, effing and blinding throughout the warzone of macho culture'
Blah Blah Blah

'Bleak, thought-provoking and brutal, *The Football Factory* has all the hallmarks of a cult novel'
Literary Review

VINTAGE

VINTAGE